DREAMHOUSE

DREAMHOUSE

Judy McConnell

Published by Yorkford Press
Minneapolis, Minnesota
2017

Cover Design by Chip Borkenhagen. All rights reserved.
ISBN-13 print   9780692612101
ISBN-10 e-book   0692612106
First edition published in 2017
Yorkford Press, Minneapolis, Minnesota
Printed in the United States of America

author's website: www.agreatbook.net

Dedicated to the memory of my father
Harold K. Bradford
who always wanted to support my writing
and whose legacy has made this
publication possible

OTHER BOOKS BY
JUDY McCONNELL

A Penny a Kiss:
Memoir of a Minnesota Girl in the Forties and Fifties
(2014)

Just Keep Shooting:
My Youth in Manhattan
Memoir of a Midwestern Girl in the 1950s and 1960s
(2016)

CHAPTER 1

⟨ornamental divider⟩

S hane lay sunk in the cavernous armchair, newspaper draped across his lap, wondering why the entire world didn't savor the glory of life the way he did. It was pleasant there in the family room buffered from the outside world, rain pelting the windows with drops that smeared along the panes. Larry was no doubt upstairs in his room, taking apart his toy radio or extending the Lego tower up the wall—by now it almost reached the ceiling. Shane looked at his daughter Megan, who sat cross-legged on the rug inserting colored tiles on a foam board, a gift from her recent tenth birthday party. Glancing at the wall clock, Shane perceived an unusual quiet pervading the room, with only the low hum of the television and the murmuring drops against the windows. Outside, the cool September air hinted of winter freeze to come. An ominous blue-black cloud bank hovered over the house, and threatening blasts of thunder could be heard across the treetops. A storm was moving in from the west. The warmth of a fire was nice, but hardly worth the effort. His wife enjoyed stirring up a crackling fire, and he left it to her. He was a simple kind of guy: seek nothing, disturb nothing, risk nothing, that was his motto, the avenue to supreme peace.

Without Larry's energetic play and his wife Radley's bustling presence, the air had relaxed, gone stale, as if some of its oxygen had been withdrawn. With Radley gone to the apartment she'd rented as a weekend retreat—another foolish whim, who could understand her?—he felt a bit reduced. The room, the house secreted an ambience, a florescent scent all its own, filled with the accumulation of eleven years of married hopes and promises—it was the house-by-the-lake they had always dreamed of, that filled their hearts and souls. This sense calmed his vision, soothed the doubts and stirs of anxiety that seeped on occasion through the placid acceptance of his nature.

When Larry hadn't come downstairs by 8:00, Shane began to worry. Reluctantly, he pulled himself from the green leather easy chair, set his highball glass on the end table, and stood, hands hanging at his sides. Wives were supposed to be at home with their family, but he had learned to acquiesce to his wife's zealous undertakings. What would she plunge into next?

His musings were suddenly interrupted by a roaring burst of thunder cracking overhead. Leaving Megan sitting on the rug, Shane went upstairs. Larry's room was empty. He scoured the house. Larry must be into another one of his nine-year-old harebrained schemes. Lately his son had taken to sneaking down to the small Reston beach on the shore of Lake Minnetonka, forbidden terrain. His impetuous impulses often carried him off beyond the scope of common sense—a threatening thunderstorm wouldn't stop that kid. Beyond the windows the sky was thickening, and a cluster of black clouds banked towards the east, barely visible in the smoky sky. With a sudden twinge of anxiety, Shane hastened his steps, checking each room, switching the light on in the storage closet where several boxes of extra toys were stored.

The events that unfolded next were hazy when Shane later attempted to piece them together—the drive, nosing the Buick through the neighborhood with Megan in the seat next to him, rain splattering against the windshield in heavy bursts, the view of the bent figure, stomping through the haze. It was Hugh Horton, trotting along the curb, floppy canvas hat dripping a watery spray around his ears. Shane had often seen Hugh, an enthusiastic sailor, towing his C-Scow past the house, headed for the Yacht Club across the bay for some sailing regatta. Despite Hugh's position as president of the Federal Reserve Bank and his forays to far, elusive corners of the bushland—penetrating the Waikato back country of New Zealand and the heights of Kilimanjaro—his demeanor when they met at neigh-borhood dinners was always friendly and modest.

Shane drew up alongside Hugh and rolled down the window.

"Have you seen Larry?"

"No, Shane, I haven't. I'm on my way to the beach to bring in my boat, which I left tied up on shore—the storm came up so suddenly, I had no time to return it to the marina." He explained that his daughter Dean had burst into the house breathless, pale, face dripping wet. Something had clearly happened. "Dean garbled something about a loose boat in the water that she was sure was my runabout, and the waves knocking it out of control and there was someone in the boat in trouble. She made no sense. You know the imagination of twelve-year-olds. I must see to it," he called as he hurried off.

Vaguely Shane recalled once glimpsing a small girl wearing an orange baseball cap fly by the house on her bike, tires screeching, tennis shoe laces flying. Radley had identified her as the Horton kid.

Shane's sense of peril increased. He drove slowly through the neigh-borhood, scanning the yards for a sight of Larry, passed down around the back road to the highway, then turned back and drove along the woods. Megan jumped out and ran to an old abandoned shed that kids from near-by neighborhoods liked to explore, but she detected no sign of life. By now the rain had lessened, falling steadily, quietly. The sky was dark.

The Buick turned in toward the beach and crept down to the water's edge. Under the filmy headlight spray lay nothing but blackness, the land and lake surfaces blending in one seamless, undefined expanse. Clicking off the motor, Shane jumped from the car and grasping Megan by the hand, scurried to the edge of the lake. Weedy lake scents hit their nostrils.

He'd forgotten umbrellas, and tiny drops wet their faces, squeezed into their eyes. The wispy light emanating from the wrought iron street lamp was swallowed by the thick blackness of the lake; they could see nothing in the vastness.

Hugh's boat wasn't in sight. Neither was Hugh. Nor were there boats to be seen out on the water. An occasional whip of lightening revealed a cold emptiness. Megan pressed close to her father as they crouched under a sudden onslaught of slapping rain. Suddenly Shane made out a figure rounding the curve of the shoreline, splashing through the shallow water, arms flailing. The beam of a high-density flashlight bobbed back and forth in front of him, illuminating the brush with a garish glow.

"Over here," Shane called. Hugh Horton emerged from the darkness, a shadowy shape behind the intense glare of his flashlight. "The headlights, Shane," he panted. Quickly, Shane leaned into the car and in the sudden glare of the headlights, Hugh's figure came into view, dark and dripping.

Shane started. Hugh's chest heaved, rain curled around his cheeks, and his face was twisted into a strange grimace.

"It's an accident . . . Shane, it's too late. Oh, God, I'm sorry."

Accident—the word ricocheted around Shane's head, pounding against his temples. Something in his gut heaved, and he stood, weighted to the ground—his son—what?—God help us! He turned towards Hugh as if in supplication and saw Hugh's face assume a take-charge expression. Something had to be done and Hugh would make sure it was.

"Shane, we have to get help. I don't know how bad it is, but it doesn't look good."

"Show me," sputtered Shane. He rushed after Hugh through the streaks of rain, following the tunnel of light from Hugh's flashlight. At first all they could make out was a mountain of crags and stones piling up the slope from the shallow water. Then the circle of light closed in on the shape of a boat, lying upside down, bow nosed in between the jaws of two rocks. As the light passed over the wreck-age, a form became visible, a small body stretched alongside the boat's hull, torso and legs sprawled like rags against the glistening surface. The tunnel of light in Hugh's hand jerked erratically through the air as he stumbled over the rocks. Shane strained to see, and in a blaze of white lightening glimpsed the pale image of Larry's red shorts and striped T-shirt lying among the swells of water.

Shane caught his breath. The small head had been outlined, lying on its side, nose and mouth crunched into the sand, its top caught between two propeller blades in what appeared to be an iron grip of death.

Moving quickly, Shane and Hugh disentangled the body and carried it to the car, careful not to disturb the sliver of a broken steel blade that protruded from the boy's skull. A thick trickle of blood ran down the sides of the little face, swept into ruby currents by the rain. Shane no longer noticed the drops running down his neck as he guided Megan into the front seat of the Buick. She leaned back, tightening her arms around her wet sweater. Shane saw her wide eyes staring at the dashboard, caught in the shock of seeing her brother torn limp and helpless, limbs drooping like a slaughtered chicken.

Carefully Shane and Hugh stretched Larry along the back seat. The boy made no movement. His mouth hung limp, and the gape in the skull looked raw, severe. Was he breathing? Shane bent over and felt his wrist for a pulse. He couldn't tell. He gazed at the little cotton t-shirt soaked with blood.

"We have to get an ambulance immediately!" Waving the beam of the flashlight in front of him, Hugh dashed through the rain to his house just down the road, his shoes sloshing along the wet curb.

Shane, numb, entered the car and flopped his arms over the wheel. It was too much to contemplate: the concept of losing his son turned his insides to stone, too cruel, too punishing . . . He kept twisting around to his son sprawled in the back seat, but could detect no sign of consciousness.

When he looked over at Megan, she stared back at him with pleading eyes. "Let's hope for the best, honey," he said, his voice cracking.

"Will they take Larry away?" Megan's little voice came through the dark.

"We'll stay with him, no matter what," Shane declared firmly, feeling a tear slip down his cheek, a streak of fear, of helpless uncertainty. Nine years old was too young for his son to die!

The wail of the ambulance drew Shane and Megan out of the car, and they watched as it pulled up and four men jumped out of the back and lifted Larry onto a stretcher and into the back of the ambulance. Father and daughter scrambled up behind them, and the ambulance shot off and plunged into the darkness, sirens full blast.

Crouched on a bench, hair matted, glasses streaked with moisture, Shane gazed with blurred vision at the limp figure of his son across from him surrounded by paramedics—it was surreal, he couldn't think. Megan scrunched at his side. The ambulance lurched over a corner curb and a branch swept across the window and broke into pieces with a sharp snap that echoed in Shane's mind like a gun-shot. For a minute, he felt his lungs swell as if he might be drowning, he clutched, then coughed, swallowed, his mind came into focus. He would be all right.

The paramedic turned to him.

"We got a heartbeat. Your son is still alive."

Thank God!

Twenty minutes later, Shane sat in the waiting room in a state of stunned suspension. Next to him, Megan was watching "All in the Family" on a 19-inch television set. Copies of *Good Housekeeping* and *Look* on the blonde coffee table seemed to emanate from another time and age. *Thank God Hugh had been there with his high-powered flashlight.* Shane began to piece together events of the evening. Hugh had followed them to the hospital in his Mercedes, gone home to wait for news, with Shane slated to phone him at the first opportunity. *Possibly Hugh felt responsible, since it was his boat that Larry had climbed into and maneuvered out into the lake. No telling how long he'd been gone or how far out he'd been when the storm hit. How it had all happened was a mystery: the only witness had been Hugh's daughter Dean, the youngster with the orange bill cap.*

The blank white walls of the waiting room enclosed them, sterile and uncaring. *Thank God Radley was on her way.*

Would the doctor ever show up? He had to know. What were Larry's injuries, how serious, would he survive? Shane's throat twitched; the desire to see his son was strangling him. A door flew open with the snap of a mouse trap. Shane stood up. It was Radley, umbrella dripping at her side, raincoat unbuttoned, her face white, looking at him anxiously.

"Shane, tell me!" Shane felt something in his gut relax, the strain in his neck lessen. The sight of her slender figure with its perpetual motion and determined air warmed him like a familiar blanket.

Shane shook his head slowly. "I don't know anything," he said. "The doctor . . ."

Just then a tall placid-faced man in a white smock and wearing an oversized silver wrist watch entered and walked over. "Are you the Gallaghers?"

"Yes," Radley said.

"I'm Dr. Soderberg. Your son Larry . . ."

The doctor looked down at his hands, then regarded them as if searching for words. His face was inscrutable. "Your son has had a close call. A sharp piece of metal penetrated his brain. It will have to be removed. Preliminary testing shows that some of his brain cells might have been damaged. We'll do everything we can."

"Will he get well?" Shane asked.

"I can't say that. I can't say anything for sure. We'll have to see."

"We must be with him," Radley cried. "Please show us to his room."

"He's in a coma," said the physician. "You can see him, but we won't know anything until the tests are run."

Radley stepped closer and lowered her voice. "Doctor, I understand there is no certainty. But you must tell us, what is your prognosis? Your best guess? In your experience?"

Seeing the scared look on Radley's face, Dr. Soderberg's placating tone of neutrality shifted. "In cases like this, with the kind of damage to the brain your son has sustained, it looks bleak. Further tests are required, but based on the multiple cases I've attended, I can't offer you much hope. If he lives he may never regain consciousness. I'm sorry," he said kindly.

CHAPTER 2

❦

They had just settled into their new, spacious house in Deephaven, and Radley was eager to contrive a new life. She searched for a foolproof idea. There must be a way to coax Shane to undertake family outings. Once on a bright day in New York they had started out for Coney Island, only to find themselves locked in a clutch of holiday traffic so stifling that Shane swerved off at the next exit and headed home. And that was it. Never again. He loathed the hassle—all the driving, wrong turns, the preparations and mess and cleanup. If you couldn't get there swiftly by subway or taxi it wasn't worth it. He would roast in hell before he'd expose himself to a department store or museum with the shoving crowds, the elevators where he was jammed with elbows and foul breath. It gave him a headache, required a shot of scotch to edge him back to normal.

Motherhood seemed as inevitable as the rising sun that burst out bright on summer mornings outside their bedroom window. After marrying Shane and two minutes later becoming pregnant, she quit her job in Manhattan with the greeting card company, locked away her box of camera lenses and poems, and threw her energies into furnishing their Upper East Side apartment and preparing for the introduction of a new life into the world. There were rompers and layettes to buy, supplies to stock in the tiny second bedroom, maternity classes, medical appointments, and baby showers, every moment filled with happy bustle.

Two years later, Larry was born. This time she was prepared, with the nursing paraphernalia assembled and Larry's crib at the side of her bed at night. She loved babies—the cuddling, the smell of talcum and skin oil, the innocent, spontaneous expressions, soft skin and silky gurgling, the way they clung to her, wanted her to be their whole world. Once they began walking and exploring, and demanding whatever fleeting impulse crossed their mind, she became hesitant, unsure. Their wants continually beat smack against what was acceptable and safe. In 1966, the family moved to Minnesota and settled in the Deephaven neighborhood where Shane began a new job with Shelby Allied foods. Now that Megan was six and Larry four, they needed to get out of the house, to explore their horizons. The challenges of parenting had become overwhelming. She needed a partner.

At last Shane gave in to her pleas. For the sake of the kids, who would benefit from an outdoor trek along the river, okay, he'd go. They would spend an entire day at the St. Croix River.

The next Sunday morning while waiting for Shane to dress, Radley stood in the screened porch, Salem cigarette in one hand and a mug of coffee in the other, feeling the warm liquid seep through her. She loved the way the bright sun skimmed through the porch and covered the white wicker furniture with summer sparkles. Behind the house, the rich green carpet of grass sloped luxuriously past a burst of white flowering spirea to a bottom row of towering cypress trees. Radley could hardly believe this paradise in the woods belonged to them. They had purchased the house— spacious, private, near the lake—shortly after moving to Minnesota from Manhattan. She had been busy ever since, furnishing one lamp at a time, searching all over town for the right brass lamp for the carved pedestal table, a Modigliani print for the bedroom, a new coffee table to replace the black monstrosity left over from her single apartment days. They had created a nest tucked away on a half-acre of woods in the remote suburbs of Minneapolis, a refuge, a realized dream. Here they would build the rest of their lives.

Gazing over the yard, she hugged her arms to her chest. It was good to be alive!

When Shane entered the kitchen and seated himself at the breakfast table, Radley was setting plates full of steaming dishes on the table. On Sundays, Shane liked scrambled eggs with paprika, sausage and pancakes. He followed daily rituals with religious-like precision: a shower each morning, the same chair in the TV room each evening, the same green- or beige-colored shirt on weekends. Life was easier that way, Shane figured. He found it hard to fathom how his wife could fly around so, always on the run, flitting through the house responding to whatever call or duty swept before her, rarely still. He'd never seen anything like it.

"How about a pitcher of martinis to go with the chicken?" Shane suggested as he watched Radley stuff containers into the wicker picnic basket. But she didn't think that a good idea when driving with the children.

Shane took his place behind the wheel and steered the dark blue Buick toward Minnetonka Boulevard, while Radley located Highway 393 on the map leading to William O'Brien Park. Until his marriage, Shane had never driven a car; the driver's license tucked in his wallet was still new and crisp. He drove looking straight ahead, hands clutching the wheel on either side, while Radley listened to the squeals from the children in the back seat, fearing a conflict would explode at any second. They'd already squabbled over who sat on which side of the seat.

"I don't want Squirrelly any more. He peed in his pajamas," Larry's voice sounded.

"He did not!" cried Megan. "He wouldn't do that! You keep him. My turn with Poker-Joe isn't up."

"He's mine. Grandma gave him to me. Give him here!"
"Quiet!" Radley cried. "The stuffed animal is Larry's." The voices toned down.

Radley studied the map. "We should hit 694 and go east to MN 97, then to 61 north to MN 95. Do you need me to watch the signs?"

"No need for that," Shane replied. "It's pretty clear."
She slipped the map back into the glove compartment. When Shane missed the 694 exit, she retrieved the map and spread it over her lap.

"Mommy, he broke my racing car," Megan cried from the back seat. "He took it and broke off a wheel and now he's got the wheel in his mouth and it's icky."

"I did not! It was already broke." Larry's voice reached a near screech. "And you stole gum from Mommy's purse I saw you so there!"

Radley flashed around. "Why don't you count the number of red cars we pass?" They counted three cars, then more scuffling. "Your dad will stop the car if you don't settle down," Radley warned.

Shane glanced at her. He preferred to ignore these things. Radley's drive to discipline the children outdistanced his—she didn't give up. He had to give her credit for trying, although her efforts had no lasting effect.

The St. Croix public parking space was full. After dropping off the family at the picnic area, Shane drove off to find a place to park. Forty minutes later he showed up with dusty clothes and a strand of hair dangling over his forehead, looking exhausted. He had left the car at the end of a dirt road a mile away, heaven only knows if he'd get a ticket. Seeing his glum expression, the I-hate-this-let-me-out-of-here look, Radley sighed and set down the canvas folding chair. Maybe this trip was a mistake.

The stretch of grass along the riverbank was covered with picnic tables, satellites, and trash cans tucked behind a clump of trees. Cars pulled up and unloaded piles of people carrying picnic baskets. People were carrying coolers, unpacking baskets or sitting in folding chairs facing the river that lapped past and sank out of sight behind the forest of hardwood trees. Shane sank into a chair and observed the scene. At the picnic table next to them a man in a plaid shirt and floppy brown hat peered through binoculars across the river. People in shorts, summer tops and hats scurried back and forth among the canoes, and two teenagers bent over swabbing the leather seats on a yellow runabout. Now that Shane was settled and pleasantly comfortable, he thought he would sit there and people watch.

After a lunch of fried chicken, potato salad, hard boiled eggs, and Jell-O mixed with fruit cocktail, and chocolate custard boats for Megan and Larry, they meandered down to the rental center, only to find that all the canoes had been rented. "Will a rowboat do?" An eight-foot rowboat with a 3-horsepower motor and a chair-seat in the stern was tethered alongside the dock. It had just been returned. Yes, they'd take that one.

The operator laughed when he heard that Shane had never touched a motor. "A city boy, huh?" he said. "A cinch. I'll show you." He hopped in the boat, steadied his body against the side of the motor with one hand and with the other gave the pull rope a hefty tug. Immediately they heard a smooth revving sound.

He clicked the motor off. "Your turn." Shane set his jaw and jerked on the pull rope. The fifth time the motor started up. He looked surprised and sat down. "You're off," the operator called cheerily. "All you have to do now is steer. Your little boy here could do it."

At that Larry jumped up. "I sure could!"

"Sit down right this minute!"

"We don't need life jackets," Larry told the operator. "We swim like fish."

"We'll take them," Radley said.

Megan and Larry squealed as the boat bounced over wakes and howled with glee when Shane forced a sharp turn and they were thrown sideways. "It's a bit choppy out here in the middle," Shane remarked. "I'm going to go closer to shore." Legs pressed together and one arm gripping the edge of the hull, he had the air of a fighter pilot maneuvering a speed dive. Radley smiled to herself. She loved watching him adjust his city talents to the outdoors of the upper Midwest—her man taking his due place at the helm.

The sun was hot, baking their cheeks. The boat glided past walking paths and tented campsites. Larry leaned over the side and plunged his hand in the water, grabbing at stray leaves swirling by, while Megan leaned against the hull, breathing in the musky odor of the river.

Bam! The rowboat lurched and a loud grinding sound breached the air. Everyone grabbed the gunwale as the boat settled back down in the water, nose pressed against the side of a tall pontoon boat. They heard worried shouts on the deck above as people rushed to the rail and stared down at the small boat. Shane waved his hand in a gesture of appeasement. Two men holding drinks, one in red shorts, the other in polka dot bathing trunks puffing on a cigar, leaned over the bow searching for damage. Shane could detect a ragged scrape along the pontoon's waterline, probably repairable, he thought hopefully.

"There's plenty of room on the river. Why don't you look where you're going?" one of the men yelled down. The two men considered jumping in the water to inspect the damage, but decided it was not worth the trouble.

Shane was full of contrition. "Really sorry. My fault." He offered them $100. The two men consulted, looking at Megan and Larry huddled in the boat next to Radley.

"It was a mistake on our part," Radley yelled. "You see my husband has never handled a boat before. We're so sorry about this."

"What's happened," a female voice called.

"We've been slammed into by a rowboat," the man in red shorts replied.

The two men conferred, highball glasses tinkling, and declined the hundred dollars with a wave and a shake of their heads. Turning back to the party, they crossed the deck and stood next to two women in flowered bathing suits and oversized sunglasses holding tall frosty glasses, apparently dismissing the rowboat and any damage it might have caused.

Radley's embarrassment gave way to relief that they had been let off so easily. Shane looked shaken. Damned ramshackle motor! "Hold on. I have to restart this." He gave a few tugs on the pull rope. A sputtering, then nothing. He stood up, tried again. More choking noises followed by stubborn silence. Minutes passed. He should have stayed home, not worth it, all this cockamamie fuss. This was not his idea of a good time!

"Let me try." Radley inched her way toward the stern. But Shane wouldn't quit. He resumed jerking the rope, over and over, elbow thrusting out behind him, until he gave up, out of breath. Frowning, he licked his mouth and looked out towards the horizon. "Blasted thing!" He sat down. He stood up. This time, after the fourth pull, the sputter elongated, coughed in quick spurts, and finally started.

"Keep hold of the handle this time," Radley said.

She thought with amusement, as the boat churned upstream clinging to the shore, that she was married to the most non-mechanical person this side of Hoboken. That growing up in a rough neighborhood protectively closeted within an apartment, Shane had failed to learn the most fundamental skills for living in the wider world. That the role model of man as take-care-of-it handyman, master of the gears of the house, driver of powered vehicles, disciplinarian, and decision-maker was in his case absurd. That here was a man who couldn't even mow a lawn—that is, the distinction between *is not able to* and *hates the thought of* was not always obvious.

Radley looked around. Megan and Larry were dangling over the side of the boat on their stomachs, butts in the air, hands plunged into the water. "Get back in the boat!" They didn't move. She raised her voice. "Did you hear me?" Their little backs remained curved over the side.

Radley felt a warm flush spreading up her neck, her frustration was gaining fire. Why did the kids continually ignore her, misbehave every time her back was turned? She sat stiffly on the bow seat, watching their every move.

By the time they returned to the picnic site, Radley's nerves had calmed. The other picnickers had cleaned up and taken off in different directions, a few were still throwing Frisbees back and forth on the grass.

She suggested they take a walk along the river.

"I think I'll sit here and watch the boats go by," Shane said, leaning back in a striped canvas chair. He never walked, Radley reflected. To walk without needing to go anywhere was against his principles. To him, walking for pleasure was the same as splitting wood in order to feel your arms ache.

She watched as Megan crawled into Shane's lap and snuggled, arms around his waist. Daddy's girl. She could tell he was in seventh heaven. Being adored suited him. Having a family suited him, anchored him to his roots, a heritage that moved through his parents and the church straight up to God and the universe.

Steady, basic—it was what Radley loved about him--an anchor to her volatility and love of novelty.

Larry had already meandered off down the lakeside path, skipping over rocks like a monkey, a bouncing figure along the mass of maple, birch, and oak trees pressing thick along the trail. Radley caught up with him, and they walked for forty minutes until the path narrowed to a rocky ledge dipping over a ravine, then turned and headed back toward the picnic area. As they rounded a bend, Radley detected a dark shape stirring behind a bramble bush cornered between the trees. Probably just an animal. Still . . . Another rustle, sharp this time.

Radley stepped off the path, curiosity growing. Pushing aside a stiff branch, she detected a head partially blocked by the brush and snatches of hair snagged in the twigs. She knelt down and peered into the shadows, then caught sight of a leg hidden among the leaves, made out arms, white and smooth, and tucked within the arms, a tiny brown form. She held her breath. As she slowly parted the branches, a pair of blue eyes turned toward her, sad, pleading.

Megan!

"Honey, what are you doing here?" Radley exclaimed. Larry peered over Radley's shoulder at his sister sitting in the leaves beneath a tangle of branches.

Megan lifted her arms, revealing a small round creature, head tilted back as if broken at the neck.

"It's Tippy. He's hurt," she said in a teary voice. "Hurt bad, his leg, he's suffering." Her arms were bleeding in several places, tiny beads of blood she didn't seem to notice.

"But why are you hiding in the brush?"

"I can take care of him," Megan sniveled. "Don't throw him in the garbage!"

"But . . ."

"This boy gave him to me, said he was almost dead and he didn't want him." Megan befriended birds that crashed into windows, wanted to rescue dead animals crushed on the road, even if flat as a pancake. The hamster cradled in Megan's shirt could barely open its eyes. Its fur was matted with blood and one of its legs dangled by a wet tendon.

"We'll take it back and see what we can do," Radley said, although it was clear the creature was doomed. "And I'll take care of your scratches, poor ducky." Pulling back the branches, she helped Megan up, and they slowly inched back to the picnic table, Megan bent over the limp bundle cradled in her shirt and humming words no one could understand.

When they reached the picnic area, Shane was gone. Along the shore, several motor boats and canoes were pulled up on the grass, and a sailboat bobbed gently against the dock. The pontoon boat tethered at the end of the dock looked familiar—Radley recognized the white railings, baby blue hull, and chairs circled under the navy and white striped awning where people chatted in loud voices. Approaching, she spied the man in the polka dot bathing trunks leaning against the railing, cigar waving, and just beyond, seated next to the railing, Shane leaned back, glass in hand, talking to a man in a Hawaiian shirt and two women with wide-brimmed straw hats with purple streamers. For the first time that day he looked cheerful. He must have had more than one. A friendly lot of partiers, Radley mused, the incident with the rowboat evidently forgotten. Shane was such a pushover for a social invitation flavored by the offer of a drink. Still, she admired his ability to get along with the just about anyone with his non-judgmental, non-discriminating friendliness. She was not so easy-going!

Radley clutched Megan's and Larry's hands as they drew closer. A man in a straw hat perched in a canvas deck chair was talking to a group of listeners, gesturing with a hand that flashed a large black and gold ring.

"Of course I couldn't go home empty-handed," he was saying. "She'd kill me. You know women. My little lady, she's romantic, I'm practical, what can I say? She even expects me to remember which one. Ten years, eleven, what difference does it make? Anyway, I was wondering how I could get flowers or candy or something at the last minute when I saw a woman come out the side door of a church and toss an armload of fresh flowers into the dumpster. I couldn't resist. I had to bend over so far to reach those gol-darn flowers I fell in! Broke my elbow in two places. Happy Anniversary! I told Myrtle I fell down the apartment steps. She nearly loved me to death. Ha, ha, ha!"

Spying Radley and the children on the dock, the partiers flashed smiles and waved them on board. Megan immediately climbed up and ran to Shane, holding out her sagging shirt. "Look, Daddy! We have to save him!"

Shane regarded the limp form, fur mottled with blood, mouth arched open. He shook his head. "Megan, we would if we could. But this little guy's a goner. Sorry, there's nothing we can do."

"Ducky, it's all right," Radley whispered, kneeling and wrapping her arms around her daughter, but Megan burst into tears, scrambled onto the dock and ran towards shore, bundle clutched against her chest. Radley hurried down the ladder after her.

Shane's gaze reverted to Larry, perched on the railing. How different his children were, he noted. While Megan was continually involved in some mishap or loss, one drama after another, Larry often took off on his own. He had a way of making things work, could figure out answers or contrive to make the answers fit. It was clear that Larry was fascinated by the pontoon boat, the plush red leather seats, the mahogany dashboard with its oversize dials, the gleaming white railings. He watched Larry lean over and swing his arms to the soft sway of the boat on the water. "The boy sure loves boats," Shane thought.

Grinning, he sat down beside a man in plaid Bermuda's chomping an unlit cigar. The man adjusted the brim of his hat and began discussing deep sea fishing. A woman in a sailor hat passed a platter of bacon-wrapped weenies stabbed with toothpicks, and drinks were refilled, including Shane's frosty glass of Bloody Mary. Sweat from the hot, insistent sun moistened his forehead. Darn, he should have brought a hat.

"I'm going to find Mom," Larry called as he skipped over to the ship ladder. Shane waved, watched as Larry swung around, clasped the handles, and disappeared over the side of the pontoon.

A woman wearing a black halter and high wedgies sat down next to him and crossed a pair of slim legs. "Hey there! I'm Maggie. Glad we got together, after that silly accident. Could have happened to anyone. Anyway, one old scratch isn't going to hurt this barge." Smiling at Shane from under her broad-brimmed hat, she took a slow sip of her drink, not taking her eyes from him.

"I'm Shane. This is our first family picnic together, and it's been one thing after another. Had to park a mile away, the apple pie fell in the dirt, we couldn't rent a canoe, and then our old rowboat with an ancient motor rammed into your pontoon. I'm really sorry. Now my six-year-old's in a stew about a dead hamster. And on top of that, it's getting so hot its suffocating. I almost wish we'd stayed home." He felt the drinks percolating through his system, and suddenly he had the urge to talk and keep on talking, never mind what he said. This woman was pretty—he took another swallow of the Bloody Mary—and she was coming on strong. But what the heck, he was a guest, shouldn't be complaining. This was his fourth drink, well, one more wouldn't hurt he thought, as someone with a thermos replenished his glass.

"I'm afraid we're out of Bloody Marys, but you'll like this." Shane took a long sip. No point in being fussy in this heat.

"You're cute. Too bad you're married," the woman next to him said, laughing unsteadily and sloshing the ice in her drink with her finger.

Shane could find no response to this, merely smiled amiably.

"I'm married too. My husband is a drag. No more oomph than a cow." She pointed to a man with a large belly who was attacking a mound of ice with a silver pick.

"He seems nice enough," Shane began, thinking he should be uncomfortable at this woman's frankness, but instead he felt an irresistible urge to laugh out loud.

"You're too nice for your own good," his companion cooed. Lifting her glass out over the deck, she slipped over onto his lap, laughing softly.

"I don't think you should do this," Shane said, pressing his hands to his sides. Even in his state of unguarded relaxation, he looked at her in shock. He *would* land with a bunch of weirdos, but heck, he had nothing else to do while his family roamed about exerting themselves.

"Your wife wouldn't like it? Well, what would *you* like?" She leaned her face close to his.

Just then, Shane felt the weight lifted abruptly off his lap and a heavy-set man wearing owl sun-glasses wielding the butt end of a rifle hovered in front of him.

His wife protested, "Gosh, we're just horsing around, Howard."

Ignoring her, Howard stood with braced feet looking down at Shane. "What the hell do you think you're doing, sap-face?" Howard yelled in a high-pitched voice, his eyes flashing. "You were invited for drinks only."

"That's what I'm doing. Drinking. That's *all* I'm doing."

"Yeah, well you've had enough liquor at our expense."

Shane set his drink on the deck and stood up slowly. He was too hot to be alert, too light-headed to protest; his single thought was to somehow escape this crazy bunch of gorillas and get back to firm land.

"Potent stuff you've got there," he said. The rocking of the boat, the firing of his insides, the pounding heat on his forehead—he wasn't sure he could remain upright. It was all so ridiculous.

"Think you can play around with my wife? Interloper! Freeloader! Pathetic drunk!" The deck of partiers had gathered around, and someone clamped a hand on Howard's arm.

"Calm down Howard . . ." his wife said soothingly.

"You drunken Don Juan!" Howard managed to shout as he lunged at Shane, before being led away by two of the men.

The man in the red shorts turned to Shane. "Forget this. Just like we're forgetting your damage to our boat."

Shane nodded, considerably shaken. *Who the heck were these people? Drug runners? Petty criminals? Hedonists?* Lowering himself down the ladder, he made his way to the picnic area and settled himself into the canvas chair. He closed his eyes. Enough commotion for one day—more than enough, ever since they'd left home it had been one thing after another. If his restless wife sought entertaining diversions, this was not the answer. There must be other ways to entertain the children.

His eyes flew open. The voice sounded urgent—Radley's voice. "Shane! Over here!" Shane pulled himself from the chair and retraced his steps to the dock. The pontoon boat was steaming slowly up river, leaving a trail of bubbles in its wake. "Shane!" As he came up to where Radley was standing, the scene made his heart sink: a crew of men in park uniforms gathered around a figure on the dock. A stab of fear propelled him, he broke into a trot. The attendants moved aside, and there, lying on his back on the dock, lay Larry, face contorted in pain, clutching at his leg.

"Fool kid!" someone was saying. "Why on earth would he try something like that?"

"What happened? I'm his father."

Larry looked up at the sound of his Shane's voice. "I could have made it," he sputtered, weeping in pain. "Really. The boat moved, it *moved*."

Chattering through his tears, Larry explained that he had leapt to the bow of a vacant Sunfish tied to the dock in order to fix a flapping sail. A wave had jiggled the boat, causing him to miss. "It was an easy shot, Mom."

A medic kneeling next to Larry announced that he had sustained no more than a bad sprain. Larry lay meekly as a medic taped the ankle and sent for a stretcher, advising him not to walk for a day or two.

Larry was always venturing into strange places, Radley reflected, following his insatiable curiosity. His lack of fear combined with unbounded confidence that he could handle anything worried her. After four swim lessons, he was able to swim the length of the club pool under water and became convinced he had mastered the aquatic world. It was an attitude that invited trouble. Still, she couldn't help but admire his initiative. No matter what, he would find a way.

Shane scoured the area to find Megan, but there was no sign of her. Probably she had retreated to some hiding place to nurse the hamster— no matter what it took she would save him, she would love him back to life. As Radley was explaining to Shane how she'd found Megan in the brush, cuddling the hamster in her arms, the girl came running out of the woods, sobbing, arms jerking, her little feet crunching on the gravel path.

"Mommy! Daddy! Oh! Tippy! He's gone!" And she flew into her mother's legs, pressed her head against her stomach, sobbing, choking the words out between gulps.

"Darling! What happened?"

"Tippy's gone! He fell in. He slipped out of my hands, I couldn't catch him. What will he do in there?"

"In where? Where is he?"

"He fell in the hole. The hole. I had to go potty. I had to lay him down for a second. And then he fell in."

Radley understood she meant the porta-potty. Good god! Their grand day out and calamities had been raining on them one after another. "You have to get him out," Megan pleaded, "You can't leave Tippy in there with all that stinky stuff. He'll be miserable. He'll die!"

"Megan, he's already dead," Shane said, looking relieved that she was safe.

"He was dead when I saw him earlier," Radley added. "Really sweetheart, he had stopped breathing by the time we finished wrapping him. You didn't notice and I didn't want to say anything to hurt you. He's totally dead. He doesn't know where he is."

Megan looked unconvinced. "I don't think he was dead. He was so soft and warm. He liked it when I stroked him. He looked at me once."

"Believe me, he's dead," Shane repeated, stifling a chuckle.

Radley shot him a warning glance—not in front of Megan. Then he let out a series of spastic giggles, as if unable to stop. *What has gotten into him? Is he drunk?* The odor of liquor was unmistakable. Radley felt a wave of disapproval rise in her. No sooner was her back turned than he unleashed himself with strangers, drinking cocktails, oblivious. He was too friendly, too easy, and left everything in her hands, assuming she had the children in sight every minute.

They walked back to the car, Megan trotting beside Shane, her hand in his. Shane kept smiling down at his daughter. Radley's mind relaxed as she contemplated his easy stride, the look of pleasure on his face as he listened to Megan's chatter. It occurred to her that that he had every right to enjoy himself, to be happy, that he accepted her and their Midwestern life in Minnesota without complaint and deserved whatever gratification he found. She in turn would accept him, uphold her part of the arrangement, linked in this life they had created together.

CHAPTER 3

❧

Pushing open the tall walnut doors, Radley entered the Holy Presbyterian Church and followed posted signs down the long hall-way. One of the chapel doors was propped open, and she peeked into the room shyly. Bodies were squeezed knee-to-knee in the pews, jack-ets across laps, purses crammed underfoot. She eased through the door, careful not to disturb the attentive hush that filled the room. The lecture had already begun. A slim man at the pulpit in a black jacket and black turtle-neck shirt was leaning forward, a strand of red hair angling over one eye, which he tossed off his forehead with a jerk of his head. All eyes, she noticed, were fixed on him as if he were about to impart the secrets of life. A single blonde hardwood cross hung on the wall behind him, simple and direct.

Whispering apologies, Radley squeezed into a pew as two listeners made room for her. She had been anxious to hear this lecture ever since she noticed the poster on the library bulletin board announcing a lecture on THE COMING REVOLUTION the following Saturday. She looked forward to getting back into the political arena, which she'd abandoned for the sweeping adventure of married life. She sat back and fixed her at-tention on the speaker.

"And then we had the Nixon Doctrine," Reverend Allerton was saying in a mellow, but resounding voice. "It appeared that Nixon was listening to us. The protestors were making a difference. Our voices were being heard. Nixon guaranteed that from now on our Asian allies would undertake their own defense. This war would be the last. That was Nixon's promise: our troops in Vietnam will be coming home!"

Murmurs rippled along the rows. The woman next to Radley clasped her hands and leaned forward attentively. "But now we learn about Operation Breakfast—United States troops sent into Cambodia *in secret.* Reports of this were kept out of the papers for weeks. How can the administration expect us to believe them again? *We are tired of being lied to.*"

This was followed by quick applause, mumblings of approval, and a loud yes! from someone to Radley's right. She glanced across the man next to her at a heavy woman in a billowy blouse who regarded the speaker with a steady gaze. Despite her obesity, with her arms crowding into the space of her neighbors, and the fleshy area under her chin, she held herself with an air of importance. The woman turned for a second and flashed a pair of opaque hazel eyes on Radley, eyes that glimmered with conviction. Then her attention reverted to the speaker, and she settled her hands in her ample lap.

"And Cambodia is only the latest of the outrages that propelled me to the pulpit this afternoon. Nixon can't bury the tragic killings that took place at My Lai." The speaker went on describing the crisis. Something must be done. His sermons weren't enough. Morality was at stake and it was their job to challenge those who value power and expedience above humanity and justice.

Radley watched him wipe his forehead with a large white handkerchief. Then he clicked on a slide that showed a photo of the My Lai Massacre published in the *New York Times*, then another and another. They stood as visual testimony to the killing by American military of 119 unarmed Vietnam civilians that had now been viewed by the entire nation. The images dissolved all boundaries of ecclesiastical restraint.

"This cold-blooded massacre is the shame of 1968," he went on. "We're entering a new, challenging decade—a decade of change, of transformation."

The projector light flickered, and a large screen on the platform flashed a grainy black and white image of two people facing each other. On the left a uniformed man aimed a long-barreled gun at a small skinny Vietnamese man whose shirt hung partially off his shoulder. The man was kneeling on the bare ground, his eyes frozen on the barrel of the gun in wide terror, his mouth twisted into a cipher of surprise. One could make out the mark on his chest where the bullet had just that instant entered.

Unable to tear her eyes from the screen, Radley bit her lip as the crowd gasped and fell into a numbed silence. She recalled the bursts of southern black killings that galvanized the student body when she was enrolled at UC Berkeley, and at the sight of the raw image in front of her she felt the swell of a new powerful outrage.

"Lieutenant William Calley," the reverend continued, "because of unprecedented media coverge, has been accused of murdering of over a hundred civilians at My Lai. What are not publicized are the cover-ups, the killings, the misinformation generated by the military, the false claims that hide the true facts." He paused. "We can no longer trust the officials who run our country to tell us the truth."

The people around Radley stirred, she noticed a wave of agreement circle the room.

"Nixon announces from one side of his mouth that troops will begin to withdraw from South Vietnam before Christmas, that the war is over, while from the other he surreptitiously sends increased forces into Cambodia. "

He lowered his voice to a confiding undertone, Radley strained to catch the words. "Protests are spreading throughout the country." Reverend Allerton's eyes scanned the rows. "Recently 250,000 to

500,000 protesters demonstrated peacefully in Washington against the Vietnam War, as it became clear that the war was not winnable. A war that wasn't justified in the first place! And get this, Spiro Agnew has denounced anyone daring to criticize the war. He called them, and I quote, an 'effete corps of impudent snobs and nattering nabobs of negativism.' The vice president has a way with words, don't you think?"

Radley joined the general laughter, looked over to see people in adjoining rows clapping wildly. The reverend straightened up, tilted his head to swing the tuft of hair from his face. "Any questions so far?"

His voice rose to a forceful pitch. "We're here to explore how we can effect change. We need action. And I know many of you are eager to participate."

Looking folksy in casual jeans and suede loafers, Reverend Allenton clutched the mic in one hand as he faced the audience. His red hair fell loosely around his face, which was alive now, his eyes glowing, his cheeks flushed with energy. It was impossible, Radley thought, not to be roused by the strength of his earnest conviction. As if unconscious of the striking, slimly handsome figure he presented, he gazed out at the uplifted faces. Radley felt his gaze light on her.

In the pew ahead of Radley a hand jerked up, and a man clutching a rolled-up magazine stood up. "Reverend Allenton, the Students for a Democratic Society convention in Chicago was recently taken over by the Weathermen. We support the aims of the S.D.S. but the Weathermen promote extreme measures against the war and are resorting to violence. I have a problem with that."

"We're talking *change* here." The reverend raised his free fist in front of him. "You're right. The Weathermen have been bombing government offices. Their goal is a revolution. That's not what I believe our movement should be about. But the Weathermen are leading the protest against the Vietnam War. We can learn from their efforts.

"Here is one of their statements." He slipped a sheet of paper from his vest pocket. "*We believe that doing nothing in a period of repression is itself a form of violence. . . . If you sit in your big house, live your white life, go to your white job, and allow the country you live in to murder people and to commit genocide, and you sit there and you don't do anything about it, that's violence.*

Radley leaned forward to catch the speaker's every word as he described how the Weathermen declared war against the United States government, bombed the Pentagon, and broke Timothy Leary out of jail. "We don't have to go to those extremes," he explained. "But to effect real change we have to collaboration. We have to find a way to unite with our brothers in action like the S.D.S., or even the Black Panthers. This group, although formed as a military force to protect black neighborhoods from the police, are riding the same trajectory of change. We can support our common goals if not their methods."

Radley nodded agreement.

A man called out, "I support our brothers in action!"

The heavy woman in the billowy blouse shot her hand up but didn't wait to be recognized. "Of course, you mean our brothers and *sisters* in action. I don't support total revolution, but we need drastic change here. We need to stop the spraying of peaceful anti-war protesters with tear gas from helicopters by the National Guard, as in California. We need to stop attacks like the one on the peaceful demonstrators at the trial of the Chicago 7." She spoke out forcefully, a voice of conviction. "The Chicago police shot a Black Panther member dead while he slept. We can't stand by and do nothing!"

On impulse, Radley said loudly, "I second that. We have a right to free speech and dissension. Something must be done." She heard a ripple of supporting yeas from around the room and felt a strong tug of commonality vibrate around the room.

"Right!" The Reverend waved his arm. "Daring actions carry consequences. Can we face that?" Radley joined the chorus of yes—yes. "But we prefer, if possible, to demonstrate without riots."

A thin woman in the front row stood up, clutching a black patent-leather purse to her stomach. "Excuse me, but Gloria Steinem is standing up for the rights of women," and hurriedly sat back down.

"Of course, we must include the rights of women, as well as the rights of Negroes, or Blacks as they now prefer to be called. You see how one injustice uncovers others." Reverend Allerton dropped his voice. "Something's happening out there. There's a fervor, an energy I've never seen sweeping the country as we move into the 1970s, and here in Minnesota we're part of it." Yes, Radley heard her mind whisper, yes, yes, yes.

"There is so much to do! We can recruit our representatives, show up at hearings and write to our leaders. We can make a difference." Wiping the sides of his chin with his handkerchief, the Reverend smiled broadly, optimism shining on his face.

"A follow-up discussion will be held in the chat room," he announced. Applause blared through the hall for a full three minutes, then people twisted in their seats to gather their belongings.

Radley felt a flow of adrenaline propelling her along with the crowd, caught the wave of expectation in the air. She hadn't been so roused since her youthful days in the fifties—those long-ago years when she'd been mesmerized by the lyrics of Pete Seeger and poems of Alan Ginsburg calling for rabble and change.

Suddenly a voice at her elbow. "Your comments were right on." Radley turned to see the large woman in the billowy blouse close by her shoulder. "I'm glad you spoke up." The two fell into step and emerged through the front doors of the church as the bright October sun washed over them. Radley found herself looking into a creamy round face framed by casually cut brown hair. Despite the softness around her chin and puffy cheeks, the set to her jaw and a forceful gaze lent the woman an intellectual air.

"I've never been especially political," the woman said, "but I can't read the papers without getting riled about the outright lies we're being fed by the administration to whitewash the true status of the war. Even though it's clear that we'll never win, the killing goes on to save face." She tugged her shoulder-strap pocketbook up on her shoulder. "I've heard of Reverend Allenton's reputation as a staunch anti-war proponent. I came to hear for myself."

Radley felt a quivering run through her. Here was someone who thought about politics, and more, thought just as she did.

"Once I was actively involved in political campaigns," Radley told her. "I campaigned for Adlai Stevenson when he ran for president back in the fifties. But these past years I've given up all that—too busy leading my life. I even cancelled my subscription to the *New York Times*."

How had that happened? How had her life become so insular? The thrill of having her own family where she was exclusively needed had obliterated everything else. The delights of an entirely new way of life, of household and babies, the mesmerizing odors of vanilla, fresh linen and talcum, sleeping every night with a man she adored, all that rounded her sense of completeness. Nothing else had mattered.

But change was in the air, and she wanted to be a part of it. She smiled at her new acquaintance.

"I know precisely what you mean," the woman said, smiling back. "Audrey and John kept me under wraps for years, but now the children are involved in school and I need an outlet. By the way, my name is Klara."

"I'm Radley." They stood on the front steps of the church, with others lingering close by, talking, some grouped on the grass, nodding and gesturing.

"Dick—my husband--works at his job with the U.S. Corps of Engineers, and spends weekends canoeing down Minnehaha Creek or cross-country skiing or playing poker," Klara went on. "I don't do any of that. But he's always home for dinner. Then he's off again. I never saw anyone so active. Has to be doing something every minute." Radley saw a tired look cross her face, as if her energy fell just thinking about it. They ambled down the steps and paused under the shade of a spreading maple tree.

"What do you like to do?" Radley asked her.

"Read. Watch TV. Cook—my spaghetti with clams and peach Lambrini sauce is to die for."

"Does your husband agree with your political views?" Radley asked.

"Mostly, but he doesn't like to get involved. Our discussions always straddle the shore, never get out to the deep end. He has a conservative streak. He believes America needs to keep the nations of the world in its orbit. You know, defend against the communists at any cost. He goes to the Methodist church; I was raised a Lutheran but gave all that up long ago. We generally go our own ways." For a moment her face clouded. "Dick's a good provider. He's just—not there for me."

Klara turned her head as a young woman in a powder blue sweater sidled up next to her. "I hope you don't mind," the woman began with a jingling laugh, "if I butt in, but I totally agree with what you said in there about the mistreatment of protesters. This is all so new to me. I've driven quite a way to hear Reverend Allenton. Isn't he great?" Her eyes swept to Radley, back to Klara. "Sorry to break up . . ."

"Not at all. We're just getting acquainted," Klara said. "I like talking with like-minded people. It's so rare out here in no-mind's land." The three laughed and Klara moved aside to make room for her.

"I live in Robinsdale in a plain old house with two boys, a dog, and a husband "We moved here last spring from Detroit when my husband switched jobs.

The woman introduced herself as Bette. "I'm just not into the domestic activities that keep the neighbor women busy," she said, fingering her knobby gold necklace. "I find it hard to break into their circles. So I sit with my coffee and read my paper. One day I saw the ad for Reverend Allerton's lecture in the local *Sun*. I'm so glad I did! Heavens, it's opened my eyes." Bette gave a perky laugh that matched her quick smile and glistening brown eyes. Despite her high-pitched voice and girlish enthusiasm, she carried herself with assurance. "I have so much to learn. This is all so exciting!"

As if in confirmation, the bright horn from a distant train rang over the church spire, piercing through the high midday sun. The groups had dispersed, and the churchyard was nearly deserted. Radley made her way with Klara, and Bette to the parking lot, dizzy with the sensation of having discovered fellow travelers and the promise of a mutual goal.

"The reverend could be our guru. I'm ready to follow him. You two seem to feel the same. Where do we go from here?" Radley asked, stopping by the rear side of her car. The three looked at each other, unsure, not wanting to part.

"All right," Radley said. "Let's go to the Turnstile Café for coffee and continue our discussion.

"Good," Klara said. "I need to sit down."

Chapter 4

I t was a notable change of lifestyle when the Gallaghers moved moved in 1966 from the apartment in Manhattan to the sedate suburb of Deephaven. The minute Radley and Shane walked into the three-bedroom white-frame and beige brick rambler they knew it was the house they'd been searching for. A large screen porch on one side enticed the summer breezes and large windows on three sides of the house caught the rays of the sun as it arced through the sky. Set high on an acre of rich green lawn bursting with blooming bushes and wrap-around gardens, it afforded just the seclusion and security in which to enjoy married life and raise a family.

A few yards from their lot, the entry to the neighborhood was marked by a wooden **RESTON** sign, under which hung a row of names on a chain listing the residents of the lower road: Gallagher, Asher, Wimbledon, and Cortland. Spaced unevenly along the roads curving up the hill, the houses, some with white brick with cerulean blue trim and beige colored siding, were partially hidden among the well-trimmed, maple, ash, and birch spread across the one-acre lots. They all had large summer porches attached on one side or else tucked in the back facing the woods. The houses were freshly painted, the borders and gardens neatly defined, and the garage doors fitted with 16 square glass panes on the upper panel.

At the end of Reston Lane an old French provincial carriage house built of stone overlooked several private mansions set along the silvery blue of Lake Minnetonka below.

Besides their spacious new quarters and the beauty of the neighborhood, both Shane and Radley were full of excitement about Shane's new job as controller at Shelby Allied Foods. A definite step up. The seven years since they'd met in New York City had whizzed by, it seemed to Radley, with rocket speed. She had first seen Shane at an Athletic Club New Year's celebration party when introduced by a mutual friend as they scooped up lobster dip in the buffet line. Radley was smitten right off with the young Irish Catholic graduate of Notre Dame, tall, handsome, with a sweet, gentle manner and enticingly aloof air. Radley found out later that he, in turn, appreciated her energy and insistent curiosity—and the way she looked at him. She was the only non-Catholic he had ever dated.

They were enjoying married life in their small apartment when a head hunter connected Shane to an established consumer goods company in Minnesota. Four months later they moved across country where Shane undertook a new job that offered a significant raise. Once back in Radley's home state—she couldn't believe her luck—they began to look for what they had always dreamed of—a house where they could spread out with chil-dren Megan and Larry and the black lab, Wolf, and make a true home.

Now they had a full dining room, with a long mahogany buffet, serving tray with drawers, and a formal table that seated twelve guests. A large breakfront displayed the rich colors of their Columbia china set, a wedding gift from Radley's parents. The decor was much like the one Radley had grown up in, where her mother served dinner parties with candelabras, brightly dressed people, and fine wine. Her mother entertained frequently, this is what wives did. Now it fell to her. It was a housewife role she had assumed upon marriage, having bought the entire package. She could do this! It was time to reach out to the neighbors, she thought excitedly—she would throw a dinner party.

She invited six couples from the neighborhood, all of whom accepted. Clean the house, cull the recipe books, buy the groceries, prepare the table, arrange the flowers, and prepare a gourmet dinner for twelve—she dove into it, caught up in the novelty. Shane drove to the store and purchased a full supply of liquor.

As Radley stood in front of the bathroom mirror, she heard the wall-clock strike six mellow bongs. She started. It was almost time for the company to arrive and there she was, hair streaming wet, no way could she dry and style it in thirty minutes. Puffing her bobbed hair with a last swipe of the blow dryer, she clipped tortoise shell barrettes on each side of her head and rushed nervously down the hall to the open stairwell.

"They'll be here soon. What are you wearing?" she yelled down over a boom of loud cackles by Peter Sellers in "The Pink Panther" issuing from the television set below.

"Shirt and pants." His voice drifted up from the paneled amusement room.

Hopefully, he had changed into one of the attractive birthday shirts stacked in the chest of drawers.

She visualized him stretched out in the recliner, martini in hand, dark hair brushed neat and clean. Highly deserved idleness, he claimed, after a full day at the office. He liked to tease Radley about her cushy job, home all day supervising naps and watching television with their two children. "Let's see if the TV set is still warm," he'd joke as he came in from work, stroking the cabinet, and she laughed with him.

Larry's voice came squealing up the stairs. "Want Mickey!"

"It's not your turn!" Megan cried. "Stop. Daddy, make him stop."

"Now kids, take turns," came Shane's mellow voice. Radley marveled how things didn't seem to get under his skin. True, his composure sometimes faded into withdrawal, until he became so remote she couldn't find him. But it was just the way he was, the way she loved him.

Radley had been swept away when the man she had her heart set on had become hers. While the same thrill no longer raced through her at such high speed, she still smiled to see him sitting across the room, she still ran to him when he walked in the door from the office, still drank in the way he looked in his charcoal suit, white shirt and tie, his six-foot-three frame towering above her, a soft, impenetrable expression on his face.

Going into the kitchen, Radley observed the cardboard box Shane had brought from the liquor store on the counter, stuffed with bottles of Beefeater gin, Scotch, vodka, several brandies, and a parade of olives, macadamia nuts, tonic and various colored mixes. My god, there was enough there for an army. Really, Shane overdid it, insisting they be prepared for any drink request imaginable.

Radley lifted the mahogany silverware box from the breakfront drawer with the words *To Radley and Shane 1960* emblazoned on the lid. She laid twelve places of Columbia china and Kirk Rose silverware carefully around the white tablecloth embroidered by her grandmother. She heard in her ears the encouraging voices of the past, echoing the traditions of women ancestors down the decades.

There was a time when Radley could not have imagined she'd be following her mother into domesticity. Allow herself to be caught in the homemaking routine that defined her mother's circle—not her! Early on, she had set her sights on life in the career world, maybe working for one of the vibrant New York magazine publishers. A life of exploring, of experimenting. Indulging her love of travel where she could search for answers to the meaning of life.

Then she fell in love with Shane. Right when her job composing jingles for greeting cards for Cowles, Crane & Co. was showing signs of losing momentum. The flush of the freewheeling single twenties had faded, and signals erupted as she swung around one corner after another that the fulfillment she was seeking did not necessarily wait on the other side.

She had protested against marriage and domesticity, vowed she would never capitulate to the norm, would be her own person, find own destiny, above all would not follow her mother's footsteps to a material and superficial life. She would not be smothered by family conformity and forced to lead a life she deplored.

But life moved on, bringing variant messages. It was more than disillusion about her mediocre career, which had not evolved into a rewarding life of creative fulfillment and associations. She had come to doubt that the fulfillment she anticipated waiting for her at the end of the road existed. Despite the wide net of exploration she had undertaken in her young free years, her adventures in foreign countries, with expectations of grand things happening, she found herself at age thirty alone in her apartment. The stack of journals in her drawer detailing her life had become repetitious, repeating the same wonderings, the same expectations, the same lacks, with no resolution.

Her days ran on smoothly enough... She had friends, a decent although repetitious job, enjoyed cocktails with men, spent warm Christmas holidays in Minnesota with her family. But her friends had gotten married or moved on or taken their typewriters and folders to the 37th floor and disappeared into executive offices. Her best friend had moved to Connecticut with her new husband. The men she dated were interchangeable. She was walking a treadmill. The future looked flat.

Time was moving on without her.

And then she met Shane. Not only was she drawn by his tall good looks, but she found his elusive manner, his tentative responses and restraint compelling. Nothing bothered her more than a guy gushing over her, pulling her in, smothering her with undiscriminating attention. The brother she had grown up with, four years older, had refused to put up with her demands for attention, her complaints and drama. He wanted none of it. He avoided her, leaving the room and disappearing out the back door with a friend. She longed to be with him, to be included in his life. When she met Shane, she sensed a familiarity. Here was someone she could respect, with whom she sensed the possibility of realizing a coveted relationship she had missed elsewhere.

They were continually with his friends, apartment parties in Manhattan, summer picnics, excursions to the beach, weekends on Fire Island. She, the serious seeker of truth, enjoyed the luxury of simple re-laxation and fun. She could pick out Shane's laugh in the crowd, warm and open like a flowing brook, coloring the atmosphere with good hu-mor. Maybe a life with this man wouldn't be so bad. In fact, as people started paring up, getting engaged, planning new lives, she longed to do the same. Enough of humdrum workdays and weary evenings at Clark's bar on Lexington Avenue. Enough rounding curves and seeing only more curves in the distance.

With Shane, the path lay straight ahead. She fell with gusto into married life. Already she'd planted rows of seedlings in the garden bed, sent to Japan for Siberian iris bulbs, planted a row of arborvitae along the edge of the yard, and massacred several recipes from *The Joy of Cooking*. She was intoxicated by Shane and life with him—a home of their own, beautiful babies, the intimacy of a committed union, the feeling of belonging, and operating in the mature world of structured society.

She'd better get a move. The guests would be arriving soon, and she still had to prepare the béarnaise sauce for the veal cutlets and locate her jade earrings. The serving dishes had to be set out, but at least the cutlets were ready to go in the oven and the Baked Alaska was firming in the freezer. The last-minute jobs could wait until later: rolls to be baked, main dishes to be served, ice water to set on the table, and everything kept piping hot until ready to eat. There was so much to do and her with only two hands. A nervous reflex shot through her wrists and into her fingers. Her first big dinner party. And her hair was still wet!

At the sound of a car rounding the circular drive, Radley scrambled into her black suede heels and hurried down the hall in another flush of nerves. She had managed to find her earrings; now to compose her face and summon a modicum of poise. She must remember to turn off the béarnaise sauce in fifteen minutes. Luckily, the children were engrossed in their kiddie programs on channel 12, with two fresh toys on the table to keep them occupied until bedtime. The bell!

"Hello Radley, hi there Shane, so nice of you to have us." Adele Horton smiled brightly. She looked chic in a slim purple pants suit with matching cream and purple *mousseline de soie* blouse. "We're so glad you invited us," she said to Radley. "I understand you're from New York and my daughter Courtney is planning to attend Columbia next year. We have a lot to talk about."

Her husband Hugh nodded amiably, taking off his fedora. "I saw you last Thursday mowing the lawn. Quite a job. And that son of yours—"

"Larry—"

"The last time I drove by he was perched at the top of the Middleton's elm tree, higher than the roof, swinging like a monkey." Chuckling, Hugh pulled a silver cigarette case from his jacket pocket. His complexion was pale, his cheekbones on the thin side, but there were lines of authority in his face and an arresting intelligence in his eyes.

Shane came up, tall and amiable, the picture of young corporate advancement. Hugh grinned at him and held out his hand. "You've already improved the place, Shane. The former owner, an older widow, had let things run down." He looked around the room approvingly.

When everyone was seated comfortably around the glass coffee table, Hugh pulled a cigarette from the case and clicked open a Zippo lighter. "So, young man, how do you find our Lake Minnetonka society? Are you interested in boats? I'm a boat man myself." He inhaled a deep puff and leaned back.

"Well, I don't know. We don't own a boat," Shane confessed.

Radley chuckled to herself. A boat! Shane had spent his young life in Queens getting around in subways and L-trains. And after their experience at the St. Croix River, she doubted he had any interest in boats.

"How about a drink?" Shane smiled with a proprietary air. "You name it." He disappeared to fill the orders. From the kitchen floated the crinkling of ice, the swish of metal shakers, the flush of vodka gimlets, lime slice perched on the glass rim, and Manhattans being poured into sheer frosty glasses.

Adele had gone over to inspect the East Indian silk print hanging above the piano. "This is exquisite," she said, lingering in front of it. "Have you seen the new local water color exhibit at the Heatherton House?"

"No." Radley moved to her side. "I haven't been in a museum in years."

"It shows local artists. You must stop in and see it." Adele lifted a Scotch and soda from Shane's tray with a gracious smile.

A car horn sounded out front, and a large figure in a flared black crepe blouse dotted with shiny black beads stepped into the room. Three-quarter length sleeves billowed around her plump arms, and her short brown hair, pulled from her face, hung in waves along her neck. Klara's husband Dick followed at her heels, wearing a floppy fatigue jacket, short khaki boots and a look of outdoor abandon. He could have dressed up, Radley thought, but she was glad to see both of them, and if he was not *comme il faut,* so much the better. After consideration, she had decided to invite Klara and Dick, although they were not Reston residents like the other guests. She wanted to introduce her new friend to the neighborhood social circle, and it didn't matter if, compared to the other couples, Klara and Dick came off as a bit on the rough side.

Klara was the one person she'd bonded with since moving to the suburbs. After meeting at Reverend Allerton's lecture on political activism, they had quickly delved into topics that Radley had almost forgotten existed: the disaster of the Vietnam War, the defeat of De Gaulle in France, John Lennon and Yoko Ono's mad bed-in performance in Quebec. Klara read profusely, quoted her Macalester College professors, and knew the history of the founding convention and the development of the Declaration of Independence in minute detail. They had started attending League of Women Voters meetings together.

Behind them, a woman in a red headband peered through the screen, laughing and chattering. "Hello," she called, breezing into the living room. Andy Cortland and her husband Stanley lived with their young son in the rambler next door to the Hortons. Andy was a woman of action; she organized and energetically carried out a battery of household projects, maintained her husband's wall of aquariums as well as her own hobbies, and managed her son's upbringing with clarity and precision. When Radley happened into her during walks with the children down the shaded streets, Andy liked to describe the history of the Reston neighborhood and the families whose mansions bordered the lake.

The last couple to arrive, Stig and Emily Ridgeway, lived in a peach and white house at the end of the road. Emily, a petite blonde with narrow shoulders, looked young and chic in a black empire dress. Close behind, her husband Stig tugged at the collar of his camel sports jacket and threw a wide, lopsided grin around the room. The Ridgway's had thrown a cocktail party the previous December, complete with a hired bartender and white-uniformed caterer. Their house was full of baseball plaques and statues of football and hockey stars that Stig had collected in his travels as marketing supervisor for a sports equipment firm.

"Hi. What'll it be?" Shane asked with a cheerful smile as people settled around the room and pulled out cigarettes. His face was open and flushed with animation, and Radley smiled on hearing his melodious laugh amid the conversation. A few guests wandered into the porch and arranged themselves on wicker furniture with yellow and green flowered cushions. The air was heavy with late summery ripeness, and the branches of the honeysuckle bushes brushed gently against the front screens.

While Shane distributed drinks, Klara outlined her plan to turn their back yard into a self-perpetuating wildflower garden—it would eliminate mowing and look quite charming.

Radley noticed that Adele, seated to her left, looked dubious. "I believe letting your yard go wild would be considered neglect. It is restricted by local ordinance," she said mildly.

"Nevertheless, it's an ideal solution if you think about it," Klara said. "I don't care for manual labor, and Dick's job keeps him too busy for yard work." She leaned over and pulled a pack of Camels from her oversized purse, then leaned back on the couch.

Suddenly a shrill whistle sounded and Radley jumped from her chair. The béarnaise sauce! "Excuse me," and she flew into the kitchen.

A saucepan on the stove was gurgling, and Radley smelled the odor of seared cream. Quickly, she grabbed a spoon and stirred. Still usable, she decided. Now to keep the sauce warm until the meal was ready. The rolls had to go in the oven immediately. Where was the silver bread basket? Yesterday she'd polished the silver, arranged the flower centerpiece, purchased the beverages, cleaned the house top to bottom, and selected the background music. Earlier, the kids, running through the house, had tripped and grabbed the dining room tablecloth, nearly toppling the dinner plates to the floor. *Not to panic!*

Just then they clamored into the kitchen—evidently toys couldn't keep a six and seven-year-old occupied for long. All right, all right, she cried as they pulled at her skirts, just not now!"

She hadn't felt this nervous since she had to give a speech to the entire student body as a sophomore in high school. Her hands were sweating; she wiped them on the apron lying over the chair, which she had forgotten to put on. Another bell: the potatoes au gratin were done. Check the rolls. Line up the dessert plates and forks on the counter. She peered in the freezer. The baked Alaska was perfection, ready to frost. She poured water from a crystal pitcher into the largest of three crystal stem glasses at each plate, dropped three cubes of ice into each, and plugged in the coffee maker.

Oh my god, the canister is almost empty. Let's see—run to a neighbor? Send Shane to the store? Dinner in ten minutes, no time. Oh thank heavens, here's another tin, Folgers, but it will have to do. With shaking fingers she ripped open the top of the bag and poured it into the metal holding cup. Never mind measuring.

After supplying Wizard of Oz coloring books for the children and settling them in the amusement room at separate kiddie tables, Radley picked up her gin and tonic and moved into the dining room. The table glowed with silver serving dishes and the green, rose, yellow and brown colors of the china plates. She'd folded the linen napkins in triangles and placed a silver candelabra and bowls of rose and yellow flower buds in the center of the table. Beautiful, she thought, pleased. If only the meal itself lived up to the promise. The thought sent her reeling back to the kitchen.

As she stood looking at the steaming crock of scalloped potatoes, a tight knot clutched in her stomach. *Would she ever master this type of production? Was it worth it? Was this dinner really superior to an outdoor barbeque in the soft summer air or a picnic on the shore of a cool lake? Who promoted this stupendous form of gourmet dining? Not busy, harried housewives. This kind of entertaining had its origins in a royal household, where god-like kings and queens commanded elaborate banquets, provided by genius artists who devoted their entire lives to their patron's pleasure. All the hostess had to do was show up.*

Back in the days of cathedrals and duels. Nothing to do with 1968 and the middle class household. She wasn't sure she liked all the polish, too grueling, nerve-racking, you couldn't enjoy your own party. Why did this royal institution continue to be imitated through the generations by the masses, the common citizen, that is, us? Maybe it was time for a change.

CHAPTER 5

❧ ❧ ❧

The clock bonged eight. The hors d'oeuvres tray had long been emptied. At Radley's announcement, the guests filed up to the table, gazing ravenously at the dishes brimming with food.

"Bring your drinks," she heard Shane say. He had been circulating, making sure that each glass was filled to the brim.

Oh my god, butter. Radley ran to the breakfront for the proper dish, back to the refrigerator to grab a stick, and sat down at the table. She noticed that she'd forgotten the second set of salt and pepper shakers, and one of the serving spoons was tarnished along the stem. A sample bite of the potatoes made her stop: barely lukewarm. *Too late for all that.*

The guests, seated around the table, didn't appear to notice. "Nice flowers," Emily said, settling her napkin daintily in her lap. Radley started passing the scalloped potatoes.

After a lengthy discussion on the newest insecticide for crab grass, Klara spoke up. "Radley and I have been studying the history of the Minnesota two-party system. Are any of you involved in local politics? She picked up a silver basket and carefully pulled a hot roll from under the cloth.

Adele said she'd once been a delegate to the republican convention, years ago. The others shook their heads.

"Klara and I," Radley said, forgetting to monitor the passing of the dishes, "have been reading Peter Arnett's article, where he refutes the military's claim that it destroyed a Vietnamese town in order to save it. Contrary to the official report, he found that hundreds of innocent people were killed. He questions the bombing of people thousands of miles from here to, quote 'protect our shores from the Communists.'"

"We have to support our military," Stan exclaimed, "grabbing his wine glass. "We must keep America strong. "

Klara shifted heavily in her chair and looked around the table, her dark eyes intense. "But don't we deserve the truth? Have you noticed, the papers never question the military, their directives are taken as gospel? The news we get is slanted—the U.S.A. can do no wrong. Did you see the *Tribune* this morning? We lost men, over 16,000, in the Tet Offensive, but the article didn't even mention the 200,000 Vietnamese killed. I guess if you're not American you don't count."

Radley cast a grateful look at Klara. Here was someone who didn't share the America-right-or-wrong mentality that seemed to exist everywhere.

Radley noticed that silence had fallen over the table. She recalled her mother's rule that formal dinner table conversation remain harmonious, agreeable, so as not to spoil the pursuit of enjoyment. Radley's college days in academia had changed all that. Gossip was fine, but surely there was a place for interesting topics among friends!

Adele dabbed her napkin on her mouth. "The killing is regrettable, but unfortunately, that's the price of defending our country," she said equably. "As a Republican I support the war, although you're quite right, our undertaking a war on such a distant country in the first place is questionable." She flashed a smile around the table. "I don't suppose we all support the same issues, but there's room for more than one point of view in a democracy."

Radley looked at her in admiration. No wonder Adele, who radiated competence with her even gaze and air of sensible authority, became president of everything she joined. It didn't diminish her reputation that her husband was president of the Federal Reserve Bank and a champion chess player.

Shane refilled the wine glasses, and everyone relaxed. Radley saw Klara's eyes twinkling, as if she were aware of the ideological gap between herself and the others.

Emily spoke up. "I vote Republican, like everyone at Stig's office. Aren't they all Republican at Prudential, Stig? But my hands are too full with the kids to bother about politics. I love being home with the children, don't you?" She gave a watery smile and emptied her wine glass, a little unsteadily. A pearl ring encircling one of her milky white fingers shone in the candlelight.

"You are to be commended for that, Emily," Adele said, "but my children are older. If I ever get a minute, I plan to join the new Art League. I need to have something to do."

"You do enough already, dear," Hugh said from across the table. "Let someone else have a chance."

With his thinning hair, graying at the temples, subtle gray eyes, and competent manner, Hugh was the picture of the amiable executive. He gave Radley the impression that no matter how much he relaxed and enjoyed the camaraderie of the evening, there was always a switchboard at the back of his mind awaiting a call to the next important matter.

"This veal is superb, Radley." Adele pierced a bite of meat with her fork. "You might like to join the local Gourmet Gals cooking group."

Radley forced a smile. Nothing interested her less than cooking, other than dumping slop buckets at winter camp. How could she admit to the immaculate, well-turned Adele that she'd never cooked in her life and that tonight she'd undertaken to prepare breaded veal cutlets for the first time from a gourmet recipe from *The Joy of Cooking,* her mother's housewarming gift? That for every dish attempted she had been forced to consult the dictionary for words like shirred, blanched, and capers?

"Thank you," she replied. "Maybe someday I'll find the time."

Shane, from his place at the head of the table, took orders for more veal. "Plenty right here." He was enjoying himself in the company of friends, drinks flowing freely, people loosening up as the wine induced a party atmosphere and the line between frankness and decorum slowly fell away.

Shane was highly satisfied with their new lifestyle. He took pride in their house in an upscale neighborhood, respectable, clean and well-kept, and an easy commute to the Shelby Foods office. He liked the security and comforts of home and a steady job where he didn't have to forage or initiate the human encounters of life. Now that they were blessed with two God-sanctioned children, he had done his duty, made his contribution.
His lifestyle exceeded the expectations of the boy growing up in the sidelines of Manhattan. Here he was, two generations away from the Irish homeland, in the heartland of American—who would have thought! He had no need for more.

Stig passed his plate to Shane and took several deep gulps of wine. "I don't take politics very seriously," he said amicably. His plate returned, he scooped his fork under a pile of potatoes. A swarthy man with a rough complexion and a close-trimmed crew cut, Stig contributed to the conversation by shooting off questions at every opportunity with boisterous friendliness. "So, what's new on the travel front, my fine friends?"

Adele smoothed her napkin on her lap. "Did you hear about Hugh's upcoming snowmobile trip to Yellowstone?"

Hugh put down his salad fork. "Yes sirree," he said. "Come January, a small group of us plan to snowmobile across the Rockies and camp at an isolated log cabin deep in the mountains. We'll be riding forty miles into the wilderness. It will be the trip of a lifetime."

"Is it dangerous?" Emily asked.

"Oh, I'll be in good hands. The Mountain Wild Association povides the most advanced equipment. Nat Nordstrom, the leader, is not only a meteorological expert, he's a pro at leading wilderness trips."

"I'm a bit worried about Hugh's stamina," Adele said. "He's not as young as he thinks he is."

"I'll be in good shape by January." Everyone glanced at Hugh, marking his slight build and the yellowish hue of his skin. "My aneurysm is no longer a problem, and I've been working out at the gym three times a week." His eyes flashed with anticipation. "I won't miss this trip."

Just then, Radley heard screams from the basement, rapid footsteps clattering up the stairs, and Larry burst into the dining room, with Megan trotting behind. At the sight of the adults circled around the table, they came to an abrupt halt.

"Megan won't let me watch *Felix*. Megan get spanked!" Larry screeched, forgetting about the company.

"He's not watching it anyway!" Megan cried, grabbing a tuft of Larry's hair, at which he uttered a sharp yell.

"Bedtime!" Radley jumped up. "Let's go kids. Say good night to everyone."

"Good night," Megan whispered under her breath, suddenly shy as all eyes turned on her.

Larry scowled and hopped up and down. "No!" Radley grabbed each of them. "I'll be back to serve the dessert," and she led them down the hallway to their bedrooms.

When the children were finally settled, she returned to the kitchen to find the coffee clinking against the top glass lid. Pulling the Baked Alaska from the freezer, she measured the egg whites and sugar for the meringue topping, plugged in the electric hand mixer and watched the mixture spin in the bowl, waiting for it to thicken. Let's see, add a little sugar at a time, how much exactly? Would it never thicken? She hoped the conversation in the dining room wasn't lagging, but she had to get this in the oven!

Radley's fingers tensed around the mixer as she bent over the bowl. At last the meringue lifted to a stiff point and she quickly set about spreading it over the ice cream dome with a spatula, forming a tall mound of creamy swirls.

As she shoved the Alaska into the 500 degree oven and set the timer for four minutes—not a second more—she heard screams and rushed down the hall to find Megan curled at the foot of her bed, head under a pillow.

"I'm scared Mommy! Can I bring Wolf in my bed, just this once?" Her face peeked out at Radley, eyes white with terror.

"No, ducky, the dog belongs in the basement." Megan's nightmares often drew Radley from her bed during the night, and she would stagger into Megan's room in a daze. *Maybe she could make up the sleep the next day. In any case, she could put up with being crabby . . . this was what it was like having kids.* And she would remind herself how lucky she was to have two beautiful robust children.

But tonight there was no time. "Here's Pooh Bear. I'll be back in ten minutes, I promise, to read you a story. Don't get out of bed." As she closed the door behind her she heard the lie bat against her ears, but in her state of desperation there was nothing else she could think to do.

When she opened the oven door, the sight made her gasp. The carved dome had disappeared. In its place a lopsided black mass lay crusted with cinder-like flakes, yellow liquid running over the edges of the pan. Nothing remained of the Alaska's former glory. Oh, my god!

A rush of adrenaline gathered in her chest, shot through her arms, her nerves, every neutron of her body exploded, and with a lurch she lobbed the plate across the kitchen and into the sink, where it landed with a thud, emitted a few gurgles, and sank like a deflated balloon.

She watched the mound disappear slowly into the drain. It was no use! Her efforts at becoming the ideal housewife, following in the footsteps of her mother to create a glowingly house, filled with healthy children and grand entertainment, were no good. Her faith in the lifestyle she'd chosen whole-heartedly was dissolving down the drain along with the ice cream. *She didn't know how to do this—she was out of her element—how could she possibly survive?*

Luckily there were two quarts of vanilla ice cream in the freezer. She doused them with hot chocolate and served the dessert and coffee with what she hoped was a composed expression, ignoring the panic burning in her stomach.

After dinner, the guests moved into the living room, where Shane served liqueur glasses of Grand Marnier. Word had gotten around that Shane was an accomplished pianist, and he was urged to play, but as usual he declined. During their dating days in New York, he had played often at parties, but a solo performance—absolutely not, he pleaded modesty, and even Radley's urging couldn't change his mind.

Radley sank back into the couch, forehead burning. Fighting an on-slaught of giddiness, she put down her drink and turned her attention to Adele and Emily, who were engaged in a lively discussion of the television miniseries, "The Forsythe Saga." Andy, ankles crossed in front of her, was telling Dick about the installation of the new swimming pool, Hugh and Stanley were discussing the results of the last Rose Bowl, and Stig was pacing back and forth asking everyone, "What school do you contribute to? Have you ever skied in Switzerland?"

Shane was pleased. It was a matter of pride that everyone kept drink-ing; it proved they were having a good time. He made sure every glass was full to the brim at all times, overriding every reluctance.

The liqueurs were followed by tall cups of Irish coffee. Voices became louder, people changed seats, wandered down the hallway. Someone knocked over a table lamp, so, so sorry.

Adele and Hugh left quietly, as the next day they needed to be up early. The conversations began to wind down, going nowhere. Andy set her cup down. "It's after midnight, we really must go," she said.

Her husband Stanley quickly waved her away. "Just one more, love, one for the road. Shane, any more of that good Scotch?"

"No, Stanley, you won't be able to see the road. We're *going*," Andy insisted.

People filtered into the bedroom to fetch their belongings. As they gathered in the front hall, Andy dashed in. "I left Stan standing right here at the front door. Now I can't find him." There was urgency in her voice.

"He was under the weather. Must have gone out to your car," Stig mumbled, bracing himself against the doorway.

"We walked over," Andy said.

A sobering hush fell over the group. A search of the basement and the rest of the house yielded nothing. Stanley Cortland had disappeared.

Shane and Stig undertook to search darkened yard, while Andy and Radley pushed up the garage door and switched on the light. A ladder and two green yard hoses hung neatly along one wall, underneath a wooden shelf holding blocks of gallon paint tins. Everything was in order. Except for one thing: the door to the Buick was wide open. Moving closer, they beheld Stanley stretched out in the back seat, one foot dangling over the threshold of the open door.

The others came rushing in.

"He must have thought he was in his own house."

"He was beyond thinking."

"He was in no shape to drive anywhere."

Shane and Stig, a bit unsteadily, grasped Stan between them and started for Stan's home singing clips of "For he's a jolly good fellow." Andy followed them down the darkened street.

Dick and Klara were the last to leave. "Hey, great time," Dick said, taking Klara by the arm as they started out the front door. "Don't usually dwnk so much. Gue by Radley. Hey Klara, steady there, thus steps look slippery. Hang on to me, I've got you, not to worry—oops! Nearly tripped there." He clung to the wobbly figure of his wife, who shuffled slowly down, leaning one way while Dick tilted the other, a precarious dependence that threatened to topple them both at any moment.

The next morning Radley shuffled to the kitchen and stood surveying the damage. Crooked stacks of sticky silverware, bleeding dishes, and pans caked with dried food lay about the Formica countertops, and the soggy remains of the baked Alaska lay in the sink where Radley had flung it, like the aftermath of a worn battlefield.

How was she going to make it through the day the way her head pounded? Her mind was strangled in a net; she could hardy focus. Somehow she had to get through the whole of Sunday, waiting for the hour when she could fall into bed and let blessed sleep restore her to normalcy.

After she'd cleaned up the dishes and wiped down the counter, Radley studied the liquor bottles on the breakfast room table, gleaming in the sun. Most were unopened. They'd spent hundreds of dollars on enough liquor for a royal wedding. Shane always went overboard, plying the guests with liquor. She wondered if any of them would step foot in the house again. The Hortons, hallmarks of constraint and propriety, were sure to disapprove of the insistent flow of liquor. She knew Klara rarely drank and didn't usually get drunk at dinner parties.

She noticed a half-full shaker of martinis standing by the refrigerator.

With a sigh, she moved to the top of the basement stairs and opened the door. High pitched voices from the Mouseketeers wafted up to her; she could picture Shane and the children scrunched in their pajamas in front of the television set.

"Do you want a martini?" she yelled down.

"How much is left?" Shane's voice drifted up.

"One drink."

"No," was the reply. "Not worth it." Evidently if there wasn't enough to acquire a buzz there was no point. She was beginning to grasp the place of liquor in her husband's routine. Well, drinking was his one amusement, his only hobby. He could be allowed. On the other hand, as she looked back on the continual partying of their courtship days, which revolved around drinking, she wondered how such a practice fit into their married roles. In the demanding era of parental responsibility, one need-ed a clear head and the fortitude of a good night's sleep.

She went downstairs, trying to keep her eyes focused. Settling on the couch, she picked up the front section of the *Tribune* from the cof-fee table. The children had been cooped up all weekend, they ought to be taken on an outing. "Why don't we do something today?" she said to Shane. "It's Sunday."

"Do what?"

"Anything. Take a picnic to Gray's Bay and watch the sailboats."

Shane put down his coffee cup and pulled a pack of Pall Malls from his shirt pocket. "I'm pretty tired," he said. "Right now I'd like to relax."

"Maybe later this afternoon," she suggested, "we could walk down by the beach or go to a movie."

"After working all week I like to stay home on weekends. The kids can find things to do here." That meant watching TV, hour after hour. She'd have to take the children out herself.

If only she could dispel the nauseous weight in her stomach. Drunken guests, hangovers, exhaustion, neglected children—Radley was unable to shake off the dark pall that hung over her.

After attempting to read the front page of the paper, she stood up abruptly and padded upstairs where the dishwasher was churning quietly. The liquor bottles stood lined up on the counter like bowling pins, the gold and brown liquid inside reflecting the sharp rays of the sun com-ing through the window. She stared at them. Finally—she couldn't stop herself—one by one, she carried each bottle to the sink, turned it upside down and watched as the circular swirls of brown and butterscotch liquid swirled down the drain out of sight, coughing up gurgles that sounded like the dying wails of a beast. She dumped the empties in the trash can.

The sun from the window felt hot on her face. All that future partying, all that expense, gone, wasted, Shane would be looking for them. She had taken a daring stance and it felt good. She knew Shane wouldn't like it, but she was sure she could count on his passivity. As for formal dinners, maybe she'd get the hang of it with practice, her dutiful good girl mind told her. Yet the evening had been a disaster, without question, and another voice, one closer to her gut, declared that never again would she attempt such a production.

Too exhausted to think about that now. She grabbed a Dr. Pepper from the fridge and shuffled back downstairs.

CHAPTER 6

I t was a hot, muggy morning, and the sun sprayed down on the roof tops unimpeded by a single whiff of cloud. Radley gazed out the kitchen window at the yard, pale and dry, not a movement in the faded turf. She must get out the sprinkler. It would be one of those August dog days that cry for window air units and ice-packs behind the neck. By noon the pavements would be scorching. Once she'd put the cereal bowls in the dishwasher, fed Wolf, and scraped off the play-doh the kids had smeared in colorful sweeps across the picture window, the entire day stretched ahead.

All summer she had been concocting things for the children to do. By now, she had exhausted every idea she could come up with.

They would go to the beach.

After rescuing their swim suits from the piles of toys, games, and clothes littering their rooms, Radley helped Larry on with his brown trunks patterned with red kites, while Megan struggled into a yellow one-piece stretch suit, wiggling her butt as she peeled the suit up her torso.

They headed for the beach four blocks away. Megan skipped along the gutters, while Radley pulled Larry in a red wagon with white stripes. He sat clutching the sides with both hands and looking up at the tree tops as if he might leap up and swing on their branches at any moment. "Go faster, Mom!" The homes in the neighborhood were silent, shadow figures could be seen stirring behind open windows. A car backed out of a driveway and hummed quietly away. They passed the Horton's yard where a sprinkler whirred, fanning water drops far over the rich green grass. Radley drank in the majesty of the soaring green trees, the clammy odor of the lake in the distance, the smoky ash scent issuing from the scattered homes.

She loved their house, set graciously into the curve of the land. She and Shane recently painted it a deep vermillion red. Radley had insisted on red, yielding to an urge to insert a spark of individuality into the neighborhood.

They found the beach area deserted. The sapphire blue lake glazed before them with a smooth shine, a few boats floated in the distance without seeming to go anywhere. The children squealed and ran to the water's edge as Radley spread out the blanket and kicked off her sandals.

"Hallo!" A cheery voice broke into her thoughts. She turned to see her neighbor Andy clipping up the path with an air of efficiency, followed by little John on his tricycle. As they neared, she gave John's tricycle a push and he spun his little feet ferociously. When he reached the end of the path, he jumped off and ran down to join Megan and Larry at the lake.

"Don't go in the water until I get there," Andy called after him.

Andy and Stan Cortland lived in a low modern house with tall narrow windows and three staggered roof levels. Inside, the walls were filled with framed needlepoint and pressed Japanese flower arrangements, examples of Andy's handiwork. Radley admired Andy's indomitable energy—she knit fancy sweaters, created large pots on the wheel, entered rose specimens in the flower show, and served up gourmet dinners on weekends. Radley watched her beat happily about the house, working a puzzle at the kitchen table with John, coaching him on the trapeze bar, or laying out the latest collage for her art class. How did she manage all this accomplishment so smoothly?

"You're so good with John," Radley told her, sitting on the blanket and pulling a tube of sun lotion from a duffle bag. "I don't know how you do it. I have a hard time controlling my two." She sighed. "It was much easier when they stayed in the playpen amusing themselves with mobiles between naps. Now they're out loose with all that *energy*!"

Andy laughed. "My Johnny is pretty placid. Most of the time he plays with Legos or watches cartoons."

"I can't imagine what that must be like."

"Oh, he still has to be disciplined. He wants what he wants when he wants it. Luckily Stan's strict and keeps him in line."

Radley felt her shoulders tighten. She thought of Shane, kind, good Shane, but utterly helpless in enforcing discipline. His ideas on child-rearing revolved around the Catholic Church. He looked to its strict commandments to keep children in line, which included the threat of eternal damnation to lash them into shape. She vowed she would never subject her children to the arbitrary authority she'd been blasted with growing up—because her father said so, no questions asked, the sanity of reason, the claims of justice abandoned. She adhered to a different approach: sympathetic guidance with a loving hand, explaining, directing small minds to the consequences of their behavior and firmly holding them within the boundaries of reality.

Just how she would manage to apply this was another matter.

"Maybe you and I could start a coffee klatch to meet regularly with other mothers. Andy looked at her eagerly, looking fresh and peppery in a crisp blue and white striped shirt and white shorts. "It would give the children a chance to interact."

"Who with? There are no other kids around here."

"So the two of us can meet," Andy said.

Radley glanced at her gratefully. It was a solution to the *What will I do with them?* problem. Anything would be preferable to the long hours at the playground, watching the kids play in the sand while the clouds inched past overhead in slow motion. How did all those composed mothers do it? She envied Shane, in a cool office bent over interesting work, while she sat on a hot bench trying to keep her mind from exploding. Nothing equaled the suffocation of sitting and doing nothing she could get her mind around.

In the old days, she reflected, children didn't require constant entertainment. They leapt under the sprinkler in the back yard, played catch, or read books while the mother bustled about in the house. Children found things to do as the days floated by defined by school hours, meals, and bedtime.

It was too bad that Andy's little John was too young for her four-and five-year-olds to play with. A coffee klatch had little appeal. Already she was tired of Tupperware parties, caught up in discussions of recipes and drapery patterns. She no longer enjoyed the novelty of gardening, sewing, cooking, and cleaning house as she had in the early days. The idea of gossiping about housework with a bunch of ladies over coffee hit her with a thud.

She did admire Andy's way with John. Scrapes, impulses, tantrums, Andy met all with a composed naturalness that held Radley in awe. Children needed a constant never-miss-a-beat guardian, a nurse, a policeman, a director, a teacher, a consoler, some paragon of patience and equanimity. And she, Radley, appeared to be none of these. Children got into trouble. It was a stamp of nature, their little bodies bursting with growth hormones that demanded an outlet, like blind creatures wound up tight and released into a spin. They required attention every second.

What was to be done? Radley's mind registered empty. She peered into a canopy of trees overhead as if trying to wring answers from the tight gnarled branches. She had to find a way to guide her children, to handle them without the cascade of emotional crises that followed their every step.

Andy met the calamities that sent Radley into a tailspin with an unflappable instinct. Nothing got to her. Was it temperament—training—intelligence—having a placid child or having only one? Homemaker, wife, mother, creator—this girl could handle most anything. It might be good to join forces with her after all.

After they had watched the children playing at the water's edge for some time, Andy stood up. "Time to get Johnny home for his nap time. See you later. Ta, ta." And with a wave she was gone.

As the ball of sun began dipping behind the tree tops, Radley toweled Megan and Larry dry, gathered up their belongings, and started for home. As they passed the Horton house, without warning Larry sprinted across the yard and scrambled up a pile of logs stacked at the edge of the woods.

"Don't climb up there," Radley yelled, hastening after him. "The logs will collapse." Larry appeared not to hear, and as he reached the top the pile wobbled and the logs began to shift. Larry paused and looked around, as if uncertain. Then, with a deft movement, he squeaked a laugh and fluttered down the pile in feathery steps, landing just before the entire pile tottered and crashed to the ground. Then he sped across the lawn, leapt sprightly over a petunia bed and stopped beside his mother.

At that moment, the back door of the Horton house opened and a girl stepped out, a tall wiry child of around ten in skinny jeans and wild black hair on which perched a bright orange baseball cap. A wide leather strap was fastened around her waist.

"What's going on? Can I play?" The girl folded her arms. Then, noticing the logs scattered over the ground, she looked at Radley and Megan with a grin. "I'm Dean. I'll bet Larry did that," she exclaimed. "Oh, boy, my dad won't like it." How did she know Larry? Radley wondered. They had not met her before.

Andy had explained during one of their walks that Dean Horton frequently got into trouble behind her parents' back. She usually managed to evade consequences by the ingenious use of deception and denial. Once she climbed a neighbor's fence, grabbed four bluebird eggs from a birdhouse, and climbing up on the garage, rolled all four of the eggs down the garage roof and watched them splash on the pavement. Emily Ridgeway saw it all from her window, Andy told her. Her antics kept the household, consisting of a responsible older sister and her parents, in continual turmoil.

Still grinning, Dean walked over to Megan and said loudly, "You kids aren't allowed on this lawn. But tell Larry I won't tell on him this time if he brings me some Milky Way bars." Megan's mouth fell open.

"Sorry about trespassing," Radley said quickly. She decided to ignore the comment. Whatever Dean was about, Radley knew it would lead to trouble and it was best to smooth things over. "Larry was thoughtless. Tell your mother we'll be back to restore the pile."

"Well, you're trespassing, that's a fact. And that boy of yours is in— cor-rig--ible." "He's not as smart as he thinks he is."

Radley, who had been about to leave, whirled around. With a father who is chief executive of a large bank, mother president of the Junior League, and sister a top honor student, Dean should understand the meaning of respect.

"Dean, my girl," Radley said, "you have a lot to learn. It takes more than big words to get successfully through life. And you would do well to show better manners." Despite her annoyance, Radley felt a grain of sympathy for the girl—who was she to judge a child whose behavior lay closer to Larry's crazy schemes than she'd like to admit?

Dean's expression changed and she began to talk as if glad for company. She liked the new swing set the Gallaghers had installed in their back yard and could she come over and try it out? She said be sure and call her Dean, that she didn't like her real name Deana but preferred a short name, it had more punch, suited her better. She would babysit Megan and

Larry, she had never done it but there was nothing she couldn't do and she would only charge ten cents an hour.

"Come on Dean, we're leaving," called a voice from the house. Dean flashed Megan a grin and scampered inside, slamming the door behind her.

The cream-colored stone house across the street that Emily and Denise Middleton lived in was barricaded behind a thick copse of oak and maple trees. One afternoon, Megan and Larry, itching for something to do, begged to go and play with the Middleton girls, whom they could hear jumping on the trampoline in their back yard.

Three days after Radley and Shane moved into the new house, Agnes Middleton had shown up with a box of home-made butterscotch cookies. She brought along her two girls, each a year younger than Megan and Larry. Students at the exclusive Clear Acre Academy, the girls appeared demure and well-mannered. Afterwards, Radley would see them drive by in the Middleton's elongated Lincoln, dressed in fresh navy collared shirts or crisp uniforms. She hadn't seen them since, either during her neighborhood walks or on hot days at the beach.

Radley watched her children prance up the curved steps to the Middleton's front door, ring the bell as she had instructed and disappear into the house. Good, they would be occupied for an hour or two, a blessed respite.

The peaceful atmosphere didn't last. Radley went into the kitch-en and began making spaghetti sauce in a cast iron frying pan, chopping Bermuda onions and stirring in cans of tomato paste. Forty minutes later, the front doorbell rang and there was Agnes, tense but constrained, herding Megan and Larry in front of her.

Agnes was direct. "I can't have this influence on my girls," she began in a level voice. She could not tolerate the way Megan and Larry threw themselves with abandon from diversion to diversion. They had broken every house rule. When Agnes sent them outside, they climbed over the shed roof and ran yelling into the woods and over to the neighbor's yard, Emily and Denise scurrying after them. Watching from the kitchen window, Agnes was horrified. She'd never seen such clamorous children. When the neighbor called to report that the four of them were rummaging in her garage, Agnes put her foot down. "Children must have some self-control and respect for boundaries. When they're at my house I expect them to behave. I'm sorry, Megan and Larry are not welcome until they learn to act civilized," she said firmly. And turning on her heel, she clipped down the front steps and disappeared into the network of foliage that veiled the stone walls of the Middleton house.

Radley closed the door, her stomach tight. *Children have short attention spans*, she thought defensively. *They don't stick to one activity, especially when enticing toys are nearby*. Her children's rambunctiousness was a sign of vim and vitality. It bothered her that she lacked control of her children, but she would never succumb to the crushing authoritarianism she had been subjected to. She would not, no matter how difficult, repeat the abrupt decisions and misjudged punishments she'd suffered growing up—being allowed only what was quiet, routine, and safe, which eliminated almost everything. Her children would be given reasons, listened to, so they *understood*. She would not resort to authoritarianism. She would not take the easy out.

Nevertheless, the word civilized reverberated through her mind. During a ladies luncheon that Agnes hosted, Radley had seen the obedient way her two girls responded to her requests. In her house, family rules were followed as a matter of course. Radley had to admire the orderly functioning of the Middleton household and the competence with which Agnes kept harmony.

There were no more playtimes with the Middleton girls. The family across the street remained enclosed behind a lofty bulwark of propriety. One Saturday night, Radley watched the throng of cars that two uniformed valets were parking along the streets by the Middleton house. Occasionally, she'd noticed the black Lincoln pulling in the garage when Mr. Middleton returned from work. More often, she'd see Agnes behind the wheel of her Ford station wagon, dressed in her Givenchy jacket and dusty pearl earrings, hair coiffed into soft curls. She would throw Radley a curt nod and Radley watched as the car swept with a disapproving choke into the garage and the overhead door slammed down with a grinding snap.

CHAPTER 7

❧❧

Radley regarded the two women across the table. They had just attended Reverend Allerton's lecture, and no one was certain how to begin. At the counter, customers lined up for freshly baked goods, while others sat scattered around the tables drinking tall mugs of coffee and nibbling on donuts. The odor of English muffins and eggs drifted over, mingling with the odor of warm sweet rolls.

Bette pulled a pack of Pall Malls out of her purse, lit one with a Zippo and drew in deeply. "I'm so glad to be meeting you both," she said. "Reverend Allerton's talk roused passions I didn't know were in me. I've never been particularly political, but when I saw the title of his lecture, "Make Your Political Voice Heard," I couldn't resist."

"I'd say," said Klara, whose plump figure bulged over either side of her chair, "that we all are chaffing from dissatisfactions that we can't voice. I know I am, and Allerton seemed to be speaking for me—for us." They all agreed that political change was needed, but that they had a long way to go to identify exactly what shape it should take.

"Seeing that this is our first meeting together, I think it would be helpful to get acquainted," Radley suggested, "and find out why we are here and where we want to go." Klara and Bette nodded agreement.

Dunking a sliver of bear claw into her coffee, Klara slipped it daintily into her mouth and took a moment to let the flavor run down her throat.

"I'll start, as the oldest." Radley and Bette waited for more. "Okay, I don't know that. The smartest. All right, don't know that either. How about the most rounded? Does that give me an edge?" She uttered a deep guffaw. The others laughed.

"You're on, Klara," Radley said.

"Okay, I'll start with some background. I've lived here in suburbia for eight years, since the Corps of Engineers transferred my husband Dick here from Brooklyn Heights."

Radley listened as her new friend described the modest house in a residential area of Deephaven where she and Dick had settled with their young children Audrey and John. Now that her kids were older and no longer required hauling to and fro day and night, Klara said she felt lost, with her husband Dick off on a job or camping or hiking with the kids— not her cup of tea.

"I miss city life, the fast pace, the intellectual stimulation," Klara said, spreading her hands on the table. "No one wants to talk about Thomas Paine or the theory of Nazi capitalism. My English major required me to memorize lines I've never forgotten." She gazed out the cafe window. "'*But look, the moon in russet mantle clad/walks o'er the dew of yon high eastward hill.*'"

"What, you don't quote Shakespeare to your neighbors?" Radley laughed.

"They would consider me a showoff or a weirdo. But I love quotes." She looked cautiously at her new friends." Do you think me a pompous show-off?"

"Don't be ridiculous."

"We know *Hamlet* when we hear it," Radley said. "Do you think we're duds?" A round of laughter.

"I don't really fit into the social network of Deephaven," Klara told them. Too bright, Radley guessed, people don't like intellectual elites, or perhaps it was tied to the prevailing prejudice against being overweight.

She listened intently as Klara related how she grew up in a middle class neighborhood in Minnesota with a banker father and school teacher mother, and had graduated from Smith on a scholarship. Her passions— here Klara's voice held a humorous edge—were reading and eating, not necessarily in that order.

A fellow reader! This was getting more and more interesting, Radley thought.

Bette spoke enthusiastically. "I find living way out here in the suburbs unbearable." With two fingers, she tucked her dark curly hair behind her ear. "I grew up in the country. Believe me, living on a farm is hard work. As the oldest of four I was in charge of my younger brother and sisters while my mother spent hours volunteering at the local church."

Drawing a quick sip from her coffee cup, she went on. "I drove truck for my uncle's beet harvest every year, and I can fix a threshing machine and milk a cow." She chuckled. "A lot of good any of that does me now."

Radley regarded her with some surprise. With her pink fingernail polish, and rounded bud of a mouth, Bette had a perky look that suggested a lighthearted, frivolous nature. It was hard to imagine her doing heavy work in overalls.

Bette's eyes sparkled as she looked from Radley to Klara. "That life wasn't for me. My goal was to get out, to find my way to the city. I wasn't much of a student, wasn't interested in college. I'm not as down-to-earth as you guys seem to be. I love pretty things, dainty dresses. I haven't done as much reading as you have, but I'm going to make up for that!" She blew out a stream of smoke with an air of determination.

"In order to find a good-paying job, I scraped off the manure, enrolled in a technical college, and started styling my hair and standing up straight. My dressing table was covered with scarlet lipsticks, mascara, and bottles of Zigane perfume." She recrossed her legs and smoothed a wrinkle in her rose colored skirt. "I dated a lot. The first boy I fell for I married—like every girl was expected to do before she got too old to be desirable."

The others nodded agreement. Radley agreed, a girl not married by age 24 was considered over the hill, everyone knew that.

Bette continued. "For the last three years I've been stuck out in Robbinsdale. My husband's always at work, he sometimes doesn't get home until after nine. There's no one to talk to. I read a lot out of sheer boredom. I've been going stir crazy, to tell the truth. And I'm so glad to meet you two!"

The waitress appeared with a pot of steaming coffee. The atmosphere in the café was warm, with its rich paneled walls and odor of buttery food. Across the room two thin women in cloche hats dunked donuts into their coffee, shopping bags propped against their knees, and to Radley's right, a man in a yellow and red lumber jacket perched on a counter stool watched customers passing back and forth.

Suddenly a gust of cool air blew into the room, and they looked up as a tall woman in gabardine shorts and a violet silk blouse burst through the door. She held the hand of a young girl with two long blond braids who was waving a bright orange pinwheel. Clipping up to the cash register, she slapped her oversized purse on the counter. "Two éclairs, no three, please, and four jelly donuts, and let's see . . ." Her voice rang out with the vibrancy of a cheerleader.

"I know what you mean about feeling isolated," Radley said, turning back to the others. "My husband comes home at 5:30 like clockwork and heads for the TV. He doesn't talk. He doesn't want to go out. He doesn't help with the kids." Radley felt a tinge of disloyalty at talking about her husband to women she hardly knew. Looking down, she snuffed out her cigarette and circled her spoon slowly in her coffee cup.

"You're not alone," the other two cried, leaning closer. A warm sense of confidence flooded through her.

"Well," she went on in a stronger voice, "after college I lived eight years in New York, where I held a fast-paced job and enjoyed the cultural opportunities continually at one's elbow in a big city." Her old single life

in the rush of Manhattan seemed galaxies away. "Life now is so different—it's like being transported to another planet. I came to marriage
knowing nothing about child rearing, or running a household, or how to
foster a relationship with your spouse—the responsibility for which appears to lie pretty much on the wife's shoulders."

The three women continued to exchange confidences, then ordered
another round of coffee, enjoying the strong sense of commonality taking
hold between them.

Radley was anxious to explore the social issues raised by Reverend
Allerton. "We're against the war and the atrocities being committed in
Vietnam that Reverend Allerton talked about," she said. "That's the bot-
tom line."

"I'm also concerned about civil rights," Klara injected. "The Negros
are finding their voice and the liberals are behind them all the way. The
protest movements erupting everywhere on college campuses mean
business."

"About time!" Bette exclaimed. "The Civil War was over decades ago
and it's time for the Negros to demand their rights."

"It almost takes a new generation to overcome prejudices imbedded in
people's minds," Klara said. "You remember Emmett Till? His brutal murder produced an outrage. The 14-year-old Negro boy who was taken to a
barn, beaten, one of his eyes gouged out, and then shot through the head-
-all because he dared address the female clerk in a southern grocery shop."

"Yes," Radley concurred. "And remember the KKK in Georgia and
Mississippi with their white sheets and bonfires stringing up Negros on
mere suspicion?" Her blood was starting to race. She quoted a haunting
poem by Abel Meeropol she'd learned long ago, "*Southern trees bear a
strange fruit/Blood on the leaves, blood on the roots.*"

Klara blew out a quick puff of smoke. "Remember when the state gov-
ernor blockaded the University of Alabama, and Eisenhower had to call
in the National Guard to escort the Negro James Hood into the building?

After that, students demanded the administration lift the ban of on-campus political activities and allow free speech."

"Yes," Radley said. "It's the domino effect. The failure of the Vietnam War in East Asia created protests across the country, then the blacks joined in with their own demands, and then women carried the cry for justice and equality to their own issues. The flame of change has grown like wildfire."

"After the Civil War, the KKK saw it as their duty to maintain white supremacy given the breakdown of law and order," Klara began.

Radley cut in. "And there was a strong need for law and order. Disenfranchised confederates and deserters plundered the countryside, and angry mobs of lawless ex-slaves, goaded by northern carpetbaggers and scalawags, destroyed property and demanded free land. Society needed protection. It's all there in *Gone with the Wind*." The KKK took over, Radley explained, and committed atrocities as they administered their own justice, admitted, but they filled a crucial need for order. "People have forgotten that side of the picture."

A silence fell at these words, and a look of disapproval passed over the faces staring at her around the table.

Bette ground her cigarette into the ashtray. "Protection! Are you kidding? They were out to get Negroes. They executed them secretly, at night, without trial. Out of pure hate."

"The Klan," Radley said, "carried on the South's determination to continue fighting the Civil War. The South was in ruins and there was no authority to deal with the lawlessness. They represented the Confederate conscience."

"You're justifying them!" Bette's face flushed above her white open-necked blouse. "How can you possibly stick up for the KKK?"

"No, I'm saying that conditions were ripe for such a group to become powerful. Of course they went too far, and their atrocities were worse than the cure. But we have to understand both sides."

The conversation paused as the waitress leaned over to refill their cups.

"Excuse me." They turned to the next table where the woman in the violet blouse sat with her little girl. "I couldn't help overhearing your conversation. I almost hear myself speaking." She held a half-eaten long john, while her daughter licked cinnamon from her lips with a red tongue.

"I saw you gals last week at the Holy Presbyterian political forum — were you as blown away as I was by Reverend Allerton's lecture?" the woman asked with an inviting smile.

Her eagerness was irresistible, and Radley pulled her purse from the empty chair. "Won't you join us?" she asked. After a few words to her daughter, who remained at the next table bent over a coloring book, the woman moved to the empty chair.

"I'm Trish," she said looking around at them. Something about her commanding air caught their attention—here was someone with confidence who allowed no small obstruction to stand in her way. It was not long before they heard her story, prompted by their curiosity.

"Okay, ladies, here it is in a nutshell: married, two years in Deephaven, one husband—an absent one—who comes home from work and retreats upstairs to his stamp collection, one six-year-old daughter, Amy, whom I am virtually raising alone." Opening her purse, she lit up a 120 Virginia Slims and set the lighter upright on the table.

"I love Amy to the top, but no more children for me," she said. "I've traveled throughout the United States, hiked two mountains, and picked coconuts in Indonesia. I didn't marry until age thirty, way past the norm. Having a child has been quite an adjustment."

"Does your husband help?" Radley inquired.

"Gracious no! He's a big-shot Xerox executive and travels constantly on business. Boring he says, but he runs up an enormous expense account so he must be having some fun." The little girl came over, leaned against her mother's chair and stared at the slice of coffee cake remaining on Bette's plate.

"Sorry I listened to your conversation, but it was too compelling," Trish went on. "The anti-war protests hadn't yet taken hold at Vassar when I was there. After two years I transferred Columbia University to be with my boyfriend. Big mistake." She drew her slender legs under her and perched on her chair yoga-style. "I missed graduating from a top-notch college in favor of a *guy*—not the one I ended up marrying."

Radley was all attention. This girl obviously had a mind of her own.

"May I?" When Trish nodded, Bette broke off a piece of her pastry and handed it to the little girl, who grinned and popped it in her mouth. "I only went to technical college." Bette said. "I never knew anyone who went to Vassar. Those circles are out of my reach."

"A lot of the elite reputation is hype," Trish said. "You can get a good education anywhere if you put your mind to it. But listen, I have to tell you, I've just finished a book that blew me away. You absolutely have to read it." She brushed a strand of blond hair from her face. "It changed my whole way of thinking, my whole outlook on being a woman. It was so *right on*."

"Tell, tell."

"I'll bet its Friedan's book," Klara said, lifting her eyebrows.

"Exactly. *The Feminine Mystique.* Friedan describes how women tend to be swept off in clouds of happiness when they get married and awake to find themselves sinking into depression. They are expected to raise their children on their own, without adult company and intellectual stimulation, to cook, clean, and discipline the children while the walls close in around them.

"Imprisoned in a house with no rights, the housewife has no identity of her own. Did you know that a short one hundred years ago women in this country couldn't inherit property? That today they can't have their own credit cards? That women are not allowed to participate in major sports? Did you know that for doing the same job a female makes $30,000 a year to a male's $50,000? My friends, need I go on?"

The protest songs of Radley's college years—the lynching of the Negros, the blocking of black student Brown from a white school—came flooding back to her. She felt her stomach tighten. Now here was more of the same: women being kept in their place, denied opportunities, denied rights and, except when concerned with child-rearing, respect.

Trish went on, "The Equal Rights for Women amendment is very straightforward: *Equality of rights under the law shall not be denied or abridged by the United States or by any State on account of sex.* All attempts to pass it have failed. Now why do you think that is?"

She regarded the three women who had set down their coffee cups and were listening intently. "Men refuse to relinquish their privileges. There's the marriage ritual: I now pronounce you man and wife—not husband and wife. The woman is an appendage and must vow to obey her husband. How primitive is that?" She pulled a tissue from her handbag, learned over and wiped her little girl's nose.

"I know women who get an allowance, parceled out at the discretion of their husband," Klara said.

"My friend Sally's husband won't let her have a car. He's afraid she won't stay home and take care of the house," Bette put in.

"While we're championing the rights of the Negros, it might behoove us to champion the rights of women," Klara said. Nods, the women clapped their hands vigorously. They laughed aloud when Amy, sitting at her mother's feet, joined in. "I'm fired. Let's all read Friedan's book and discuss it further."

"So when shall we start?" Trish asked. "If you'll include me." Radley agreed readily, along with the other women. They were on to something and although not sure exactly what or where they were headed, it was a journey she and her new friends were anxious to embark on.

When they stood to leave, Radley's saw her neighbor Adele enter the café, accompanied by her daughter Dean. As they passed, Dean stopped, planted herself in front of Radley, and grinned. "Hello, Mrs. Gallagher. We're picking up cakes for a party." Behind the child's cheerful words, Radley detected brashness, and recalled the times Dean had showed up when they were at the beach and plopped down on the blanket, wanting to be included in whatever they were doing. *A little too cocky for my taste,* Radley thought.

"Hello, Adele. Hello, Dean."

"I'm going to get a giant gingerbread man," Dean said proudly.

"I don't think they make gingerbread men here," Radley said.

"You're wrong. For me they will! Mom will pay extra."

Her mother urged her forward. "We'll see, darling," she said, smiling goodbye as the two walked away.

Radley turned to her friends. "That girl lacks respect for her elders," she explained apologetically. The others nodded understanding.

"I've been brought up to respect authority," Trish said. "But I feel that respect eroding as I seriously question the authoritative powers running our country. So what do you say? Let's get to it!"

It was agreed: they would meet again in two weeks at Klara's. Radley couldn't believe it. A women's group! A new adventure. The women looked at each other as they gathered their things and made their way out of the café, each marveling at the luck of meeting such interesting, promising friends. Exhilarated, they filed into the parking lot. The lined-up cars were shining in the sunny summer afternoon, and from one of them came the strains of a new song that was topping the charts that very week. The words were familiar, and they hummed along as the tune reverberated above their heads. Even Klara added her raspy voice.

Little boxes on the hillside
Little boxes made of ticky tacky
Little boxes on the hillside

Little boxes all the same.
And they all play on the golf course
And drink their martinis dry
And they all have pretty children...
And they come out all the same...

Bette gave a delighted cry. "There it is!" she exclaimed. "Malvina Reynold's song of sixpence written just for us." She skipped a few steps and waved her arms wildly in the air. Klara's face glowed as she approached her over-sized Oldsmobile, and she walked more quickly than usual. Trish swung Amy into her arms: "Places to go; things to do. See you guys later!"

As for Radley, she pulled her keys from her purse, opened the car door and gave herself a hug as she slipped into the driver's seat. The lift in her heart lasted all the way back to the house.

CHAPTER 8

Mrs. Merlin's call had taken her by surprise. Yes, she would be happy to meet at Clear Springs School to confer about Megan, even though regular conferences were not scheduled until the end of the year. Mrs. Merlin hadn't mentioned what it was about, but the note of caution in the teacher's voice stirred Radley's curiosity.

The first grade classroom contained rows of small chairs with attached writing desks, and crayoned drawings of lumpy pumpkins and colorful stick figures stretched neatly around the walls. Mrs. Merlin, standing behind her desk in a trim navy and white suit, held out her hand. In her thin-framed spectacles, she presented the look of neat propriety one would expect in a formal elementary school teacher. Nothing in the room was out of place. Clearly order and efficiency reigned here.

"Thank you for coming, Mrs. Gallagher. Do sit down." Mrs. Merlin motioned Radley to a stiff wooden chair, seated herself on the other side of the desk and with a swift gesture straightened a neat pile of papers. Then she interlocked her hands on the desk and looked cordially at her guest.

Radley had looked forward to this meeting and anticipated sharing Megan's progress with a concerned adult, someone who took an interest and could understand Megan's tendency to drift away with her own thoughts, abandoning the reality of the moment.

"Mrs. Gallagher, I called you because I'm concerned about Megan. She's a sweet girl, but I have to tell you she's not happy here."

Radley's color rose and she stared at the composed woman seated across from her. Those were the last words she'd expected to hear. For a minute she was speechless.

"What's the matter?" she said at last.

"When the class undertakes a learning module, Megan has trouble maintaining interest. She shows no patience learning to write, and instead of copying letters on her desk she stares out the window."

"Do you think she has an IQ deficiency?"

Mrs. Merlin sat rod-tight in her chair. "I certainly don't know. I can't say that. Of course it takes longer for some children than others to catch on to an enforced schedule. Most of my children come to school with some preparation. But Megan may very well get used to it. That's not what worries me."

My god, there was more? What preparation? Megan had spent the last two years in a Montessori classroom and worked on all kinds of projects. She had taken well to the Montessori emphasis on self-direction and interactive support, had been commended for her willingness to help the younger ones.

"Megan keeps to herself and is reluctant to answer questions." Mrs. Merlin paused and straightened the pile of papers in front of her. "I don't think she thinks very highly of herself. Last Monday something happened. No one saw it. That is until brave little Jill Hartman came forward. I confronted the entire class with the situation. It's important that these things be a learning experience for the students."

"Yes?" Radley sat frozen in her seat.

"I'm afraid," Mrs. Merlin shook her head disapprovingly, "that Megan stole ten dollars from a coat hanging in the cloak room."

She stopped and waited for her words to sink in. "And then lied to me about it."

"What? Why on earth would she do that?" Radley's mind reeled. "There's no way she can spend money without my knowing. The ten dollars would be useless to her," she floundered. Lying and stealing—how could that happen with a child brought up in a household where integrity was honored above all else?

Mrs. Merlin went on. "Nevertheless, Henry missed a ten dollar bill his mother had given him that morning, and when the class reassembled after lunch break, Jill reported she'd seen Megan rifling through the coats. I immediately called Megan up to the front. We found the bill in her back pocket."

Her tone had become more severe, and she smoothed her hair, clamped into a chignon at the back of her neck. "She claimed she didn't know how it got there. It was obvious she'd taken it. If you can assure me that that you haven't given her money, I am certain." Mrs. Merlin continued as if reading Radley's mind. "But then these things don't always make sense. She probably saw Henry with the bill, she wanted it, and she took it. Some children are unable to control their impulses."

Mrs. Merlin had no answers, claimed she had no psychological expertise, was at a loss. Her thick heels clicked metallically on the floor as she led Radley to the classroom door. "I hope you understand that your daughter needs help. She persists in her denial and nothing will persuade her to confess. I would say," she said pointedly, "the child begs for affirmation." Mrs. Merlin's demeanor suggested a concern for Megan's welfare, along with the implication that this type of thing wasn't tolerated on her watch.

What was to be done? After collecting Megan from the watchful eye of the librarian, Radley strode out to the car, face grim, holding her daughter's hand tightly. Faced with Mrs. Merlin's severity, she became anxious, almost as if she herself were guilty. In a sense, as Megan's guide and mentor, she was. How in the world was she to handle her daughter's trans-gression, for which she could see no possible motive? It was impossible to think, her brain a mass of confusion. It wasn't uncommon for things to disappear in the house, losses impossible to trace. She'd missed a charm bracelet, a gold China box from the bookshelf, and several of Larry's farm animals, but they could easily have fallen in the trash or been lost. She could prove nothing.

After installing Megan in the back seat and collecting Larry from Mrs. Draper's by-the-hour day-care in Excelsior, Radley drove the blue Buick slowly, oblivious to the giggling noises issuing from the back, her glazed eyes on the road ahead as she struggled to find a way to cope with the growing realization that Megan had a serious problem.

"Mommy, turn on the radio," Larry called from the back seat. "We're bored." She turned the knob and notes of a Mozart sonata rose through the car. "No, no, not that!"

"You know that shrill rock music gets on my nerves and drives me crazy," Radley countered.

"That junk you play gets on our nerves and drives *us* crazy!"

"How about a compromise? We'll take turns: five minutes of classical, then five minutes of something jazzy," she suggested.

After two minutes, Megan stood and shouted into her ear, "That's awful. Our turn!"

"Hurry, change it," Larry chimed in.

Radley slapped one hand against her cheek. "Stop it! Right now! SIT-DOWN-IN-YOUR -SEATS! If I have to listen to that blaring electronic music, you have to listen to some of the best music ever composed."

"Your music stinks," Megan protested.

It was no use; they would never let up.

Last May on the drive to the Excelsior Amusement Park the children had passed the time by ripping pages from a magazine one by one and tossing them out the window. The shrill siren and the face of the policeman at the car window had taken her by surprise—no, officer, she was not aware of what was going on in the back seat. He had let her off with a warning.

How had her parents coped? She thought of her father with his over-powering temper. In his house there was no argument, no digression, no discursive pleading that wore him down until he gave in. He decided and that was that. It was a method she'd despised. Now she longed for its strength.

She switched off the radio. A hundred times she had silenced it, only to be coaxed into turning it on once more, hoping to keep the kids occupied. She vowed her next car would have no radio.

They hadn't gone ten blocks when she heard angry voices from the back seat. "He's pulling my sock off!" Megan screamed.

Another wail, this time Larry's shrill cry, "She kicked me in the stomach, Mommy, and it hurt!"

"I did not, you liar."

"Did too!"

"Stop, he's pulling my hair, ooh, ouch, make him stop!"

"She's kicking me with her shoe."

Hadley's face burned, but she checked herself. She would not yell. She would deal with this some other way. But nothing else worked. They paid no attention to reason, pleading, threats, or bribes. There was only one way, the final solution that never failed to stop them in their tracks: her voice. It was her only power.

She wouldn't give in. Here was a chance to try the techniques of Rudolf Dreikurs she'd been reading about in *Children the Challenge* and some of the other child behavior modification books that lay on her dresser. Pulling the car to a stop, she announced she would not move the car until they settled down. Several minutes passed. Silence in the back seat. She watched two squirrels chase each other around a tree trunk.

Finally, she turned around. Megan and Larry were sitting on either side of the car seat, looking at her silently. "Are you going to remain quiet?" No response. "I need a yes before I start the car."

She heard two feeble yeses.

At the next intersection, she turned down a narrow road without traffic, a shortcut she had used before. Best to get home as soon as possible, get the kids into the house and occupied. The road curved, bent by the shape of Lake Minnetonka. They passed a stretch of houses hidden behind banks of shrubbery, then nothing but woodland and fields of shag grass. The car rounded another curve and moved along a sunken swamp, brown stalks encircling the shallow shoreline, a green milky film coating the surface. For a moment she felt lost in the middle of nowhere, without civilization or anchor. Her mind strained for some resolution, then fell blank as she gave in to the surrounding emptiness. Finally! A row of houses and up ahead a traffic light. With a weak sign of relief she turned onto a main road and pointed the car towards home.

That night after the kids were tucked in bed, Radley sat across from Shane on the couch waiting for the last strains of *Hawaii Five O* to fade. It was time to talk.

"Something has come up. Do you mind if I turn off the television?" Shane shook his head. He was still wearing the navy suit and Louis Feraud tie Char had given him for Christmas.

"It's Megan," she began. As she related the interview and Megan's theft of the ten dollar bill, Shane's eyes didn't leave her face. "Mrs. Merlin was snippy and rather self-righteous. She offered no advice or solutions. But she made it clear that such behavior was not to be tolerated. I guess she's right in that."

Shane shook his head. "Megan hasn't stolen anything around here. What would she do with ten dollars, since she couldn't spend it without being discovered?"

"That's just it. Things in the house have gone missing, but there's no proof. They could have been misplaced."

"Megan must be taught that stealing is wrong," Shane said flatly. "I suppose she'd better be punished."

"What do you suggest?"

"She has to learn that it is wrong to steal and lie." He pulled out a white cotton handkerchief from his pocket and blew his nose. "Maybe she should be confined to her room."

"But she has to *understand*." Radley spread her hands over her knees. "This afternoon I pulled her on my lap and explained the importance of trust and respect for possessions. I told her that if she wanted a good life she'd better learn to make different choices. Then I offered to forego punishment if she'd own up and say she was sorry. She denied everything. When I said she'd been *seen* taking the money, she hung her head and refused to say more. It was like she'd vanished and I was facing an empty shell."

"You need to put your foot down."

"And how do I do that?" Radley asked.

Shane shrugged.

"I don't think she feels good about herself." Radley had the feeling the walls were closing in and boxing her in a dark corner. How could anyone deal with something so nebulous?

Shane said, "I think we should consult the priest. He might have some ideas."

Radley's heart sank. What in heaven would a priest know about child behavior? There was nothing in the scriptures about behavior modification.

"What can a priest do?" She wanted to be fair; the church had ruled Shane's entire life, it soothed daily bumps and tamed the mysteries of the universe. It was what he had. Naturally he would turn to its authority in a crisis.

"He deals with family issues as part of his work. It's worth a try."

It was not the first time Shane had wanted to fling their problems into the lap of the church. She needed more than prayers this time. She stood up impatiently. As he reached for a cigarette, her eyes fell on his face, looking serious and humble under the illumination of the brass floor lamp. Something in her softened. It occurred to her that the two of them had been shaped at the opposite ends of the universe.

The clock chimed midnight. Radley had gone upstairs to bed, but Shane stayed sitting with the television off, paper in front of him. He hadn't been able to read a line. With the weight in the back of his head, he couldn't sleep. His wife had become more and more antagonistic against the church. He couldn't understand the change in her.

During their engagement, Radley had attended catechism classes faithfully, and after their marriage, they had attended the Latin mass together, her hair covered by a black veil, kneeling on the prie-dieu, joining in the Hail Mary, every Sunday. Then without warning, she showed signs of cooling and finally refused to attend services at all. The church's restriction on birth control had been hard for her to swallow, and he repressed his opposition when she started using birth control. It wasn't easy, cutting off potential life, but what could he do but make allowances? Like he had done so often as the extent of their differences intruded into their marriage. Her stance on abortion had taken over her thinking—damn that Abortion Rights Action League and its pro-choice nonsense.

Radley kept saying she didn't come into the marriage an empty vessel. Well, what had she expected? That the church would make life harmonious and wipe out all their problems?

Their attendance at mass on Sunday mornings ceased. To Shane, it wasn't worth the fight, he preferred the path of accommodation. For him, the marriage took priority, and the sacrifices demanded of him would be rewarded in the hereafter by a just and forgiving God. His solid Irish Catholic faith remained unshakable—although he wondered for a split moment if a crack had formed in his perfect understanding.

She would not seek help for Megan through the church. It looked like they were on their own. And he was without a clue.

CHAPTER 9

R adley and the other women were seated around the bulky coffee table in Klara's amusement room, purses stashed at their feet. The room had a casual, lived-in look, with books strewn here and there and throw blankets piled on a chair next to the console television cabinet. A table fan whirred quietly from atop a low bookcase.

She was perched on the couch next to Bette and Trish. Across from her were three newcomers, sitting with their legs crossed, whom Klara introduced as Maureen, Cookie and Barbara.

"Now," Klara said, circling her gaze, "let's get started. It's our first meeting. Nothing is defined, nothing is set. We're all against the war. We all support civil rights, that's a given. Now, let's begin with getting better acquainted." She laid her clipboard on the coffee table and lowered her bulk into a large swayback chair. "What are our individual reasons for being here?"

"I'll start," Trish said. "I'm Trish. I ran across Klara, Radley and Bette in a café a few weeks ago after a political lecture by Reverend Allerton—talk about serendipity!" A brass floor lamp cast a glow over her face, and her blue-green eyes sparkled under black lashes. She displayed a jaunty air that struck Radley as a fortuitous sign—here was someone who wasn't afraid of a challenge.

"My husband brought the family here from New York five years ago because of his job," Trish told them, brushing a crumb of coffee cake from her mouth. "He travels extensively on business, which affords me a great deal of freedom to do as I like. I absolutely must have economic independence as well, so I intend to return to college and obtain a master's. My duty to Amy comes first, of course, but I am perfectly capable of melding motherhood into the career path I have mapped out for myself."

Maureen, a tall girl with chestnut hair pulled from her face by a black velvet headband, told them that she had grown up on a farm outstate, but had escaped to college and a wider existence as soon as she was able. Now, she was looking to expand her anti-war activities be-yond the confines of the Catholic Church. "My husband is supportive," Maureen said. He understands that I am an activist at heart and is a wonderful father to our three children."

Barbara and Cookie pronounced themselves typical housewives, from Ohio and California respectively. The publicity about the war and the need for social change had stirred something in them and they wanted to get involved. The bulletin board notice announcing the start-up of a women's group for political action had caught their eye. To Radley, they looked ready to take on the world.

"I loathe the term housewife," Bette said when it was her turn. "The house and the wife are entwined, as if there's no separation. Being a daughter and wife and mother and church-goer are fine. But there should be more, there should be options.

The idea that her life of family domesticity, which she had thrown herself into with all the strength and conviction of one who has found the Holy Grail, was so limited, stuck Radley with a rush. Maybe her lack of aptitude for this role had a basis in society. Maybe she wasn't entirely at fault.

"It's clear to me," Trish said, after everyone had sketched their background stories, "that we all back the right of the Vietnamese people to live in freedom and the right of Negroes to be treated decently. Isn't that true of women as well?"

Everyone agreed.

"There's no sense in trying to correct the errors of the war if we can't fix the problems in our own lives. Let's start there." She snapped shut the lid of her Zippo and looked at the others with conviction.

Radley noted with satisfaction that they were getting to the core of the issue, the place they had to launch from: dissatisfaction with their own roles as housewives. They had to get personal, it seemed to her, in order to understand and connect with the suffering of others.

Everyone had experiences to relate. Bette's daughter was not allowed to play on her high school's baseball team, even though she played like a pro. She'll hurt herself. She'll distract the boys. She'll require shower accommodations. She'll be a liability.

Trish and her husband led separate lives, their marriage a mere convenience. Her daughter Amy, the love of her life, made up for the lack of intimacy.

"My husband," Cookie explained, "considers his paycheck his, and only allows me a portion. I have to keep track of what I spend, as if I were a child.

The women's frustrations grew more intense as each delved into unexplored territory; these were subjects they did not usually discuss.

When it was her turn to speak, Radley found herself hesitant to share the bald facts of her life with Shane and the children to this group of relative strangers, but as she heard the others' stories, her reluctance eased. Who but these women would understand without judgment, since they seemed to have the same problems?

"I—well, I don't know how to say this." She hesitated. "My life sometimes seems out of alignment. That is, I mean, I'm not very domestic;

once I undertake a new project, like cooking or sewing, I get interested, then it becomes boring. My husband drinks, he always has, so I should have known, but this is different. His drinking scares me. And I don't know how to handle the children, to get through to them, and as for discipline, Shane, my husband, hasn't a clue, his favorite word is whatever—this must sound so negative . . ." But they urged her to go on, and she continued to express the frustrations that had been festering slowly at the edge of her consciousness. As she spoke, her words took on a life of their own, as if they had finally found a release for their buried existence. When she had done, relief washed over her like a current of fresh air.

By this time, the room had warmed, the coffee cups had been refilled repeatedly, and the room crackled with energy. Fetching a fresh cup of coffee from the sideboard cabinet, Radley mulled over what she had heard, ideas that cut straight to her sense of truth. A wife's financial dependence. Her sole responsibility for raising children while husbands escaped to their jobs. Her craving to use her mind in some capacity. Her isolation inside a house surrounded by moats of suburban propriety. It became more and more clear that these ideas, this new focus had touched some undefined need in her, and she was ready to pick up the thread and follow it to the end.

Barbara reached for her bottle of Pepsi. "Listen to this. When I was a graduate student at the University of Minnesota, I had access to the medical facilities. When I visited a gynecologist at the University hospital, he flatly refused to tie my tubes. Said I was too young, that I should keep open the option of having children." Taking a gulp of the Pepsi, she set the bottle on the table next to her and gave her full attention to the group. "Even though this is what my husband and I wanted."

Radley agreed with the others that the freedom to make decisions about child-bearing was non-negotiable; adult women who gave birth, tended to, and devoted their lives to raising children should not be dictated to by outsiders, especially men. Male physicians clearly didn't understand women's issues.

"My doctor," Cookie related, "called my depression housewife fatigue. Said I was bored and recommended I go to a movie once a week. How ridiculous. Then he prescribed a tranquilizer. I had just been reading about this in Betty Friedan's book—I was to have become one of the millions of American women given Miltown and Valium to keep them content." She raised Friedan's book from her lap, bracelets tinkling along her arm.

They were interrupted by footsteps clumping down the stairs, and a girl wearing a pink blouse and mules appeared carrying a tray of bismarks, a sliced bundt cake, napkins, and a fresh pot of coffee. "I heated the rolls," the girl said, sliding the tray on the oversized coffee table beside a large marble ashtray stuffed with cigarette butts.

"This is my daughter, Audrey," Klara said.

"Hi." The girl nodded without looking up. She was tall, with a plumpish shape that showed signs of resembling her mother's.

"You better stick around, Audrey. This is women stuff. You qualify," Trish remarked as the young girl filled one of the cups.

"You don't have to serve us," Barbara said. "We can pour our own coffee."

"I *like* to serve," Audrey retorted, lifting up another cup. "I like all that." She stood for a second, shoulders back, looking under her lashes at the array of bodies seated around the room. Her air of assurance, bordering on disdain, suggested she did not agree with what she'd heard as she descended the stairs. "I like being feminine and caring for the house and don't see the need to upset everything," she said abruptly. A coat of red lipstick covered her lips and her eyebrows had been plucked to a thin line. Everything about her, the defiant edge to her voice, the lines of insecurity around her mouth and her flighty gestures as she dumped the cigarette butts into a soiled bowl suggested the awkward in-between age.

Audrey set the coffee pot on the sideboard. "I have homework to do."

"I can't tell her anything," Klara confided in a low voice as Audrey disappeared up the stairs, mules whopping. "She's determined to go her own way. I love to teach, but she's cut me off. All that hard-earned knowledge going to waste!"

"Her turn will come," said Trish said.

After all the trials I'm having with my children, I still have the teenage years to deal with! Radley despaired of Audrey's attitude, while at the same time admired her forthrightness and determination to be her own person.

"Your daughter has a point," Barbara said. "I think it's satisfying to look good, to feel feminine, to give unselfishly to others. As long as we don't lose ourselves in the process."

"On my wedding day, my mother admonished me to look attractive for my husband at all times." Trish coddled her coffee cup in her hands. "To dress nicely and wear lipstick at breakfast. Of course, no one ever tells a man to take care of his stinky breath and wash under his arms."

"But I *like* to look attractive. Not for my man, but for me," Cookie protested. She had been following the discussion with wide eyes, sunk back in her chair. Every so often she pulled a Milk Dud from her purse and popped it into her mouth.

"At seven in the morning? Do you fancy sitting at the breakfast table dolled up like Mrs. Gottrocks across from Godzilla in an undershirt? Trish asked.

Everyone laughed. Radley giggled as she reached for a butter bun. Such outspokenness was liberating, gave her the comforting freedom to say what was on her mind. This group definitely had possibilities.

CHAPTER 10

❧

At 2 p.m. on the dot the doorbell rang. Right on time. On the other side of the screen stood a tall man dressed in black, an official-looking smile on his face. Radley had been hesitant to agree to this visit. His phone call had taken her aback. Father who? Why would he be calling her? "Don't you want to speak to Shane?"

Cough on the other end of the line. "I'm Father Marten. Actually, I've spoken to Shane. You are the one I need to talk to. I'd like to pay you a visit. May I?" Radley felt her stomach harden. She had drawn away from religion, no longer attended mass; with the challenges of married life theoretical concepts had faded into the background.

But she couldn't say no. And now here was Father Martin at the door. The priest smiled and held out his hand.

She took it and smiled back. "Come in. I've made some coffee. How do you take it?"

"Black," he replied. "Black and bitter." Something about his frank demeanor disarmed her. He seated himself on a peacock patterned chair and gazed around the room, nodding his thanks when she handed him a steaming mug. She was not sure what to make of this tall, spindly man with his arched eyebrows and mass of red hair bunched in layers around his head. A white starched collar full of clean, bleached propriety circled his neck. He tapped the tips of his long antennae fingers together nervously.

The morning sun filtered through a net of tree branches and dropped abstract patches of light over the rose living room carpet in front of him. "It's a nice home you have here," her visitor said congenially, casting his eyes around the room at the brass umbrella rack with the embossed grapes and vines in the hall, the Cezanne print in a gilt frame over the couch, the matching scarlet and gold peacock chairs, and the Mexican ebony Chac Mool in the brass bookcase.

"It's taken years to get the house furnished," Radley said proudly. "We started during our scrappy newlywed days. Now we have it all—children, dog, beautiful home. Our dream home."

The priest nodded. "I'm here to pay a neighborly visit and see if you and Shane have any concerns I can help with. I haven't seen you at mass for some time." He regarded her openly. "I've missed conversing with Shane after the service. He's a fine young man."

"I've . . . stopped going to church. You see, I'm not actually Catholic. I tried, but, well . . ." Twisting the silver serpentine ring on her middle finger, she looked up to find his eyes planted full on her face. She had taken the plunge, joined the church, and now here she was, wrapped up in the fight for free choice and family planning, going in an entirely different direction. She tried to rationalize, to allay her guilt at disappointing Shane when he has expected so much of her. *But how could she deny her principles, the causes that drew her more and more strongly to action?*

And here was Father Martin, gazing at her with an intensity that pressed her to reveal her thoughts. She understood: he was here to woo her back to the faith, but it was more than that. His expression was one of inquiry, not accusation. She decided to be honest and not conceal the qualms that had plagued her for some time.

"I understand you were baptized into the mother church," Father Marten said gently. Shane had explained that Father Marten was a Jesuit, a high recommendation to Shane, who had been educated in Jesuit schools. He characterized the Jesuits as intellectual protectors of the faith, masters of the intricacies of church doctrine, able to out-rationalize, out-argue, out-last, and pierce through the fiercest critic. She straightened up in her chair, determined to hold her ground without hedging the truth.

"True, but it didn't take," she said, setting her coffee cup on the coffee table and resisting the urge to pull out a cigarette. "Father Marten, I find my own beliefs too often compromised. While I respect the power and good works of the church, there's too much that doesn't work for me."

"I'm certain you did not undertake the sacrament of baptism without reflection," Father Marten said. "I assume your reservations were addressed during instruction with the guiding priest, were they not?" It dawned on her that behind his amiable manner lay a bank of steel. Father Marten drew his wiry fingers apart and tapped them together with precision. "Are there issues you'd like me to clear up? I have, my child, much experience in this area. You are not alone in your doubts."

Radley's mind flashed back to New York, to the pre-baptismal meeting in the priest's small office. After holding out for a year she had given in. She would be inducted into the exclusive realm of the universal church. It was time to unify the family, now including a three-month-old baby. She would give up her last thread of resistance, the defiance, some said, that kept her new life from its final resolution. A large carved crucifix dominated on one wall and the attractive young priest sat behind a neat oak desk, upright and alert in his white clerical collar. She could ask anything, he was there for her, he assured her.

She clasped her pocketbook more securely in her lap. "Well . . ." She had no questions, but didn't want to disappoint the expectations of this nice young priest. "The concept of heaven. How exactly do you define it?"

The priest looked confident. He'd been here before. "Heaven is the most bountiful, beautiful paradise you can conceive of. It is everything you ever desired." His opal eyes shone and he looked at her with radiant understanding. "In the sight of God, you will be reunited with your loved ones, your family, your friends, you will live, laugh and play together, be healthy and happy, deformities will be healed, you will want for nothing. Everything you've ever lost will be returned to you and everything you've dreamed of will be fulfilled. Sunshine will cover you for eternity. The glory of it never fades; you will live in bliss forever."

Radley blinked. "And sex? Can you have sex?"

"Yes, there will be sex, all you could ever want, without restriction. Whatever you need or desire will be yours in perpetuity, bathed in golden light. It is almost inconceivable."

A sinking feeling filled Radley's chest. It was not *almost* inconceivable. It was absurd. Not to panic, she thought. She must maintain sincerity at all costs. She didn't want to be disingenuous with this holy man, but she was aware of how far removed she was from his vision. She'd already confided to Shane that devotion evaded her, she felt no waves of epiphany stirring inside her.

She made one last attempt. "My understanding is that the administration of the baptismal sacrament confers grace that will deepen my belief and unite me with God."

The priest leaned toward her, his eyes deep with understanding. "That is exactly so. It's in God's hands. That's the beauty. He never stops caring for His children."

But it hadn't happened. The ceremony performed, her forehead sprinkled, the papers signed and stamped, over the months she had felt no illumination with her entry into the ranks of the chosen. The seeds had not branched into the certainty of faith.

Her mind returned to Father Marten, sitting in the living room across from her, legs crossed, fingers tapping back and forth in his lap.

"Do I have issues to clear up?" she asked. "No, nothing." In truth, she did admire the moral guidance that Catholicism provided, with the do's and don'ts of life clearly laid out. The problem was that any behavior not specifically forbidden was free territory; there was no intellectual space to deal with the gaps. In most religions, the precise admonitions allow an ocean of possibilities that have to be figured out on one's own. Church rules can't cover every instance, and the creative thinking needed to deal with the in-between areas doesn't exist. When people are commanded to follow the law blindly, the individual is left without the impetus or capability to devise individual solutions.

She realized that voicing these thoughts would only offend this kindly priest, who sincerely desired to lead her into the arms of salvation. "There are too many areas where I with the teachings," she said simply.

"I would like to hear your frustrations, if you're willing to share them," he said.

"There are many, Father Martin. I feel strongly about the right of women to have abortions and the right of children to be wanted. I don't think it's fair to force women to have children because they've had sex. Forced into back-alley abortions, women die."

Her visitor, leaning back in the high-backed chair, listened attentively as she continued, tapping his fingertips together one at a time as if running scales on a keyboard, over and over in rhythmic repetition.

"Poor women in third-world countries have thirteen, fourteen children because they don't know how to prevent pregnancy. Without charity, these families are often underfed and starving. It's cruel and inhumane." She laid her hands on the skirt of her shirtwaist dress and watched Father Marten's face, worried that such a direct challenge would offend him.

Father Marten continued tapping his fingers on his lap. "I can show you how strongly the Catholic Church supports life," he declared.

'I've heard all the arguments. Father Marten." Radley felt a pang of hopelessness at the extent of their differences.

"I won't try to persuade you. I didn't come here with iron gloves," he said. "But many, both religious and non-religious, are against what they see as the destroying of a life. Every soul that is conceived belongs in the arms of God, through birth and baptism." He shifted his legs under the folds of his black robe and rested his hands on his lap.

"I assure you," he went on, "The Church encourages people to explore their doubts. If one of the fold strays, the power of the holy scriptures and the holy passion will eventually reveal the sacred truth.

"Remember," and here he jumped up and strode to the bookcase, picked up the obsidian Chac Mool, stared at it, then shook it as if to remove the dust. "The Church will always be there. You have been baptized, you are one of us."

She knew Father Martin meant that no matter what path she took, she would enter heaven with the rest of the chosen to spend eternity with those who had been baptized in the faith. She was struck by the injustice of this, given her withdrawal.

He was watching her with a gentle expression. His fingertips resumed tapping back and forth slowly.

"The Church can offer help," he said after several moments of silence.

She needed help, desperately, in being an effective mother, but what would a single man bound in spiritual dogma know about that? Eternal suffering in hell and the promise of everlasting life might have persuasive value to spiritual thinkers, but she needed more than that.

She decided to face him honestly with her reservations. Maybe he could understand. Surprisingly, the words rushed from her.

"Many of the Church's rules contradict my beliefs. I'm required to select a saint's name for my child. I'm forbidden to use birth control, even though I can barely handle two kids as it is. The threat of damnation is used to terrorize children into obedience. I can't attend a non-Catholic service since non-Catholics are considered heathens. I can only reach God through the intervention of the church hierarchy. Innocent newborns are considered sinners." She sucked in her breath.

Maybe she'd gone too far, but how else could they understand each other?

Father Marten sat quietly, his face emblazoned by a circle of red hair. There was no sign of judgment in his pale blue eyes, as if he'd faced these arguments a thousand times. "I can see you are convinced. I appreciate your openness. I have faith in you. But I've taken too much of your time for one afternoon. Might we have a further dialogue sometime?" He stood up. "I believe I can help."

She watched as the priest moved briskly down the front steps toward his green Pinto, black robe billowing behind him. What was the use? Buried in his wiry frame he was immovable. His goal was not to support her beliefs but to lead, she understood this. There was no question of changing his thinking. Only hers was up for negotiation.

CHAPTER 11

W hen Jack O'Malley, manager of overseas inventory and supply operation at Shelby Allied Foods, invited Shane and Radley to his fortieth birthday party, they were excited. For Radley, it was a rare chance to spend an evening out. With a burst of enthusiasm, she ran down to Young Quinlan's and purchased a new violet dress with velvet embroidery at the neck and mother-of-pearl-buttons.

They went out very little. Neighborhood cocktail parties had dwindled along with Radley's enthusiasm for entertaining—she shunned the stress, the oppressive hangovers blotting out the entire next day. Invitations were rare.

By the time they arrived the O'Malley's home, the party was in full swing. Eleanor O'Malley escorted them into the living room filled with groups chatting, glasses clinking, voices rising. Men in pullover sweaters were talking to women in gold hoop earrings and full organdy skirts, and the odor of meatballs and bubbling cheese drifted from a side table.

Shane headed for the bar, grinning. He looked at ease, Radley noted. Well, why not? This was his idea of a good time: relaxing with booze and good cheer. The strain of living with her and her struggles, her expectations of him to be different, must wear on him. He was no doubt relieved to lose himself in the festive atmosphere. She watched him blend into the group of men clustered around the bar, drink in one hand, cigarette in the other, nodding and cracking jokes.

The evening passed quickly. After a buffet dinner of honeyed ham, tossed salad, au gratin potatoes, and green beans with slivered almonds, the men retreated to the amusement room to toss darts and reminisce about the Twins and George Mikan of the Minneapolis Lakers. Man talk, Radley thought—and an unlimited supply of drinks and freedom from female approbation, saved from the boredom of listening to the endless babble of curtain fabrics and Knorr soup recipes.

By two a.m., the few remaining guests sprawled about the living room drooped in chairs or settled on couches mumbling indistinct conversations. A short man with black curly hair sat on a stool balancing a can of Budweiser on his head. Another was slumped to the floor, snoozing, feet bent around the legs of a chair. Radley, standing in the doorway, looked about for Shane. She had passed from the threshold of intoxication into the realm of exhaustion. She couldn't swallow another ounce of liquor, her head buzzed with a dull roar, her stomach felt twisted, and a thirty-mile drive home loomed ahead.

She found Shane at the dining room table in the midst of a rambling conversation with Jack O'Malley. When she tried to pry him away, he shook her off, absorbed in Jack's story about a sailing accident involving an errant speedboat. As she watched Shane laughing, eyes bright and glazed, she was pulled back to their courting days back East, the packed weekends with Shane's Irish friends that brought partying to a new height of raucous gaiety. All merriment and camaraderie, letting off steam as they graduated from college and headed into careers and marriage. Back in their single days, when everyone was free from ties and could sleep till noon and nurse their hangovers in private, glad to pay the price of all that exhilaration. Tomorrow she would have to get up at the crack of dawn, see to the children, fix the meals, and drag up and down the stairs as she counted the time moment by moment until the blessed hour she could fall into bed and let the balm of sleep restore her to normalcy.

'You don't have to go yet," Jack urged. Shane grinned as if Jack were his best buddy in the world.

"We have a sitter," Radley told him. "Mrs. Craymer will be anxious. It's late."

Highball glass in one hand, knees crossed, cigarette balanced on a bean-bag ashtray beside him, Shane clearly was not in the mood to leave.

"We must go, Shane!"

He wanted just one more; it was going on three o'clock when at last they tumbled out the front door, Shane's sport coat tucked over Radley's arm. When Radley took hold of his elbow, he shook her off, careened down the front steps and pulled open the car door.

"I'd better drive." Radley brushed in front of him, and before he knew it, she had gained the driver's seat and inserted the key in the ignition.

Shane's mood changed abruptly. "No you don't! *I* will drive, I'm fine. Very fine." He could too walk straight. She didn't know what she was talking about. When he saw that his wife wasn't about to budge, he opened the back door and heaved himself into the back seat, muttering to himself. *No way I'm sitting in the front with her. Damn woman, breaking up the party! Won't let a guy have a little fun, old stick-in-the-mud. Always runs things, has her own way, thinks she can tell me what to do . . .*

Radley, ignoring his mumbled complaints, adjusted the rear-view mirror, started the car, and pulled away from the curb. They had a long way to go, but it shouldn't be too difficult if she could just get to Highway I-94. She followed the road for some time until she saw a dim sign ahead that read ANOKA. On the corner she made out a dark Holliday filling station that looked vaguely familiar. Stopping the car at the intersection, she hesitated. "Do you remember which turn to take," she asked into the silence.

"Find yerself. I don't give a slam damn," came from the back seat. She turned to the right, counting on instinct. At this hour the landscape stretched dark and empty. A yard light in the distance flickered between fields of trees. Then nothing. The only sounds were the drone of the motor and Shane's labored breathing in the back seat.

Suddenly a heavy rain began to pound against the windshield, thick drops that smeared into each other. With visibility near zero, she peered anxiously along the road for markers or signs.

Shane's grumbling resumed. "*I know the way home.*" Radley said nothing. "Miss all the fun . . . great party. . ." More silence. "Jack and I were shooten' the breeze, having good time."

The words shocked her. It was the first time she'd seen Shane like this. Who was this person she'd been married to for eight years? What had become of the gentle, passive man from whom she rarely heard a cross word? She had considered, in better moments, his equanimity to be a balance to her volatile nature. The sane man she knew existed no longer, had flown beyond all bounds of reason.

She squinted to see the white center line, barely visible in the darkness. The windshield wipers slashed back and forth, smearing thick drops across the glass. As the Buick rounded a curve, the headlights lit up a yellow sign ahead SLICK WHEN WET.

Radley slowed the car to a crawl. Inside, a musty silence hovered under the pounding of rain on all sides.

"I can barely see. I might have to stop," she said, surprised at the nervousness she felt at addressing him. Probably better to remain quiet, maybe as the liquor wore off he would settle down.

"Oh, what do you know?" Shane growled from the back seat. Radley tightened her fingers around the wheel. "You don't even know how to drive. You think you know everything. Just ruin everything. What mashe you so high and mighty? Juss butt out. You think you know so much. Who hell do you think you are?" His voice kept on, shooting out every invective he could think of in a steady stream that encircled her in a tight grip. "She doshn't know what she's doing. Pull up, I'll get us home."

Stunned, she couldn't think of what to say. She felt a fire creep up her neck and flush over her face, and with each verbal lash flutters jerked in her stomach like swarms of tiny fish caught in a net. "Oh will you be quiet? You're drunk, admit it," she said in a meeker voice than she intended. She had been used to his acceptance giving her strength; now all sense of security eroded in the face of the unknown, the vitriol that rose like a Trojan sea monster from the back seat.

"Am not! Can't have a few drinks!"

Her hands trembled on the steering wheel.

Then, "You, Miss hoity toity, you can find your own way home. I hope it takes all night. "

The car sped along the wet highway, she could only hope in the right direction. Her hands gripped the wheel as if she were drowning. She had a sinking feeling that she was on her own, alone in the vast wilderness of the night. She had grown to hate these parties, these brawls where everyone got drunk and laughed at every stupid thing that was said. Usually, when she tried to drag him home, she gave in and stayed, but no longer was she willing to pay the price. The children would be up at seven the next morning, only four hours from now. She needed a clear head. This time, she had insisted and was paying the price.

Clearly, Shane would not stand for his desire for alcohol to be thwarted. He continued to launch a barrage of insults, calling her every name that entered his swirling mind, like a record spinning in a single groove.

Usually, loaded with drink, he became outgoing, affable, buddy-to-buddy. Yet here was a new entity emerged full-blown from the figure of her husband, holding judicial court in the back seat.

They rarely argued, bound by a mutual restraint that avoided the threat of real exposure. Spats were followed by long periods of non-speaking, for a day or two or three, until the feelings languished and present reality drew them back to routine. But she had a feeling this time would be different. She would not forget this.

Out of the darkness ahead an electric sign suddenly appeared, flashing a blaze of yellow and red letters. Two of the round O's blinked off and on, off and on in jerks that struck her like wild laughter, as if elated at the blasts of rain she was drowning in. With a shudder, Radley swerved and with a bang the car hit something solid, she couldn't tell through the watery midst. She jerked the wheel and regained the lane, shoulders shaking.

"Idiot!" came from the back seat.

She made no reply, but strained to see ahead, afraid the pelting rain would block her view, that all light would vanish and the road would disappear into blackness forever and the car with it. She licked her lips, they were wet—tears she hadn't noticed creeping down her face.

The rain had thinned, and she fastened her gaze on the empty highway that stretched ahead, streaked with pools of black rain. They were nearing Cresthaven and closer to her pressing goal to get into the garage and the safety of the house.

If she could just get home, out of this hell car! So far she'd made the right turns, out of pure luck, with the road signs sucked into the dark and the streetlights curtained by the rain. At last, up ahead, she recognized a major highway. Thank heavens! She knew exactly where she was. She guided the car into the exit and sped south, sucking in a breath of relief.

She felt drenched inside as she struggled to break through her fear. Rational, she must be rational and think this through and maintain her sanity. Some powerful drive had transformed her husband. Had booze become his God? Or had the depth of his drunkenness loosened traits that he normally subdued under a mantle of decency and harmony? Who was this person she had pledged her life to? From the figure of her dream-man a stranger had emerged, and at each revelation her sense of emptiness grew. She felt the bubble of her happiness shriveling. How could she keep up the good life, maintain the bright marriage she thought they had created together, when she felt her ideals dimming month by month, a subtle collapse of all she had imagined in her naive youth?

Tomorrow would they speak of this? Would they talk it out at last? She didn't know. Just let the tension and exhaustion go away. Right now, that's all she wanted.

CHAPTER 12

꩜

R adley wiped her hands on the towel hanging through the refrigerator door handle and hurried to answer the doorbell, leaving the lunch dishes soaking in the sink. She brightened at the sight of Klara's friendly face. "Thank heavens you're here. We have to talk." She'd never been so glad to see someone. "Come on in. Shane is downstairs watching his shows. We have the living room to ourselves."

"When I heard your voice on the phone, I knew it was serious," Klara said, lowering her ample torso onto the couch. "Tell me everything, as one feminist sister to another." She dug deep into her oversized leather bag, pulled out a thin brown cigarette and lighter, and settled back like a den mother.

Radley seated herself on the peacock-patterned chair, took a Salem from the silver cigarette box on the table and regarded her friend. It was good to have someone who listened with spotlight intensity, as if your concerns were the center of the universe. Since the formation of the women's group, she and Klara had spent long afternoons on Klara's porch rehashing the group meetings, analyzing their motives, and discussing Nixon's latest campaign speeches. Radley appreciated Klara's voracious curiosity and gift for recall, her ability to probe with crucial questions, and the way she kept everyone laughing with continual wisecracks.

Klara obtained a degree at Macalester College in three years on a scholarship, then snared an at-home job editing textbooks for Academic Press. After marrying Dick, she quit and devoted herself to reading and juggling the schedules of Dick and the children. Now that the children had become teenagers, she found time to study Thomas Paine and take extension classes at the University. The family didn't seem to mind that the house was a mess and that evening meals were of the slap-dash kind, produced from tin cans, frozen food boxes, and fortified instant hamburger mixes. "We're used to each other. I pretty much let the kids go their own way," she had explained. "I'm not terribly domestic. But they can always find me in the den, bent over a good book."

Radley took a deep inhale of her Salem. Something about the looseness of this arrangement didn't seem right. If Radley let go of the reins in such a manner, mayhem would ensue, the house would crumble in shards of broken toys and limbs. Still, Klara had a warm, open relationship with her children. She must be doing something right.

"Klara," she began, "how do you do it? I mean keep your children in line so they do what you ask and behave respectfully?"

Klara unclasped her hands, leaned forward, and regarded her friend sympathetically. "Is that what's bothering you? Tell me."

"My two drive me crazy!" Radley grabbed a lighter from the table, flicked it open and shut. "I'm at my wits end. My adorable, beautiful children are wild, unmanageable, they fuss and fight, ignore my requests, do as they please. I don't know what to do! I can't stand to be around them." With that, she dropped to the back of the chair, head drooping, clasping the lighter in her fist.

"That's a great deal of power for such little tykes," Klara said.

Radley pulled herself upright. "You hit it. I'm helpless. And I worry about Larry. He's reckless, will try anything. He'd throw himself off a building confident that the person below would catch him." Lifting her arms, she stared at her friend for a moment before letting them drop to her lap. "The child knows no fear, has no concept of reality and total confidence in his own ability. I daren't be distracted for a minute. He's bound to get into trouble.

"And Megan has trouble separating right and wrong. She operates on impulse and responds according to what she wants to happen as if truth didn't exist. Is it possible for someone to be born without a conscience?" She picked up her cigarette, took a long drag and let the smoke filter out through her mouth and nose slowly, then flicked her cigarette ashes into the ashtray with little finger taps.

"Megan's teacher believes Megan has low self-esteem. She sticks to herself. Since the theft of money, the students have shunned her. She seems to have given up."

"Once, several girls demanded to know where Megan got the red and gold knit sweater she was wearing. Megan looked confused, and when they insisted, mumbled that she got it for her birthday. They accused her of stealing it. Megan ran into the bathroom in tears. I had given her the sweater for her seventh birthday."

"It must be dreadful for her."

"When the teacher called on her with the question, 'Why do snowmen melt?' she answered, 'Because they get bored.' The class roared, not kindly. Now Megan won't respond at all. Some of her classmates perceive her as on the slow side. Mrs. Merlin thinks it's psychological."

"Maybe Mrs. Merlin can help," Klara suggested.

"She claims she has no answers."

"What about Shane?"

"Shane was an only child. An obedient, quiet one, with no experience dealing with sibling squabbles. What his parents said ruled, his wants were overruled and that was that. With our children, he complies with whatever they want. They need discipline. I would not subject them to the blind injustice of the autocratic, arbitrary approach of my own childhood, but I have no idea of what to do instead. I'm at a loss, Klara."

"Can your mother help?"

"My mother! Get real. She left the discipline up to my father. When I leave the children with her, she hires a sitter."

Klara smiled. "My friend, I don't excel in any of those things. But I've a big lap and my kids can always count on me to take their part and guide them from the sidelines. Discipline is not my forté. Dick's a super father, is firm about rules, and brings one or the other into his room for parental talks." She lit another skinny brown cigarette, snapped the Zippo shut, and draped an arm over the back of the couch. "He takes them canoeing—right now they're floating down Minnehaha Creek—and camping, not my cup of tea. Me, I let them make their own decisions."

"But they have to be trained to make good ones!" Her friend was fortunate, Radley thought enviously. She guessed, from what she had seen at Klara's, that her husband Dick ruled with a strict hand, that as Audrey and John were enjoying the many outings and capers he took them on, he made them behave. Klara could afford to be relaxed.

"Do you recall the money Megan stole?" Radley went on. "She still won't own up to it, she behaves as if nothing had happened. I stressed that she was never to do it again, that stealing and lying were wrong and would damage her life. Nothing gets through to her."

"What else did you tell her?"

"What do you mean? Those are the facts."

"You have to lay it out, explain *why* it's wrong and *how* it affects her life, her friendships, her feeling about herself, how it affects others—you know. A cold lecture isn't sufficient."

"I . . . I guess so." Setting her floral coffee cup and saucer on the coffee table Radley scrunched her forehead. "But I don't think a seven-year-old can understand theories about trust and relationships and integrity."

"You have to be more immediate. Did you draw her out? Ask her what she wants? Ask her what she thought? What her feelings are about money? Suggest other methods of getting things? Did you tell her you love her no matter what?"

Radley shook her head sadly. "I did none of that. It never occurred to me." She covered her face with her hands and closed her eyes.

"How did counseling work out?"

"Oh, Mr. Poppele, a highly recommended child specialist, was no help at all. This Mr. Poppele sat behind his desk looking noncommittal and asked me questions, the very ones I had come to ask him."

"What advice did he give?"

"None. Evidently, he gets you to posit the problems and allows you to figure them out yourself. It's a form of professional mirroring." Radley gave an incredulous laugh. "Finally, he stuck his neck out and suggested I reward good behavior with candy. My kids aren't allowed candy, dentist's orders. The session was a waste of time." She shook her head, frowning. "So was the Rudolph Dreikurs' workshop on child management Shane and I have been attending. Hasn't made any difference that I can tell."

Klara balanced her cigarette on the edge of the marble ashtray. "I think she's crying for attention."

"Attention? I'm with her day in and day out, every minute she's not in school. I pick her up, run her to the dentist, buy her clothes, fix her meals, clean her room, read her stories at bedtime, take her to the zoo." Radley clamped her jaw. "I really can't imagine what she wants. Hasn't she got everything she needs?"

"Simmer down. All I know is kids need to be swamped with love and tend to act out if they don't receive it."

"I'd throw myself in front of a speeding train for those kids. They're my world. They're the most important thing in my life!"

"You still don't get it. She needs you to share her life and reach out to her emotionally."

Radley shook her head ruefully, looking down. "I don't know how to do that."

Klara reached over and laid a plump hand on Radley's arm. "I can tell you, Megan with her bouncy enthusiasm is so easy to love. Just do it." For some moments she sat still, as if letting her words sink in, finally lifted her gaze. "I may not run an organized shop, but I do know how to do that." Then, as if rousing herself from a spell, she abruptly changed her tone. "Sorry, I have to use the little girl's room. Even though that doesn't describe me." She coughed a throaty cigarette laugh as she lifted herself up and padded from the room.

Radley sat staring out the window. Strains of dialogue from the television seeped from the amusement room below. As Klara resettled herself on the couch, they heard footsteps clipping up the stairs, and Shane appeared in the hallway.

"Hello, ladies.' He stood tall in a Kelly green shirt, wearing the tan leather slippers she'd given him for Christmas. The sight of him drew a smile to her lips. "I'm getting a Fresca. Want one?"

They demurred, indicating the coffee cups on the table between them.

"Shane, Radley tells me you two have been studying *Children the Challenge*," Klara said.

"Sure have," Shane said good-naturedly, stuffing his hands in his pockets and moving into the room.

"So what do you think of his methods?"

"Well . . . Sure worth a try."

"Everyone pinpoints Dreikurs as the top authority on child behavior," Klara said.

"Dreikurs advocates rewarding good behavior and ignoring the bad," Radley said, "and the use of natural consequences to modify their actions. For example, if the child is not ready in time to catch the school bus, the child has to walk to school. Do away with power struggles and blame. It makes sense."

"Is it working?" Klara asked.

"No."

"Too soon to tell," Shane put in. A muffled voice trailed up the stairs from below. "Excuse me, *Dennis the Menace* is starting. Never miss it." Raising a hand in farewell, Shane smiled, fetched a Fresca from the kitchen, and trundled down the stairs.

"Shane seems like a good man."

"Oh, he is."

Klara drew a roll of butterscotch drops from her purse and popped one into her mouth. "You love Shane, don't' you?" she asked in a soft voice.

Radley's head jerked up. Of course she did. Maybe not like she had at the beginning—the glow had receded, sucked into the swirl of child-rearing, the everyday skirmish of household demands, and the bouts of drinking. Yet, there was more, something had been slipping over the years, had been lost. The question was, what remained?

"I admit I sometimes feel disenchanted. I need more than a breadwinner." She pressed her fingers to her eyes, but after a moment straightened up. "I do love Shane, but sometimes I feel like I have three children to care for instead of two." She brought the coffee cup to her lips, sucked in a deep swallow of the warm liquid. "It looks like I'll have to deal with the kids on my own. So—that's what I'll do."

"You're already doing it," Klara said with her usual equanimity. "Don't give up. Kids are resilient. They'll survive."

Tears formed in the corners of Radley's eyes and trickled down her cheeks. "Will *I* get through this?" she asked, then realized how feeble that sounded—she was the adult, she had the advantage. "Maybe I'm just not cut out for the mothering role."

"You have to care for yourself if you're to be strong for them."

How glad she was to have Klara as a friend! They hadn't reached a single conclusion or formed a plan, but she felt as if her body had loosened and that somewhere in the tangle of random ideas there was hope.

Shane glanced up as Radley entered the amusement room. Klara must have left. He watched a few more minutes of *Howdy Doody*, then during the commercial pulled a mystery from the magazine rack next to his leather lounge chair, re-crossed his legs on the leg rest and opened the book to read.

It was pleasant sitting here with his family, sun streaming in through the wide expanse of windows. Perched on a stool, Larry held the ear flaps of a stuffed elephant with white button eyes and was twirling it faster and faster around his head. Megan sat on the floor poking the nipple of a baby bottle into the mouth of a curly-headed doll.

Across from him, Radley flipped a page of *Time*. "Larry, you're going to break something," she said sternly, lowering the magazine.

Shane noticed her frequent glances in his direction. Something was on her mind. He guessed she was waiting for a chance to corner him for a talk. He detested these talks. She always wanted something and he always came up short. He suspected it was another bout with the children that called for discipline, in which he would be called on to find solutions. He would be squeezed to the limits of resistance.

A nerve tightened around the edges of his spine. What was he supposed to do? He had no answers. This was not his bailiwick. Handling the children was her realm, her end of the marriage partnership.

Maybe he should consult the priest. A few catechism classes would straighten Megan and Larry out. Discipline that guided their wills through the rewards and punishments embedded in church doctrine, that's what was needed. But Radley would have none of it. Declared she wouldn't use the threat of hellfire to make them behave. But the idea of eternal punishment had deterred sin for centuries, how else were people to be guided except by the hope of heaven and fear of suffering? It was the basis of human motivation.

Since his wife obdurately refused to turn to the church, he was stymied. He could, he reflected, slip out to mass on his own, but he didn't want to create another source of protest. That its spiritual power had failed to bring Radley into the mother fold perplexed him, and he wondered if something might be lacking in the ironclad tenets of the faith.

Shane's life had been formed by the church, his early schooling, high school, college, all couched in religious doctrine, stretching back through his parents to the old country, to his deep Irish roots. Sin is redeemable and suffering endurable in the arms of the church. Sins, absorbed into your very bones, racking one with guilt, can be exorcised through the church. Suffering, a condition of life, can be alleviated by turning power over to God. All the faithful have to do is obey—Shane had been told that obedience was the hardest vow in the Catholic Church to follow. Responsibility is shifted to a Higher Power, leaving you with a sense of relief. Shane learned to trust fate to God, to let go, to give it up and take life as it is.

No, nothing he could do. It was in God's hands. The children would survive. His family was his life, and he would go along, it was the only way. He would offer up this sacrifice, confident of reward in the next world.

He sat for a while, staring out the window at the long oak branches arching over the lawn, letting the waves of sadness pass through him, filling his every cavity, without resistance. He reminded himself of how much he had to be thankful for, but this time it did no good. He felt too heavy to move. A sense of helplessness gripped him.

He sat still for some time, lost in thought. Then, closing the unread book, he got up and stood at the open door leading to the patio. Through the screen he could see the spirea bushes cascading in a stream of white blossoms along the edge of the sloping lawn.

"I think I'll go for a walk," he said without turning around.

"You never go for walks," Radley said from the couch. "You hate to walk."

"Well, I'm going for a walk now."

"Why don't you take the kids?"

He opened the screen door, stepped out on the patio and stood on the flagstone walk. "I'm just going to stand here. Get some fresh air," he said over his shoulder.

The sun, for days hiding behind an ocean of grey clouds, had emerged, a yellow ball that beamed waves of brightness over the lawn. Shane regarded the red geraniums scattered in boxes among the white wrought-iron patio furniture, the green sweep of yard, and the gleaming treetops crowding the edges. The view filled him with a fresh peace. As he watched, a cardinal swooped onto a tree branch and flicked its tail, jerking its head from side to side. He never tired of watching birds, winging back and forth to the feeder, their dainty antics, the colorful streaks of white, red, and yellow feathers.

His mind went back to the yellow parakeet that hung in a cage by the apartment window when he was growing up. The brick wall of the apartment building next door blocked much of the light, casting the corners of the small living room in perpetual shadows. Opposite the print-covered couch on one side of the room sat a 19-inch TV and next to it a folding table, topped with a white doily runner, which was pulled into the center of the room when there was company for dinner. The cheerful bird brightened the room with its gay yellow color and ringing tweets. Shane watched it by the hour, fascinated by the soft eyes that looked at him, until one summer a drunken aunt inadvertently left the cage door ajar and it flew out the open window.

Shane mourned for weeks, convinced that the bird didn't desire its freedom, that it coveted the love and protection that he, Shane, would give it. Such a delicate creature, not meant to be abandoned, and the silly thing had seen an open door and flown off to its inevitable doom. Well, if it could find its way back, by some miracle, Shane would be there, waiting.

Shane sat down in one of the patio chairs. Yes, he would be there, solid and reliable, he would stay and care for his own.

CHAPTER 13

❧

I t was a crisp Sunday afternoon. The sun snoozed behind a blanket of clouds while branches of bronze and gold leaves spread a languid canopy over the house. Inside, Shane relaxed before the crackling wood fire in his navy sweater and leather slippers as he perused the Sunday paper. Radley had carried in logs from the garage, stuffed the kindling, and stirred up soft ruddy flames. A warm golden glow filled the amusement room. The sounds of his family upstairs, the murmuring fire, and the aura of sleepiness outside the windows sent waves of contentment through him.

Radley was dressing the kids for an outing to the science museum. He hated museums, department stores, and freeways—anything that involved crowds or traffic. The jostling and commotion rattled him, almost drove him to drink. Growing up in a two-bedroom walk-up apartment amid neighborhood pockets of Italians, Jews, Blacks, Puerto Ricans, and Irish, he had been reined in from the rough and tumble, the fights and crimes that swarmed the streets below. His was a quiet, protected home of routine and matriarchal efficiency, guarded within the close walls of the apartment. A quiet, structured life, getting together with Irish relatives on holidays, meeting at Aunt Bridie's after Easter morning service.

He and his wife's backgrounds couldn't be more different, he reflected, sighing, and here he was in her world, in the foreign reaches of suburbia—no wandering down the street for a coffee. He would have to adjust, he could adjust. He was really quite pleased with the drastic turn his life had taken since he married Radley. If only he could divine what was expected of him—sometimes he felt as if this new world were about to swallow him.

He listened as his wife hustled the kids into the garage, and the Buick swung out the driveway and sped off with a roar. She had not been in a good mood, had grumbled that she had to do everything, perturbed that Shane did not build fires, repair shower fixtures, or change light bulbs. "We can't call the superintendent, we live in a *house*," she had exclaimed as she emerged from the garage, logs piled up to her chin. It irritated him that she continually threw him reproving looks as she went about these chores. What did she expect? He worked hard all week. Why couldn't she leave him alone? He retreated into a subdued resignation.

After all, he did his best. He glanced at *Children the Challenge* lying on the coffee table, which he'd read from cover to cover while they attended the Dreikurs' classes. All that talk of natural consequences, analyzing and plotting reactions to every incident, of ignoring bad actions and "catching" the good, was beyond him. Bad behavior was to be reprimanded, beyond that, they would learn as time went on.

He turned his gaze to the fire and watched the flames, now reduced to tiny licks between the logs. As he thought of her whipping up a fire in the fireplace, stoking the logs with an air of efficiency and reproach, his lazy mood evaporated and the soft tenor of Sunday tranquility seemed to vanish up the chimney in smoke.

Last night had been too much. It confounded him to be under the gun like that. Char and Wilson had stopped by for one of their regular visits, and while sipping Tom Collins, they chatted about the children, a new leaf blower Wilson had purchased through a Montgomery Ward catalogue, the new surround sound stereo system Radley recently had installed in the living room. Megan and Larry dressed in the matching sailor outfits—gifts from Char—sat on the floor building a Byzantine tower with tinker toys. As the tower grew tall and needle-thin, it began to wobble. Conversation ceased and everyone held their breath as Larry placed a large turret at the top of the tower, and watched as, after tottering for a moment, the entire structure toppled to the ground. They all laughed.

Radley turned to Shane. "Shane, please play us a Chopin piece," she urged.

Char often played at parties and family gatherings, folk songs that everyone knew from childhood. She'd been delighted to discover that Shane had studied for ten years at Juilliard. "I am very fond of classical music. Oh, do play something!"

Shane's back stiffened. He had been through this before. The pressure, he knew, would mount, the insistence that he perform. When he demurred, claiming that he was rusty, hadn't played in years, they persisted. You're too modest! But they expected too much of him; he absolutely would not touch the piano.

"Come on, at least play some popular songs for us," Radley urged. "It would be so easy for you. We love to sing!" Shane remained adamant. Hot pokers wouldn't move him.

Char chimed in. "Shane, do be a dear."

"Don't' be so stubborn!" Radley added. But he clamped his lips and wouldn't budge.

As he thought of last night's scene, he could feel the blood firing through his body. They wouldn't let up, pushing him, pressing him into a corner like a wad of putty. The combination of resistance and guilt at denying them made his skull pound.

"God damn it!" he exploded aloud. To be the cause of such disappointment, the target of such disapproval! Afterwards, his wife continued to probe him for reasons, she couldn't comprehend his reluctance, but all he could do was shake his head. His only recourse was to give in. But for once, he would stand his ground!

Feeling shaky, he got up, went to the bar and refilled his whiskey sour from the stainless steel cocktail shaker. He took a sip. Then another. He felt his muscles loosen as he returned to his seat. How could he tell Radley what he didn't know himself? His refusal to perform at the piano was just—but he couldn't tell. He only knew he would never give in. The assumption of his genius, the anticipation of musical clouds of heavenly purity, froze every nerve in his fingers. He hadn't played for too long. There was no way he would allow himself to be spotlighted in front of the entire clan.

Why couldn't Radley respect his wishes, release her bulldog grip? Yes, when they were dating he had played at all the parties, with her hovering around the piano like a butterfly, but those days were over. Damn her! He worked hard all week while she stayed home and played with the children—yes, she had much to do, but none of it was complicated. She didn't have to deal with irascible bosses, ignorant co-workers, demanding memos, threats of deadlines. She wasn't forced to toe the line. Her time was her own; she ran the household at her pleasure. It appeared to him a far easier business.

He was overcome with how unappreciated he was.

"Damn her!" A spurt of anger rose in his belly, submerging the sense of inadequacy she always managed to make him feel. He stood up. "Damn her and her fucking family."

He had no options. To forsake his present life and return to his past, alone and family-less, was unthinkable. The immutability of his position swept over him and he felt confused, almost unhinged. His contained, orderly system of living had been violated, and he felt a surge of raging protest.

Moving to the window, he stared at the patio and sloping lawn scattered with leaves he was supposed to have raked weeks ago. The yard and the surrounding woods held a foreign edge, as if he'd just awakened and found himself in an alien country.

The ice clinked in his glass and he gulped down a large swallow. As he started back to his chair, his foot hit one of the bar stools and he tottered and fell heavily against the bar, grimacing as his glass flew from his hand and hit the counter with a sharp crack, splattering the drink in all directions.

His heart pounded as if he'd run a mile. With an abrupt swing of heel, he turned and headed for the piano. Whipping open the bench lid he grabbed the stacks of sheet music lying neatly inside, one handful after another. Then, arms full, he marched to the fireplace and stood glaring at the charred logs among the glowing embers.

The only sound in the room was the Mexican calendar clock on the paneled wall that emitted a faint *ti-ti-ti-ti* with the movement of the second hand. It reminded Shane that he was alone in the house, that Radley and the children would be having lunch with Char after the museum and would be away for hours. With a fierce grunt, he drew aside the sliding screen and plunged the frayed pages into the fire, stack after stack. The flames quickly found their prey, licking the edges of the papers. He watched transfixed as they quickly blazed and then fizzled into a heap of orange ashes.

A surge of relief flooded through him. Putting his feelings into motion had strengthened his resolve, added resin to his limbs. His muscles relaxed, his stomach unfurled, and a sense of satisfaction passed through him. For one moment he was his own man. Contemplating the repercussions of his act, the questions and protests that would be heaped on him when Radley discovered what he'd done, he conjured a stony wall behind which he would retreat with equanimity. His armor of silence was well in place and, as he had learned so many times in ten years of married life, would serve him well.

Flinging himself into the easy chair, he took a gulp of the whiskey sour and felt his body relax. His eyes lit on the pool of liquid and broken glass on the floor by the bar, but he did not get up. Let the mess remain on the floor, let it fester, something in him was churning round and around in his gut. Before he could conjure what it was, he fell into a troubled sleep.

When he opened his eyes, the room had darkened. Beyond the window, a thick bank of clouds hung low in the sky. The clock on the wall marked 5 o'clock. He pulled himself to his feet and entered the small half-bath at the foot of the stairs and soaped his hands under the faucet. The mirror above the sink reflected the gleam of his dark hair with the hint of a widow's peak, his handsome well-proportioned face, and sensitive mouth. He wiped his hands carefully on the peach trimmed hand towel and averted his eyes. He was not an introspective guy, he knew that. He'd always counted on the certainty of faith and structure. He liked to keep things simple and take life as it came, with forbearance, without demands or preferences.

It was then he saw a ripple running diagonally across the mirror surface, a subtle imperfection in the glass he hadn't noticed before, glaring across his face like a whiplash. It struck him that maybe his system didn't work as well as he had supposed, that closing himself within his unflagging belief system cut him off from the world he relied on.

He stared at himself without moving until the light from the window faded behind the clouds and the image in the mirror disappeared.

Chapter 14

❧

Larry pranced into the living room, bold in a red and black cowboy suit and boots, vest with hanging fringes, a silver pistol riding at his hip. "Look Mom, I'm a dude," he said, patting the holster. He could wear whatever he wanted, and he selected the cowboy suit his mother had purchased for his birthday from FAO Schwarz.

The guests arrived at four and traipsed onto the dining room, where clumps of balloons festooned the walls. The table was spread with party napkins, bowls of favors wrapped in colored crepe paper, jelly beans in a glass rooster dish, and bandana blowouts. The children fluttered up to the upholstered chairs like humming birds, giggling, shy, pressing thumbs into the bright wrapped favors by their plates. A banner strung across the wall read HAPPY 8TH BIRTHDAY LARRY.

Larry relished his role as King of the Day, surrounded by six small guests in pink crinoline dresses and suits or vests, chomping on jelly beans, faces twisting here and there. He smothered his hot dog with ketchup, gobbled it down and pointed to the empty chair next to him. "Okay, Mom, we've finished eating, now Wolf can join us. You promised!" He had managed to persuade his mother, it being his birthday and all.

What would he think of next? Smiling, Radley coaxed a hesitant Wolf into the chair. The dog sat on her haunches, tail tapping, sniffing in every direction. At the sight, the children burst into hysterical laughter. "Give him some jelly beans," one of them urged.

"No, candy's not good for him. He gets a present, though," exclaimed Larry. "I wrapped it myself." Everyone looked at the box covered in red wrapping paper.

"Open it, open it!" cries around the table.

"All right," his mother said, "go ahead, while I bring the cake."

Larry tore off the red wrapping paper and removed the lid from a small box. Heads twisted to see what was inside. There lay a large steak bone, tidbits of dried meat clinging to the edges.

Radley set the chocolate-frosted cake next to Larry. "He cannot eat that bone at the table."

"But Mom . . ."

"No. That's NO. He has to take it outside."

The dog trotted willingly to the front door, a crusty T-bone between his teeth. The children, having lost the last vestiges of timidity, were talking and poking each other as they stuffed chocolate cake into their mouths. Radley couldn't help smiling as she watched Larry slicing and passing pieces of cake, directing from the head chair. He had a way of invigorating every event, always improvising some new game or projecting some new or surprising twist that set everyone laughing.

It was time to start the telephone game. "I've got it!" Larry exclaimed. He leaned over and cupping his hand whispered to the girl next to him. "*If you are smart and talk fast you will become a millionaire.*" The message circled around the table, whispered from ear to ear, until it reached the last child next to Larry, a lad with wide button eyes and swirls of curly hair. The boy swept his bangs aside and announced, "*If you fart in the grass you can't go to the fair.*" A moment of silence—that word!—then an eruption of wild giggles. Radley shook her head—oh dear, the mothers would hear what went on at the Gallagher house!

By the time Radley's parents arrived, the children had left, picked up by cars swinging up the curved drive. Shane was in the front yard throwing sticks for the dog. "I just stand here and throw. Wolf does all the work," he said. He was in a good mood, Radley noticed, this balmy Sunday afternoon. And why not? He was surrounded by family, celebrating with his son, and now here were Char and Wilson requiring drinks. They would sit and talk about the day-to-day doings of the children. The day was bright, sun bright, happiness bright.

Soon they were circled in the living room with gin fizzes.

"Wilson, will you take off that god-awful fishing hat?"Char said to her husband.

Wilson slipped the hat into his lap. "I was just showing Larry my good-luck hat. I caught a twenty-pound Muskie wearing this hat. It will be his someday."

"When are you taking me fishing again, Grandpa? Can I wear my cowboy hat instead?"

"Yes, if it helps you catch more fish," Wilson replied.

"Larry's Tinker Toy Taj Mahal won the third-grade Architect Design contest," Radley announced.

"He sure is a clever one," Wilson said, a gleam of pride in his eyes. "Larry will go far, not a lazy bone in his body. This boy will leave no stone unturned."

Radley wasn't surprised by his words. Her father bragged shamelessly, liked to speculate how Larry would go on to achieve success—a future attorney, architect, or interstellar spaceship pilot.

Her mother agreed. "With his handsome good looks," she remarked, "and likeable personality he will go far in life."

Radley saw that Larry, bent over a new erector set, beamed at this.

Megan, who had curled in her father's lap, jumped to her feet. "Watch this," she exclaimed. All eyes turned to her.

"I've taught Wolf a trick. He can tell us when he has to go. Watch this. Wolf!" The dog stared up at her, all alertness. "OUTSIDE." His tail swished faster. "WOLF, OUTSIDE." Quickly the dog nosed the toe of Megan's shoe, then gave it a quick tap. "Good dog!" Megan exclaimed, throwing her arms around the dog's neck. "Oh, I love you so much!"

"But how do you know when he actually has to go?" Larry cried.

"He hasn't learned that part yet," Megan confessed. "That's next."

Radley saw Megan look around expectantly, but all eyes had turned to the tower Larry was erecting, which was threatening to topple as he added another beam at the top. Megan sank back against the couch, a hurt look in her eyes, then sprang up and raced from the room. Radley looked after her with a sudden surge of regret. No one had acknowledged Megan's efforts or appreciated the kinship she had with animals that responded so willingly to her touch. She was continually outshone by her brother, Radley thought. She had often seen her recoil, abandoning her lead role as the oldest. Larry had a way of dominating with his initiative and quick thinking.

What was she as a mother to do? This was Larry's day, nothing to be done for it.

A lilac branch brushed softly against a far windowpane and the fringes of a vermillion sunset backlit the trees across the street. Inside, the seeping darkness drew the room close. Radley looked around at the King Arthur figures in medieval attire, a plastic bowling set, an Arctic explorer kit, and four colored sport shirts stamped with HE MAN, and beyond in the hallway, the warm tones of the antique pendulum clock and next to them sets of ice skates piled on the hall rug. The sound of children's laughter echoed in her head, and there was Larry looking up at her with delight, and across from her those she cared most about, her world. A tight swell rose and caught in her throat.

Radley watched Larry smile his sweet, I-can-do-no-wrong smile and settle himself on the couch between Wilson and Char. "Where's my present?" he asked, looking at them with sun-lit blue eyes.

"We're waiting to hear what you want. What's your heart's desire?" Char asked.

"If I tell you will I get it? Promise?

"Well, dear, we certainly will if it's reasonable," Char replied.

"Okay, good. I know just what I want." He paused, looking around at Radley, Shane, Char, Wilson, and Megan, who sat waiting. "Well—I saw it in a magazine at school, you know, one of those picture magazines about foreign countries." He pulled from his pocket a page splashed with colorful illustrations. "See? This is what I want."

Radley stared at a photo of a monkey in a yellow suit, next to the words MONKEYS. TAME. EAT SCRAPS. ONLY $99.95. SHIPPED DIRECTLY TO YOUR DOOR.

"It's *alive*," Char exclaimed.

"It could get sick," Shane said.

"Wolf would hate it," Radley said.

"Oh, he's adorable," Megan cried.

"A monkey has to be trained and cared for," Wilson said.

Larry was finally mollified when Radley stated that if the monkey came into the house Wolf would have to go, that was all there was to it. Tomorrow they would take him to Schwartz' and he could pick out whatever he wanted.

As she tucked him in, Radley sat on Larry's bed and placed a kiss on his forehead. "Good night, sweetheart."

His black eyelashes fluttered sleepily. "I love you, Mom," he mumbled. The words startled her. She ran her hand through his mop of blonde hair. Where had he learned to say that? Neither she nor Shane was in the habit of expressing intimate feelings. Did this expression of affection originate directly from his soul, like an eruption of primordial life? She studied him with a tender feeling of awe.

Larry lay quietly, energy spent. In the low circle of light from the hall his face looked serene, almost angelic. She thought how hard it was to fathom what lay inside a child beyond the instinctive drive to immediate gratification. But there was more, she could feel it. Needs buried, unknown. Did he perceive that Megan, with her continual mishaps and setbacks, received a mammoth share of her parents' attention, leaving him isolated in the shadows? *Did he feel the need excel, to shine, to improvise a place for himself in the family to authenticate his existence?*

"I love you, too," she breathed. "So much!" But Larry had fallen asleep.

The next day she told him. Whispered in his ear.

Does this mean I get my present? Larry asked.

He had to be satisfied with a stuffed gorilla that stood as tall as he did and chomped its teeth when you pulled a string.

CHAPTER 15

❦

"*West Suburban Council for Women's Liberation*. Wow. That's a mouthful," Cookie exclaimed.

"I approve of our new name. Says exactly who we are," Trish said. She sat upright in her chair fingering the gold Byzantine chain that rested on her green sweater. Across from her, Radley leaned back, legs drawn up, observing the piles of books stacked by the fireplace and National Geographic prints lining the walls of Klara's living room. She liked these weekly meetings, conversing casually, munching sweet rolls as people refilled coffee cups from the pot on the low table, stretched out or curled up, pumped full of caffeine.

By now the group had devoured *The Female Eunuch*, *Voices from Women's Liberation*, *Sisterhood is Powerful*, and *Ms* Magazine. The words of these bold women dispelled the general malaise that had been gripping her and filled her with a new hope and excitement.

"So many housewives are depressed. They tend to blame it on their husbands, but often it's their homebound lifestyle," Trish said. She stretched her legs in front of her, displaying a pair of yellow Indian moccasins and heavy gold anklets.

Maureen spoke up. "I have to differ with you gals. I like managing my home. There were five kids in my family, and I find family life rewarding for its own sake. But I admit, once married, my identity disappeared behind my husband. It wasn't long ago that I couldn't own my home, and even now I can't have a credit card in my own name, although I handle our finances and pay the bills. I find it unacceptable that working women receive sixty percent of what men do for the same job and that men trained for months by a woman are promoted to be her supervisor." Maureen's calm, no-nonsense manner held everyone's attention.

"My sister wanted to be an attorney," Barbara said, "but kept being directed to the female slots of secretary, teacher, or nurse." Radley noticed that she wasn't sitting as primly as usual.

"My cousin was fired from her teaching job for getting pregnant," Cookie said. "No hints of sexuality allowed in the classroom!" She laughed, a surprisingly full sound coming from such a tiny figure. Her round face with her thick straight bangs and snub nose flashed with humor.

"When I went into a liquor store last week for a bottle of wine, the men acted as if I'd invaded the men's room. They couldn't stop staring," Barbara said.

"Men are not used to seeing unescorted women in liquor stores or in bars, pumping gas, operating tractors, lifting weights, or sitting on a jury," Trish observed.

Klara leaned forward, arms lined along the arms of her chair. "Ever notice that the newspapers describe males just out of knickers as *men* and females of any age as *girls*? That there is no male equivalent to the female term *old maid*? That when women—and I'm dropping the term *girl* from now on, swear on my slaving grandmother's head—act forcefully they are considered aggressive and abrasive and are termed *bitch*, whereas for the same behavior men are strong, commanding, and powerful?" Heads nodded vehemently.

"Look at the semantics," she continued. "Pure refers to untouched and inexperienced, and protected equates with isolation. The woman-child is a goddess, while the sexual woman is a slut. It's all there in the vocabulary." Seeing agreement on everyone's face, she blew smoke rings into the air and watched them burst against the lamp shade.

They agreed. No more calling themselves girls. The decision seemed gigantic—something had happened, something was different, something that tasted of conviction and progress.

Radley's bond with these energetic women strengthened every time they met. They seemed to be born from the same cloth and pointed in the same direction, united in a common quest and hunger for fulfillment. Women throughout the country were challenging the conventional norms, and by some miracle, she thought, way out here in the conservative suburbs, they had found each other.

She looked at her friends seated around the room: Straight-as-a rod Maureen, chatty Cookie with her dangling gold bracelets, Barbara with her stern, arched demeanor, Trish her womanly confidence, Bette her cute stubbed nose and black curls—she was infused with warmth as she listened to their tales of the heart.

And of course intellectual Klara, now her best friend.
Barbara held up a copy of *House Beautiful*. "Aptly named, I'd say," she said. "Look, here's a picture of a housewife showing off her gleaming dishes. Betty Friedan says the *Women's Home Companion* is based on the premise that the desires of women are fulfilled in the home, that the home is her domain, her identity. The kitchen is her sanctuary, the castle where she reigns. She spends the days devoted exclusively to child care and housework." Barbara looked up, peering through her black cat-eye glasses. "Is this what I went through four years of college for?"

Cookie spoke up. "But wait a minute. What about girls—I mean women—who like staying at home, who love these things? Maybe this is what fulfills them. Can't some women be happy just because this isn't for us?

"You're right, Cookie," Barbara said. "But I think that women should have a choice."

The others nodded.

"Last spring I attended a seminar on Sexism in Education." Maureen pushed aside an ashtray and set a black notebook full of clippings on the coffee table. "The 26 of us were separated into small discussion groups and told to choose a leader. Guess what? All five groups selected a man. And there were only six men at the seminar." She took a drag of her cigarette. "And it was the women who suggested it! They simply turned to the men as a matter of course, and the men jumped right in."

"Did anyone question this, given the topic of the seminar?" Radley asked.

"No. I squirmed, but said nothing. No one else seemed to notice." Maureen pressed her lips together. "I should have spoken up, I see that now. In my home church I'm more forthright. Last Sunday I brought up the idea of married women keeping their maiden names and the ladies were horrified. They insisted they were proud to bear the name of their husband and would stand behind him in all things. It was best, they said, to give themselves unselfishly to their family."

Maureen paused. "Women need an identify to secure their rights. I reminded them that women have not been allowed to own or control property or obtain their own credit cards. Also, that not long ago women couldn't be on a jury, the male legislators considered women to be too fragile to hear the grisly details of crimes and too sympathetic by nature to remain objective about the accused." She looked at each listener in turn. "None of that influenced my women friends at church. They said they preferred to be protected."

So that's why she has ventured beyond her lifelong church group! Radley had wondered why Maureen, so straight and conservative, had thrown with their free-floating revisionist women's group.

"My husband," Barbara said, "claims that women belong on a pedestal to be adored, guided, and protected, to remain pure above the vulgarities of the world."

"Another word for that," Klara said, "is ostracized."

"How about weak?" someone put in.

Trish described her recent lobbying effort for pro-abortion at the Minnesota state capital. The legislators her team interviewed didn't want to hear about pro-choice or Roe versus Wade. When she mentioned the National Association for the Repeal of Abortion Laws, they snickered or drew their gaze to some far-off piece of furniture. At this, Radley perked up; the freedom of women to choose whether or not to bear children was a cause dear to her heart, and she felt a shot of anger. Each story brought renewed aggravation. This could not be! This must not be left to stand!

"As we left," Trish went on, "well-dressed men in dark business suits crowded into the elevator, hissing in lowered voices about the damn feminists, should be minding their families. We detected words like ball-breaker, dyke, bitch, man-hater—men normally so gentlemanly and polite, opening doors with a smile, now scornful and hostile."

Each person spoke in turn, relating personal experiences once taken for granted, now viewed with new insight. After much discussion, Radley noticed the sun was sinking beyond the window, and the room had taken on a mellow flavor. People sat around the room stretched out in various poses. The coffee cups had been emptied, refilled, the ashtray bulged with cigarette stubs, and pastry crumbs lay drying on the plates.

Klara roused up and switched on the table lamp, flinging an orange-yellow light over the furniture. A bookcase stuffed with oversized books and magazines that protruded every which way retreated to the shadows. "To quote Gloria Steinem, 'If men could get pregnant, abortion would be a sacrament,'" she remarked, sitting back down.

"You realize that all this is challenging the male order?" Barbara said.

"If exposing injustice and male prerogative means toppling the normal order, so be it," Trish said. "It's a price that must be paid."

"I hope we're not going to end up hating men," Cookie said, scrunching a Milk Dud between her teeth.

"Only their antiquated behavior," Trish replied. "Unfortunately, they have no idea what we want. They just don't get it." She was stretched out on the floor, head cushioned against the couch.

Radley heard a door slam, drawers being open and shut in the other room. Audrey had returned from band practice, Klara explained. A few minutes later, Audrey entered, followed by a whiff of vanilla and fresh- baked bread. How young she looked, Radley thought, in a crepe rose-colored blouse and her cheeks aglow and her mouth glowing with pink lipstick.

"Hello, ladies. I stopped by the bakery and I'm willing to share," she said grinning, looking as if she relished the hostess role as she passed a plate of pastries with poise beyond her fifteen years.

"We are now officially The West Suburban Council for Women's Liberation," her mother said, selecting a cake. "Do you want to join us?"

Radley watched her, wondering if the obvious disapproval she had voiced at Klara's last meeting had softened—all this friendliness! Klara must have talked to her.

"Women's Liberation! You aren't becoming one of those men-bashing groups, I hope." Frowning, Audrey tucked a fringe of brown hair behind one ear and lowered a basket of napkins to the table.

"Believe me, Audrey," Radley said from her perch on the arm of the couch. "We don't dislike men. But their behavior can block us from achievement, self-esteem, power. Really, you don't like to be referred to as a chick, do you? Like a pet."

"Call me a chick if you want, it's nothing to me. It's sweet. I *like* being thought cute or pretty. I want to wear makeup. I want silky hair and creamy skin. I like it when boys open the door for me. It makes me feel special. I like the feel of a strong hand. " Klara's daughter clearly had a mind of her own.

"But if that hand holds you back? If it keeps you in your place? " Bette asked.

"Don't you think women should have equal rights?" Barbara put in, nursing her fourth cup of coffee.

Audrey, as if propelled by the overwhelming resistance she was facing, burst out fiercely, "I'm young. I want boys to like me. Do you think any boy is going to stick around if I spout all that stuff about independence and not needing men?" She stood straight as a stick, one hand on her hip. "I'm sick of feminist lectures and trying to make me into your image. I'd rather die than be like you." And setting down the plate of goodies, she swirled and left the room. Radley heard the echo of disappearing footsteps stamping down the hallway.

The women turned to each other in astonishment. "That girl has a fighting spirit," Trish said, breaking the silence. "She'll go far."

"If she survives her teen-age years," someone added.

"If *I* survive her teen-age years," Klara exclaimed. "I live with this. Sweet as saccharine one day, vitriolic the next. I let her find her way. She's a smart person, with ideas on everything. She just needs to get over the bumps."

Finding your true identity, Radley suggested, was difficult, especially during the first flush of adolescence. Everyone agreed that with experience Audrey would no doubt come to view the cause of women in a new light.

Bette snuffed out her cigarette and bit into a slice of bundt cake. "I usually look in the mirror when I eat sweets," she cracked. "Have to watch my figure."

Popping a Milk Dud into her mouth, Cookie proclaimed the coffee delicious but feared the bitter coffee taste in her mouth would repulse her husband. "Forget I said that," she screeched, clapping her hand over her mouth. They all laughed, Cookie the loudest. They were in a mood to be delighted with anything.

Lingering on the front porch after the others had gone, Radley, Klara, and Bette, bathed contentedly in the semi-darkness.

"I guess I'll have to read *Sisterhood is Powerful* again," Bette mused, stretching her arms lazily.

"I thought you'd already read it," Radley said.

'Oh, I skimmed it, you know, enough to get the gist."

"That's not the same!" Really Bette! She found Bette unsubstantial, with her fluttery charm, the way she chattered on with her cute, flirtatious manner. Often she didn't do the readings at all. Her airiness bordered on the frivolous. "You really don't gain command of the material without understanding the nuances," she suggested.

Radley turned to Klara, who was braced with pillows on the porch swing. "Have you read Masters and Johnson's new book?"

"What book is that?" Bette asked, brushing a dark loop of curl from her forehead.

"You don't——? It's called *Human Sexual Response*."

"I just finished it last night."

"I don't know when you two have time to do all that reading," Bette said. "You honor students are so serious, you know all the literature. All you want to do is study, you've been at it for years. I'll never catch up."

"Of course you will," Klara said. "Just do the reading and bring your questions to the group. We'll all pitch in."

"You want to know the truth? I grew up on a farm. I was taught to cook with chicken grease and smile when you were with a date. You two were educated in private schools, you're used to privilege. Well, in my opinion it takes more than advanced degrees and fine houses to have a good life."

"Bette, one is not responsible for one's upbringing. Such an attitude could be termed reverse discrimination." Radley kept her voice even.

"Hey—we all have different personalities, with different experiences." Klara smoothed the skirt of her crumpled muumuu. "What we've been learning is how insignificant the differences are. We have something together that is far stronger than our varied backgrounds."

The porch swing squeaked gently back and forth. Radley listened to the rustling sounds issuing from the darkened yard, the buzz of cicadas and the occasional crunch of trampled leaves. The three of them might have different profiles, she mused, but silhouetted in the darkness, signs of individuality obscured, they formed equal partners.

As Radley walked down the darkened steps to her car, the night around her held an ethereal sheen, as if masking some mystery. She experienced a soaring feeling of exhilaration. Whatever she was getting into with these thought-provoking women, she had a feeling that her life would be changed forever. She headed home to make dinner with her head in the clouds, having decided that tonight it would be beef stroganoff—her family deserved the best.

CHAPTER 16

❧

"Would you like a refill, little mother?" Wilson asked amiably, setting his highball on the glass patio table and standing up. He looked relaxed in the colorful parrot yellow and green shirt acquired during their last winter's vacation in Florida.

"Not yet, thanks Dad," Radley replied.

"How about you, Grandma?"

"Don't call me that," Char said. "Makes me feel old. Yes, I'd like another drink. And I'd like a cherry this time, please." She held up her glass and a jingling silver charm bracelet rolled down her wrist, clattering like icicles, echoing the sound of her lilting laugh. Char laughed easily, Radley noted, part of a continual cheerfulness she carried with her everywhere. As she lifted her arm, the bracelet slipped under the cuff of her pink pongee blouse.

"Coming right up," Wilson said, opening the sliding French door into the house.

It was pleasant on the patio. Radley and her mother leaned back in the white wicker chairs without speaking. On the opposite bank, clumps of full-branched elm and aspen trees ran along the large pond, bird calls rang from the distance, and the air hung fragrant with milkweed and moist grass. They watched Megan and Larry playing at the pond's edge at the bottom of the slope, tossing sand pebbles into a toy boat with a red and white striped sail that floated several yards out on a tether.

Wilson returned with refills and settled in his chair. Radley watched her father's eyes light on his grandson, heard him chuckle. She knew that Wilson saw his years of labor and dreams of generational success fulfilled in this bright, enterprising child. For birthdays he presented Larry with BB guns, Gopher football caps and fishing lure kits. Once in Boca Raton she had heard him bragging to the Culberson's on his grandson's independence as Larry steered their cabin cruiser up the canal.

Her parents recently sold the big house and moved into smaller, empty-nest quarters on a quiet pond, filling their days with dinner parties, sightseeing trips, and golf. Her father had devoted his life to carving out a career, had climbed to the top of the corporate world of industrial design and made a name for himself. Radley knew the story by heart: his rise from modest circumstances to become president of a corporate enterprise by aggressively pursuing an advanced education, studying nights as the family grew and devoting seventy hours a week to building his company to a pinnacle of success. But his sacrifices didn't allow much time to interact with his children. To Radley he had always been a distant figure, awesome, bigger than life, untouchable.

The responsibility for emotional connection fell to Char. Or was supposed to. When it came to children, her mother remained at a loss. The loud exuberance and demands of children were beyond her tolerance, clashed with her craving for harmony and peace. But she contributed what she could. As a grandmother, she showered the grandchildren with electric woodcutting sets, life-size stuffed pandas, battery-operated walkie-talkies, and outfits from FAO Schwarz. Radley loved her mother on a rational, material level, where she felt protected and important, if not touched and understood.

Char stood up, her skirt falling gracefully around her legs. "I'd better see to dinner—pork chops smothered in mushroom sauce." She disappeared into the house through the sliding French doors.

Her dad smiled at her, and Radley could tell the conversation was about to take a personal turn, now that they were alone. "And how are things in Deephaven? Need anything? Your mother and I want to send out a contractor to repair your front steps. All right with you?"

"Sure, if you want to." But she cringed at the thought of his whipping out his checkbook. Her parents had done enough, demanding nothing in return. They did everything for her, always had, ever since her college days when they perceived her as a variant, noticed that she was veering in the wrong direction, away from the tried and true, away from them. At a loss, they plied her with anything she wanted, an attempt, she thought, to compensate for some lack in her upbringing, or maybe they just wanted to see her happy. To Radley it felt demeaning, being covered with generos-ity, having her needs smothered under a blanket of accommodation.

Her father ran his fingers in little taps across his knee. She noticed he wore his usual expression of parental concern that appeared whenever they happened to be alone. "How do you like life in the suburbs? You and Shane are such city slickers. Everything all right?"

"I'm fine, Dad," she said. What could she say? That she was having doubts about her marriage? That she felt pulled in a different direction? He would worry—the very prospect of a family breakup—divorce was just not acceptable. And she didn't think with his conservative views her father would understand her drive for equality, change, protest. Besides, despite the troubles of the past months, she was not yet ready to abandon the dream, the life of fulfillment she and Shane had built in the sweet sanctum of the suburbs.

Radley took a long swallow of her gin fizz and smiled. "We're doing fine. The neighborhood is beautiful, the living is clean, the streets are safe, who could ask for anything more?" She felt a bizarre urge to break into song—*I got rhythm, I got music, I got my man* . . . What was coming over her?

"To tell the truth I'm not sure marriage is right for me," she burst out before she could stop herself. There, she'd said it. Punctured the perfect bubble her parents promoted and she had gratefully assumed she wanted. She bit her lower lip, stifling the urge to cry. "I tried to be domestic. But I don't fit in. And," she gulped, "I can't handle the children. They wear me to the bone. I feel helpless."

"I can't pretend to understand precisely what you're looking for, never have," Wilson said, putting his drink down. "But maybe my desire to have you lead what Mother and I consider the good life was misguided. I've always believed in hard work, good education, and devotion to family. Maybe you'd have been happier if you'd remained in New York with Shane and his circle." The lines around his eyes were tight and his face looked drawn.

Radley restrained an urge to grab him, hug him, anything to shake that look off his face. "No . . ." she murmured. "Dad, it was a great opportunity for Shane. For us." Immediately, a layer of doubt covered her words. Maybe they should have stayed out east where the balance of power favored Shane with his intimate network of friends and family. They could have continued to participate in the endless variety and vitality of Manhattan. Instead of the endless isolation of their secluded hideaway.

Char would claim it's the wife's job to bring structure to the family, her duty to create a happy, harmonious household, to make sacrifices. In Char's view, the man creates a career outside the home while the woman coordinates everything inside the home. But in Radley's opinion, justice requires equality. In terms of options, those two responsibilities are not at all equal.

A brown-speckled flicker perched on the patio wall uttered a series of piercing cries, tipping its beak to the sky. Wilson and Radley laughed, and the atmosphere loosened.

"That guy has something on his mind," Wilson said.

"I think he's telling us to stop being serious," Radley said, "to lighten up, sing a song, throw our worries to the sky."

At that moment, they heard sounds of a yell and excited jabbering from the bottom of the slope. The flicker flew off. Char rushed out carrying a spatula.

"Look!"

They watched as Larry trotted up the hill carrying a wiggling bundle in his arms, Megan running behind him. "I caught him by myself!"

Radley looked in surprise at the plump creature squirming inside the folds of Larry's long shirt. A head streaked with iridescent green and purple protruded from one end. As Larry came to a halt, it uttered a loud *squawk, squawk*.

"Yee gads!" Char cried. "He's got one of the ducks. Take it away, dear, you mustn't touch the wildlife. Wilson, do something."

"But Grandma Char, he's beautiful. I caught him. He didn't want to be caught. I had to coax him with bread." He pulled one of Char's dinner rolls from his sleeve. "And fast like a fox I pounced on him with my shirt." The form under the shirt gave several quick jerks. "Can I take him home? I'll feed him, I promise."

"We'll have to return him to the water and let him go," Wilson said, suppressing a smile. "He doesn't belong to us."

"Ducks can't be pets," Radley explained. "He would die if you took him home. He needs to be free in the pond."

"Come on, son. Let's return him to the water and watch what he does." Wilson put his hand on the boy's shoulder.

"Well . . ." Realizing that argument was useless, Larry turned and headed down the slope, clutching the wiggling bundle against his chest. The others followed, anxious to watch its release. Suddenly the bird let out a series of thunderous squawks, whereupon Larry began to run, swaying as his prize started to edge free from the confines of the sweater, and as he gained momentum he stumbled, jerked to one side and frantically clutching the bird to his chest, fell with a thud to the ground. The duck gave one last ghastly shriek and fell silent.

Larry leapt up and stared with disbelief at the heap lying immobile on the ground.

Radley hurried to her son's side and grabbed his shoulders. "Are you all right, Larry?"

Larry nodded, lips quivering, unable to utter a word. Radley saw Wilson reach down and push the limp bird over with his hand. There, protruding from the bird's mottled breast, was a long shard of glass, edged with blood that trickled down the feathers in thin streams.

Wilson picked up several pieces of shattered glass. "It looks, like Larry has fallen on a broken whiskey bottle, and a large piece has stabbed the duck like a knife."

"At least," Radley said, shaken but relieved, "the bird acted as a shield and Larry's not hurt."

"We better take the bird to the doctor," Larry pleaded, finding his voice.

"It's dead, son," Wilson replied softly.

Larry's cheeks were pale, he stared at his hands spotted with blood. "I fell," he gasped. "I murdered the duck!"

"Of course you didn't," Char said quickly. "It was an accident."

Radley grimaced as Wilson pulled several bloody piece of glass from the bird's chest and held them up. "There were only three breaks. Unfortunately, one of them pierced the bird's heart. It's a fluke accident. Larry, you're not to blame."

"It's all right, Larry. Let's go get you into some dry clothes," Radley said, taking Larry's hand.

Wilson picked up the dead creature with amused forbearance. "That child," Char said to him under her breath, "has a knack for creating trouble. I'm afraid one day he'll go too far and get himself hurt, heaven forbid."

Megan went over and ran her hand along the duck's yellow beak. A few sobs escaped from her throat. "Poor bird," she choked. "Can we bury him?"

Her grandfather shook his head. "I'm afraid here's no place to bury him here," he said. "It's against the rules."

"What will happen to him?" Megan asked.

"He'll go into the garbage," Larry said. "That's what."

Megan stood up, glared at Larry, and with a sob ran up the slope and disappeared into the house.

"I think she needs to be alone for a bit," Radley said.

"Yes," Char said. "Let's go in, dinner will be ready in a jiffy."

After Larry had been bathed and outfitted in one of Wilson's old shirts, he hastened the garage to find a box for the duck. No one had seen him since. Radley was about to go in search of him when she heard the front door open and slam shut, a few footsteps clipped along the floor, and Larry appeared in the doorway, a triumphant gleam on his face. He looked around as if expecting everyone to share the excitement.

"What, Larry?" Radley exclaimed. What had he been up to now?

"Well," he said with a quick smile. "I found a place for the duck where he'll be happy. It's perfect."

"What do you mean?" Radley cried. "Where? You buried him?"

"Oh no, Gramps said not to. I just saw it, next door . . ." He didn't finish the sentence. A loud bang sounded at the front door and two over-wrought people flew into the dining room.

"Your son—we saw him—a dead bird, for God's sake! It's ruined," cried the woman, grasping her face with one hand. "There's blood, it will never come out. Why don't you control your child? It's too much! And Jeremy dead only twelve hours!"

Wilson spoke first. "Try to calm down, Mrs. Maguire. What happened, exactly?"

Sucking in a deep breath, Mrs. Maguire explained that their adopted Indian son had died that morning and they were honoring his religious background by holding a service in their home. The casket had been placed in the hall, waiting for the funeral home to pick it up and drive it to the local Shirdi Sai cemetery.

"The casket had been sitting there for only a few minutes while the delivery truck was parking, and when Clive saw Larry disappear through the bushes, he investigated and when he opened the casket he found this disgusting dead bird," Mrs. Maguire cried. "What kind of a trick was that?" She looked about to cry, but anger overpowered her.

Larry stared at his hands.

Char moaned. "Larry!"

"I'm very sorry, Mrs. Maguire," Wilson said. "Of course we will pay for any damages."

"Yes, of course," Radley echoed. "The child's only eight, but he was definitely out of line."

"How dreadful for you, Mrs. Maguire," Char said, glancing at Radley. "Larry will be punished, you may rest assured."

"But how could he have done such a thing?" pursued Mrs. Maguire. "To deliberately ruin a sacred container, Jeremy's last resting place . . ." She started to weep, tears dropping down her cheeks.

"But it didn't ruin anything!" Larry lifted his head. "I cleaned him up. There was room for both of them in the box. The duck will keep him company. They will both be safe forever."

"If you were so innocent, why did you run off when you saw us?" Mr. Maguire accused.

"I heard Mommy calling me for dinner," Larry said evenly. Ever quick on the draw, Radley thought, shaking her head.

In the face of general disapproval, Larry's expression grew contrite—he had done something wrong. But Radley could detect the pride that lurked in his eyes. She divined what he was thinking. Hadn't he found the perfect, foolproof solution?—a casket, plenty of room for two, both dead, no problem—if it weren't for those panicky Maguires.

The dilemma ended when it was decided to bury the bird in the stretch of woods alongside the Gallagher's house, complete with metal box and stone marker. It would be a secret grave. Larry would be in charge of the burial.

When it was time to leave, Larry carried the tin box to the car, looking pleased with himself. "Everyone says the accident was not my fault, and now we're going to have a dandy funeral to make up for the mean Maguires," he told his mother. Besides, he claimed, if it hadn't been for him the duck would have been thrown in the garbage.

While the children piled into the back seat of the Buick, Wilson turned to his daughter. "Shane is a good man," he said with a serious look. "We all like him. When he returns from his business trip to Mexico, we'll have you all over for dinner."

Yes, he's a good man, Radley thought to herself, but his virtues don't seem to be doing me any good.

Her mother kissed her on the cheek. "Don't be a stranger."

Parents never stop being parents, Radley mused as they drove off, waving out the window. *Maybe we never stop needing them. Maybe I better learn how to do this.*

CHAPTER 17

❧

Radley slipped another log on the smoldering fire, stuffed clumps of balled newspaper around it, and lit the edges from a jumbo matchbox. With the children safely tucked in bed, she looked forward to an hour of reading on the couch. "Tomorrow's Saturday. Let's do something with the children," she said as the flames snaked up between the logs.

She glanced at Shane, reclined in his green leather chair watching *Colombo*. She wondered what excursion she could devise that would tempt him to leave the comfort of his Olympian seat. A solid family man, Shane didn't appear to consider that his role included entertaining or interpreting life to his children. Just to be there was enough, providing a secure environment for them to grow up in, protecting them, loving them.

"Too cold to go out." His eyes remained fixed on Peter Falk facing a scar-riddled man brandishing a pair of steel cleavers.

"For heaven's sake, this is Minnesota. It's cold for seven months of the year. Are you going to remain inside all winter?"

He shrugged. The minute she saw the lift of his shoulders under the white business shirt she knew she was heading down a path that went nowhere. He kept his eyes fastened on the television screen, backed up out of reach, leaving her without a presence to react with. They would sit home all weekend, as usual.

Throughout their marriage, they had avoided carrying grievances too far, fearful of igniting a Pandora's box of raw emotions that would leap out and wound them both. Suddenly a blaze of resistance shot through her.

"I'm sick of staying home all the time, of dealing with screeching kids day and night, seven days a week," she cried, swirling around and facing Shane. "Chores, chores, that's my life!" Anger brought a flush to her face. "It's too hard to take the kids to the museum by myself, what with the two of them dashing through the rooms, yelling, leaping on statues, flying over ropes. I know you find museums tiring, but then think of something else! I'm going stir crazy."

Shane glanced at her, back to the TV screen. He did not understand his wife's restlessness. She was always fretting, wanting things to be different. He felt tired just thinking about it. His watchword was *endure*, he would go along with whatever presented itself. After all, he was the first of his Irish family to attend college, had obtained a law degree and now held a professional job, enjoyed a beautiful home and family and lived in a fine house in a smart suburb. He had melded into the mainstream American life. He had it all. He was satisfied. It was best to accept things as they were.

He shuffled to the bar to refresh his drink. "Where do you want to go?" he said as he lifted a bottle of Johnny Walker from the shelf, filled his glass, and reached into the miniature fridge for a handful of ice cubes.

"I don't care! Sledding, the movies, a museum, drive to a mountain top. Anything."

Shane sank down in the green recliner, lifted his feet to the footstool, one ankle over the other, and took a deep swallow from his glass. "I'm gone all week. I work hard. I like to spend time at home," he said.

Radley grabbed the iron poker and thrust it into the smoldering logs, stabbing at them until they flared and the heat pushed her back. As she stood, watching the carefree flicker of the flames, visions of the old courtship days flashed into her mind: the lively parties with friends, the honeymoon hideaway by the ocean, the delightful follies of being in love—how they had flown joyfully about, had adored each other, how she couldn't wait to be in his arms.

After ten years, the flavor had ebbed, the novelty of domestic tasks had simmered to a dull routine, even lovemaking had lost its urgency. Disagreements flared briefly and died in silence until gradually life resumed, a little less vibrant. Shane showed no interest in socializing with his co-workers or cultivating the work relationships that would advance him up the office ladder. He didn't seek people out. He didn't aspire to greater things. He spent all his time at home, Radley reflected, where his mute acquiescence had become stifling.

Carried back further, watching the flames curl around the log, to her college dorm room, rousing speeches by young bearded men and charismatic black crusaders promising revolt, and the voice of Pete Seeger singing promises of a world of freedom in words that caused her heart to tighten, made her want to rise up and strike out.

We'll walk hand in hand, we'll walk hand in hand
The truth shall make us free, the truth shall make us free
We shall live in peace . . .
Oh, deep in my heart, I do believe, we shall overcome some day.

She moved down the hall to the bedroom and flicked on the light switch. On the bureau loomed a large portrait of Shane wearing an Irish green sweater over an open-collared white shirt. It captured his soft grey eyes, his look of guileless pleasure, his sweet, gentle smile. Each time she gazed at it, she would think how lucky she was to have this guy as a husband, with his handsome looks and fundamental, inflexible decency.

But the photo had aged, a water mark etched a round circle on the cheek.

The door opened and Shane walked in, over to the chair on his side of the bed and began to remove his shoes. Radley went into the small walk-in closet and lifted her nightgown off the hook. They undressed under the cover of darkness, just as they make love, without discussion. Emerging from the closet, Radley stared at Shane, who had changed into his blue striped cotton pajamas and was laying his wrist watch on the night stand. Arrested by her expression, he stopped, watch hanging in one hand. "What?" he asked.

She stared at the sight of the dangling watch swaying helplessly in the air like a lost bird. Suddenly, an avalanche of pent-up frustration shot through her. "I can't stand this," she burst out. "We never go anywhere. I have to get out, have some fun, do something interesting. Shane, I'm not happy!" She took a deep gulp of air. The rush of adrenaline pulsing through her blocked out all caution. At last she was saying what she thought. "Don't you care?"

Shane stared at her in surprise. "You could be happy," he said testily, "if you'd stop hankering after what you don't have. But you know something? --you'll never be satisfied." The look of defensiveness with which he usually responded to her complaints was gone from his face. "I thought this was what you wanted," he murmured. "Can't you make a life for yourself here?"

"How can I? I'm continually on duty," she cried. "I don't fit into the church and neighborhood domestic scene. I don't enjoy the tea-parties, the coffee klatches, the Avon socials." Her pulse was throbbing; whatever was happening was scary, but she couldn't stop. Her emotions had embarked on a flight of their own and were racing their way to the end.

"This house is nothing but bouts of screaming uncontrolled children separated by brief periods of pure dullness"—nothing could stop her—"I buy the most powerful toilet cleansers, know what brand of bleach produces smiling white sheets, and my dust cloth is intimately familiar with every tabletop, every cranny in the house." She paused to stem to force of her emotion.

"I walk the dog daily no matter how exhausted I am, feed, wash and groom it, I mow the lawn, sweep the garage, sew tears in the kids' cover-alls, paint the back fence, hang the swing from that old oak tree. All this with no assistance from you." She stood trembling at the end of the bed, oblivious to the nightgown strap that had slipped down over one shoulder. "You and your chair in the basement are Siamese twins—they'll have to craft you a special coffin so that you can enter the hereafter together."

Stopping for breath, she caught on to the footboard of the bed. Shane was staring at her as if she'd materialized from another planet. "You—you take out the garbage."

"I work all week," he said, sitting down on the bed, his jaw clenched. "Your job is the house and children. You have every minute of every day to take care of things. I don't see why that isn't enough."

"You get evenings and weekends free," Radley cried. "I'm on call 24 hours, seven days a week. You have a job that uses your advanced college degree. You commiserate with co-workers, face intellectual challenges. Me, I'm no good at housework. I've never done housework before."

"What's there to be good at?" Shane exclaimed. "Anyone can do housework, it doesn't take a degree to run a vacuum cleaner. You have your political books to read. You have your women's group."

"Those things take only one-half of one percent of my time. Besides, I crave alone time, to breathe."

Shane stood up, nosed open the cream floor-length curtain, peered out at the blackness, turned back toward the bed. "I get damn tired of going to work, hitting the same books, ledgers, legal forms, day after day," he said heatedly. "You think it's easy at the office? I have to do what I'm told and like it. I don't complain. What's the point? I don't go out with buddies. I don't have the option of spending my days as I like, meeting friends, going to amusing places with the kids, being able to improvise what I do each day."

"It's not like that! The meetings with my women's group keeps me sane, but those amusing outings with the kids are nothing but grueling." Her heart was racing. She felt the space closing in around her as they stood facing each other across the bed. His figure was rigid, and she detected a faint odor of bleach from his cotton pajamas. "I can't go on like this. Why can't you understand?"

"I understand that you have a constant need for change, for things to be different," he said. "That's not what life is about. I like things the way they are. I like comfort, I like to relax and watch television. When I find a restaurant I like, I keep going; what's the point of always looking for something new, hoping something else will be better? After graduation from law school, I knew pretty quick I didn't want to work in the legal field. I didn't like the confrontation, the politics. So I switched to accounting. Reliable, predictable, straightforward. You can be as flighty, as daring as you want, I'm fine with that, but I'm not like that. I'm just a simple guy. Why can't you accept me for who I am?" He looked directly at her, his face tight. "Why can't you grow up?"

Radley spun around, walked to the door, opened it, shut it, and stood staring at the wooden frame.

Finally, she turned. "It's your—your silence. You never put yourself out to make conversation. I miss having someone to talk to about what matters to me. I miss having a friend. I miss—everything I used to have!"

"I don't stand in your way." Shane's voice floated low and deliberate. "You can do whatever you want. You know that. You even take the pill and I don't interfere, even though I don't approve." His voice was tense, as if trying to hold himself in check. "I know I'm not the sophisticated well-heeled guy you're used to dating. But I thought you had what you wanted."

He picked up his cigarette from the porcelain ashtray on the bed stand and inhaled deeply, looking at her. A waft of smoke curled around the edges of his wire-framed glasses.

"That's not it!" she cried. "I'm not sophisticated and I'm not used to and don't need well-heeled. It's just—you're like dead. You have no interests. You have no wants. You won't go anywhere, do anything. Everything is too much trouble. Now that we are no longer wrangling about Catholic theology, there are no more discussions, no more topics. We have nothing in common!" Her eyes flashed.

"We're a family. We have the children, they come first," Shane said evenly. He shifted his six-foot-two frame and stood, arms hanging at his side. "That's more important than anything else."

"You don't understand. Sometimes I can't bear my children." A flush lit her cheeks, she felt suddenly hot. How could she say such a thing?

Shane's color darkened. "The trouble with you, all you think about is yourself. You're the queen of the kingdom. What *you* want, what makes *you* happy? You expect everything to be your way, to please you. Did you ever hear of sacrifice?" The cigarette trembled in his hands. "You're a spoiled brat, you're worse than the kids." With that he turned and sat on the edge of the bed, elbows clamped over his knees.

The words pounded on the side of Radley's head as conflicting emotions flooded through her body. She searched the room for relief, but the curtains were closed, the shades on the lamps on the bed stands were lowered, and the stiff walls of the room gave no signs of escape.

"I hate everything! I hate you!" Leaping to the bureau, she grabbed the portrait of Shane and brought it crashing down on the polished footboard of the bed. Neither of them moved as the glass hit the wood and a galaxy of shards scattered onto the rug with a crackling sound and lay still. Her body tingled, drawn to an alert tension as if ready to take off.

Shane didn't stir. She regarded his back, stiff and unmoving on the edge of the bed, and leaping up behind him, she pummeled him with her fists, over and over, breathing in heavy puffs. Shane didn't move; she could tell he was not going to respond. She drew back. It was no good; nothing she could do would change him. She was behaving like an idiot.

The bed remained still. She had to see his face, his reaction, and as she shifted next to him, glancing over intently, almost shyly, she saw a tear, then two, three, inching down his cheeks. Her remaining anger, released with each blow on his back, dissolved in a flash. She couldn't move.

Then, "Radley, your life here is not different from that of other housewives. What is it you really want?" he asked with resignation.

She took a deep breath. "I don't know what I want," she said in a subdued voice. "I want—I want—I want you to love me."

"Of course I love you." Shane angled around to face her. His voice held a strange undertone of hope, as if an opening had occurred.

"You think you do. Devotion is not the same. You would be lost without me, I grant you, but not because of who I am. I'm the wife and mother, the keeper of the family—it could be anybody. You don't know me at all."

Shane shook his head, but she went on. "You haven't the slightest interest in me as a person."

She leaned against the bed and broke into tears. They were from different planets. He would never understand. It was hopeless.

When she returned from brushing her teeth, Shane was tucked under the covers. She slipped in next to him. It was not true that she hated everything. She loved this house and the earth-bound woods and her children, Megan, miss blue eyes, with her easy-going, loving nature, and Larry, the daredevil, with his blond locks and mischievous eyes, marveled that she'd actually produced these beautiful beings that would be part of her forever.

And Shane—if she could just stop thrusting her frustrations on him and allow her natural instinct to be close to him be enough . . .

She turned her gaze to her husband's back, curved under the covers beside her. "What is it *you* want?" she said aloud. But he was already asleep. She clicked off the table light and with a deep, cleansing breath stretched out her legs and felt the sheets cool and fresh against her arms and the warmth of Shane's body next to her in the dark.

CHAPTER 18

❧

"Ralph doesn't want me to be here." Radley fixed her eyes on the woman in the checkered shirt and black Capri pants seated on the wicker chair. Barbara adjusted her cat-eye glasses. Her soft dark hair curling loose on her cheeks contrasted with the tight set of her mouth and sharp chin. She wore no lipstick or adornments.

"But I'm here," she said with a quick smile. Radley could see that she felt uneasy.

It was their fourth meeting—no one had missed—and the women's group had settled into an easy rapport. As Radley expressed it: no one but us, no barriers, no rules, just us cut off on our island of hope. There were no social conventions to uphold, no familial relationships to appease, they could unload whatever they wanted to into the pool of female acceptance that had formed without anyone even trying.

The air in Bette's porch was still in the late July afternoon. Surrounding the porch, a freshly-watered yard, clipped trees, and along the front a row of lilac bushes that cascaded house-to-house down the block—Lilac Lane, Bette called it. Inside, the dog snoozed on the rug, while a fan drew wisps of air through the long living room. Bette had greeted them at the door, laughing. "Look at me. The standard American housewife: husband, two kids, dog, house in burbs, living in quiet contentment—and here I am, stirring the pot, calling for revolution. Ha!"

She turned to Barbara. "Of course, you're here. Where else would you be?"

"Here we're alive. That is, real," Trish said. "Let's face it: our name includes the words Women's Liberation and that's enough to raise hackles on some people's backs."

"When I said I wouldn't quit the group, Ralph decided I could go any-time, as long as I have his dinner on the table when he gets home."

Radley frowned and like the others, shook her head.

Without warning, Barbara burst into tears, pressing her clutch hand-bag to her stomach. "You're my friends," she began, but a hiccup of sobs escaped her and she clasped her hand over her mouth. Maureen jumped up and put her arm around Barbara's drooping shoulder. Radley grabbed her free hand.

Without looking up, Barbara burst out, "I'm never going back. It's too much. Ralph—I don't care if I love him. I've tried so hard. Everything to please him. Can I help it if I'm—I'm—if I don't like sex?"

They had gleaned, analyzed, evaluated every subject except this one, withheld in the last vestiges of privacy. Having penetrated so many other areas, they were ready to crash the last American inner sanctum.

"Go on—we've been there."

"I shouldn't be telling you this," she stammered, stifling her tears, "It's so personal. I can't help it. If Ralph won't have sex with me ever again I don't know what I'll do. Oh, I feel like such a schmuck, a real failure."

"Tell us everything."

Barbara rubbed her fingertips along her cheeks, tucked a strand of dark hair behind her ear, and took a deep breath. "I'm so glad I made it here. This group has meant so much to me—so many things I'd never even thought of before. I don't talk about any of this to my husband. But I'm starting to stick up for myself. He doesn't like that. He gets angry. I know you'll understand. But," she paused, "it's too personal, I don't know . . ."

"For heaven's sake, Barbara," Trish cried out, "I'm sure we've experienced worse. You're not unique."

While Barbara collected her thoughts, Bette tiptoed to the porch door to let out the dog, who had been whining at the threshold. Radley stood up and filled the empty glasses with lemonade from an amber glass pitcher, helped herself to a cluster of purple grapes, and sat back down on the porch swing.

"Ralph won't have sex with me anymore," Barbara said at last. "Says I'm frigid. He's sick of my deadbeat participation, says I'm not sensual enough, I never initiate or show pleasure, and he feels deprived. He wants a real partner." She pushed back her cat-eye glasses. "I guess I can't blame him. I'm too skinny, and to tell the truth," she confessed, "I don't like sex. I just do it to please Ralph."

"Does Ralph ever please you?" Trish asked. "Does he stimulate you, bring you along, or is he the one, two, three, go type? What about his part in this?"

Barbara looked at her as if she had pulled out a knife and aimed it at her. "I've never been pleased. I don't know if I want to be."

"Once you're really aroused, you'll change your tune. I've never told this to a living soul." Bette raised her head and sucked in a deep breath. "I've never had an orgasm." The women stirred in their chairs. The taboo topic!

"I finally took to faking orgasms. I couldn't bare the strain. Arlan tried at first, but he was like a bull in a china shop. He didn't know what to do. I knew even less." Leaning forward, she lowered her voice. "To tell the truth, it's become a pretend game. Arlan doesn't suspect a thing. He's happy and I no longer dread facing my sexual inadequacy night after night."

Bette's lack of self-consciousness astonished Radley, who hadn't had a frank discussion about sex since seventh grade, when she and her girlfriend Gretchen found her brother's book on positions depicting stick figures. They were able to figure out that sex was something weird await-ing them in the future, and that boys held some element of mystery that set them in a different light. Through all the years since, she had never revealed her sexual experiences, not even to her best girlfriend.

"I couldn't have orgasms at first," Trish said. "I sought advice from my physician. He didn't seem to know what I was talking about. Finally, Jerry and I got the hang of it, with coaching from me, and it blossomed from there. I now have eight or ten at a time."

The women stared in disbelief.

"Ten!" Bette exclaimed

"Trish! How do you and your husband manage that?" Barbara swiveled in her chair.

Trish laughed and adjusted the orange silk scarf round her neck. "Oh, they aren't with my husband, Jerry. He's good in bed, he's large and he takes it slowly," she said. "But Sebastian knows how to stimulate my clitoris. Once I have the first climax, the others follow close behind, like a series of explosions. He knows how to make that happen. You're surprised I have a lover?" She smiled at the shocked looks. Lifting a fig Newton to her mouth, she kicked off her wedges and sank back onto the flowered cushion.

"I lived in New Orleans for three years, sailed along the coasts of Australia, traveled through Japan, and have three university degrees. I knew when I was seventeen that the conventional life programmed by a puritanical society was not for me. Sebastian is fascinating, artistic, and doesn't threaten my family. Women and men's bodies don't work the same sexually and Sebastian knows how to synchronize the differences."

Radley gazed at her in wonderment, while several women revealed that they had how-to books on sexual techniques stashed under the mat-tress or in a closet drawer.

Trish went on. "I like married life. Jerry is a good man but he's a bore. He travels a lot and when he is around we have nothing to say to each other. All he cares about is work and his coin collection. I either give up my marriage or find an outlet. So, I have a lover." She picked up her glass of lemonade and dropped a lemon peel into it. "I leave Jerry to his hobbies. My daughter Amy is happy—she has two parents who love her and an intact home. It works just fine."

"I'd feel guilty," Barbara cried.

"But it's deceptive. Isn't marriage based on trust?" Radley asked. Adultery broke the marriage bond, robbed one partner of the emotional and sensual interest of the other, which was being exhausted elsewhere. Just how far would this group go in its quest for reform? Everything must be questioned, yes, but a line of moral principle must be drawn somewhere.

Bette considered that if such an arrangement worked for Trish, it was probably better than a divorce. Maureen advised that they were there to learn, not judge.

"Why should we be restrained when men sleep around blamelessly?" Trish asked. "None of the restrictions apply to men. Adultery is denounced in front of wives and preachers but greeted in the old boy's network with winks and whistles."

Radley realized how much she liked these women. It felt so good to have things said straight out, smack in the air without ambiguity or strings.

The women were ignited, everyone had a story. They all admitted they'd had never had a frank discussion of sex with their spouses and that attempting such a thing would be like plunging naked into arctic waters in the dead of night. Sex took place after they had changed clothes in the bathroom and slipped into bed, and what followed happened wordlessly, without fanfare, blended into the darkness.

Maureen listened quietly. "People think I have it all together, but my marriage is lacking as well. My husband is tired when he gets home from work. We have sex, which I would classify as satisfactory, but that isn't so important to me. Andrew is a good father and provider, faithful, devoted to the Catholic Church, and loves me in his reserved way. I get lonely, but I throw myself into political action work. That's enough, and when it isn't I make do."

As usual during their discussions, Radley noted, once the experiences started rolling they caught on, like a roller coaster gaining speed.

"I've always liked sex with Shane," Radley said, hooking her arms around the throw pillow beside her and drawing it to her chest. "I love the way he always responds when I reach across the bed to him, his lingering kisses, the feel of his weight on me. We never talk, except to say I love you from time to time; being carried away gives us permission to express our deepest feelings—it's the only time we mention love, as if there were some danger in the word. Sex allows us to express what we feel. I didn't have orgasms for the longest time, then it just happened. I'd almost given up, I enjoyed love-making anyway, but I was thrilled. So was Shane.

It's only when my anger begins to fester and I became disenchanted with him that my interest in sex wanes. There's more to love-making than physical exchange. I find my libido is affected by the tenor of my emotions and my feelings about our relationship.

Cookie spoke up next. "Count your blessings! I have a different problem. Tom wants it continually, sometimes two or three times in a row. He's constantly grabbing me from behind as I lean over the stove, pulling me into his lap as we're watching TV. 'Won't take a minute,' he says. It drives me crazy." She pressed two fingers to her mouth, as if considering. "What I want is to be left alone until I feel sexy, until I want it and can go at my own pace, but I haven't felt the urge for years. It turns me off if I am bombarded with sex, and I never get a chance to want it.

"We have to start opening up and telling our husbands what we like and how we work," Bette said. "What if the husband needs it every night and the wife once a week? Who prevails?"

A discussion erupted on the vagaries of sexual behavior and the value of masturbation. Radley could feel the intimacy between them grow. She had never shared these things with anyone, and she felt overcome with relief. It was like a fresh breath of air breaching the unspoken secrets of the ages.

Setting down her freshly-filled coffee mug, Maureen addressed the group. "The reading we've been doing has got me thinking. It seems to me we revolve our lives around our husbands and rely on him to get our intimate needs met. Often, he can't give us what we need, so we feel abandoned and alone. This is not fair to him. It's a terrific weight to saddle him with."

Radley regarded her appreciatively. Exactly so; they needed to stop depending on their partner to do it all.

"An important aspect of this," Barbara said, "is our self-image. Recently I looked at my nude body in a full-length mirror—in horror. I studied my sharp elbows, scrawny buttocks, moles, uneven teeth and bulbous Adam's apple. My body wouldn't sell a pot of glue." She laughed. "But, prompted by what I'd read, I noticed that my skin was smooth and white, my breasts well-shaped, and my hair thick and glossy. Even my back had a rather graceful curve."

"I do *not* want to look at myself in the mirror!" Klara exclaimed.

"It's about accepting ourselves as we are. It's our feelings that should change, not our bodies."

"I can't be expected to like my breasts!" Bette cried. "On my back I look like a pancake, so during sex I position myself on top so that what little I have will hang down."

"You think you have a problem," Cookie chimed in. "My breasts are so heavy I can hardly stand up. Forget trying to buy clothes that fit."

Trish suggested they read *Our Bodies, Our Selves* for the next meeting and find out about Kegel exercises. "Our motto is: *learn to love our bodies*." Everyone was to strip and study their body in the mirror—not in comparison with the flawless images of women in commercial ads, but in a tender labor of love.

Maureen stood up, slipped her leather pocketbook strap over her shoulder and gathered her papers from the coffee table. "This is important, but I think it's time to think about action. We're been discussing deep personal issues, but remember, we originally convened in order tie into the political scene. I understand that change begins at home, but I think we're ready to initiate a community project." The others agreed; they were ready! "The social action group at St. Theresa's is currently studying the civil rights movement. If you agree, I'll prepare something for our next meeting," Maureen concluded.

"Next week our bodies. The week after that the world!" someone exclaimed. Laughing, tugging on shoes and collecting purses, they separated in a cloud of camaraderie, marveling at the sweet scent of honeysuckle in the front yard and their luck in knowing each other.

CHAPTER 19

❧

I t was a dim day, still and overcast, going nowhere, without promise or
energy, a day without inspiration. For a long time Radley stared out the
window at the grey sky and its fleet of white streamers. There must be a
way to quell the sense of unease that clogged her chest.

Her gaze shifted to the white expanse of ceiling overhead, she felt
herself relaxing slowly into the whiteness and her mind drifted into a
sleepy blankness. Slowly an image of Megan's face projected above her, a
soft face, a little red bow in her hair, wearing a red and navy dress with a
red velvet belt and the shiny black Mary Jane's they had purchased for the
occasion. Radley had photographed her standing on the front stoop of the
house, minutes before they left for Lucy Blake's seventh birthday party.
She hugged a long birthday box wrapped in balloon-covered paper. Inside
was the wooden Pinocchio in a green and brown suit with a tiny felt collar
and forest green loops sewn on a wide belt, picked by Megan herself from
a row of storybook dolls. It had been an unfortunate accident, the doll
had been soaked through and through, but Radley had used a hair dryer,
smoothed out the damp costume so the damage was barely noticeable.

As Megan stood meekly next to the iron railing submitting to the stare
of the camera. Gloom darkened her face, Radley recalled the scene viv-
idly. Megan and Larry had gotten into a fight, Megan had been slammed
against the tub and the Pinocchio doll had tumbled into the tub and been
swallowed by the soapy water.

Amid the screams, the mad chaos of the dripping doll, the cries of blame and denial, Radley had lost it, her temper had taken hold, taken a life of its own, become a force of unstoppable strength, flooding out all else and her voice sent the children scurrying terrified to their rooms.

She could see it on the face in the 4 x 6 photo. The child was in trouble. Radley had blown the anger from her system, but for a seven-year old, there was no such path of relief. Her eyes dark, her mouth sunk, her cheeks streaked with tears, Megan stared unfocused past the camera. Her face held a conviction of ruin and behind the wide puzzled eyes lurked the shame of defeat. And utter helplessness.

Radley's heart lurched. The sight pierced through her. That look. And she had put it there.

She would have ripped up the photo, but Megan, when she saw herself dressed up with the colorful balloon box, wanted to keep it. So reluctantly Radley pasted the four black corner pieces on the album page and slipped in the photo—captured for posterity.

What to do? Megan was forever losing things, forgetting she was supposed to be somewhere, mixing up instructions. A look of bewilderment would cross her face, her bubbly, outgoing chatter replaced by a dull tentativeness. When assured that mistakes were inevitable, allowed, she would perk up and run to give her Baby Doe doll a bath. But her tendency to misjudge, to choose the wrong alternative, followed her everywhere. Radley's anxiety grew as she discovered money missing from her purse, traced to Megan's drawer, or caught her lying and sneaking across the street to the neighbor's swing set. Reprimands sent her darting to her room in tears.

If only she could find a way to teach her daughter to walk a straight line. If only she could reach out for guidance—but where?

During the children's first years, Radley had not worried about Megan, with her strong graceful body, even teeth, creamy skin, beautiful golden brown hair, and wide eyes. Miss Blue Eyes, people called her. Sweet tempered, agreeable, everyone's favorite. She'd always thought

Larry was the one to watch, a flippant, aggressive boy who slipped out of control before she knew it. Despite his antics, Larry always managed to get out of scrapes unscathed, buoyed by some innate agility. But as Radley watched Megan turn more and more inward, she realized that it was Megan who needed attention.

Megan would not admit to stealing the ten-dollar bill at school. The girl withdrew whenever the subject came up. Radley struggled to find out what to do, would say nothing until then. Best for the time being to show how unacceptable her behavior was with coolness, by withdrawing the approval and affection Megan was constantly seeking. If she bathed her in love, the child would think she'd been forgiven, that her act was of little importance. That must not happen.

She, her mother, must find an approach that would bring Megan around, a rational, sympathetic appeal to puncture Megan's determined denial. No clear method had materialized. But it had to be done.

One afternoon, after picking her daughter up at school, she led Megan into the master bedroom and sat down next to her on the bed. The minute the door shut Megan's face tightened, and she bent her head and began running her fingers along the crewelwork pattern of the bedspread.

"It's time we had a talk," Radley said. "Megan, stealing money is very serious. It's important that you understand that."

Previous attempts at eliciting remorse from her daughter had brought only yes and no responses. No sign of understanding. This time she listed the pitfalls of stealing: how one just didn't do it, how no one would trust her, she would have no friends, would face disastrous consequences throughout her life. As she continued, Megan kept her head down, eyes on the floor. "Now that you've had time to think, I bet you regret doing it." She paused. "Do you?"

Megan squirmed, pulled a pillow into her lap and buried her chin in it. "Yes," she said without looking up.

"Do you understand why stealing is bad?" Radley pursued.

"Yes."

"Why?"

"Because I might get caught." She stole a glance at her mother. "Because it's bad," she amended.

"Megan, don't you understand that you can't just go around taking things that don't belong to you? Don't you realize how important trust is? For heaven's sake, can't you see that?"

Megan nodded. The passivity of her daughter confronted her like a steel wall. "Megan, you have to cooperate here. Why did you take the money? Why didn't you ask me, let me help you?"

"I don't know."

"Of course, you know I won't just hand over ten dollars to you, but if there's something you want, we can talk about that. Exactly want did you want the money for?"

"I don't know."

"Oh, Megan, what is the matter with you? I don't know what to do with you. My god, can't you try to understand?" Megan pressed the pillow to her chest and stared at her knees. "Megan, please look at me. I want you to participate in this discussion."

Megan straightened up and thrust her fist into her mouth, looking up at her mother from under her bangs.

Radley moistened her lips. This was not going well. Megan remained out of reach..

"I just—don't—know what to do with you," Radley muttered, almost to herself. It was important that Megan develop a strong sense of right and wrong. The basic foundation of her character, her very integrity was at stake. "Go to your room and think about what I've said. I'll come in later."

Something in Radley collapsed, she knew she had failed, taken the wrong approach. Everything she'd said had been shallow and irrelevant to her daughter. The why or how of it escaped her. She lifted the pillow, still warm from Megan's imprint, and drawing her arms around the soft material, clasped it to her chest.

The Driekers classes, held at the downtown child behavior clinic, involved reading, homework, and individual sessions. "At the age of seven, I'm not sure she can understand the concept of right and wrong," Radley told Shane one evening when he returned from work. He was in the bedroom, removing his suit jacket and tie in the closet. "Remember, Driekers tells us to let children find their own way. Megan will learn, with time," he said.

Honestly! Driekers doesn't mean do nothing at all! She swung about on her heels and left the room, resisting the urge to slam the door behind her.

The Driekers sessions didn't help. It had been her one hope. She inundated Megan and Larry with praise and compliments: their drawings were beautiful, their pan of burnt brownies had come out perfect, their blares on the flute were lovely. But nothing changed. Natural consequences—all well and rational, but after missing the bus for the third time and being obliged to walk to school, Megan still didn't get ready on time. These Driekers' methods took too much letting go—how could she sit still with a book while the two of them battled it out in the other room, screaming on and on at each other—impossible. Children and adults were not equal, children lacked experience. To "let them make their own choices" meant they did what they pleased, which was often not for their own good. Really! She read *Children the Challenge* three times, the words sounded like silver truths on the page, but this was not reality! Reward good behavior, well and good, but how could she reward them with candy when she didn't allow sugar? Logical consequences.

Avoid power struggles. Talk, don't nag. Let them settle their own disputes. Follow talk with consistent action. Nothing she did interfered with the household drone of constant chaos.

Not that Shane didn't try to help. Sometimes he'd say, "You're doing a good job, Radley," but more often he'd tell her, "I've been here in my chair, I'm not a witness." He encouraged her to leave them alone to work things out, in other words, she thought, give it up. She could only stand the fighting and arguing and resistance for so long. When was the behavioral change going to kick in?

Walking to the window, she ran her gaze over the surrounding woods and neighborhood rooftops veiled under an early evening drizzle. All was quiet with no sign of life. There was only the narrow road that stretched into the distance, curling round a corner and leading into acres of nothingness.

CHAPTER 20

❦

I t was a snowy day, almost a blizzard, gusts of snow packed the walk-
ways. Trish slid her passenger van into a slot in the small ramp and the
four of them tumbled out wrapped in winter coats and wool caps, plaid
scarves twined around their necks. Cheeks pink, snowflakes catching in
their lashes, they trudged single file along the path that angled round the
side of the 1908 four-story brick building,

"Hey, people, are we nervous?" Trish asked as they rounded the corner and headed toward the front entrance of the club.

'No!" Bette and Maureen said with determination, "Excited." None of
them had ever undertaken a public confrontation, and they pressed closer
as the snow stacked a coating of flakes across their shoulders.

"Act perfectly natural," Radley said. "We're four friends having lunch
together. Nothing more usual. Half the lunch customers will be women."
The dark lobby, spread with deep leather seating and heavy mahogany
tables, was nearly deserted. A lone male sat in a plump easy chair by the
window reading a newspaper.

Behind the front desk, two men wearing navy suits, crisp white shirts
and identical navy and blue striped ties were marking entries in a ledger.
Sucking in her breath, Radley removed her glove and spread her hand on
the counter as if claiming space. The men's eyes swept over the women
and landed directly on Radley.

"We have a reservation for lunch . . ." she began evenly.

One of the men interrupted. "This is a men's club. Girls are not allowed to enter the club by the front door. You'll have to leave at once."

"It's storming out there," Radley said, injecting her tone with as much confidence as she could muster. "I'm a member here, a subsidiary member."

"That doesn't matter," the other man said. "You can't come in this way. You'll have to go around to the rear door."

"But my father's a member. He's also on the board of directors. This is his card." She laid an embossed business card on the marble top.

The clerks exchanged indignant glances, shaking their heads. Radley reflected that she and her friends weren't dressed in the heels, suits and hats of the usual female clientele; in fact, blown by the gusts that whistled around the building, they must look windblown and scruffy.

"Really, it's pointless to go all the way around to the back door in this weather," Radley pursued. "Since we're already here. My friend has bronchitis. Please let us pass."

"Out of the question. It's a standard Marquette Club rule. No female has passed through those front doors up to now, and it won't happen on my watch."

Radley felt her blood rise. Keep your cool, she reminded herself. The men were the ones being tested. "We're not leaving," she stated evenly, trying to sound matter of fact.

The men considered, whispering. "We're just enforcing the rules. You girls skedaddle," one said in a low diplomatic tone. The men stood locked side by side, an immovable block.

"We want to see the manager," Radley demanded.

"I am the manager."

"The president of the club then." Her voice rang across the lobby.

"He's not in."

The women searched each other's faces. Trish moved forward and stood facing the men at eye level. "This is a popular club located in the heart of downtown, where a great deal of corporate business occurs. Because women are denied membership, they miss out on invaluable networking opportunities. But our gripe is not about membership. We protest that you force female guests to use the back entrance like servants or criminals."

The two men stared.

"You can take it up with your superiors. Now we're going to honor our lunch reservation."

"Oh, no you're not!"

As if propelled from a spring, the two men charged from behind the desk and clipped in front of the women, arms outstretched like two penguins protecting their young.

"What's going on here?" All heads turned to see three men advancing across the lobby toward the front desk, conservatively dressed in dark business suits and starched collars, white handkerchief triangles protruding from their jacket pockets. A man seated in a plump leather chair by the window laid down his paper, and a smartly dressed couple heading for the elevator turned curious eyes in their direction.

The clerks fluttered their arms to their sides. "These girls entered by the front door and refuse to go round to the back entrance."

"Now, what is it you girls want?" one of the men demanded, planting his feet in a wide stance.

"To enter the club by the front door," Radley replied.

"It's against Marquette Club rules."

"Yes, we know," Bette said. "We're challenging that. It's discrimination."

"Everyone uses the back door. It is just steps from the parking ramp. Hardly anyone uses the front entrance," one of the men countered.

"That's not the point."

"Look, this is a men's club, and like all clubs we have rules. Ladies are to enter by the back door only. It's out of our hands. I don't know what you hope to gain by making a fuss. No one else has complained. Other women don't mind." The man spoke in a conciliatory tone.

"Don't give us that bunk." Trish's gaze pinpointed each man in turn. "You have no idea what women mind. You expect women to be polite and accept the status quo. But we're not patsy housewives. I'm telling you, we won't stop protesting until the discriminatory rule is rescinded. It's a simple request. What could you possibly stand to lose by allowing women to enter through the main door?"

"Their sense of privilege and superiority," Bette said.

Radley noticed the couple standing by the elevator next to a large sand-filled pot darted with cigarette butts, looking in their direction. After glancing around the lobby, the men relented, motioning the women into the lobby. "Enjoy your lunch," one said.

"You need to change your discriminatory rule," Maureen told them. "Tell your directors that we're the West Suburban Council for Women's Liberation, you'll be getting a letter from us," she added as the men strode off and disappeared into the elevator, looking straight ahead as the doors snapped shut in front of them.

"You women's libbers had better watch your step," a voice growled. They turned to see a man in a pinstripe suit and wide purple and orange tie throw his newspaper down and stride across the lobby toward them. "This is a men's club. You have no place here." He stopped in the middle of the room and glared at them.

"And just who are you?" Radley asked.

"Fuck off," Trish cried, inching over and planting herself in front of him. The man glared at them as if they had materialized from the lower depths. Without bothering to answer, he twisted his mouth into a grimace and plunged his hand into his jacket pocket.

"There's only one way to deal with your types," he said, and with a steady, purposeful gesture he pulled out a small pistol and aimed it at the four women.

As one unit, the women stepped backward, too stunned to speak. A moment of silence. Radley noticed the clerks had their heads buried in paperwork, oblivious, possibly unaware of the weapon, which was blocked by the four women. With the rest of the lobby empty, there were no witnesses, had they needed one, although none of the women believed that the man would actually pull the trigger—this wasn't a slum district, this was the last place they expected to be confronted by a madman. He was bluffing, of course—well-dressed, sober, standing there glaring at them, his wits under full control. Driven, Radley guessed, by a conviction of male entitlement. Still they froze, staring, unable to think of a single recourse.

The man laughed at their fright—it's empty, you wildcats!—turned his back and started to return to his chair, but Trish followed him, informing him in a loud voice that only a coward needed a weapon to get his point across, that his hot-headedness was matched only by his crudeness, and that the police would put him where he belonged.

As the women retraced their steps out the front entranceway, they heard his piercing voice behind them, "Don't bother, I have friends on the force. Hey, do you girls want to go to a party tonight?"

As they passed the front desk, the one remaining clerk was bent over a ledger, the top of his blonde head encircled in the light of the coil-necked desk lamp. He did not look up.

Outside it still snowed, but they didn't mind. They were thrilled. The flakes cooled their faces as they trudged back to the parking ramp, smiling, laughing. Mission completed! Faced with hostility, they had nevertheless transmitted a message. That was enough for the present.

CHAPTER 21

❧

Three days later, the women's group convened in Bette's living room for its regular meeting. Radley, Bette, Trish, and Maureen proclaimed their confrontation with the gatekeepers at the Minneapolis Club a success. Not that they had changed a thing, Radley admitted that the rule requiring women to use the back door stood intact, but they had ruffled feathers, had taken a stand, prodded the upper levels of management. They were under no illusion that the club would change a traditional policy just because four snow-covered women walked in the front door and made demands.

But they had done it! Radley didn't know when she'd been so stirred. Smiling, she passed around a letter she had sent that morning to the club CEOs demanding a change in the rules. A small effort, yes, but she felt a kinship with the demonstrators who bussed to Washington, D.C. and the student equal rights protests on campuses. The excitement at having performed a symbolic act infused everyone in the room.

All during 1970, the women had been getting more and more fired. Radley was attending Minnesota Organization for Repeal of Abortion Laws meetings. Trish reported on the Social Workers Party headquarters where the Trotskyites promoted world revolution. Maureen led her active church group to a civil rights rally at the state capitol.

Trish and Bette joined the University of Minnesota Feminists, where they heard women openly relate their experiences of being raped. "The stories were mind-blowing," they reported. "Many rapes are committed by family members, and all of them covered up. Women keep quiet because they're made to feel it's their fault for being the temptress. One woman told how her boyfriend raped her five-year-old daughter after she had crawled up on the bed and touched his thigh. The judge let him off, claiming that men are hormonally unable to resist such temptation."

"Aren't there instances where the woman does actually parade her sexuality inappropriately?" After all, Radley thought, they had to be fair and consider both sides.

At these words, Trish lifted Morgan's *Sisterhood is Powerful* from the table and rifled through the pages. "Listen to this."

"Let's put to rest for all time the lie that men are oppressed . . . by sexism—and the lie that there can be such a thing as 'men's liberation groups.' Oppression is something that one group of people commits against another group specifically because of . . . skin color or sex or age, etc. The oppressors are indeed *fucked up* by being masters (racism hurts whites, sexual stereotypes are harmful to men) but those masters are not *oppressed.* Any master has the alternative of divesting himself of sexism or racism—the oppressed have no alternative—for they have no power—but to fight. In the long run, Women's Liberation is going to *cost* men a lot of privilege, which no one gives up unwillingly . . . ."

Of course, she was right. The bonding these friends had achieved amazed Radley. From widely different backgrounds—Klara with advanced degrees, Bette raised on a Minnesota farm, Trish the free-spirit from Los Angeles, Barbara, a former teacher from Chicago, with Maureen, Cookie and Radley raised in Minneapolis—they had found a commonality in their search for better lives, for others as well as their own, had developed an openness and honesty deeper than they'd ever known. Regardless of background, Radley sensed they were alike, bound together by their roles and the drive to make a difference.

Radley took a swallow of coffee. A feeling of purpose had stolen over her life. Reading feminist literature, devouring the latest protest happenings, exchanging life-altering ideas on the phone—it was as if she had come alive.

Bette brought in a fresh pot of coffee and set a plate piled with a variety of cookies on the coffee table. "More sweets!" Trish said with a shake of her head. "Will you women stop with the goddamn goodies all the time? You've got to get rid of your tea-party mentality."

"I need my energy," Klara said, sliding the plate to her end of the table.

""I have to tell you guys," Cookie said, lifting two butterscotch wafers from the pile. I've decided to change my name." She bit into the warm dough. "I was looking for a name similar to my present one, but couldn't come up with one. . ."

"I've an idea, what about Rookie?" Radley said.

"Or Nookie might do the trick," added Trish.

Cookie laughed good-naturedly, twisting her silk neckerchief in her fingers. "From now on call me Mirat."

"Original," Trish said.

"You're definitely striking out on your own, girl," Bette remarked.

"I'd go to a bar and celebrate, if it were allowed," Cookie, now Mirat, said. "Those Boston women who recently chained themselves to their bar stools to protest the law banning unescorted women from public bars—weren't they fantastic?" Her blue eyes flashed. "These are the brave souls who make things happen. And guess what? Victory! The law was changed. We're now free to go into a public bar for a few relaxing drinks if we like without being accompanied by a man."

Radley reached across the couch and clasped Cookie's—Mirat's—hand. "You have grown so much in the two years since we first met. You speak with a confidence you didn't have before. I'm so glad you're with us."

"Me too," Mirat said, glowing. "I'm getting into the swing of protesting."

"Do you mind paying the price, Cookie—I mean Mirat?" Trish asked. "You will be considered by some as abrasive and crude."

"Bring it on!" Mirat cried.

Maureen had been sitting quietly, arms resting along the arm-rests, following the proceedings with interest. "I suggest, my friends, now that we have our feet wet, that we go on to a more rigorous action." Maureen's serious tone caught everyone's attention. "I suggest that we set ourselves a new target." She sat upright and drew her hands to her lap. All eyes turned to her.

"Let me tell you the story of my aunt Emma. For years—during her entire marriage—my aunt handled the household bills. Her husband, however, continually over-charged their credit account and ignored the warnings and overdrawn bank notices. For 18 years she covered his careless extravagances. But when they divorced in 1968, Sherwood Bain refused to issue a card her own name—even though she'd paid the bills all those years without fail." A murmur of recognition circled the room. "All the stores where she'd been a faithful customer cancelled her credit cards." Maureen lifted her coffee slowly, took a deep sip and replaced it on the table.

Radley held her breath; she divined what was coming.

"After hearing this, I tried to get Sherwood Bain to change the joint card with my husband to my name," she continued. "I got a flat-out no. Against their policy. As an unemployed woman with an employed husband, I have no credit identity. My letters of protest to the CEO and the other department store officers have been ignored."

"This means," Barbara cried, breaking in, "that if I get divorced I will have to wait years to build up a credit rating. I'm getting knots in my stomach."

"So I'm suggesting we create a public demonstration aimed at Sherwood Bain's policy. Something that will grab the attention of the media."

Assent careened round the room.

"Good. I'm glad you're all with me. There must be hundreds with the same problem, women who don't have a voice. Here's my plan: we do some research and plenty of thinking and come up with a public protest action that will shake Sherwood Bain's socks off."

Trish gripped her hands together. "I like it!"

"Perfect. As Minneapolis' flagship department store, Sherwood Bain is a good target," Bette agreed.

Maureen looked around with shining eyes. "I think I can get the Midwest Council of Churches to back the event. And we can corral other religious groups. Reverend Allerton promised to back our effort with his ecumenical clout. The media won't be able to ignore this one."

"I could get my husband to help," Mirat offered. The others groaned. Absolutely not! No husbands. Men would take over. This has to be for, about, and by women.

"Force of habit," Mirat said quickly. "I wasn't thinking."

Radley looked at Klara, who voiced a reluctance to show herself in public. "I take pride in my mind, not my body," she said.

"I'm not crazy about speaking or being photographed in public, but people need to hear what we have to say," Bette said. "When they understand, they'll support us. Whatever it takes, I'm willing."

"I suggest we plan a brainstorming session," Radley said, eager to move.

"Well," Klara said after a time, "I want to stick with all of you and to be an equal partner in our actions." She studied her hands, then lifted her gaze to the Picasso print on the far wall. "Damn the torpedoes. Count me in," she cried at last, smashing her cigarette into the side of an ashtray. "I'll stick with the group no matter where it leads." Pulling a Pall Mall from a crumpled pack, she lit another one.

"Damn the torpedoes—full speed ahead!" Mirat echoed, brimming with excitement. "I'll just take this last one home," she added smiling as she tucked a frosted cookie into her purse.

CHAPTER 22

Radley pulled her coat tight against the frosty October weather as the women gathered on the sidewalk in front of Sherwood Bain, the popular department store in the heart of downtown Minneapolis. The bank of clouds overhead blocked all but a few persistent rays of sunlight, not propitious for the Big Event, but never mind, she mused, the frost would keep them on their toes. The sidewalks flowed with Saturday shoppers carrying striped department store bags from Sherwood Bain, Donaldson's, Power's, or Young-Quinlan's. People peered in display windows at the new fall pleated skirts, matching cardigans and Courrèges pants suits draped on plastic mannequins with chins lifted and arms akimbo. Across Nicollet Avenue, men in business suits emerged from The Magic Pan, toothpicks sticking out of their mouths. The faint odor of French perfume and shoe polish swept along the sidewalks, and the swish of swinging doors sounded from tall buildings.

Klara walked up to a store window clutching several bulging packages against the front of her black wool cape. "How are you going to climb up the ladder with all those packages?" Radley asked, watching as two men stretched a boundary tape along a stretch of the curb near them, adjusting the poles at either end to form a protective barrier. She wondered how Klara, who refused to walk farther than a few yards from her car in winter, would keep warm with only slacks under her yellow skirt and thin cape over her long-sleeved white calico blouse.

"I have no intention of climbing up any ladder. I'll leave that to you skinny ones. My role is that of comfort dispenser." Klara lined the bundles on the sidewalk alongside the Sherwood Bain building: two white bakery boxes trailing whiffs of sugar, a silver thermos, a stiff-handled duffle bag bulging with pamphlets, a wood-cane umbrella, a coin purse filled with quarters, and various aluminum-wrapped food packages.

"Klara, what have you got there? Are you planning to seduce the television crew with treats?" Trish asked with a lively expression on her rosy face, looking tall and confident as she surveyed the scene.

Klara laughed. "These, I'll have you know, are fresh donuts straight from Dunkin' Donuts. With this frisky October air, we'll need them in case we get cold."

"Oh, peachy keen—just what we need, donuts to warm our stomachs. I always turn to donuts when I need heat. Indispensable," Trish said.

"You got that right!" Klara said.

As Radley stood surveying the pedestrians, Maureen arrived with two men carrying a fold-out ladder. Setting it up next to the curb, Maureen clipped a large sign to the top rung reading WEST SUBURBAN COUNCIL FOR WOMEN'S LIBERATION. Next to it on the sidewalk, she erected an A-frame sign that displayed WOMEN'S RIGHTS. A crowd forming on either side of the street eyed the goings on with curiosity. The women were dressed in an array of frontier style costumes, with layers of long underwear underneath. Radley and Maureen wore long-sleeved calico dresses, Barbara had tied a white full-length apron over a blue and brown print frock, and Trish sported black button-up shoes she'd found at a Stillwater antique shop. They all had on yellow or blue bonnets with stiffened brims that tied under the chin. Holding up picket signs: WOMEN BOYCOTT SHERWOOD BAIN— SHERWOOD BAIN UNFAIR TO WOMEN —WOMEN SHOPPERS UNITE —WOMEN DEMAND YOUR OWN CREDIT CARDS, they circled around the ladder.

"I hope people understand the significance of these outfits." Barbara tugged the bow of her bonnet tighter under her chin and squinted up at the ladder, having tucked her cat-eye glasses into her purse.

"They will before we're done speaking," Radley said, feeling conspicuous standing on a public sidewalk dressed in stage costume. She reminded herself it was for the cause. She had faith in Maureen, the mastermind of this caper, all would run smoothly in her hands. But she felt her confidence waver as the crowd grew, and she stood back shyly, not certain she wanted to be this exposed.

"Do I look rugged and independent," Mirat asked, tucking a rogue strand of hair into her cap, "like a female who circles the wagons and skins buffalo in the back country?"

"You look like a hostess about to welcome guests to dinner," Klara said. "Put a serious look on your face. You've got to stop smiling like we're hosting a party. We are brave women facing the elements and determined to do or die."

"I'm not smiling," Mirat retorted. "I'm too cold to smile." But her eyes were twinkling. Radley noticed how trim she looked nowadays, her arms free of the clinking gold bracelets and her bright scarlet lipstick replaced with a natural pink.

"I'm afraid we look like Halloween leftovers," Barbara said. "This idea sounded good on paper, but I feel like a fool in this dress."

"Don't you think I feel ridiculous swamped in this butter yellow outfit?" Klara asked. "This bonnet makes me feel like a milk maid, and I'm definitely not the milk maid type."

"Where are the hundreds of supporters that were supposed to show up?" Barbara asked dubiously. "After weeks of phone calls, distributing leaflets, and speaking at university and political functions, where are they all?

Radley was determined to project optimism. "Just wait," she said.

"The crowd is bound to grow," Maureen assured her. "I expect many from various church groups and the protest movements we've contacted to show up. They support us one hundred percent. And a large number of Reverend Allerton's followers will be here."

Hugging their arms to their bodies for warmth, the women stood facing the growing crowd. Radley's mind reverted back to her university years, when earnest young boys strummed the guitar in dorm rooms packed with students: *This Land was Made for You and Me.*

"I've invited everyone I know," Mirat said.

"I haven't," Barbara said. "I don't want anyone I know to see me if this flops."

"I haven't," Bette said. "I don't know anyone."

"What's the matter with you two?" Mirat said, adjusting the waistband of her gingham skirt. "We're making a statement, *doing* something, putting our beliefs into action. I feel like a farmer girl who milks goats in the day and spins straw into gold at night. I'm having a grand time." She joggled the vintage drawstring bag dangling from her wrist.

Radley smiled at her friend. Good old Cookie, well, okay, Mirat. It was hard to believe that once she had considered her friend lightweight, lacking significance. Now she felt like hugging her.

Two network news vans with ABC and NBC blazed on their sides drew up alongside the curb, followed by two police cars. A television crew in black turtlenecks began unloading heavy television cameras and tripods, setting up electrical hookups and running cables to the ladder. As the crowd thickened, the women raised their placards over their heads. Faces appeared in the windows of the surrounding buildings, pressing to see out.

On the far side of the street, Radley spied a man wearing a black cap from which a tuff of red hair protruded. A long red and white striped scarf around his neck whipped out behind him like a streamer in the wind as he threaded his way to the television vans, spoke a few words to the crew, and threw a grin of assurance to the women in frontier garb. Then he leapt to the top of the ladder and stood arched above the heads of the crowd, towering tall in his long black coat.

"Look," Radley said, "it's Allerton. He's going to introduce us." Raising his jagged eyebrows, the Reverend waved a hand to the crowd, flung one end of his red and white scarf over his shoulder, and lifted a bullhorn to his mouth.

"You are about to witness," his deep voice rang out over the mass of heads, "a drama that represents you or someone you know." People moved toward the ladder, pressing closer together. "Pay attention to these women you see here, these women are you, your wives, daughters, friends, colleagues. These women are members of the West Suburban Council for Women's Liberation. They stand here today representing over fifty local organizations advocating women's rights, including the National Organization of Women, the American Association of University Women, the New Torin Citizens League, the National Black Feminist Organization, the Women's Equity Action League, and the American Indian Movement. To name only a few."

Shoppers whirling from the revolving doors of Sherwood Bain paused on the sidewalk, and people trailed across the street to get closer. Reverend Allerton squinted as the sun broke through and illuminated his flushed face. "Now it's time for you to hear their story. It will speak for itself." Sweeping his arm toward the women hovering around the ladder, Reverend Allerton slid to the ground and positioned himself next to a black and white television van.

Radley noticed that the onlookers had increased, quieter now—men in trench coats, matrons with blue-grey hair, women in bucket hats and fur collars. A man in a striped business suit stepped up to the curb and whispered a few words to Maureen. At her nod, Barbara, Bette, Radley and Mirat strode into the growing mass of people and began passing out leaflets. Maureen climbed up the ladder and waved at the familiar faces of supporters peppered through the crowd.

"Way to go!" cried a voice standing across the street in front of Woolworth's Five and Dime.

"It's a bit breezy," remarked a short man in a pea jacket standing by the curb. "You ladies better get your coats on."

Radley looked over. "We prefer to be called women, not ladies. Ladies is too antiseptic, too remote," she said politely. "We don't want to be restricted up on a pedestal."

"Then you better get off that ladder," another male voice called amid a titter of laughter.

Nearby, a well-dressed man in a black coat with a velvet collar gave a loud guffaw. He leaned against a street light, ankles crossed, and fixed his eyes on Radley in a laser stare, his head tilted forward, his small aquiline nose and narrow eyes sunk in a concave face. Even from a distance, she felt the intensity of his gaze focused unrelenting on her.

"You're on," one of the crew men called. Radley exchanged glances with the other women. They were in this together and the moment of truth had arrived.

Maureen climbed the ladder and surveyed the crowd, faces tilted upward expectantly. Her companions had spread out in a line on the sidewalk below, placards lifted above their heads. Maureen lifted the microphone and fixed her dark gaze on the crowd. Her words shot out clear and distinct.

"I want to tell you why we're out here in the cold on a busy Saturday afternoon in front of Sherwood Bain. We're here because we want to right a wrong. We speak for all women." Her voice strengthened as she spoke. "We speak for all women who are responsible, reliable citizens, who have earned a top credit rating, who often manage the household bookkeeping and pay the bills. Yet these women *cannot get a charge account in their own name at Sherwood Bain Department Store.*"

The street had lapsed into silence, waiting. "Many of you don't realize that when a woman is listed in her husband's name, when she is Mrs. John Smith, she is buried in his history and has no identity of her own."

"What are you gals up to?" a voice yelled from the sidewalk. "My wife has a credit card. Easy as pie."

Tossing a glance in the man's direction, Maureen continued. "Hear me out. I'd like to tell you of one woman's experience." She looked at Radley and held the microphone closer. Radley nodded encouragement.

"I'd like to tell you a true story. About Amy Feldman, mother of three, a former accountant, now a housewife." She went on to describe the years of bad debts that plagued the family, the warning phone calls and threatening messages from creditors, and how Amy had struggled to curtail her husband's trips to Las Vegas, his compulsive spending on fancy fly-fishing equipment and airlifted fishing jaunts to Alaska. How she turned away trucks threatening to remove unpaid furniture and took in sewing to cover her husband's debts." Here she paused, raising a hand for emphasis. "Her husband remained oblivious, then defiant. Finally she gave up the struggle and the marriage.

"When their marriage ended, so did Amy's access to shopping credit, even though she'd paid the bills responsibly for years. She applied to Sherwood Bain for a credit card in her own name. Sherwood Bain refused, and all the credit she had built up over the years reverted to her ex-husband.

Radley noticed with satisfaction that Maureen's voice carried over the street loud and strong. "You can see that something has to be done! That's why we're here."

The crowd grew as people pressed around to hear. "Hey, girls!" a male voice yelled. "You're blocking the sidewalk. Put your complaints in a letter."

Maureen whipped her head around. "The struggle has to be in the streets," she boomed into the microphone. "We approached the president of Sherwood Bain with a letter signed by over thirty organizations. No one higher than the division manager would see us." She paused to let her words hang in the air. "We asked to be recognized as individuals and not appendages to our husbands. The manager, Mr. Harriman, supplied us with ice water, commended our enthusiasm, pledged to pass on our request, and ushered us out of the office. The department store did not respond to a letter threatening a store boycott. Four weeks later I received a boilerplate letter stating that they were unable to change their policy at this time and hoping that they could be of further service in the future."

The crowd murmured, stirred uneasily.

"We need to spread the word, to gather supporters, to keep fighting for our rights. That's why we're here."

Standing tall on the ladder, all eyes fastened on her, Maureen continued to relate examples of women who attempted to claim their own identity so they could take charge of their economic future. Today she was serving as their voice.

Two TV cameras on the nearby vans were pointed directly at Maureen, panning occasionally along the mass of heads and the costumed women on the curb waiting to speak. Radley caught sight of the man in the black velvet-collared coat worming his way towards them. Something about the eel-like smoothness of his approach bothered her.

Gripping the microphone, Maureen described her own family and her long-term involvement in church work. Radley noted that the crowd listened respectfully, many heads nodding. Maureen, church activist, wife and mother with her plain wind-blown hair and wholesome demeanor in a calico dress, did not present the picture of a far-out radical. Her heartfelt explanations seemed to be winning them over.

"You may ask why we are wearing these dresses," Maureen went on. "None of us has ever demonstrated before. Ours is an act of desperation. We've approached Sherwood Bain by every possible means. They refuse to listen. By taking to the street, we're striking out, just as our forbearers did when they blazed western trails to the unknown wilderness of our country."

She paused, looking out over the slew of faces looking on with interest, a few with amused grins or pinched looks of open hostility.

"We need your support. We urge you *not to shop at Sherwood Bain until they amend their policy.* The only route is through their pocketbooks. Women, let us fight for credit cards in our own names. Men join us. We deserve an individual credit rating. We demand it."

"Why should you girls possess your own cards?" called a tall man standing in the center of the crowd." One of the cameras swirled around and fixed on him. "You're married, you don't work, you don't produce income. Without employment you have no financial basis and are therefore a risk. On what grounds can you expect credit on your own?"

Maureen spoke evenly into the microphone. "In a marriage the salary of the man is owned equally by the husband and wife. Her work in the home is every bit as important as his in the workplace, and her remuneration is included in his income. You can't expect the wife to hold down a full-time homemaker job for nothing."

"The salary belongs to the husband!" came another male voice.

"That's a fallacy," Maureen replied. "Under the marriage bargain, the woman works in the home and the man on the job. His salary pays for both efforts and belongs to each, half and half."

"Much ado about nothing," a man in the front row growled. "What will they think of next?"

Another voice shot out. "You tootsies are cute, but you best get back where you belong."

A hoot issued from the sidelines, "You girls have too much leisure time."

More remarks followed with bullet-like rapidity. "I'll bet you gals aren't as innocent as you look in those getups."

"If you're pioneers, I'm a bare-assed caveman."

A trickle of laughter followed these remarks. Radley looked on, astonished. Who were these blockheads? The crowd swayed, straining to view the source of the jeers. "You're not only a caveman, you're also a pig," a female voice yelled from somewhere in the back. Several hands clapped amid a ripple of women's laughter. Women's voices began yelling, "You only want to be waited on!" and "Male chauvinist pigs!" More shouts rang out, unintelligible. Heads turned this way and that, feet shuffled uneasily. An unruly streak fired through the crowd.

Maureen had finished, it was Radley's turn. She climbed up the ladder and leaned her thighs against the rungs, clutching the microphone tightly. The trembling in her knees was steadied by a surge of anger at the outright hostility of those, she believed, who were fighting to maintain the status quo at any price.

One face inched up to the front and stared up at her, slit-eyed and half-smiling—it was the man with the black velvet collar. He wore black gloves and held a white package tied with royal blue ribbon. She noticed something odd about his steely gaze.

The crowd quieted. She must concentrate—never mind the little man, just tell her story. Grasping the mic with both hands, she began.

"I'd like to tell you about myself." Taking a deep breath, Radley described growing up in Minneapolis, attending UC Berkeley, where she participated in various political action rallies. Adjusting her feet on the rung of the ladder, she looked out over the swarm of heads, past the familiar stores lined along Nicollet Mall, with the lone spire of the Foshay Tower rising behind them—a street she'd combed so many times, woven into the fabric of her childhood —never had she imagined a public demonstration taking place here.

"Our women's liberation group you see here today was inspired by Reverend Allerton," she continued. "After hearing his lectures on civil rights, a group of us set out to investigate the rights of all oppressed people, including the rights of women. What we uncovered was mind-blowing!"

She felt her calico skirt lift in the breeze and quickly tucked it between her knees. "We found so many rights that women lack, so many ways they are excluded from male dominated enterprises." Radley ran her gaze over the crowd. The sight of the lifted faces watching her quietly gave her courage. She felt light, inspired, sure of her purpose. "We are seeking a simple right—the right of equality in a store where women are the main customers. A right on which this country is based."

A male voice cut through the mass of heads. "The constitution states that all *men* are created equal."

"It's an inclusive term, although *women* would be a better choice, since it actually includes the word men," a female voice rang out angrily. People stirred, looked at their neighbors with heated expressions.

When Radley had finished, Trish and Bette mounted the ladder and told their personal stories, describing how the movement for rights had changed their lives. Each talk was followed by enthusiastic applause.

Maureen remounted the ladder to broadcast the final words. "We women go on record saying that if Sherwood Bain doesn't address our needs we will NOT SHOP AT SHERWOOD BAIN. We ask you to take up this cause with us." A chorus of yeah's went up from the crowd, female voices, loud and defiant. Radley held her breath in excitement: *They are with us!*

Just then a male voice shot out, "Why aren't you gals at home watching your children? What about your marriage vow, when you took your husband's name? That's your name now." Several male voices shot out in agreement. As jeers and counter accusations flew back and forth, people strained to see what would happen next.

A man standing next to a lamp post yelled, "You girls need to fall on your backs and let a good man fix you. That'll put smiles on your faces." Not far from him two businessmen in sports jackets, white button-down collars and ties stood with folded arms, smiling and nodding.

Radley's blood, already churning, ran faster. She noticed that Maureen, perched on the ladder, kept a composed countenance. The women had anticipated the inevitable naysayers. They had agreed the best tactic would be to keep the demonstration orderly, civilized. They didn't want to appear like the Washington protestors whose camps disrupted traffic or the rioters in Los Angeles who smashed store windows and terrorized the streets.

"Look," she exclaimed suddenly. A few feet away the man in the black velvet collar was bearing down on them. In his gloved hands he gripped a box tied with a blue ribbon secured by an enormous blue bow. He slithered up and extending his arms, shoved the white box into Radley's hands.

"You women should get what you deserve," the man cried out, "And here it is," Without waiting for a response, he backed up and with a quick pirouette dissolved into the crowd.

People hushed, curious, straining to see what was happening. The box felt hard in Radley's hands, and with some trepidation she pulled the blue ribbon loose and carefully removed the lid. There, encrusted in wads of white tissue, was a dark moist mound, still warm, followed by a stench that fumed out over the sidewalk.

The crowd gasped. "What is it?" someone called. "Hold your nose!" another cried. The stench was knock-out strong. Even with the lid clamped back on, the box continued to eke out a hot, smoldering smell.

Trish climbed up the ladder and raised the open box high above her head. "Someone just handed us this sign of their support," she yelled. Heads strained to see. "It's excrement," she called out. "An entire box full." Groans were heard, titters, exclamations of disbelief. "I want everyone to see this." She lifted the box higher. "The man who thrust this box on us," she shouted, "has disappeared. So here we have, in a nutshell you might say, an example of what women who want to exercise their inalienable rights are up against."

"It's just more male shit!" Bette yelled, ripping off her yellow bonnet and waving it over the crowd. "Now you see what we have to deal with."

"It's an example of the hatred felt by men when we ask for our rights!" a fiery female voice called. "Ignore it."

"Yes!" another yelled. "It's an adolescent prank. It doesn't warrant a reply."

By now many in the audience were smiling, even some of the men. As the crowd broke up, a mass of women pressed around the ladder, pledging their support.

Radley's throat relaxed. It was over. They'd done it! The women of the West Suburban Council for Women's Liberation burned with excitement. The drama had enflamed the crowd, had been picked up quickly by the press and would run on the evening news. The poop man, as they called him, was a nut—a perfect symbol of the opposition.

Klara took a fold-up umbrella from her bulbous purse and without opening it snapped it along her thigh.

"It's not about to rain. What are you doing?" Radley asked.

"Any more surprise boxes and someone's going to get it in the ribs. Enough of this prissy housewife image. Men better understand that we mean business." The women laughed. This was only the first step. They were prepared to go further, to plunge into pits of fire if necessary. Whatever it took.

CHAPTER 23

❦

Reverend Allerton stood alongside Trish, Bette, Maureen, and Barbara at one end of the parishioner's lounge. The red and white scarf he'd worn that afternoon was still draped around his neck. He peered over the roomful of people who had gathered, sitting or standing, a few clustered around a serving table holding a blue punch bowl and blue punch glasses. He smiled warmly, nodding to familiar faces. Behind him, a large silver cross gleamed on the wall and next to it a gold-bordered banner stamped with ENTER ALL INTO THE WORLD in gold letters.

Standing with Klara a few feet away, Radley watched him in admiration. Never had she known one so dedicated, so passionate about political transformation.

"Thank you all for coming to Holy Presbyterian to honor the efforts of these women today. The demonstration could only have succeeded with the participation of many supporters—some right here in this room—who arranged for busloads to attend the demonstration, obtained permits, and set up media contacts."

Radley looked on as Reverend Allerton clasped his hands in front of him. A tuft of red hair was curled over one ear. "Watch the evening news tonight. Our message is out there. We don't know what Sherwood Bain will do. We shall see." He looked around at the women grouped at his side. "In conclusion, I want to congratulate you seven women on the success of your daring efforts!"

This was met by loud applause from the listeners.

"There are hundreds of us," Maureen said to the crowd, smiling widely. And this is only the beginning."

"I don't know how you had the guts to pull it off," a woman exclaimed.

Radley stepped forward. "This is new territory for me," she said. "I never imagined I would be on top of a ladder speaking to a mass of strangers. But I could do it! And even more, I found I relished the opportunity for self-expression. It made me feel I could do anything.

"I was there," someone said. "How could you endure all the taunts and insults hurled against you?"

Radley had already considered the question. "The hostility of our opponents was recorded and transmitted by local TV stations for the world to see. We think it adds drama and actually draw people to our side."

"I can promise you I will not enter Sherwood Bain store again until I walk in with my own credit card," a woman in a three-piece suit exclaimed.

"I'm for you gals absolutely. My physician has prescribed tranquillizers so that I'll settle down and accept my lot," said a young woman holding a baby in a blue flannel bunting. "This has to stop."

"My girlfriends and I have read Friedan." A women in a yellow sweatshirt moved forward from the back of the room. "We're with you a hundred percent."

"I feel a real sense of sisterhood in this room," Trish said heatedly. "Together we can make a difference.

A woman in a leopard-trimmed suit and matching pillbox hat stepped up. Radley thought she had seen her among the mass of onlookers outside Sherwood Bain. "I'm a member of this church," she began. "These women should not be parading themselves in public. What kind of woman would display herself in such a brazen fashion? It's unladylike and unfeminine." She held herself with an air of authority. "These women are feminists. They only talk about one side. Sherwood Bain will never give in to their demands."

"On what do you base that opinion?" a female voice yelled across the room.

The woman adjusted the collar of her jacket. "I'll tell you. Why should Sherwood Bain issue a card to an individual with no job, no income? No intelligent organization would assume such a risk. Women should be home with their families where they're needed. I believe it is pure self-indulgence." This wealthy matron, Radley judged, no doubt lived in a lakeside mansion and had not felt oppressed a day in her life. "You say you want to get your needs met," the woman continued. "Women are meant to sacrifice for others, it's their nature. It's what the world needs. Not demeaning dramas in the streets. Women talk about freedom—what they mean is freedom from their Godly duties, from their primary re-sponsibility, their family. I for one am proud to stand behind my husband, to assume his name. It's in the natural order of things. If it's freedom you prize, the freedom to exercise your "rights," then remain single."

People shifted their feet uneasily, some glared at the speaker. Radley suppressed her anger. *This woman shows no sympathy for the needs of others. Clearly, she cannot be persuaded. But she should be allowed her say.*

The Reverend spoke up. "Everyone has a right to voice their opinion here," he said in an even tone, "if offered with respect."

At that moment, Radley elbowed Klara's ribcage.

"What?"

Radley tilted her head, and Klara followed her gaze across the room. There, half-hidden behind a metal rack of coats, stood Klara's daughter Audrey, wearing a tam hat, eyes flickering furtively around the room.

"What is Audrey doing here, hiding like a lost pigeon behind the coats?" Radley knew Audrey scorned what she termed her mother's lax fanatical friends and the disgrace of exposing themselves to ridicule by parading publicly in their stupid frontier getups. Audrey wanted no part of it.

"I'm sure I don't know," Klara replied. "She pooh-poohs our efforts. Says we are reverting to adolescence and that she will dye her hair and change schools if she sees me on TV tottering on a ladder." Her daughter had not yet spotted them. "Best to leave her alone. She gets uppity if I infringe on her moods. I try to give her space."

Klara and Radley watched as Audrey approached, inching forward in turtle-like steps as if she were heading towards the guillotine.

"Hello, Audrey," Klara said smiling. "Glad you could make it. The protest appeared to have been successful."

"I know. I was there." Audrey threw her mother a look of such despair that Klara and Radley were speechless. "I—I had to see for myself what my own mother was up to. Of course, I don't approve of these corny displays, but I really do agree with your take on the credit cards. And," she brushed a wayward string of damp hair from her cheek, "I was alone in the house. I couldn't stand it. Mrs. Armstrong gave me a lift. I . . . I watched everything." Her voice was thin, hesitant.

"Audrey, what is it?"

This is quite a turnaround, Radley thought. Something had happened, she couldn't imagine what. She and Klara waited breathlessly.

'Nothing, nothing." One hand covering her stomach, Audrey tottered, tilted to one side, then straightened and darted her large watery eyes around the room as if searching for something. "I'm fine. There're too many people."

Klara studied her daughter. "Come with me," she said, straightening from the table she had been leaning against. "You too" she added when she saw Radley hesitate. The two followed her down the hallway and into an unlit meeting room where a cluster of armchairs circled a large round wooden coffee table. The drapes were partially closed, leaving a desk and scattered chairs recessed in semi-darkness.

"You better sit down," Klara said. Audrey sank onto one of the chairs while her mother and Radley seated themselves next to her.

Audrey folded her hands primly in her lap, a look of desperation on her face.

"Audrey, love, out with it," Klara urged, placing her hand on Audrey's knee. "What is it?"

Audrey pushed back against the chair as if pinned by invisible wires. It looked as if she might stop breathing.

"Nothing. I'm pregnant that's all." The two women stared. Fifteen! Miss Proper! Complaining, Radley recalled, that the women's calls for freedom were nothing but female imaginations run amuck. That Audrey yearned for a traditional family with a father and mother who went out together and had sit-down family meals and did things the way they'd been done forever. Radley bit her lip—this was hard to believe. Yet Audrey's tortured countenance showed the news to be only too true.

"It's all right, honey. We'll deal with it." Klara stroked her daughter's shoulder. Radley admired Klara's unfailing composure. Nothing seemed to rouse her from the complacency with which she faced the cares of everyday life. Radley had never seen her friend trembling with urgency or flushed with anger. She envied such consistency, always coasting on an even keel.

Audrey choked back a stab in her throat and looked up. Her coat had fallen open revealing a navy jumper, white poplin blouse, and a rhinestone starfish hanging at her neck. Sitting with rounded back, twisting her fingers together, she looked more like a small child than a blooming teenager. Klara looked sympathetically into the distraught girl's face.

"Thanks, Mom." Ignoring her wet eyelashes, Audrey looked up directly at the two women focused on her. "I—don't ask me to explain. I know you want to know who it was."

"Maybe I should leave," Radley said. "This is private . . ."

"No need," Audrey said, her voice steadier. "You're my mom's best friend. You might as well hear."

"It would help if I knew." Klara leaned forward in her chair.

"All right, I'll tell you. It was just a guy. I had way too many beers, there were just the four of us, the couple in the front seat was doing it— the guy who had played so hard to get suddenly became amorous . . . he was so insistent . . . I let it happen. Break out of the mold! Don't be ruled by false dictates! Like you're always saying, Mom. Assert equality! I don't know." She pressed her hands to her throat, fingering the rhinestone star-fish. Then she straightened her shoulders.

"I know, I got myself into this . . . I guess I sort of lost it. It wasn't as if I were stoned or anything. One time!" She lowered her eyes and her hands fell to her lap. "Oh, what a train wreck! I don't know what to do. I don't believe in abortion. But can you see me with a child? I'm still in school!" She tried to force a laugh, but produced only a gurgle. Klara and Radley exchanged glances. She'd just squelched what had im- mediately leapt to their minds.

At the lost look on Audrey's face, Radley felt a rush of sympathy.

Klara reached for her daughter's hands. "First of all," she began in an even, determined tone, "we won't tell your dad. Not yet. Second, I'm with you. We'll see this through. That's enough for now. We both have some thinking to do. And we certainly can't do that on an empty stomach." Audrey's expression relaxed for the first time, her shoulders released their arch.

Radley offered to contact Bonnie Benjamin, president of the board of the National Association for Repeal of Abortion Laws, to explore options, including the choice of adoption.

"So much," Radley said to lighten the mood as they strode down the hallway, "for the National Breakdown of American Moral Structure Due to the Complete Distrust of the Ruling Establishment." They walked down the front steps holding hands, the three of them, looking straight ahead.

That night, Radley watched clips of the of Sherwood Bain demonstration on the ten o'clock national news, including excerpts from Maureen's speech as she stood coatless and windblown on the ladder, the women in long calico dresses clustered at the bottom. Sherwood Bain store windows loomed in the background, while the anchorman at ABC, Harry Reasoner, explained the women's demand. He avoided taking sides, but the scene spoke for itself. Close-ups captured the cheers and jeers from the crowd, including male insults and fist-shaking. There was no sign of the manure box; the network had left the scene by then. The store management declined to comment, beyond implying that the little skit had been too meager to notice.

The next morning the Minneapolis *Tribune* carried a four-paragraph notice of the event in the society section, squeezed between the funnies and the daily horoscope.

The women's expectations fell. Radley was disappointed. Two lousy minutes on the evening news, with no accompanying support, and no editorials glorifying their cause. They were backed by solid supporters, but what about the rest of the community, the bulk of society? Never mind, the engine had been started, the boat had pulled out of the slip towards deeper waters, and the waves were beginning to ripple.

CHAPTER 24

❧

I t was Sunday morning and the family was relaxing in the amusement
room. Radley read a book by Eugene McCarthy, while the children
wrestled on Shane's lap as they watched *Tom and Jerry* cartoons. Larry
balanced on his abdomen, bobbing back and forth, and Megan's elbow
dug into his side, all of which Shane bore stoically. He never got angry, or
set limits, they really should learn some restraint, she thought, but he let
them do anything. Radley wished he would show some backbone.

The three of them laughed as Tom drove Jerry through a door that
slammed on Tom's nose as he tried to grab the mouse by the tail.

"That's you," Shane chided, squeezing Larry's shoulder. "You're Tom."

"I wanna be Tom!" Megan cried.

"No, I'm the best Tom. I'm a boy," Larry said. They watched Tom bite
into a sandwich that made his mouth pucker and he grabbed his throat,
while Jerry laughed hysterically from inside a white mix-master on the
kitchen counter.

"I guess I'll be Jerry instead, because I'm smart!" Megan said.

Shane chuckled. Radley watched him smoke his Camel down to the
burning tip, noticed an ugly stain of tobacco on the insides of his fingers.
She wished he didn't smoke so much. The blare of the television filled
the entire house. That's all they ever did, watch television. Whenever she
asked if he wanted to invite the Cortland's over for dinner, Shane would

shrug. It was an easy yes or no question. Couldn't he at least take the trouble to activate his voice? His acquiescence to anything she said or did was maddening.

Following the celebratory assembly with Reverend Allerton after the Sherwood Bain demonstration, Radley went about the house cleaning and seeing to everyday chores with new energy, buoyed by a feeling of purpose. She had a cause; she and the group were now part of a new march toward liberation. The public had witnessed, many had responded. Yet, as the weeks passed and things drifted back to normal, the sense of loss, of something missing in her life, had gradually resurfaced.

Putting the book down, she trundled upstairs, aimless, and wandered from room to room. She could hear the far-away hum of the three voices downstairs and the low buzz of television. Trails of pale light drifted up the stairwell as she wandered alone through the silent upstairs darkness.

Finally, she entered the bedroom and stood by the window, gazing outside. The woods were dark, shadowy, the sun caught behind a boulder of dark clouds. There must be a solution out there, some force that would come exploding from the trees and explain this malaise within her.

How could her feelings have changed so much from those first years with Shane, swept with happiness, marriage, children, house, all piling in joyful newness? Had it only been eleven years since she met Shane at the Coast Club bar, where he was schmoozing with his Irish friends? They had hit it off immediately, talking about nothing much, eying each other all evening across the table. Shane's calm laidback approach diffused her energetic non-stop pursuit of the next move. The two of them relished the contrast, joked that together they formed a harmonious whole—they were clearly meant for each other.

But now she wasn't sure she wanted the traditional marriage where women kept the nest and provided the nurturing, while men provided the pocketbook. There were times *she* needed nurturing. Yet, wives were expected to furnish physical and emotional balm to the trials and tribulations of life. If she couldn't provide this, Shane was cheated, bereft of wifely love. Maybe she wasn't capable of love. Through a window in her mind, she saw both of them deprived, saw herself and Shane at a sorrowful impasse.

She continued to gaze sadly into the woods, where the trees hung still in the shadows as if they had stopped breathing. No answers were forthcoming. Certainly, she belonged in this house—with her children and husband, where her position as wife and mother, cherished by all the creeds of society, held her secure. Yet, the thought plagued her that here in paradise a piece had been broken off and was sweeping her out to sea.

CHAPTER 25

❧❦❧

M aureen was late. The others waited anxiously, seated in Radley's living room amid tables cluttered with cigarette packs and trays of newspaper clippings. Char had stopped by to take Shane and the kids to lunch in Wayzata, so the group had the house to themselves. As she poured coffee, Radley listened for the sound of Maureen's car driving up in front of the house.

Since that blustery day when they had hoisted themselves aloft on the ladder, exposed to reactions on all sides, the women had gained confidence. Radley believed that what they stood for was far greater than the objections of those who held to the status quo. Having taken the plunge, as the women called it, they'd found their squeamishness eroding, replaced by a shared fighting spirit. The tremendous outpourings of support proved to them how much their efforts were needed and how many women felt buried with them in the confines of domesticity.

Radley had never been so close to a group of women before. Since the demonstration, the women had been in constant contact by phone, alerting each other whenever a favorable news article or reference to what some referred to as their "daring protest" appeared. Other reports were less sympathetic, treating the event as something of a community circus. Several local *Sun* papers ran photos of them in their calico dresses and Maureen perched on the ladder with the microphone. The *Star* ran a brief paragraph quoting the Sherwood Bain management's report that the financial interests of the store did not warrant a change in policy at this time, but that the matter was still under careful study. They indicated that special in-house discounts to honor the ladies were currently being arranged.

Their supporters, infuriated by the evasive response of Sherwood Bain and its feeble attempts to pacify them with one-time discounts, mailed batches of credit cards, cut in half, directly to the president of the company. Churches delivered packets of protest statements signed by thousands and threatened to set up a statewide boycott of the department store if the demands weren't met. So far, no response.

At last Maureen entered, out of breath. She stood in the center of the room, clutching her purse to her stomach as if she could feel the hot outline of the contents under her fingers. Klara and Barbara set their coffee cups on the table. The group turned and waited for the words that would give a final claim to their efforts.

"Well, here it is!" she said, eyes glistening. Snapping open her purse, she pulled out a long white envelope. Bette pulled herself upright. Klara flicked a long ash off her cigarette and Barbara straightened her cat-eye glasses. All eyes were riveted on the speaker.

"It's a letter from Sherwood Bain." Maureen held up the envelope. "The response we've been expecting for five months." The silence in the room was broken by the rustle of paper as Maureen withdrew an ivory linen sheet and read:

This is to inform you that in consideration of the inconvenience to some of our customers in regard to our credit identification policy, Sherwood Bain has made the decision to reverse this policy and allow women to open credit accounts in their own names.

Accordingly, at your convenience, you may submit a written request to our administration office to change your name from Mrs. John Doe to Jane Doe.

Sherwood Bain further promised to transmit this announcement to every credit card holder and send press releases to the local papers.

For a second no one breathed. Then the room seemed to spin into action. Maureen laughed aloud as Mirat rushed up to hug her. "I don't believe it!" came from Barbara on the couch. "Ohmygosh!" Mirat screeched. Bette leapt to her feet. "Hot damn! You guys! We won!"

"Do you know what this means?" Trish asked.

"We get our own cards!" Mirat cried.

"Besides that, you coot, it means we can move on to our next action, that we have clout. We may be small, but we are a small force to be reckoned with!"

"Yeah," Barbara said, eyes wet as she tried to contain her emotion. "Now we can consider ourselves actual movers, not just a bunch of disgruntled housewives."

Radley, gripped by a charge of energy, threw her arms around Klara's substantial body. "Now we're part of a wave sweeping the country. We've joined a movement uniting women at all levels, along with Betty Friedan and Gloria Steinem. A national phenomenon is taking place, and we're part of it!"

Everyone gathered around Maureen as they discussed the ramifications of this latest development. "You were fantastic, Maureen," Mirat said, her breath catching.

Trish's voice sounded above the rest. "It's time to look forward! There are so many women's issues to publicize. How many people know that women can't get a bank loan without a male signature? Or that universities are locked into hiring ratios that favor men? We have to decide what to take on next."

Mirat started laughing. "Next? My husband has been holding his breath until I finish what he calls my doodling around with political action and return to my senses. Go ahead, get the steam out of your system, he says. But then you're needed here at home."

"Ralph also wants me to settle down and to quit creating productions and stirring up publicity," Barbara said. "The guys at the office are giving him flack."

"And what did you say to that?"

"I told him if flack was all I had to deal with I wouldn't have to take to the streets."

"My husband thinks I've done enough," Bette said. "He wants me with him, but hardly says a word from dinner to bedtime. I suppose it's in case he might need me."

Their spouses, it appeared, anticipated a return to normalcy and more concentration on the household and on them. The protest at the Marquette Club and the credit card demonstration and had served their purpose, but now they had done their thing, it had gone far enough. Even Klara's liberal-minded husband thought she was wasting her time. It was okay to participate in the local political caucuses, but leave the revolutionary tactics to the extremists like Abbie Hoffman, Angela Davis, and Tom Hayden. Revolution was a full-time job, for people without family responsibilities. Want to effect change? Use your vote.

"While we're on husbands, let's talk about what we need to address on the home front," Trish said. Scrunched on the couch, she drew her legs under her and fingered her silver anklet. "I've thought about my own situation. I love my daughter and my husband, but I want to move beyond homemaking. After eight years of being a mother, I need something more." The hiatus she'd taken to marry and have a child was over. She intended to return to work.

"What I want is a sex life," Bette said. "Lately, my husband has lost interest in sex. Don't tell me to masturbate, it's not the same as lovemaking."

Mirat drew her legs to a lotus position on the rug and set a bean-bag ashtray in front of her. "I want to be taken seriously. Not chucked under the chin or helped over a puddle or pacified with rosebuds. To be listened to, not indulged. I'm sick of Cutesy Cookie. No one will call me Mirat. They say it's too hard. My mother thinks I've lost my beans." The others laughed.

Klara spoke next. "As for me," I want to be accepted, not discounted because of—because of my weight. I've tried many times to get back to the size eight of my high school years. But it's no use. Others hide their problems. Mine is so damned *obvious*."

It was the first time Klara had mentioned her weight. Radley looked at her friend with sympathy.

"I spent my youth in our backyard orchard leaning against a tree with a book and munching Haralson apples and date nut bread. I was the fat girl, the odd one out. You people accept me for who I am. That's all I want." Klara's face flushed, her lips trembled. For the first time, her composure failed her. Several hands reached out and touched her arm. A chorus of "we love you's" spiraled around her.

At her turn, Radley didn't know where to begin. "Like all of you, my parents considered a husband and children the only road to happiness for a woman. I knew that wasn't for me. I set out to build a career and was modestly successful, but a job spitting out greeting cards wasn't enough. Then when I met Shane, my reservations scattered to the winds and I set out on the path of romance and rose petals." She unclasped her hands and looked at the others. "But now I find I'm cut off from a part of life that's crucial to me, but I haven't yet figured out what it is. I want to know— what's missing?"

"Listen to Virginia Woolf," Trish said, drawing a book from her tote bag. "I've read this novel four times. Here's a passage from *To the Lighthouse* describing why women in the home are so necessary to the male, of how women sustain life, how they give sustenance. The question women must ask: who provides sustenance to them?" She slipped on her glasses and opened the book.

"Mrs. Ramsey braced herself, and half turning, seemed to raise herself with an effort, and at once to pour erect into the air a rain of energy, a column of spray, looking at the same time animated and alive as if all her energies were being fused into force, burning and illuminating . . . and into this delicious fecundity, this fountain and spray of life, the fatal sterility of the male plunged itself . . . barren and bare."

The passage had a familiar ring. Radley was certain Woolf was stashed somewhere in her bookshelves, not opened since college. She vowed to locate it as soon as she returned home.

CHAPTER 26

꧁ ꧂

T he Sherwood Bain protest of September 1970, had made a brief
splash. The group had received some congratulatory phone calls
and requests to speak at community meetings. But the inquiries trickled off, and after the success of what was after all a baby step—their
single achievement would soon be filed away in the back archives—they
hankered to do more, to meld their efforts with those of unsatisfied
women everywhere. They wanted to be part of the tide of feminism
and the surge for equality, peace, and justice demands that were'
crashing through America.

Despite the grumblings of their husbands, the women were not about
to relinquish the course of change they were on. Klara and Radley joined
a fiery young feminist group at the University of Minnesota; Trish accompanied a busload of anti-war protestors to Washington, D. C. for a
National Peace Action Coalition demonstration; and Mirat and Bette participated in organizational meetings set up by two wealthy women pa-
trons to establish the first safe house for battered women in the state.

Opposition from those who labeled them radical naysayers only increased the women's resolve. One afternoon Radley, Bette, and Mirat
returned from the state capitol in a state of shock. They had arrived at
the office of a state legislator to lobby for women's rights, a man who
welcomed them cordially with a non-committal smile, yes, what can I

do for you? As Radley explained that they were citizen advocates for pro-choice and pointed out the suffering caused by back-alley abortions and the moral right of women to choose when and if to bear children, the expression on the senator's face tightened, his glance jerked several times to the window. Of course, he fully understood their position, please leave a written report. He stood up. Clearly the man on the far side of the desk did not agree with them, and further, was not amenable to females invading his office and taking up his time. Two subsequent interviews with male legislators at the other end of the hall revealed the same reluctance. The women sensed that the controversial subject involving women's functions was one the men preferred to avoid altogether.

Disappointed, they headed toward the elevators, through throngs of men and a few secretaries clicking down the hall in high heels, past closed doors behind which servants of the state pursued their male priorities. They saw no sign of the four females who were members of the Minnesota legislature in 1971. Inside the crowded elevator, the men eyed Radley, Bette, and Mirat with hostility—these are female lobbyists, the looks said, troublemakers who go about overstepping their bounds and stirring up trouble. When the car reached the first floor, the herd of men marched out, brushing past them and out the elevator. As they walked off, the women felt the looks of condescension on their backs, scornful comments floating after them that contained the words bitch and ball-breakers.

These were not the gentlemen they met in living rooms and sat next to at dinner tables, the polite men who opened doors, removed hats, and stood when a woman entered the room, brimming with deference. Something had changed drastically.

They had just encountered the strongest dose of misogyny they had ever experienced. The group agreed—it was not to be tolerated!

One quiet summer afternoon, as the neighborhood napped under a sun-drenched sky, Radley's friends arrived at her front door full of energy, arms piled with gifts. Trish and Bette scurried into the kitchen with brown bags of food, while Klara, Barbara and Mirat followed Radley down the stairs to the patio. The faint odor of honeysuckle rose from nearby bushes, and the muted tone of a trilling bird issued from the woods. Radley pushed open the table umbrella, sliding it up the pole until it shed a wide shadow, under which the women seated themselves in white wrought iron chairs.

Sitting between Klara and Bette, Radley gazed contentedly at the rich green yard sprawling beyond the patio, girded by a band of thick woods that blocked out the surrounding neighbors so that she could, in idle moments, remove her shirt and bra and lie on her back while the sun baked her skin. She liked having her friends around her, companions who had stood close during these last crazy months. Caught up in a national whirl of change, the women rallied, phoning and dropping in on each other, offering waves of support. Now, here they were seated around the glass patio table, celebrating Radley's thirty-eighth birthday.

As the circle of women seated themselves around the glass table, Radley was aware of an empty spot. Maureen had left the group to return to family and plunge into a political study group she had organized at her church. She still supported them in spirit, but pressing duties drew her back to home base. Radley proposed a toast in memory of their absent friend, and their uplifted tea glasses sparkled in the bright afternoon sun.

People were digging into the spinach dip, joking and exchanging stories when they heard a noise. Fanfare! Accompanied by a staccato run of booms on a pan, Trish strode from the house holding a covered platter high in front of her, followed by Bette carrying a tray of small plates and forks. "Radley, this is for you from all of us." Trish flashed a broad smile and everyone shifted in anticipation, grinning widely and exchanging glances. All eyes were on Radley.

"We've brought you the birthday cake to top all birthday cakes, to complete all dreams—custom made I'll have you know. A prize-winner, this!" Trish placed the platter on the table and swept off the cover. There, in full chocolate glory, was a devil's food cake in the shape of male genitals. At the surprise on Radley's face, everyone laughed. "A penis cake," she cried, overcome with surprise and laughing with them. The elongated cake in front of her was resplendent with chocolate icing carved into waves and covered with swirls of tiny candles. It represented a symbol, Klara explained, of sexual freedom, the breakdown of inflexible rules, the liberation from female coyness.

"Well, this is a first," Radley said, thrilled at the daring of the object staring at her from the plate. "You all are wonderful!" She pressed her hands against her stomach, laughing helplessly.

"We wanted to present you with something different." Trish turned the platter around to show off all sides of the cake.

"Where on earth did you find it?" Radley asked.

"Well!" Trish rubbed her palms together. "You wouldn't believe the trouble Klara and I had. The first bakery didn't understand, didn't seem to know the meaning of the word penis, the clerks just shook their shoulders and scooted off to the back room for the manager, who acted as if we were asking them to implant a bomb. 'Not on our style list,' he said in a voice like ice. I asked him if he ever made boob cakes, and he looked evasive—I know the answer was yes!"

Her listeners erupted in hoots of laughter. "It became clear that the men did not like to talk of male parts. At the next three bakeries, everyone acted insulted, wanted to know what we wanted the cake for, said they didn't have a penis pan, offered a wide variety of animal shapes that would do just as well. 'We could fix you up a nice duck.'" Mirat and Bette sank into their chairs, choking with glee and holding on to their throats. "Why were nice girls like us being so dirty? It was not in their repertoire and that was that."

They all agreed, between bouts of laughter, that this exhibited the double standard: naked women jumping out of cakes, fine, but men's parts so much as mentioned, *verboten*.

"So," Radley asked, "how did you finally obtain the cake?"

"The seventh shop wanted the business and was able to see the humor of it. The baker, a tall man with sideburns and a pony-tail, who assured us he could improvise with pan shapes and make it work, no problem," Trish said.

The cake stood big as life in front of them, emitting the delectable odor of rich chocolate. "Don't you think the balls are too large in comparison to the penis?" Mirat asked Barbara.

"How can I tell? I have nothing to compare it with. I've never seen Ralph naked," Barbara said.

"Radley," Trish held out a silver cake knife, "to you the honors. Time to dig in." At the ironical look on Radley's face as she poised the knife, more laughter. By now, the women had fallen into uncontrollable spasms of giggles, and the slightest remark sent them into more gales. It had been a long time, Radley realized, since she'd had so much fun. It felt good to laugh, to let go and give in to the explosion of play.

"Come on," Klara urged. "Let's eat."

"All right, Klara, do you want a shaft or a ball?" Radley clutched the knife and with a sweep of her hand cut off the tip of the penis and edged it onto a plate. "Who wants this choice piece?"

Just then Wolf ambled up and rested his nose on the edge of the umbrella table, tail wagging and a pleading look on his face.

"Give it to the dog!"

"He's not supposed to have sweets."

"He's a retriever, I'll bet he'd like one of the balls."

"Just this once." Radley lowered the plate to the ground and the dog snatched the piece, trotted off to the grass and lay down next to a bush, licking cake crumbs from his muzzle.

"Who's next?"

CHAPTER 27

Radley parked on the sidewalk in front of a dark brick building. Letting herself in the main entry, she traipsed up the narrow stairs to the third floor, turned down the hallway and inserted a key in the door to apartment #8. The room was sparsely furnished with a single bed, a hand-assembled chest-of-drawers, a leggy chrome kitchen table, and a faded arm chair. A long folding table stretched along one wall, where a large ream of photographic paper was set next to an enlarger, several shallow developing trays, bottles of chemical solutions, and other darkroom equipment. Boxes containing a few changes of clothes, pots and pans scrounged from the local Goodwill, and books and other reading material were lined next to the bed.

Still clutching the key, she looked around. It was only her second weekend here, and she could hardly believe that she was in sole possession of her own studio. It had been years since she'd experienced alone space, without the fluttering of an entire household surrounding her. The air hung stale; she tugged at the sash window and was finally able to lift it open. Chips of paint and dried dirt were scattered along the window base. It was not *House Beautiful*, but she'd had enough *House Beautiful*. She thrilled at the plainness of the room that would not have to be tended or beautified; here she could think, expand, work. Ever since she'd learned to develop negatives for a high school science project and held a job in a local camera shop, photography had become a hobby, and she carried her 35mm Leica with her everywhere. Now at last—her own darkroom!

She'd attempted to stamp the room with her signature. A colorful East Indian throw blanket covered the steel-framed bed, an Otto Heino ceramic bowl sat on the counter, filled with fruit. On one wall she had attached an oversized poster obtained at a University of Minnesota feminist rally depicting a young woman in a checkered apron, feet planted firmly apart, arms outstretched and each hand holding one half of a broken broom. The words **FUCK HOUSEWORK** blazed across the top in large red letters.

This word, considered the most obnoxious, never-to-be-uttered word in the English language, said it all: they were about serious business, radical business. Its blatant note of defiance declared that she and her friends were not to be taken lightly, despite those who claimed such language demoralized the civilized social order. She watched with amuse-ment as comedian George Carlin proclaimed over the airways The Seven Words You Can Never Say on Television, outdated prissiness, the words rendered more shocking by their ban. As a feminist, the so-called f-word represented defiance, a break-through, loud and clear—let the moralists take note.

She was alone at the studio, but she didn't feel lonely, not as she had at the Reston house. This was peaceful, sufficient. A place to spend occasional weekends and work. To take stock, figure things out, get herself on a track that would make sense of her life. She needed something, but what? Sometimes she missed her Manhattan work life, going into an office every day, exchanging ideas with co-workers. Her former job writing greeting-card jingles for Cowles & Crane hadn't been ideal at first— called for no real talent, just an ear for quick rhyme— but she threw herself into her work. Her colleagues were ambitious young people, braving the competition of the big city, full of ideas and vitality. Along with two other college graduates she created rhymes that attempted to express sentiments of sympathy and love in a humorous vein. They tried to outdo each other in offbeat jingles, the more outlandish the better.

There was a young gal from Bastille
She'd broken her bones at the wheel,
The medicine was gross
But she swallowed each dose
And soon saw her jagged bones heal.

After several years on the bunny team, she was promoted to group leader and was sent to scour the country, camera in hand, gathering ideas for jingles and artwork. At the time she had complained about the meager verses and endless repetition, but now, looking back . . . now she viewed things in a new perspective.

She had discovered the studio by pure luck one afternoon when she and Klara were posting announcements for NARAL (National Association for the Repeal of Abortion Laws). Wanting to expand beyond the suburban areas, they drove into an older neighborhood near downtown Minneapolis. Klara maneuvered her Olds past a corner grocery store, a dry-cleaners shop window that announced ONE DAY SERVICE, and a barber shop displaying a large red and white ad for Burma Shave that read NO LADY LIKES TO SNUGGLE OR DINE ACCOMPANIED BY A PORCUPINE. Rounding a corner, she noticed a sign in the window of a brick apartment building—one of many strung together down the block—STUDIO FOR RENT. The apartment turned out to be small, cheap, and available. Radley signed a six-month lease.

Shane could not understand why she wanted to leave a perfectly nice home to go sit in a bare room in the slums—as he called it—but watched her go with resignation. Let her get out of the house once in a while, give the itch burning in her system a chance to simmer down. Maybe she wouldn't be so grumpy, so short with the children. She had already ceased her constant complaining and no longer sought his advice. He was afraid she was giving up. Maybe a change would help. If only she would settle down and work at managing the family, like other wives. When she walked out the front door, suitcase in hand, the color drained from his face. "It's only for one night every other weekend, Shane." And she was gone.

A few hours later, she lay on the skinny bed in the studio reading Eugene McCarthy's *The Limits of Power: America's Role in the World*. It was one of those melancholy evenings when the sun released its hold on the sidewalks and buildings and sank into the horizon, sucking waves of pinkish-orange across the sky. From outside the window she could hear the occasional rev of a motorcycle, the yip of an excited dog and the clatter of passing voices. Inside, the studio was quiet except for the gurgle of water pipes rumbling in one corner of the room. No television, no phone, not even a radio. That afternoon she had walked downtown and stocked up on dark-room supplies; tomorrow she would get busy and develop her latest rolls of film, street scenes of the South Nicollet neighborhood.

After reading an hour, she lowered *The Limits of Power* onto her lap and stared out the narrow window at the oak branch sweeping across the wall of the brick building next door. She shifted her gaze around the bare room. How liberating it felt! The possession of her own space with the freedom to move, go, stay, to follow her inner calling, was exhilarating. Here she could be her best herself, not a floundering mother but a competent functioning person.

Then a cry burst outside the room, of an angry bird or maybe a child behind the window across the way. She was reminded of the last sound she heard as she left the house that morning, the voice of Megan, her face pressed against her bedroom window screen as she watched Radley back the car out of the garage, back seat stuffed with goods for the studio. Mommy, don't go, please Mommy. The words came back her, plaintive, she couldn't get them out of her head. *Maybe she wasn't such a wash after all at this motherhood thing, maybe Megan and Larry needed whatever she had to offer—paltry as it might be—more than she knew.* If only she could hang on, could suffer the trials of the early years, they would be grown in no time at all. They were energetic, happy, eager to learn. She would get the hang of it, would learn to be flexible and rebound, and soon enough they would outgrow the difficult years and turn into people who could be reasoned with, confided in. The next instant—the thought resonated in the pit of her stomach—she realized that this was the family she longed for, had always longed for, ever since that day when she was 12 and had vowed to herself that someday she would have a family of her own, one that worked. It seemed she had always wanted this. Her beautiful children—they would learn from life, and she could learn to take whatever they served up. She felt her heart expand as she realized how much she wanted this.

She craved freedom. She loved her family more than life. Maybe here in this woman-cave some miraculous solution would reveal itself.

Meanwhile, the evening loomed ahead. She had envisioned the weekend as alone time, but maybe she'd call Klara after all, just this once. Impossible to relax with the sounds of life sounding high notes just outside the window. Then she remembered that Klara was home fixing beans and burgers for John's Boy Scout troop. Oh well. Might as well take it easy.

Then it hit her. Now was her chance. A night on the town by herself, something she'd wanted to do ever since the evening she'd spent with Bette and Klara discussing Germaine Greer's *The Female Eunuch* at Leland's Roadhouse. Tossing her book on the night stand, she got up and cooked a hamburger on the miniature stove, topped it with beef tomatoes, cheese, simmered onions and ketchup, pulled a Pepsi from the fridge and settled on the sway-back chair next to the kitchen table. Was it really a good idea to go out? A little reading, a night of peaceful sleep to ready her to plunge into work tomorrow, would be preferable.

No, peaceful sleep was not in her blood tonight. At nine o'clock she slipped on a pair of jeans, pulled a wool sweater over her light blue silk blouse and strolled six blocks down Nicollet Avenue to a bar she'd passed several times earlier. A sign in orange and green lights stating

CURLEY'S CAROUSEL hung under the second story eave, and in the window tin block signs advertised Bud and Coors beer. Pulling open the door, she stepped inside.

Immediately she was met by the sound of voices and human bustling. She moved past a row of stools at the bar lined with business men in black trench coats, workers wearing newsboy caps, and balding guys in drooping leather jackets. Male heads turned in unison to look at her curiously, trying to guess her mission. She felt invigorated by the high-pitched chatter, the warm movement of bodies, the moaning of the music—it had been so long, felt so foreign to be out, away from the usual routine. It reminded her of the New York night life during her single days, something she'd long left behind.

Approaching the next room, she heard the loud babble of voices and detected the scent of bitter lime and tobacco. The room was jammed with people, chairs were full, and on one side, under a string of signs advertising car racing events and bubbling soft drinks, a four-piece band seated on a miniature stage played *Hound Dog,* a low horn sounding the melody. She located a vacant corner table and slid into a curve-backed wooden chair. At the next table, two young couples clutched tall mugs of tap beer. Most people in the room wore jeans and collared shirts, the styles of males and females differed very little these days, Radley noted. Among these young people, she saw no sign of the sculpted hairdos, tight sweaters and heavy makeup of the early sixties. There was definitely change in the air, a trend toward the natural look consistent with an emerging emphasis on sexual equality. Impulsively, she pulled off her wedding rings and stuffed them deep into her jeans pocket—better to blend in with the exuberance of the youthful crowd.

A waiter carrying a tray jammed with glasses appeared at her shoulder and Radley ordered a Budweiser. At first she felt conspicuous at a table alone, but no one seemed to notice. Sipping her beer, she watched the people around her, young faces tilted and laughing, abandoned to the moment. Two boys, cigarettes dangling from their mouths, squeezed through the curtain of smoke, side-stepping around tables, and headed in her direction. They scanned the room with scuffing, hail-fellow-well-met expressions—the type of university students who skipped classes and didn't bother with homework until the night before the exam, she guessed. To her surprise they stopped at her table. No seats. Could they sit down? When she nodded, the boys, one blonde in a checkered shirt open carelessly at the throat and the other wearing horn-rimmed glasses and a black turtleneck sweater, pulled up two chairs and drew close. One tossed a Minnesota Gophers sweat shirt on the empty chair next to him.

The band started another song, making it impossible to talk without shouting. The boy in a black turtleneck held out his hand. "I'm Gus," he yelled. "And this is Charlie here." Charlie nodded and grinned.

"Drink?" Gus mouthed, nodding at Radley's empty glass.

"Sure. Vodka Gimlet."

Gus nodded and set out for the bar.

Radley and the boy in the checkered shirt listened to the band and blew circles of smoke into the dense air. "Nice band," he shouted over the din, smashing his cigarette butt in the ashtray and pulling another from a squashed pack in his shirt pocket. "Hey, listen to this one. They're playing *Knock Three Times*. You like it?" he asked.

Before she could answer, Gus returned balancing three drinks and resumed his seat.

"Oh, yes," she replied, straining to hear the melody through the clogging din of voices. It was unfamiliar, she was not up on the latest favorites. She seemed to be sitting in the midst of another, louder generation. At the thought, she took a deep swallow of her gimlet. Her university days had become dim, part of a distant past. For the first time, she felt old—at thirty-eight! Well, she was still full of energy. She wasn't sure about these boys, but at least they had shown up—something of an adventure in itself.

"Whatever happened to "*How Much is That Doggie in the Window?*" she asked, recalling the top Hit Parade favorites from the fifties.

The boys looked at her as if she'd said her favorite drink was Ovaltine. "You don't hear that much anymore," the blonde one said.

Gus laughed. "It's okay. My mother likes it."

They wanted to know what high school she'd graduated from. Wow! No one had asked her that for a hundred years. The dim light must be deceiving—high school! "South High," she said quickly. They nodded and turned back to their drinks without asking what year, to her relief.

"I live over on 19th Street. I'm just a poor student," she went on. The lies slid out like water from a spring, without allowing her mind to interfere. She explained that she was saving her pennies to finish an advanced degree in marketing. Luckily their curiosity extended no further. She hadn't intended to lie, but the stark awareness of how much older she was from these boys, from most of the people in the bar, chilled her. This must be a University hangout. So much the better. No one would care who she was or why she was there.

"So, what are you doing here?" Charlie asked.

"Well, ah, I just moved nearby and had nothing to do, so thought I'd check out the neighborhood. I like trying things on my own."

As they regarded her, she interpreted their expressions: here was a girl with a mind of her own. They nodded; they could accept that.

As the night went on, the conversation, amid the din, included how far the boys had to walk to class from their apartment in Dinkytown; the second-hand De Soto Gus had just bought for a song, complete with new tires; the latest Twins game; and how you could buy cut-rate cigarettes at Luigi's on Washington Avenue if you purchased four drinks.

Emptying the last of her drink, Radley relaxed, enjoying the sensation that she was in a time warp, transported to another era. Even if the noise beat against her head and the dense smoke clogged her nostrils.

Charlie fetched another round of drinks. The cacophony of instruments and voices in the room grew more intense, and they leaned back in their chairs and watched the dancers. Charlie turned to Radley and when she nodded led her to the dance floor. After a fast number, the band launched into Presley's *Love Me Tender.* As the guitar vibrated sweet notes across the room, Charlie pulled her close. She could feel his breath along her ear, his cheek barely touching hers, the warmth of his chest brushing against her sweater. She felt her pulse quicken, felt his arms tuck across her back, slip down to her waist. She intended to pull away but didn't. A familiar thrill she had almost forgotten, a sense of slow expectation, subtly promising, fluttered in her chest. When the music stopped, Gus moved in to take his place for a fast one. His dancing was assured, expansive, and they soon lost themselves in the beat.

"You're good," he exclaimed. Her body fell into the swing rhythm, directed by his improvised twists, and it came back to her, the dancing she had adored so much all those years ago in another life.

The crowd became boisterous, the room smokier. Chairs scraped, voices yelled over each other, and men helped their dates weave through the tables to the dance floor for a last spin before the bar closed. Back at the table, the two boys looked at Radley in silence. They appeared to be assessing what she was up to.

"So why are you here alone?" Gus asked without warning.

She looked back at him steadily, barely able to think, the pulse of the music echoing through her head. "Why not? It was a last-minute impulse. Everyone else is busy on a Saturday night."

Charlie reached in front of her to stub out his cigarette in the pewter ashtray, and she noticed the black bold-faced Bulova watch on his wrist, the thin blonde hairs flowing over his bronzed arm.

"I also wanted to see what it would be like to go to a place like this alone, as a single woman. To spend an idle evening out, which men do all the time."

The boys exchanged glances. "Are you a feminist?" Gus asked, tilting his head to look at her.

Something warned her to be careful. The word feminist had divergent connotations—you could be denounced as a radical bra-burner or praised as a fighter for God-given civil rights.

"Yes," she said. She was not a Judas, would not repudiate the cause. She drew her coat over her arm and stood up. "Time for me to leave," she said. "I enjoyed your company, guys. Thanks for the drinks." The boys had turned down her offer to pay, clearly intending to perform their role as males. She was not in the mood to argue the fine points of equality.

Smiling, she pushed in her chair and slipping through the crowd, edged through the swinging doors and out to the sidewalk. Charlie and Gus scurried after her. The three of them stood on the sidewalk, circled in the glare of flickering orange and green light from the window.

"Say, Radley." She had revealed her name, but only the first. "Do you want to come home with us?" Charlie asked softly. He eyed her expectantly, head slightly bowed, a tuft of blonde hair hanging over his forehead.

The idea of an adventure was appealing. It was so far out of her usual routine it staggered her mind. She knew what she was doing—she wasn't afraid of these two snappy students. Besides, looking at Charlie leaning on one leg, sleeves pushed up carelessly, she felt drawn, almost hypnotically, imagined his arms slipping around her waist, his breath...

Seeing her hesitate, Gus grinned. He'd been the outgoing one all evening, and now he grabbed her arm and moved her into the shadow of the building. His hair, disheveled from the dancing, rose in spiked tufts behind his ears. As he removed his glasses and pulled out a white handkerchief to wipe the lens, his face took on a serious look.

"You like us, don't you?" he asked, releasing his breath on the lens.

"Well, yes," she replied.

He paused, slipped the glasses back on. "Look, my friend Charlie is in the dumps because his girlfriend left him. High and dry. It's been several weeks and he's trying to get over her. I could hardly get him to go out tonight. What do you say? He likes you. He thinks you're pretty."

Radley scrutinized his face. The expectations were clear. Charlie wanted some cheering up. This was taking a strange turn.

"He's great in bed. Girls have told me. Why don't you—well, could you come to our apartment and take care of him. It's been a long time. I know he wants you, he told me so. He's shy because he's been hurt. You understand."

Go to bed with Charlie! He was cute, with his youthful blond looks and sensual blue eyes. She looked over at him studying his nails in his open jacket, tall, male, warm. For some time the thrill of sex with Shane had dimmed. She wondered if it had been their only form of intimacy.

She looked up. Gus waited patiently, head cocked. She slid her hand down and felt the bump where her wedding ring lay tucked at the bottom of her jeans pocket. For a brief evening she passed as single. The way was open. The opportunity was there for the grasping.

Gus looked at her as if she were weighing the opportunity of a lifetime that she would forever regret missing. Charlie stood nearby on the curb, hands thrust deep into his pants pockets. People were exiting the bar in two and threes, pulling the collars of their coats tight against the night air. She looked from one to the other of her companions. Because of her politics they assumed she was a free-for-all. A vision flashed in her mind of the two boys driving her to Dinkytown and ushering her into a dingy apartment where one would wait in one room while she serviced the other in the next. All at once these newfound companions seemed to belong to another era, another milieu. Her senses froze as if shot with ice water, and she felt the magic of the evening deflate, disappearing like smoke into the night air.

She clutched her shoulder bag strap and pulled it high on her shoulder. The scheme filled her with disgust. "I can't," she said with a take-charge air. "My car's right around the corner. Goodbye." She tightened her scarf around her neck. "Try one of the dorms."

Without looking at them, she spun and walked towards her apartment. She'd gone to the brink, almost fallen off the edge. She couldn't blame them. A rare woman alone, single, free, displaying independence and freedom over drink after drink. What had she been doing? She was crazy. But so were the two boys, making assumptions about her. So was Reston, expecting her to conform like a round peg in a square hole. So was the entire world.

As she reached the apartment building and made her way up the bumpy brick pathway, she felt a disturbing sense of isolation. Not a soul was about. Most of the windows in her building were dark. Where was everyone? An overhead bulb in the entrance hall eked out a thin grayish light that had earlier looked charmingly bohemian but now looked merely grubby, almost ominous, like a warning light in a storm. She climbed the stairs, conscious of the shadows and the faint smell of oil and old garbage coming from the hallways. When she reached her apartment door, she saw a narrow brown envelope protruding from the crack. No one in the building knew she was there except the superintendent. None of the other doors had an envelope stuck to it, so it couldn't be an advertisement.

Pulling out the envelope, she unlocked the door and switched on a lamp. The cheap Woolworth clock on the wall above the stove showed one-thirty.

It was a Western Union message. She whipped open the yellow sheet of paper and stared at the words strung in two lines across the page. For some minutes the words didn't sink in. Then, shaking her head and refo-cusing her vision, she read it again.

RADLEY GALLAGHER STOP LARRY IN SERIOUS ACCIDENT STOP COME IMMEDIATELY TO METHODIST HOSPITAL DEEPHAVEN 4100 GERARD STREET STOP SHANE

CHAPTER 28

Radley stared out the front windshield in a daze. Slowly edging around the familiar turns, she turned onto Reston Way and pulled into their driveway. Purple streams from the sinking sun cast a violet veil over the yard. The house had an abandoned look, as if the inhabitants had long left for distant parts. Traipsing from the garage and up the back stairs, her movements awakened the house, the click of her heels, the soft brush of her slacks, even her breath seemed to vibrate through the vacant, dusty rooms.

Passing the living room, she became aware of the beautifully coordinated décor created so assiduously over the years: the gold and purple gleam of the fleur-de-lis wallpaper; the rich carved oak of the cabinets; the brilliant brass knobs on the doors; the peacock-patterned matching chairs; the bright rose marble table lamp. Fabricated beauty, faded beauty, now filtered behind a dusty haze of neglect. Useless, she thought, without the clamor of family activities to bring it to life.

She reached the bedroom and lowered herself to the edge of the bed, trying to shake off the catatonic state she'd been in since she sat by Larry's bedside gazing at his immobile face on the pillow. Her son hadn't moved since the accident. He lay in a coma, tubes and catheters attached to his body, gauze coiled around his head, sucking shallow breaths from a machine. The medics told them that he was fortunate to be alive, considering his injuries. They didn't know if he would survive.

As she sat on her bed, she imagined the accident as Hugh Horton had described it, flashed on Larry as he must have floundered out in the boat, caught mercilessly in the heaves of the storm, flying into the rocks, lying crushed and bleeding under the hull. The thought of him withering in pain make her nauseous.

Her mind hovered in a nether-nether zone where all she could do was exist—and wait. The air around her had gone dormant. She had the sinking feeling that normal life would never exist again.

She longed to be back at the hospital where she and Shane had virtually lived for the past two weeks, sleeping in a hospital guest room on the twelfth floor. She'd returned to the house to check on things and pick up some fresh clothes. One night's rest, that's all she'd stay for—jump into bed, let darkness enclose her, and soon she'd be back at Larry's bedside.

The next morning Radley pulled a batch of laundry from the Maytag, slapped cold water on her face, and drove back to the hospital. Larry lay on his back, head sunk in the pillow. She stationed herself in the cushioned chair next to his bed, book on her lap, and watched Larry's chest move in and out under the covers, clinging to the fact that he was alive. She tried to get used to the sight of his body buried among the mass of ventilators, urinary catheters, infusion pumps, monitoring equipment, and pulse oximeter machines connected by a web of sensors and tubes that seemed to be devouring him with octopus arms. He had not opened his eyes since the accident.

It was possible he never would.

There had been much speculation on what exactly had happened the night of the accident. Painstakingly, the pieces were fit together from the three witnesses. Hugh Horton described how he had discovered Larry's body. His daughter Dean claimed she saw Larry from her bedroom window heading towards the lake, tossing a rubber ball in the air, and curious, decided to follow him. Evidently Larry, succumbing to his passion for boats, went down to the beach where Hugh had been tethering his runabout for the past several days. Since there was no dock, Hugh secured the boat to a steel post on one side of the landing. No doubt oblivious of the approaching mounds of black clouds, Larry launched the runabout—the key must have been left in an obvious location—and headed into open water. As Dean watched, the gusts from the advancing storm grew threatening, and she saw him bring the boat about and head towards shore. A powerful blast of wind and a ferocious downpour caught the boat in its grip and threw it against the chopping waves. Moments later, it crashed into a mound of giant rocks piled against the shore. Upon later inspection, the deep gashes along the hull and the twisted state of the engine propellers revealed the boat had taken a heavy beating.

Hugh, arriving to pull his runabout up on shore, discovered Larry pinned by the gunwale of the overturned boat. His head was crunched into the sand, only his nose and chin protruding from the water. Something metal seemed to be lodged in his skull and blood had dripped down his face and soaked into the neckband of his T-shirt.

Larry's obsession with boats was well known. He clamored to take the wheel of every boat he'd ever been on, convinced that he could handle anything that floated. The reconstruction of the event made perfect sense.

Since then, Radley had stayed by Larry's bed, waiting anxiously for the hospital technicians to complete the tests and analyses. Finally, Dr. Soderberg called them into his office for a conclusive report.

"We base our conclusions on extensive testing and a complete review of Larry's medical state. Understand, it is impossible to predict the progress of a coma. The prognosis for Larry is poor. The steel blade pierced a part of his brain that could regenerate, under the right conditions, but in your son's case it is not happening. For all intents and purposes, he is mentally dead. Chances that he will recover are next to zero. There is no telling how long the coma will continue. His bodily functioning is quite good so that soon he can exist on his own without artificial support, and family home care should be sufficient.

"But that's the most we can expect. Of course, every case is unique and one can always hope for a miracle. I'm sorry, that's all I can offer."

It was over. It was over. It was over. Their son, whipped from their lives—one storm, a crash, and he was gone, a placeholder in a hospital bed, fate uncertain.

Shane, pale, reached out and put his hand on Radley's. She looked at him in surprise, and they walked slowly down the hallway towards Larry's room without speaking. What was there to say? Nothing would change the fact that they had lost their son. Yet he lived, and as long as he was alive they saw a thin ray of hope, irrational, but a life raft they clung to desperately. The worst fate imaginable, they had believed, would be that Larry would die. Now they had received the gift that their son would live—but the gift proved false, it wasn't really Larry, he was no more than a shell. It almost seemed to Radley that death would be better, a definitive end.

The soft gurgling of machines surrounded Larry's bed like a breathing bevy of animals, the one sign of life in the aura of his existence. They gazed at his inert form as if at a specter, awed at the colossal power that ruled over people's lives. It was Larry's form, but the Larry they knew, with his affectionate burst of smiles, his keen curiosity, wasn't there. Nothing. Nothing left. They could hardly bear to look at the pale face pretending to be Larry, yet couldn't break away, staring at his pallid skin, his still limbs, his remains.

Radley's mother arrived at the hospital the next day to say good-bye to her adored grandson, arms overflowing with daffodils and red roses. Char gazed soberly at his form lying on the hospital bed, hooked up to a spaghetti web of hanging tubes and catheters, and the colored charts lining the counters. Radley understood when Char refused to accept that Larry would not regain consciousness. "There's always hope. The experts will come up with something," Char said wistfully.

"We have some thinking to do, Mom," Radley told her. "Dr. Soderberg informs us that there is no hope. How long can we allow him to languish under 24-hour care with no end in sight? Months, years? It's an overwhelming decision. Shane agrees with the general medical standard that life is to be maintained at any cost. I believe that when all hope is lost there is no point in prolonging a life that is not of this world."

There was nothing more to be done. Radley packed up Larry's toys and clothes, leaving the family photo on the bedside table should he by some miracle wake up. They fell back into their usual routine, at least on the surface, with Shane catching up on assignments at work and Megan back in school full-time. Radley wandered the house, carrying laundry baskets, scrubbing the shelves in the pantry, going over the bookshelves with a feather duster, calling the plumber to silence a gurgling toilet. While awaiting the physicians' verdict, Radley and Shane had worked together arranging shifts at the hospital and visiting Megan at the grandparent's house. Now, life must continue, and Radley fell into her duties like a drum major marching in rhythm. After all, Larry had not died, and everyone kept repeating that where there was life there was hope. Dreamers, they didn't understand the debilitating effect of ambiguity.

Aside from regular visits to the hospital, life went on, but it wasn't the same, the bustling had been replaced with a dull resignation. Her treasured artwork had lost its luster, the bird calls that greeted her each morning drifted by dry and irrelevant, and conversations droned on and on. She stayed closeted at home, sitting for hours on the porch as the sun lowered behind the bushes, staring into space, caught up in a sense of loss and a crushing weight of emptiness. Larry's removal from their life—which closed around her, even as his body remained as an appalling reminder—cast a shadow on everything she did. The ache in her stomach drove her to his room, and she clutched his giraffe pajamas, burying her nose in them to catch his lingering scent. At the women's group meetings, the lively discussions swirled around her like ghosts from another era. Shane, she noticed, kept his feelings to himself, even more distant as he went about the usual routines with a drawn face. Once he slipped his arm around her in a hug, but she saw his eyes redden and he withdrew back into his paper.

The days inched on, one after the other. Eventually, the knowledge that Larry would not regain consciousness settled into place. The book on grieving, which Radley read twice, described the astounding ability of the human spirit to adapt to the unacceptable, and slowly Radley felt a sense of normalcy returning to the daily activities.

One morning, sitting on the wicker settee with a mug of coffee watching the shaft of early sunlight move up the lawn towards the house, she felt a sudden lurch in her stomach, and a trickle of anger spread through her veins, sneaky, slippery like a snake inching for its game. The words of poet Dylan Thomas flashed in her mind: *Rage rage against the dying of the light*!

Gradually, a fog lifted and her mind moved into active mode. Thoughts of reality began to surface, reminding her that she had decisions to make, a household to uphold for her daughter and husband, a life to live. She took Megan and her girlfriend ice skating, and invited Shane's buddy from work over for dinner. For the first time since the accident, she called Klara and Bette and met them for lunch at Hanna's Corner.

One evening, Radley stood by the stove, waiting for the spaghetti water to heat. Shane would be home soon. Pulling the last cigarette from a Marlborough pack, she lit it, glancing idly at the boxed print on the back. Since cancer warnings were now printed on all packs, everyone was thinking of quitting but no one was actually doing it.

She took deep drags of the cigarette. It was time to pull herself together, to think. They couldn't go on like this. It had been five months since Larry's accident. She had to discover how she felt about Shane. His clamped silences irritated her, she couldn't get past them. Affection between them was non-existent. She recalled with wistfulness her parents' warm kisses when her dad entered the house after work, the endearing nick-names, the snuggling on the couch, the exchange of laughs. Shane had retreated behind a defensive wall, they barely communicated. His adamant stance against divorce for any reason—a sin against God—allowed no out. She was certain his devotion had nothing to do with love—without her, the kids, the house, everything would fall apart. She filled a role, no more.

Watching the steam drift out of the boiling pan, she felt a pang of longing. When Shane flew to Mexico for Shelby Allied during the summer of 1970, it was the first time they had been apart. It surprised her how strange the house had seemed without him, some vital presence had been missing. When she'd seen the mail truck pull to a stop in front, she dashed outside and down the steps. Pulling out a pile of mail from the box, she thumbed quickly through an electric bill, an advertisement for crabgrass fungicide, a notice for an upcoming DFL caucus, a National Geographic magazine, and tucked at the bottom a letter from Shane.

Quickly she tore it open and drew out a light blue sheet with *Hotel Plaza Reforma* embossed on the top.

Dear Radley,

    I arrived safely. The hotel is close to the plant and I'm picked up every day by a co-worker. I don't know how long I'll be here. I hope Megan and Larry are fine. Miss you all.

    Sincerely yours, Shane

She dropped down on the concrete step, holding the letter in one hand. Exactly what she'd anticipated—a dry letter with nobody in it. She shouldn't be disappointed. This was Shane, the Shane she knew, Shane who would never change. She read the letter again, searching for something behind the barren text. The words floated off the page, fluttered in front of her eyes. Why couldn't she cease expecting something from him? Why couldn't she give up the struggle and let go?

She'd have to look elsewhere to have her passion kindled, to feel embraced, to feel acknowledged as a person. Maybe her women friends provided a lifeline, one that she ought to take.

Retracing her steps to the house, she threw out the letter and with it her disappointment. She tried not to think of it, another rift in her life. Since Larry's accident, there were more important issues to face, and now the fact of Larry's virtually brain-dead state and the need to come to terms with a life without him outweighed all concerns.

As she stood at the stove musing and poking spaghetti noodles into a pan of hot water with a prong, Shane walked in, followed by Megan. Laying the afternoon paper on the kitchen table, he sat down and pulled Megan on his lap.

Since Larry's tragedy, Shane had maintained a distant air. She hardly dared approach him, knowing his response would wave her away. She wondered if he blamed himself for allowing Larry to go missing under his watch the night of the accident. Or, also possible, if he blamed her for going off to her own apartment and not being home at the time. Not that he'd ever said anything. *She should have been home caring for the children, not off on some ego trip of her own*. Nor had she mentioned it. They grieved silently, each in their separate corner. Grief was a private thing, what was there to say?

The water was boiling loudly on the stove, and she turned down the heat and looked over at Shane. Megan, curled against his chest, lifted her blue eyes to her mother.

"Tired, sweetie?" Radley asked. Megan smiled and closed her eyes. Shane tightened his arm around Megan's back.

"How was your day?" Radley asked him. The usual question he never knew how to answer. If he said "Same as yesterday," she would get irritated, would stand at the counter chopping onions faster and faster. "Surely you can think of *something*," she would say. 'It doesn't have to hit the headlines."

She didn't understand, nothing happened; every day was the same. He had to make up a story. The effort exhausted him. "Went pretty well," he began, trying to think. "Jerry and I sat at the same table at lunch today."

"What did you have to eat?"

"Chipped beef, peas, peach salad, coffee." Chop, chop, chop, followed by the sound of diced onion sizzling in the iron skillet. "And I reviewed the ledgers to ensure tax compliance for the upcoming audit. Mostly it was crunching the numbers as usual."

Other couples had it, she'd seen it on screens, at performances, in homes of friends, on quiet park streets, couples embracing or gazing at each other across a table, couples radiating ideas and curiosity, gestures of affection. Other marriages had that. Why couldn't hers?

Holding a head of dripping lettuce leaves under the faucet, she felt lost. Everywhere women were forsaking the marriage bond, striking out on their own. Bette was in the process of divorce; Barbara was planning to move into her own place and had had taken a job selling ads for local newspapers. She had also signed up for the Program in Human Sexuality at the University, where women stripped and used a speculum to explore and appreciate their bodies. Society was changing. Women no longer had to make do, endure the great sacrifice, no longer did they need a man to bring up a family.

She shut off the water, watched a single drop linger at the edge of the faucet then drop into the drain hole and disappear. She wrapped the head of lettuce in a dish towel, patting it dry with mechanical motions. Her heart wasn't in it. Since Larry's diagnosis he had lain inert on his hospital bed, effectively remove from their lives. Something had dried up in her, as if the loss had robbed her of feelings and she had nothing left to give. The air in the house had become dry, Shane's figure moved like a specter in the background. Something in the house was not right.

The implication that her marriage was over stared her in the face.

Still, giving up without a struggle was not an option. She had decided that morning, brushing Megan's silky hair in the bedroom, that she had to make an effort on her side. Longing wasn't enough.

"I'm hungry," Megan peeped up.

"Just another ten minutes," Radley said.

"You and I will wait right here," Shane said, ruffling her bangs. "We're a team, you and I." With a giggle, Megan threw her arms around her dad and squeezed hard until her muscles bulged. "Don't do me in. I'm the only dad you've got," Shane groaned.

Megan buried her head in his chest, then without warning she hopped to the floor and darted from the room, scooping up a slice of apple from the counter, blue overalls billowing out behind her. Her little feet clicked down the hallway.

Watching Megan run off, Shane felt bereft, sitting stiff and empty-lapped as if the tide had suddenly retreated, carrying everything on the sand with it.

A bluebird flapped against the pane, senselessly beating its wings back and forth. Shane smiled. He loved to watch the antics of the birds, their quick movements, the lightness of their wings, the way they cocked their heads. During the lunch hour, he often wandered down to the pond behind Shelby Allied Foods headquarters and tossed bread chunks to the ducks. He enjoyed working at Shelby Allied. His duties required just enough challenge to keep him on his toes. Mr. Henderson had reassured him more than once that he was valued by the company. "You do good work. Your analytical skills are brilliant." Shane was pleased.

No, he had no complaints on the job front. But his home—nothing stayed the same. His family had shrunk, just the three of them now. Change unnerved him. He would find solace in the family that remained, those who were everything to him, who made up his life.

Now he felt tired. Since Larry's prognosis, something in him had shrunk. Grief seemed to have turned Radley inward and she remained distant, lost in another world. He was not sure what she wanted or where she was headed. Now that she had taken her own studio, he felt a distance growing between them. He feared his world was crumbling.

We cannot judge God's plans for us, he thought, drawing himself up. He would give himself over to his faith, to a power stronger and more glo-rified than any one being's ability to comprehend. He was not in a position to make demands. He would rely on his Christian faith and the unknown intentions of God. It was what he could do.

He heard Radley at the sink pouring out the boiling spaghetti water, the click of the pan as she set it on the counter. Before he knew it, she was sitting down next to him. "What is it Shane? Why are you bent over?"

Shane raised his head. Her presence, the warmth of her, stirred something in him, drew him out of his head and a light flashed behind his eyes, as if a floodgate had opened and let lose a swell of sunlight. "We'll get through this," he told her. "I'll help. You're not on your own, you know." He wanted her to be happy, them all to be happy. He struggled to put his shaken feelings into words.

"I know it's hard . . ." she laid a hand on his sleeve.
He was reminded of the impulsive hugs and cheek rubs that once ac-companied her happy moods, moods that had faded with the years. He missed that.

"Things will change," she said gently.

He could do more. He wanted it with every fiber of his being. He would have to change.

He straightened up as Megan walked in wearing oversized polka-dot sun glasses and a yellow bandana tied under her chin. She was followed by Wolf, red bandana tied around his neck, ears alert as if ready for action. "Mommy!" Sidling up, Megan pressed against her mother's knees. "Wolf won't roll over when I tell him to," she moaned. "I'm bored."

"I'll play slap jack with you," Shane said. Radley gave him a surprised look.

"Okay!" Megan trotted to the next room to fetch a deck of cards from the top drawer of the buffet. She dealt out the cards slowly, one to her dad, one to herself, and straightened her pile neatly. Shane noticed that Megan was more at ease lately. Since he and Radley discovered that Larry would not recover and no longer spent every waking moment at his side. Megan had been thrown into the role of only child. Radley taught her to do the ironing just like a grown-up, took her shopping and let her select macaroni and cheese boxes and Spaghetti O's from the grocery shelves. She accompanied Shane when he drove Wolf to the vet's to get his distemper shot, pointing out the route. Wilson even took her to see the Minnesota Vikings play the Green Bay Packers, and she dragged her grandfather to the car, skipping. Shane knew she relished being center of the family, now that her parents were not distracted by what Megan called Larry's dumb tricks to always grab attention—a trouble-maker of a brother. But now she got all the portions, all the privi-leges, all the attention.

One afternoon Megan phoned from school. "Will you pick us up? I said I would stay and help clean up after the art fair. LeAnn stayed too. Can I bring her home with me? She's really nice." Radley pressed her lips in sat-isfaction and clasped her second hand around the receiver. It warmed her to see her daughter flourish; lately she had been taking the initiative, had suggested outings to her favorite amusements, sat calmly in a chair over a new activity book, and now she'd found a new friend. The hours of read-ing to her, recounting stories of her own childhood and the goofy things she'd done as she and Megan sat together on the porch with fresh lemon-ade—after school, when Megan walked in, lost, looking for something to do—were producing subtle changes. Megan would run up, face alight, to drive to the library for puppet story time or they would sit at the piano and sing *Playmates* or *You Are My Sunshine* together. At first Radley entered into these activities rather dutifully, seeking an outcome, but soon began to look forward to the time together and smiled with pride when Megan shyly performed one of the songs in front of her grandparents.

But Radley could tell Megan missed her brother. She admitted to missing what she termed her dippy brother's crazy tricks—like sneaking off to tie Wolf in the woods to see how long before his absence would be noticed—that had been such a lark. Radley imagined that her privileges had lost their novelty, and that Megan's claim to a toy didn't seem so special if Larry wasn't around to be envious.

"Dinner! Cards away, Shane. You too, little miss blue eyes."

Radley placed plates of piping hot spaghetti simmering with chicken Alfredo sauce in front of them, followed by glasses of milk, garlic bread soaked in melted butter, lettuce leaves topped with new green peas, cucumber slices, and bright red beefsteak tomatoes tumbled in colorful confusion. New red salt and pepper shakers and butter dish matched the plain vermillion dinner plates. In the center, a bud vase of iris added a touch of purple. The table glowed with color and the rising aroma of tomato sauce and garlic. Why the special occasion? Shane wanted to know. It's like Christmas! Megan cooed.

"What's special is that we're together, as a family, that's what's special," Radley said. "We've been a long time in limbo, balancing on a limb, anxious about the future. We might not like the resolution, but now we can get back to living again and be thankful that we have each other."

They sat in silence, overwhelmed, soaking in the sound of promise. Amen, whispered Shane.

Radley sat still, amazed at the overflow emotions she felt, of relief, of expansive love, of gratitude. Was it because this was the first sit-down home dinner they'd had together in weeks, or the sight of the Shane and Megan locked in each other's arms, or the realization that the tone of the household depended on her, needed her as an anchor? Dazzling sprays of last-minute sunlight flooded through the windows and poured a pinkish gold glow over the kitchen table where they sat, before slowly drifting out of sight behind the trees.

Megan picked up her fork, then froze. "Look!" The bluebird was back, fluttering against the window, bobbing its head in jerky little motions. "It wants to get in. Please, it wants to be with us. Let it come in!"

"Poor thing," Shane said. "Never gives up. Sorry honey, he wouldn't be able to survive indoors."

"The bluebird is just confused. It has a nest and a family it wants to be with." Radley smiled at her daughter. "That's where it belongs." Megan smiled reluctantly as the bird, with a last rat-a-tap-tap against the pane, lifted its wings and flew off.

As they were finishing dinner, the door buzzer sounded. During the first week after the accident, the neighbors had inundated them with generous food dishes. Adele and Hugh Horton's daughter Courtney arrived with flowers from the family, and Andy showed up with an armload of home-made pizzas. People sent casseroles, sympathy cards and fruit baskets, they inquired about Larry. But no one had showed up for some time.

The buzzer sounded again. They weren't expecting anyone. When Radley opened, there was Dean Horton, standing one foot atop the other, shoelaces splayed in all directions, orange bill cap pulled over her forehead. Radley had not seen her since Larry's accident and assumed she was in camp or at their cabin on Lake Sylvia. Occasionally she brought packages up to Radley's front door from the curbside mailbox, shaking each one briskly. "Save you a trip," she'd say with a crafty look. Radley had heard of her reputation as a tomboy, full of piss and vinegar, as someone put it. She always looked like she was up to something.

"Hi, Mrs. Gallagher," Dean said. "I just wondered if you needed anything. I mean, I'm between vacations right now so I'm available. I'm a baby sitter. I also mow the lawn, sweep the garage, go shopping for groceries. I don't do hard labor, but I can take a load off your hands. My prices have gone up, but that's because I've gained so much experience. Oh, and one more thing. I don't work on Tuesday afternoons when *Count Dracula* is on TV, and I don't allow anyone to watch me work."

Suppressing a chuckle, Radley folded her arms. The sly fox! She detected a thinly hidden audacity behind Dean's politeness. None of the neighbors would use Dean as a baby sitter, she scorned all rules, and the younger children always got into trouble. "Sorry Dean, I do everything myself. And I'm not sure if twelve is old enough to baby sit quite yet. But if you'll tell me where I can get one of those funky orange caps, I'll give you an armful of lilies from my garden."

"No thank you, its money I'm after," Dean said with a shake of her head. "And if Larry wakes up, tell him he won't get away with it," and she bounced down the front steps, shoe laces flying behind her.

Radley frowned, watching the girl stride off, hands swinging confidently. What did she mean? What had Larry possibly to do with anything involving Dean? Probably just another of her provocative taunts, meant to stir trouble. She didn't trust that girl as far as she could throw a concrete slab.

CHAPTER 29

A few days later, Radley was bumping up the stairs, clothes basket under one arm, when the buzzer rang. Opening the door, she saw a woman's silhouette outlined against the bright sky.

"Radley! I saw your car in the drive. I have bad news. Can I come in?"

Radley quickly stepped back and pulled the door open as a breathless Adele Horton bustled in clutching a patent leather purse, hair askew, countenance strained, quite unlike her usual composed self. Streaks of powder were caked along her cheeks suggesting the flow of tears. Even her neatly-belted linen dress looked slept in. Something was terribly wrong.

"Adele, come and sit . . ." Radley began, but Adele cut her off.

"I can't stay. But I had to let you know. Hugh didn't make it." She gazed evenly at Radley, as if voicing the message steadied her.

Radley stared at her.

"On second thought, I think I'd better sit down and compose myself." Adele dropped onto the living-room couch, placed her purse in her lap and folded her hands on top. "I must get home. My mother will be arriving this evening with Courtney and Dean. But you've been such good neighbors. I know what you and Shane have been through, and it seemed a good idea to let you know right away. It might help for us to share our trials."

finally worked through it. Their relationship wasn't perfect, but with accommodation and compromise the marriage had during the last year had blossomed at a new level. At these candid words, something in Radley snapped, as if the hinges in her mind had reconnected. She found herself telling Adele everything, her worries about Shane, her inadequacies, her dreams, her inability to move in any direction, frozen in indecision.

She sank down and laid her head on Adele's shoulder. "Shane is an empty well, and I need to find another source of nourishment to remain alive," she choked in a little girl voice.

Adele looked at her thoughtfully. "What is it you seek out there in the world that you can't have at home?"

The question struck Radley in the pit of her stomach. She had no idea.

"Your family needs you now." Adele looked at her kindly. "You are not to blame for the sorrow your kids go through. Disappointment is part of growing up. Kids have to get used to not having things the way they want them to be. Maturity is not gained by being happy all the time. We shouldn't shield them from life's teachings."

Raising her head, Radley turned a tear-blotched face to her friend. "I'm so glad you're here. Life's teachings never seem to end, do they?"

The chime of the clock striking three sounded from the hallway. Adele stood up. "Goodness, I've been here two hours! It's been for me good to talk. Thank you, my dear."

Radley stood at the door for some minutes and watched Adele descend the front steps and head across the road. Until now, she had not known Adele at all, as if her neighbor's humanity had been buried in the scope of Reston social propriety. Radley lifted her hand and felt her cheek, dry now, and inside a warmth drew through her, strangely enervating, that illuminated every corner of her body.

Her eyes lit on a photo hanging under the hallway light: She and Shane, holding hands on the front steps of their Manhattan apartment building, dressed in their Sunday best. Shane looked irresistibly handsome—Shane, straight and predictable, go-by-the-rules, plain and simple, a take it or leave it guy. Early on she decided she'd take it, that is if she could get it. She couldn't stop looking at the photo—those early, happy days when she and Shane laughed and the earth stood still.

Even now . . .

He was a good guy. Solid. Once he said something he stood by it, no wavering, no roundabout second guesses. "Be good to each other," Shane's mother had advised as the two families hugged good-bye in front of the Pinehurst Athletic Club after the wedding reception. They had attempted to fill their roles. She found that Shane's role was to provide. Her role was to maintain life. Sam was a good provider, devoted, good-humored and agreeable. Notwithstanding his wife's vacillations and tempers, he ad-hered to her lifestyle without complaint, doing his best to fit in. Everyone liked Shane, his basic decency, his tall, broad-shouldered good looks, his pleasant, easy-going manner.

How could she not love him?

But slowly he had become withdrawn and distant. It struck her, as she gazed at the photo, that not once had she reached out a hand or encouraged him, had not explained herself or offered him affection, guidance, reassurance, understanding—the very things she wanted herself. She'd been immersed, she thought ruefully, in her own needs, trying to reformulate the entire scope of her world from her own perspective.

More than once Char warned her that it was up to the woman to cre-ate a positive tone in the home, which seemed to be exclusively a female talent. Had she done that? Had she contributed to their happiness? She had devoted herself to struggle and resistance, beating against the limits of convention with criticism and anger. Fleeing from the helplessness she felt as a parent, she had turned to outside affairs, caught up in her own agenda. Of course, these pursuits were important—but where did they belong in terms of priority?

Her brain whirled. She had to think this through, ferret out answers. Shane asked for nothing. He was willing to agree to anything to make her happy. Maybe he felt crushed under her merciless eye. Maybe her continual criticism had pushed him into the corners of retreat where he now existed.

Something split in her and she found it difficult to breathe.

Maybe it's not my life I hate, or Shane. Maybe it's myself.

Of course, she couldn't be sure. She wasn't sure of anything anymore. Except that Larry was gone from their lives and nothing would be the same. And it was up to her to put the world of make-believe and reality back together into some sort of whole.

CHAPTER 30

❧◦❧◦❧

Radley and Megan walked across the adjacent parking lot and around to the front entrance. The revolving door hissed behind them as they swept into the front lobby, then caught the elevator to the seventh floor and headed down the long corridor toward room 713. It had been ten months since the accident, and these visits had become a Friday ritual. Shane would join them at the hospital after work and they would gather around Larry's bed with trays of cafeteria food, not saying much, acutely aware of the prone presence on the bed, of his breathing, which seemed to fill the room with silent vibrations. This, plus scattered visits during the week to plant a kiss on Larry's cheek and consult with the nursing staff, comforted them, gave them the sense that Larry still lived, was alive. At first, it made the emptiness at home a little easier to bear, made it easier to pretend that he was merely recuperating from a temporary illness or off on an extended vacation. Their expectations hung in limbo; while there was hope, he was still with them. But with time, the hope had faded, and Radley's attitude turned to resignation. Life called on her to let go, to give it her unalloyed attention.

As they approached the central station, the two nurses in white starched uniforms smiled at them broadly, faces full of expectation. What was up? Radley wondered. At the far end of the hall, a group stood talking outside of Larry's room. Tightening her hold on Megan's hand, Radley quickened her steps. A family of five, one woman carrying a baby with a tube in its nose, approached, and Radley and Megan pressed against the wall to let them pass. As they reached the end of the hall, Radley could make out several aides and nurses commiserating, gesturing and nodding in unison. Something was going on.

Radley ran up, Megan trotting beside her. The staff looked at Radley pointedly as she pushed open the door and entered Larry's room.

Inside, several physicians in white lab coats conversed in low tones. She recognized Norma, Larry's regular nurse, as well as a fill-in nurse she'd seen occasionally, and Dr. Soderberg. She halted, felt her stomach clutch. Dr. Soderberg stepped towards her holding a pile of manila folders in one arm.

"Mrs. Gallagher, we've been trying to reach you. Something has happened." She glanced at Larry's bed, surrounded by a soft grey curtain. Nora closed the door quietly. An eerie silence filled the room, an unusual tension lurked behind the low tone of Dr. Soderberg's voice. "Be prepared for a shock. Maybe you should sit down."

Radley felt them staring at her. Norma opened the window, and a cool beam of fresh air struck the edges of the grey curtain, causing it to flutter gently. Why was the bed curtain closed? It smacked of finality.

"What is it? I don't need the padding." The words flew out of Radley's mouth. Her fingers dug into the sides of her thigh.

"Twenty minutes ago Larry opened his eyes." Dr. Soderberg pressed the folders to his chest and looked directly at Radley. She stared at him as a flush of emotion caught in her throat. "Nurse Norma was moving his limbs for his daily exercise routine when he woke up. She immediately pulled the curtain to shield him from direct light. His eyes closed shortly afterwards, and when I arrived at his bedside he opened them again and focused directly on me. We've checked his vitals and none have changed, but healing has been going on that has broken through the coma. It looks like he's going to recover."

A tight pressure gathered in Radley's head, ready to explode. She felt dizzy. She and Shane had been trying for months to accept the fact that their son was lost to them forever. And now, just as they had begun to concentrate on getting on with their lives, were beginning to adapt, the inconceivable had occurred. Pulling herself together, she looked around for Megan, who moved up and pressed against her side.

Dr. Soderberg's eyes softened and he lay his hand on Radley's upper arm. "I can't tell you how glad I am. Though unexpected, these recoveries do occur, even after years, out of nowhere. Of course, we never want to encourage false hopes."

One of the nurses pulled back the curtain. Radley stepped over and looked down at her son. Larry's small pallid hand lay across his stomach on the white sheet, and his hair, flat and dull from constant pressure against the pillow, hung listlessly around his ears. She held her breath. This Larry looked no different from the inert body that had lain immobile on the bed month after month barely hanging on to life. But then she noticed that his head was tilted slightly against the pillow, the sunken, otherworldly look of his face had shifted to a more natural relaxation, and his complexion had taken on a pinkish hue.

Radley stared at the limp body on the bed, Megan pressed to her side, looking on with wonder. The scene didn't seem real. She wanted to take Larry in her arms, but didn't dare touch him, the spell might come crashing down and she would be left with the remnant of a mirage.

Shane! How to reach him? His flight from Mexico City was due to arrive at five that evening. He was at that moment heading toward them through the clouds. He would come straight to the hospital, as planned. Would the shock be too much, should she somehow warn him before he entered the room? But it would be best to have Dr. Soderberg with them, with the facts at hand. She decided to wait, to let him be confronted with the happy surprise.

Dr. Soderberg laid a hand on Radley's shoulder. He had an appointment but promised to return and fill her in on the details when Shane arrived. There was a lot to discuss. "Larry should sleep for some time. A warning: we don't know what his recovery will look like. Meanwhile, try to brace yourself for the upcoming adjustments ahead of you." She watched his white coat float out the door, a reassuring cloud of efficiency.

Megan leaned against Larry's bed and gazed at her brother with wide eyes, crumpling an edge of the white bedcover between her fingers.

"When will he wake up, Mommy?"

"We'll have to wait and see, darling."

Megan looked expectant, as if waiting for him to awake and rejoin them and life would resume. "Please let him wake up!" Megan whispered, clasping her hands together.

Suddenly, Radley drew Megan into her arms and pressed their cheeks together as if afraid to let go. She wanted to hold her little girl forever, so warm against her, so vulnerable. Megan had always been a sensitive little thing. When playing, she had a bubbling, happy face; when she messed up or felt the prick of criticism, a look of suffering burned in her eyes. One Saturday afternoon she had arrived home and found Megan curled on the floor clutching Wolf in her arms, her face buried in the dog's neck, sobbing. Dean Horton was sprawled nearby on the couch, legs curled under her. At her side sat a wooden crate with a small black rabbit inside, lying on its side and breathing heavily.

"Megan, what——?" On seeing her mother, Megan ran up and grabbed the front of her shirt.

"Mommy, she stuck a ball in Tipsy's mouth and tied her ears with a rubber band and she wouldn't stop . . ." She looked tearfully up at her mother with a pleading expression. "And she hit Wolf with a poker—see, there it is on the floor."

With an air of nonchalance, Dean twisted the orange cap on her head. "Megan has it all wrong. I was just teasing. Tipsy has such long ears and makes such funny faces. And I was just playing dodge with the dog. She was having fun. It was a game."

"No! The rabbit hated it, Wolf hated it!" cried Megan. Radley looked at the rabbit lying suspiciously still in the crate, fur mussed, a wounded look on its face.

Dean jumped from the couch and grabbed the crate in her arms. "You wanted to see the rabbit and I did you a favor and brought it over. She's got it wrong, Mrs. Gallagher. Look, there's no mark on the dog." Dean strode across the living room. "Gotta go," and without waiting for a reply, she shot out the door and slammed it behind her.

"Megan, what was Dean Horton doing here?" Radley asked, sitting down on the couch. She picked up the poker in question from the rug. There was no mark on it, nor was there any sign on Wolf that he had been abused. But a poker! That Horton girl! What would she do next? There was something about the girl—the word sinister came to mind. Probably too dark to apply to a youngster of twelve. But something about her indicated more than mere mischief.

"She came to show me the rabbit. She said we'd play. But Tipsy was so scared!" Megan pulled herself onto her mother's lap and tucked her arms around her. Wolf's tail thumped slowly at their feet. Radley stroked her daughter's hair, brushed her fingers gently down Megan's cheek and pulled her shirt tail down around her curled bottom. Finally, Megan fell asleep, head against her mother's breast. As she felt the warm body against hers, it seemed that nothing existed more precious than this being, a part of herself, bigger than herself, this little blue eyes who depended on her for every other breath. Aside from this, everything was dreamland.

Her mind reverted to the present where they sat together by Larry's bed, waiting in awed silence for Larry to come to life and acknowledge them. "Daddy will be here soon," she whispered in her daughter's ear. "Everything will be all right." She was filled with a strange emotion. The silky breeze brushing in from the open window, the warm light surrounding Larry's blond head, the brilliant blue coffee cup on the nightstand, the pure white Peter Pan collar resting on the curve of Megan's soft neck, and the photo of Shane on the counter, bathed in amber light: everything had become precious, glowed with a new resonance. Never before had the objects around her been filled with such vitality. Everything she'd ever needed was right here in this room. Anyone who looked for more was a fool!

Two hours later, as the nurse walked out the door carrying a tray of vials, Char gushed into the room. "Oh, my dear! My favorite grandson restored—will miracles ever cease?" Laying her alligator clutch bag on the chair, she tiptoed to the side of Larry's bed and stood gazing down at him.

"He hasn't moved since we arrived," Radley said, speaking in a whisper. "But he opened his eyes this morning for a few moments and looked at the nurse! We're been sitting here waiting for him to wake up."

At that moment Larry's eyes fluttered open and he looked directly at Char.

Both women gasped.

"My Lord! Does he see me? Does he recognize me?" Char asked, lowering into a nearby chair in slow motion, as if afraid to disturb the air.

"I don't know. . ." choked Radley. She moved closer and leaned over the bed. Slowly Larry turned his head toward her. She touched his arm gingerly and felt the warmth of his skin through the nightshirt. Suddenly, she felt as if she were falling, floating in a honeycomb of air, unable to touch ground.

A gurgle sounded from Larry's throat. To Radley it sounded vaguely like the word mommy. "Larry's back," she cried, "Mom, Megan, he's really here!"

Larry tilted his head on the pillow and shifted his eyes around the room, then planted them on his mother. She tried to speak, but shock, relief and expectation shook her in an avalanche of emotions. Before she could move or think his eyelids closed again. It had lasted only a few minutes, but she had glimpsed a gleam of life behind the blue spheres.

More waiting, through the bleak afternoon, with the sounds of feet tapping along the hospital corridor, the wail of bells, low voices mixed in confidential urgency. Darkness gathered outside. Char left to call Wilson at his downtown office, leaving a stack of *House Beautifulll* magazines on the table. Megan sat next to the window bent over a coloring book. Full of anxiety about what would be revealed next, Radley watched Norma as she checked the gauges and charts. Finally, one of the physicians returned, perused the charts, and ordered the equipment removed, leaving Larry attached to a single tube of intravenous support and a tall monitoring machine.

Radley drew up the shades and remnants of afternoon sun flooded the room with a yellow haze. Below, she saw a thread of miniature pedestrians, heads bobbing along the sidewalk. She noticed one in particular, taller than the rest, and as it drew closer she recognized the wide brow, the swing of the arms, palms facing the rear, advancing in even strides. Shane! She clapped her palms together.

"Daddy's coming!" she cried to Megan. Megan jumped from her chair, spilling a fan of crayons along the floor.

Since Shane had left for Mexico, her time had been consumed with women's group meetings, lunch with Adele at the Binayshee Art Society, and quiet evenings with Megan over some board game or other. Faced with Larry's tragedy, their differences had been submerged in mutual grief and they operated in a pact of silence. Now the image of his gentle smile, his tall, broad-shouldered frame, the calm pool of equanimity in his eyes steadied her. Something in her expanded, she felt a lightness and joy that made her want to reach out and envelop the world. The store of wrongs that needed correcting, the weight of unfilled expectations, the spiral of her conflicting needs, became mere fabrications, stories told by the wind. Her whole body anticipated the familiar weight of Shane's presence.

Her husband rushed in flustered, his jacket flung open. He scanned the room. "What's going on?"

With a cry of delight, Megan rushed to her father and crushed herself around his legs. "Daddy, you're back!" She buried her face in his pants leg, and then looked up at him, blue eyes beaming.

"Yes, and guess who else is back?" Radley blurted to her husband, laughing, her eyes riveted to his face.

Shane stopped short. Megan and Radley both began talking at once. From their breathless chatter, he was able to make out that the impossible had happened and that his son had reentered the world of conscious life. His muscles locked, all he could do was stand and stare at Larry under the sheet, face up, hands at his side, the same form he'd seen during hundreds of former visits.

Radley took his arm and led him over to the bed. "The doctor was in the room when Larry regained consciousness this morning. Since then he's been sleeping."

Before she could say more, Larry opened his eyes and looked up. He turned his head slowly, robot-like, as if trying to register the tube in his arm, the oxygen tank at his bedside, the ruffle of flowers in a pink vase. Radley noticed that his eyes surveyed the room without focusing on any one object.

She held his hand gingerly, and took a deep breath. "Larry, sweetheart, can you hear me?" she asked loudly.

"Yes, Mom. Do you think I'm deaf?"

Radley coughed a laugh, and the sudden quickening of her heart pounded in her ears.

Shane swallowed. He moves! He speaks!

The door clicked open and Char and Wilson rushed in. Wilson carried a pile of hoagie sandwiches from the cafeteria.

"Look. Larry just woke up."

Char rushed over. "Oh, my soul! Call the doctor," she cried in a tizzy, unable to think of what else to say.

Radley giggled absurdly, tears running down her cheeks. "Larry, you're back! Oh, Larry!"

"Have I been somewhere? Mom, I feel weird. What's this thing on my arm? Is Dad here?" He spoke with a cracked voice, as from the other end of a tunnel.

"Here," Shane cried.

"We're all here, darling, Radley said. "Dad, Megan, Grandma, Grandpa."

A pause. "Grandma, did you bring my favorite candy, you know, those candy corns they have at Halloween?"

"I'll get you some, dear," Char cried, moving closer.

For a second Larry's expression livened, then he sank back and his eyes drooped half-mast. His next words were barely audible. "Get me Hot Tamales and chocolate Twinkies . . ." His voice sank, and one corner of the blue nightshirt slipped off his shoulder. They thought he was falling asleep, but suddenly he straightened up, looked around.

"Where's Mom? Where's Dad? Why can't I see anyone?"

The room fell quiet. His listeners froze, exchanged glances as the shock of his words sunk in. Could it be . . .

Shane wiped a stream of tears from his face with his handkerchief.

At this moment, Dr. Soderberg entered the room. His grey-streaked hair hung loosely behind his ears, and he beamed at them through gold-rimmed glasses. He gave Shane a hearty handshake and turned to the figure on the bed.

"How are you, young fellow?"

"I feel fine," Larry said weakly.

"You're a very lucky chap to have broken out of the coma. But there are residuals from the brain injury. Larry's vision has been affected. He has no more than 80 percent perception in both eyes. That means he is partially blind." He folded his clipboard against his white lab coat. "But his return to consciousness is miraculous. You have much to be thankful for."

After listening to further words of encouragement, Larry's energy appeared to drain as fast as it had appeared, and he fell into a deep sleep.

Dr. Soderberg turned to Radley and Shane, who were focused on him expectantly. "Well. You are one lucky family. Larry will probably recall nothing of the accident. Not uncommon in these cases, at least initially," he said reassuringly.

"You see, we found few detectible signs of damage to explain his coma," he went on, "aside from the peripheral damage to his occipital lobe, which seems to be healing nicely. Every traumatic brain injury is unique and diagnosis is rarely simple. The radiography results found no focal lesions in the brain nor were there signs of intracranial injury. Usually when an object pierces the skull and breaches the dura mater, we see diffuse axonal injury and edema, but the signs were indeterminate. We've yet to test his motor coordination, which requires slow extension due to the length of time the patient's been inactive."

"Doctor, could you rephrase all that in laymen's terms?" Radley asked, shaking her head in happy disbelief. Dr. Soderberg had been an attentive and sympathetic advocate all these months, but he needed lessons in patient communication.

"The upshot is," Dr. Soderberg said patiently, "it will take time to determine what, if any, residual problems remain from his injury. Of course, his loss of vision is severe, but we have methods of strengthening his eyes. Your son will begin a program of physical and occupational therapy and be monitored closely for several weeks." His face flushed with gratification as he scanned the happy, anxious faces before him.

"And keep in mind, patient characteristics also influence the prognosis. From what you've told me, your son is high on the determination scale." He smiled. "There are no indications that he won't fully recover with proper follow-up care. Of course, it is far too early to give a prognosis after ten months in a coma. It could range from severe defects to full recovery. He will in all probability remain partially blind; some residual disability is common. But he has returned to conscious living and can lead a normal life. You have every reason to celebrate."

The next morning Larry woke up to find Radley and Shane sitting by his bed. Despite his pale skin and shaky, feeble movements, his face held a look of alert curiosity.

"Can you see us?" Radley asked gently, her voice thick.

"Kind of. I can tell who you are by your voice."

Radley took his hand and stroked it. "Larry, you've been very sick. You've been unconscious for a long time. We will have to work hard to restore your eyesight. Honey, do you recall the boat accident you had when a big storm came up?" she asked.

Larry furrowed his brow. No, he didn't know what boat she was talking about. Afraid of tiring him, she said no more.

"Let's see how this brave young chap is doing." Dr. Soderberg, arriving for the morning check-in, marched over to the bed. "It will take time to determine if Larry's sight can be improved. Meanwhile, he can see light, enough to navigate on his own with corrective physical aids." Radley heard Shane whisper a prayer of gratitude under his breath. She reached over and pressed his hand.

Pulling down the thin muslin blanket, the doctor asked Larry if he thought he could stand up. Gingerly, Larry slipped off the bed, pulled his body upright and stood shakily, looking down at the floor. Then, pulling his hand from Dr. Soderberg's, he lifted his hands in the air and looked up at the doctor.

"That's fine, lad," Dr. Soderberg said. "Excellent! It will take a while to get your strength back. You'll have to learn to walk."

"But I can walk now," Larry said breezily, lifting and planting a trembling leg. In a daze of happy emotion, Radley could only look on, torn between disapproval and elation at this unexpected show of energy. Never had she welcomed such a display of blind overconfidence.

"Enough for now. Back into bed with you, my boy." With a boost from the doctor, Larry pulled himself onto the bed, leaned back into the pillows, and dropped instantly to sleep, legs askew, head turned against the pillow, one hand stretched out over the bed.

CHAPTER 31

❦

"Can I join the festivities?" boomed a voice from the doorway, and Wilson walked in, a dozen red roses clasped in one arm. Setting his leather briefcase on the floor, he laid his hat and overcoat over a side chair and surveyed the room. Radley sat smiling at him over her book, Char beamed at him expectantly from her chair, and Shane looked over the evening paper he had been reading and grinned from ear to ear. Before Wilson could catch his breath, he felt himself bombarded with hugs. "Hey!" He uttered his deep baritone laugh, "You'll have *me* under doctor's care in a minute." He laid the bundle of flowers in Char's arms. "How's my grandson?"

With all eyes fixed on him, Wilson moved over and looked down at Larry sleeping peacefully, much like his old self, except for a few scaly patches of skin, crescent pockets around his eyes, and a white bandage circling his forehead. Without warning, Larry opened his eyes, looked directly at his grandfather, and what could have been a smile moved around his mouth. Then his eyes drifted shut. Wilson paled, and a haunted look passed over his face. "Welcome back," he said under his breath, and a reverent hush fell over the room.

"He's done that a couple of times," Char said. "We have to wait. I'll get the nurse to put these flowers in water." She pressed a bright red fingertip against the call button.

"Is he awake?" Megan ran in from the playroom and threw herself against the side of the bed. "I'm not to touch, am I?" she asked, fingering the blanket. "I want to ask him where he put my slinky."

"Better not wake him, dear. He needs his sleep," Char said.

"But Grandpa's here," Megan said. "He'll want to see Grandpa right away. He can sleep later. He'll be mad."

"No, honey, not when he sees how happy we are and that he's the star," Radley said.

"Bring out the champagne! It's time to celebrate." Char laughed in her tinkling voice, and reaching into her purse for a hanky, she dabbed at her eyes. "Shane, would you fetch my black leather bag from the cloak room down the hall? There's a bottle of Dom Perignon inside."

"Sure." Shane instantly pulled his hands from his pockets and strode out of the room.

Norma poked her head in the door. "We need a vase for the flowers, please," Wilson told her.

"And could you find us some champagne glasses?" Char added.

"Oh, and bring along a can of caviar," Radley said, her face lit up behind a smile.

"Of course, I have one in my lunch pail." Norma's white-smocked figure clipped off down the hall.

When Shane returned with the champagne, everyone lifted their glass in unison and expressed awe at the power of nature; Shane gave thanks to the mercy of a beneficent God; Wilson commended the strength of the family where one person's presence was so crucial; and everyone attested to the power of inscrutable luck.

"When I heard the news I nearly fainted," Char said. "I tried to say something, but my mouth wouldn't move." She laughed, bracelet tinkling as she took a sip from her glass. Radley smiled.

"I knew the minute I walked in something was up," Shane said enthusiastically. "Radley looked conflicted, as if she didn't know how to tell me something. And then, with Megan jumping around like a grasshopper and everyone chattering at once, I feared the worst. . . . But, when I went up and saw Larry on the bed, looking normal, and the words sank in, I felt like I was hit by a thunderbolt. A welcome blow!

"The next thing I know Larry is sitting up in bed looking at me!"

"I put on my hat as soon as I heard the news and continued to work at my desk with my hat on until my business was finished," Wilson said.

They sat conversing, although Radley could tell they were hardly paying attention to what they were saying. She heard Shane's easy laugh thread through the conversation. No one wanted to get up and leave.

"We'll go out and celebrate properly when Larry's back on his feet," Wilson said at last, when the nurse appeared to give Larry his shot. "We'll treat him to all he can eat at Shakey's Pizza." He slipped Char's chinchilla jacket over her shoulders and fetched his overcoat and scarf from the chair. "Be sure and keep us posted," Char urged, kissing each of them on the cheek.

After they had gone and Radley had left to take Megan home, Shane drew the brown armchair close to Larry's bed and leaned back. He had no desire to sleep. The joy of being home after the grueling assignment in Mexico made him feel alive. He had endured the trip stoically. Each slog down a narrow street lined with ancient buildings and foreign signs, with people in strange garb scurrying unpredictably about, surrounded by jabbering foreign words he didn't understand, filled him with loneliness.

To be home was the last stop before heaven—the place which, although he struggled with his wife's discontent, her resentment towards him, towards everything it seemed, was still the only home he knew, the sacrosanct seat of his family, his life stretching to the next world.

To be home, and then to be greeted by the miracle of his son's unexpected recovery—it was too much to absorb all at once.

As the minutes ticked by and the corridors fell silent, Shane was invaded by a pervasive sadness. This miracle did not erase the fact that his marriage had toppled into discord. For some time now Radley had been restless and full of complaints. Her distaste for domesticity, her frustration with the kids, and her erupting temper permeated the household. She was tormented, her unease hung over the house like a black cloud. She was a bird pressing to flee the cage, a firecracker ready to explode. What did she want? Always striving, seeking, nothing was ever enough. Why did she want more when they had so much? What on earth was she looking for?

Her need to find meaning sounded to him like useless forays into a bottomless pit. If only she could learn to live life as it presented itself, to leave things alone, that she didn't have to solve life's problems or achieve perfection in this life. If only her spiritual sense were more developed. He had to admit she'd tried, in the beginning had joined the church, but something blocked her effort to settle into a ritualized religion. He often wondered what it was.

It was his faith in God that sustained him. How could she not see that?

The children were everything to him, the core of his existence. Unlike Radley, he never complained, never questioned his role as father. While Radley spent more and more of her days off on some feminist quest or attending political meetings, he remained faithfully at home with the children. He didn't feel the need to take them to exciting play dates, it was enough that he was there at home with them at all times, available, looking out for things. They knew he loved them and that he would be there for them no matter what.

Marriage bound for life. A home with Radley afforded his total comfort and purpose. He would not go slinking back East, tail between his legs. She was the link to everything he wanted.

Although Radley had never hinted that he held any responsibility for Larry's accident, waves of remorse washed over him at odd moments. Larry had left the house on his watch, there was no getting around it. Radley insisted that Larry had slipped away like an eel, had been gone in a flash and no one could have seen him or stopped him in time. Still . . . the accident weighed on him, and he sat deep in thought, pondering, struck by a tight stir of conscience.

"No," he shook his head at the nurse's inquiry. "I'll sleep here in the chair tonight. Larry might wake up." Norma cleaned Larry's face and arms with a washcloth, checked his vitals, and brought in fresh blankets and pillows. He heard the door click as she extinguished all but a dim table light and left the room.

Late the next morning after a deep twelve-hour sleep, Larry woke up refreshed and began talking eagerly, almost like his former self. There was a bounce to his voice.

"Mom, can I have something to eat?" he said, pulling his arms from under the covers.

"How about soft-boiled eggs and toast?"

"How about pancakes with lots of syrup and sausages?"

Radley put down her book. It was hard to believe that this figure, prone and inert for so many months, was actually functioning. She and Shane were anxious to learn the full measure of his recovery and resolve at last what had actually happened on the lake during the violent storm nearly a year ago.

"How do you feel?" Shane asked.

"I donno. I'm hungry. Why can't I see you? How long have I been here? When can I go home?"

"You've been sick a long time, honey," Radley said. "You were hurt in an accident, but you're getting better. The part of your brain that affects your eyesight was damaged, and you'll need help to get around." An irresistible urge seized her to feel him, to verify that this apparition with a voice was really viable. She drew her arms around his shoulders. "It will take some getting used to, Larry." As she held him, a swell of emotion overcame her, she could hardly breathe.

Larry's eyes looked straight ahead, pupils drooping listlessly, as if floating on water. His hand was limp in hers. He could see, he said, light and some blurry shapes and that was all. How would he ever, Radley wondered, adjust his prodigious energy to this new handicap?

Now that he was back in the land of the living, it was time to learn the truth about what happened the night of the accident. "Honey, do you remember what happened the last time you were awake? Anything at all?"

"Sure I do." He wiggled himself up and Radley propped another pillow behind his head and tucked in his Flying Dutchman pajama top.

"Do you remember the motorboat on the lake, Larry," she said. "The storm, the accident . . .?"

"Well . . . let's see. The boat, Mr. Horton's boat, he let me use it a couple of times, let me start the motor and everything, once he let me drive it to the yacht club. Well, I found it down on the beach, no one was there." He stopped as if suddenly realizing he had left the house without permission and on top of that had taken out the boat alone. "And then, well, that's all."

It took some urging and assurances that Larry would not be held responsible, that they only desired to find the truth, and their primary concern was his recovery. Any mistakes were forgiven, he had already paid a heavy price. Besides, it might help the doctors to treat him if they knew how he had received his injuries. With this, Larry admitted that he had found the key in a dashboard tray, untied the boat and pushed it out into the water. Yes, a storm had come up, all of a sudden like. At that point, he paused, and after a feeble resistance sank back on the pillows and closed his eyes.

It looked like soon she and Shane would at last learn what had happened that stormy night. Lifting her head, she looked around. Where was Megan? Her daughter had been hanging at the foot of the bed listening to Larry's words in silence, but now she was gone. Searching the playroom, she perceived a mound crammed on a sofa, a small white tennis shoe protruding from it.

Megan . . .?

Unfolding Megan from the corner of the couch, she lay down beside her and drew her close. "Larry will be all right, Megan honey," she breathed.

"But he's blind."

"He's alive. He's himself. He can lead a good life, with our help. And we will be there for him, you and Daddy and I. You will help, won't you Megan?"

"Yes. Yes. Oh, I will."

Later that afternoon, Larry, freshly bathed and wearing clean orange and brown giraffe pajamas, sat cross-legged on the hospital bed. Posters of penguins, turtles, and a Nantucket whaleboat lined the walls. A small bookcase held boxes of games and toys, and Larry's clothes were piled neatly in a large cardboard box against one wall. Having consumed a meal of cottage cheese, Jell-O, and lentil broth—he insisted on feeding himself without assistance—he was investigating with his hands a set of block toys sprawled on his lap, touching everything in sight, familiarizing himself with his surroundings.

"We'd like to ask you more about the accident. Can you tell us how you came to take the boat out, honey?" Radley began.

"It was Dean."

What? Radley glanced at Shane, who looked at her questioningly. No one had suspected the Horton girl's presence or that she had played a part in the events of that calamitous day.

Radley turned to Shane. "Better fetch Megan from the playroom. It would be good for her to hear this, so she understands what actually happened." Shane nodded and left, returning in a few minutes with Megan in tow.

"Say hi to your sister," Radley suggested.

"Hi to your sister," Larry said.

"Dopey," Megan said.

"Dopey yourself," Larry said. They both laughed.

"Go ahead and tell us the story, sweetheart," Radley said.

"Okay, I untied the boat and was about to give it a spin—just around, I wasn't going anywhere, no one would know the difference. And no one would mind anyway because I knew what I was doing and nothing bad would happen. And then Dean Horton showed up—I saw her orange baseball cap."

Larry's tale gained fluency as the images flooded back to him. When he had finished and Radley finally grasped Larry's account of the accident and what led up to it, she sat frozen in her chair—as did Shane. It couldn't be! In a few minutes the straightforward version of Larry sneaking out on Hugh's runabout for a quick spin and getting lashed by a sudden storm had been dashed to smithereens.

The next day the sky turned a crisp cornflower blue and the sun burst out for the first time in a week, throwing bright sparkles over the whitewashed buildings and into Larry's hospital room. Radley and Megan sat on Larry's bed playing Go Fish. Larry said he couldn't distinguish the cards enough to play, but he followed their moves with a look of delight, laughing as Megan took three cards in a row from her mother's hand. Shane was reading the morning *Tribune* in the scruffy brown armchair he'd sat in so many times, when the door burst open and in walked Dean Horton.

Yesterday, Radley phoned Adele with Larry's recital of the events of the accident, including her daughter Dean's participation in it, of which Adele had no inkling. Adele determined to find out exactly what happened. Now here she was in person, following Dean into the room. She greeted everyone briskly and, refusing a chair, declared that she had heard Dean's side of the story and now wanted to hear what Larry had to say.

"I appreciate your contacting me," she began with her usual composure. "I couldn't be more thankful for Larry's spectacular recovery." Radley thought she detected coolness in her tone. "You are correct, we need to get to the bottom of this."

Placing her purse on the table she drew Dean to her side. "After your phone call, Radley, I sat down with Dean and pressed her to tell me everything exactly as it happened. She provided such a different version of the accident from Larry's that I had to come see you."

Nodding agreement, Radley convinced Adele to sit down. Larry sat on the bed listening with a mixed expression of amusement and apprehension.

"Dean and I have had a long talk, and she's here to explain. Go ahead, tell them what you told me." Adele looked at Dean with a no-nonsense air.

The girl raised her head, full of lively confidence. "Well, like I told you, I saw Larry on the boat. You know it was raining and no one else was about, and I was down there to let poor Buddy go, to give him his freedom. Buddy? That's the turtle, and I put him in the water and watched him swim away free as a bird and just then I saw Larry come down and get in Dad's boat and take off. It was him for sure. Then I went home."

Radley stared at Adele's daughter in disbelief. "Dean," she asked. "Are you sure? You didn't get in the boat with Larry?"

"No, no I didn't. It was raining too hard."

"So that's the truth?" Shane asked. His face was livid.

"Mom, Dad, that's not what happened! Really!" Larry, sitting cross-legged in his pajamas, turned toward Dean's voice. "Tell them you made me take you to the yacht—you know, the one across the bay we see all the time in front of the Cresthaven Yacht Club. She said if I didn't she would cut the feet off the turtle—said she wanted to see if it could swim with its legs alone. When we got there, she got on the yacht and took the gold dagger."

"Adele," Radley said, "Larry has told us consistently that Dean threatened to tell on him and also to dismember the pet turtle unless he drove her out to the yacht." She looked directly at Dean, standing rigidly at her mother's side.

"I said no such thing!" Dean cried.

"Larry says that the yacht was too far away," Radley continued, "and he didn't want to do it in the dark."

"According to Larry, Dean's express aim was to take the dagger," Shane put in. "But we haven't seen the dagger."

"Show them, Dean." At her mother's words, Dean pulled a long emerald-studded object from a canvas bag and held it out for all to see. "Larry gave it to me."

"That's it," Larry cried. "That's the dagger and she took it."

One of the children was lying, and Radley was pretty sure it wasn't Larry. "According to Larry," she continued, "Dean forced him to take her to the yacht, then she climbed up the ladder, returned with the dagger and when they returned to the beach Dean jumped in the water, waded to shore and vanished."

"The ladder is always pulled up when the yacht is not in use. I've been in that boat many times," Adele refuted.

"Larry could hardly steer as the storm was falling in waves." Radley went on, her eyes fixed on Adele seated upright, her slim hands folded in her lap. "He was trying to reach shore when suddenly a powerful thrust swept the boat sideways and the last thing he says he saw was a mountain of craggy rocks bearing down on him in the darkness."

A clatter of footsteps passed the closed door of their hospital room and faded down the hallway.

"If the ladder was missing, there's no way either one of them could have boarded the boat," Shane exclaimed heatedly, rising from his chair and standing, hands deep in his pockets.

Radley looked over at him, tall, fetching in a brown herringbone sports jacket and light blue shirt. It felt good to have him involved, to have him engage with such energy.

There followed a moment of uncomfortable silence.

"But I got us to the yacht and back! Didn't I do good, Mom?" Larry took pride for what he considered the success of the venture. Assured by his parents' consoling attitude, he scoffed at any idea of danger. The entire episode had been a daring, exciting adventure.

"I have an idea," Adele said, tucking her purse under her arm. "I will return shortly."

While they waited, Radley pondered Dean's story. Larry had been wrong in taking out the runabout. But it wasn't likely that he would try to take it to the yacht on the other side of the lake. A nine-year-old could hardly have carried out such an exploit on his own, and everyone in the neighborhood knew of Dean's devious reputation. Yet, if as Dean claimed the dagger came from the yacht, when and how it happened had yet to be determined.

Twenty minutes went by. What was Adele up to?

Finally, she strode in, her face crinkled, eyes set like steel. The news did not appear promising. They watched her anxiously.

"It's been settled. I was able to reach Clem, the watchman for the yacht. He tells me that on that particular evening, busy securing the craft for the approaching storm, he had neglected to pull up the ladder. And," she wet her lips and threw Dean a close look, "that's not all. Clem saw a child leap from the ladder into a small boat and two children took off into the night."

Silence. Dean shuffled her feet and looked down. "One of the children was a girl. The smaller one a boy," Adele added.

"It wasn't me!" Dean cried.

"He recognized one of them. The one he'd seen on board as a guest several times. Her name was Dean Horton."

Later that afternoon, Adele phoned and informed the Gallaghers that Dean had returned the dagger to its owner with apologies and would be spending the next two months doing clean-up work on the yacht.

"Expect her at your house to apologize."

Later that evening, Dr. Soderberg took Radley and Shane aside. "This will be brief. I just completed complicated crainiopagus surgery on conjoined twins, but I want to update you on the possibilities for Larry's further recovery." The doctor's white coat was smudged and dark bags drooped under his eyes.

"After ten months in a coma, it will take some time for Larry to re-cover," he said. "You had better be prepared. There is no predicting the long-term effects of the damage to his brain." He dug a roll of butter-scotch mints from his breast pocket and pulled one off with his teeth. "Excuse me, this is my break," he said in a tired voice.

"What's the prognosis for full recovery, doctor? Shane asked.

"It's possible he'll have some permanent neurological damage," Dr. Soderberg replied. "His blurry vision could improve—many cases have regained partial eyesight, but one never knows, every patient is different. He will be outfitted with home safety equipment and pos-sibly a guide dog. He'll require physical rehab and constant care for some time."

"But he seems like the same boy—our Larry. What is the likelihood of further problems showing up?" Radley asked.

"There is a possibility. But his immediate recovery has been astonish-ing." Dr. Soderberg's positive expression filled Radley with hope. "It looks like there is no memory loss, which is encouraging. He's young, coura-geous, and he has strong family support, a crucial factor. There's every hope that he will eventually resume full bodily functioning."

Shane nodded and breathed yes, yes in a loud voice. Radley thanked Dr. Soderberg profusely, in a small voice, dabbing a tissue at her eyes. It astounded her that they would have their son back, all of him, and he was expected to have a good, healthy life. Whatever it took to further this happy scenario, they would do it.

With a weary smile, the doctor shook both their hands. "I'll have the documentation on his present condition brought up right away. Tomorrow we'll sit down in my office for a more detailed report on your son. You look beat. You'd best get a good night's sleep." They listened to his feet tapping rapidly down the hallway and gradually fading.

Radley turned toward Shane. He was looking at her with a mixed expression of wonder and loss she had not seen before. Moving over to him, she laid her hand on his arm, scrunching against his brown jacket. His arm encircled her back slowly, deliberately, and as their bodies touched she looked up at him, finally, and met his eyes.

"I think it's time we talked to a counselor," he said in a soft voice.

CHAPTER 32

The women's group sprawled in the familiar comfort of Klara's back porch discussing the latest developments in their lives. It was a lazy afternoon, with the warm air spreading around them a sheet of feline relaxation. The sprinkler outside swished back and forth and the odor of wet grass seeped in through the screens.

Over the past months, there had been a noticeable change in the way the women dressed. Everyone had become much more casual. The chic crispy dresses hung untouched in closets, fine jewelry lay neglected on velveteen liners. No more lipstick and eyeliner; house dresses had been replaced with over-sized collared shirts and blue jeans. Everyone except Bette had let their hair grow long—she claimed curly hair only looked good short. No adornments—this was who they were. They preferred to look tan, healthy, and plain. The artifice, the elitism of costuming oneself to look better than others contradicted their quest for truth and freedom. They couldn't bother dolling up when there were more important things to concentrate on, too busy following the boiling surge of revolutionary voices heard everywhere.

Radley returned from a reception and tossed her six pair of pumps and sling-back heels into the trash can, unwilling to distress her feet in order to entice the opposite sex (men hid their bodies behind identical box suits). Mirat exchanged her house dress for jeans and a forest green

T-shirt and abandoned her clinking bracelets. Barbara, sitting upright in her chair, long legs crossed, wore bell-bottom jeans and a halter, black cat glasses perched on her nose. Klara, in a blue and white caftan, hair brushed simply back as usual, claimed she didn't need to change her style, she had been natural all along.

""You're getting to be a real hippie," Char observed on seeing her daughter's scrubbed unadorned face and stick straight hair falling down her back. Shane took her commitment to simplicity in stride. Far be it from him to insist on being fancy.

Bette brushed her hair behind her ears and filed for divorce. Since moving with her two sons into an apartment in a six-story brick building in Bryn Mawr, she had entered a computer operator training program and was dating two guys, one she'd met at the school, the other at a We Care divorce group at St. Theresa Cabrini Church.

She sat in the porch chair, looking unusually spiffy in a bright red leather jacket. Her friends pelted her with questions about her upcoming date, intrigued at the long-forgotten phenomenon of dating men.

Bette put down her cigarette and leaned forward. "Do you want to hear the latest? This one guy, Devon, cute as a bug, took me to a party Saturday night. We discovered a group in the basement sitting cross-legged in a circle. Except for candles, the room was dark, you could barely make out people's faces. Everyone was smoking pot. I tried a joint. Everybody's doing it!" She looked around at her friends. "Yes, pot."

Radley was aware of marijuana's popularity, although she knew that up until now only Trish had tried it.

"Go on!"

"Well, soon I was feeling really good. We finished our drinks, between drags, and floated up the stairs, loose and mellowed out." As the party escalated, people dropped onto couches, danced in dark alcoves, or disappeared down hallways. They searched the house unsuccessfully, until they found a small room with a double bed on which sprawled an inert male figure, shirt scrunched around his chest, pressed face-first against the wall. The two of them stretched out and in a burst of giggles wrapped their arms around each other. The inert figure didn't move.

"It was the only spot in the house," Bette continued. "We started kissing and time didn't exist and space didn't exist and the bed seemed to be floating on air, objects became fuzzy, and we kind of got carried away. When Devon moved on top of me and began serious love-making, I fell completely into the moment. Like I was in another world. It was the most passionate experience I've ever had. Devon knew what he was doing. He touched me in a way that brought my body to life. And it was so effortless, so easy. And," she paused as if waiting for the air to part, "I had my first orgasm!"

The women reacted with some shock at the extent of their friend's daring, coupled with admiration at her wild abandon. They understood that Bette, now single, was totally free to explore her sexuality.

"I've never experienced anything like this with my husband," Bette went on.

"But the strange man in the bed?" Radley asked incredulously.

"When we got up to leave he was peering at us under half-shaded eyes. Strangely enough, we didn't mind," Bette said. "It was all out in the open." Her smile flashed around the porch.

Trish laughed. "Well, I think that's just peachy keen. Bette, you're really putting your new freedom into practice." She drew out a Marlboro, flicked open her lighter and drew deeply. "Nobody cares these days. Any rules are better than the ones we've got. In the name of experimentation, you can do what you like sexually. A woman recently told me she was going away with her boyfriend the following weekend and taking her vibrator with her. Made thing easier."

Radley listened to her friends' comments with interest.

Barbara shook her head. "I could never do group sex," she recrossed her legs, "although I'm ready to try something new. Ralph has no interest in sex, thinks it's over-rated. I suppose I'm not voluptuous enough for him, being so skinny and all, and, let's face it, plain compared to Ralph. I want to have sex, if only to prove I'm not cold. I think I'm missing something."

She took a sip of lemonade, watched the ice cubes click together in the glass. "But I'm sticking. I have no source of income and the children need two parents. Ralph and I go our own way. He lets me do what I want. There's only one solution: take a lover. I don't think Ralph would even care."

Radley admired her initiative. Brave words—how far she'd come from the Barbara who walked into their midst all those months ago with a dark, scared look, clutching a book on political activism.

"Where are you going to find a lover?" Mirat asked.

Barbara laughed, stretched out her legs, sucked in a deep breath, let it out. "Maybe I'll take a university class, like Bette. Maybe I'll go dancing or take up skiing. You know the saying: when the cat comes out, the tiger appears."

"Just don't get eaten, my friend," Klara exclaimed. "I smell a great deal of trouble pulling that off. Think of the sneaking and lying required to protect the children, stealing an hour here and there, not enough time together to reach true compatibility." Klara took her burning cigarette from the ashtray. "But hey, I'm not judging!"

"So people," Mirat said, setting her box of Milk Duds on the table, "we have become part of a new society moving into sexual freedom, we are sleeping with guys, masturbating, taking lovers—does this mean that we now move into group sex, open marriage, and nudist living? How far are we willing to go?"

"Anything's better than the old dictate that a bride must be a virgin, while the man is patted on the back for taking it where he can get it," Bette said.

"We have to throw it out, throw it all out. It's the only way change will occur," Trish cried, leaping to her feet. She walked to the edge of the porch and gazed out over the back yard, arms folded. "These manicured lawns will have to go, the perfect houses with exquisitely decorated rooms, the two and a half children and dog, the perfect nuclear enclaves set in steel, inside which wives perform their designated roles. We need more than a ripple of change, we need a tidal wave."

"Where are you in all this, Radley?" Klara asked. "You haven't said anything."

"Of course, I agree that we absolutely must create different standards for women." She turned from gazing through the screen, a hint of sadness deepening her face.

"Now that Larry has emerged from his coma, we have to wait and see how his recovery will progress, how he has changed, what his limitations are. Anything can develop. I spend a lot of time at the hospital. Besides that, I am dealing with my relationship with Shane—our marriage is in limbo. That's my life now."

The group seated around the porch became silent. All that could be heard was the whish, whish, whish of the sprinkler, round and round, and the sound of drops hitting dry leaves. Abruptly, the family dog nosed open the outside door, trotted into the porch and stood shaking, flinging tiny droplets over the braided area rug.

"Jasper! Out!" Klara yelled from the recliner and the dog trotted obediently into the hallway.

"I'll have to see. "Radley looked up and smiled. "I know nothing right now. Except one thing: how glad I am to have you as my friends. I want you to know that I hope to have you as my friends forever."

CHAPTER 33

❦

As they walked along Reston Lane, the soft evening air brushed against their faces, the lowering sun followed them with a dying intensity. Radley had put on the Adidas lace-ups she wore for long hikes around the neighborhood and Shane was still in the Oxford shoes from his day at the office. The walk had been Shane's suggestion, surprising her, since they'd never before taken a walk together. He wanted to talk. Another first. The waters of Lake Minnetonka gleamed beyond the roof tops as they turned towards Reston Beach.

At the end of the white gravel drive, they stopped and stood at the edge of the lake, looking out over at the blue-grey water that stretched all the way to the horizon, as far away as the rest of their lives, or the next tomorrow. *We are a singular couple, a mismatch*, Radley mused—she in her tie-died blouse tied in a knot at the waist and long straight hair, Shane in his navy business suit, crisp white shirt and wide-striped tie—two cultures crossing at one lone desert intersection.

Shane picked up a stone, tossed it in the water and they watched it disappear, leaving concentric circles swirling on the surface. It had been Shane who insisted on counseling—this from Shane who had always considered therapy a con game for lost souls, a female thing

When Shane said he wanted to talk to a counselor, she had replied more briskly than intended, "It's not a counselor I want to talk to, it's *you.*"

But she immediately agreed. *At last he might be willing to open up!* Radley thought. *There was a possibility that things might be different.* Given their impasse it was the only way. Every Tuesday evening they drove off, leaving the children with Char watching "Leave It to Beaver." They sat side by side in Mr. Phillip's office, facing a man in a corduroy jacket and brown tie planted on the other side of the walnut desk, who regarded them with placid expectancy. Thin streaks of light from the partially closed blinds behind him stretched across the room, giving it a hushed look.

Radley had no problem launching her list of complaints. The therapist probed her to explore the feelings behind each one. He waited patiently, hands folded, while she circled her eyes around the room looking for clues to her inner motivations. If only she could pinpoint what they were, but what drove her seemed embedded in the fabric of her depression, impossible to disentangle.

"What is it you expect from Shane?" Mr. Phillips asked as she floundered for words.

"I need him to help discipline the children," she said. "And at parties he drinks himself under the table. And me, I'm tired of waking up with a pounding head and having to manage the kids all day on my own."

"So you object to your own drinking as well?" the therapist prompted.

"Well, yes." As Mr. Phillip kept turning her objections back to her own behavior, glimmers of truth seeped in into her mind. Her first thought had been to wonder how Shane could have allowed Larry to leave the house in the storm, yet she hadn't been there with her usual vigilance. She resented his lack of interest in her feminist projects, yet she did not share with him or even attempt to explain what the group was trying to do. Shane continually came up short, yet, guided by Mr. Phillip, she found herself looking inward.

"Shane never wants to go out," she told Mr. Phillip.

"I like to stay home," Shane always said. "You like to go out. I like to stay home."

How could she argue with that? The therapist pushed her further. "How about other relationships?" She'd never had many friends; when people came close—she struggled to explain—their flaws continually emerged as a straining gap between them.

In her eyes, Shane could do nothing right. She seemed unable to accept him as he was. She sat limp in the chair. A wave of sadness rose up in her chest. It struck her like a bolt that while she craved love, maybe she herself wasn't so lovable.

Maybe *she* would have to change.

Since the therapy sessions, she had noticed subtle alterations in Shane. He had started reading the morning paper at breakfast, even went so far as to remark that the latest student protest at UC Berkeley had uncovered some little known facts about war atrocities and the press was taking notice. His shoulders as he walked swung more loosely, less like a wooden soldier, swaying with the rhythm of his steps. She thought things must be going well at the office—for some reason he was feeling better about himself.

"Look, I want this to work." He tossed another stone into the lake and turned to look at her. "I can change—it won't be easy. I like life easy, comfortable, predictable, the less fuss the better. I'm like an elephant, I plod along and take what comes. I'm not very good at delving into feelings and deciphering relationships. But I accept that marriage isn't easy and I will make a robust effort.

"I don't know, Shane . . . ." *It's too late*, she thought, watching another set of concentric circles disappear into the placid water. There was no going back. The bond between them had been severed, no way could they possibly revive a love that had dissolved into the walls of the house, leaving it barren. How could their marriage be saved after she'd given up all hope of connecting with Shane and had in the process lost all desire to do so? Could he ever really change? Could she? How much could she sacrifice without compromising her core self? Could a marriage that she no longer wanted endure?

Or did she?

His lack of initiative drove her to a state of near-mad exasperation. And yet, inexplicably, during his trips to Mexico, an emptiness had invaded the house. She felt the specter of his presence in every room, pressed around her person, as if the flush of his memory gave her substance. She found herself running to the mailbox every day and tearing open his letters.

Was it Shane or some romantic ideal of him she missed? It appeared to her that a disconnect existed between the attitudes concocted by the brain and the hidden desires of the psyche. On one hand, she buried Shane in complaints about his behavior, on the other when he wasn't there she harbored desires to be with him and have his warm presence infiltrate her life. How was one to decipher it all? She sensed mysterious forces about her, invisible currents entirely out of her control. Her head spun.

She and Shane left the beach and continued along the length of road until it U-turned and doubled back along the row of stone-fronted houses with circular drives and freshly watered lawns. They strolled back to the house in silence, watching in mutual wonder as a fuzzy orange ring of sun withered and sank behind the trees.

Radley finally broke down and told her father everything. Well, not quite everything. As they sat facing each other over shrimp cocktails at the Marquette Club, she blurted out, "Last month I told Shane I want a divorce." The words came out of nowhere, in response to his innocent, How are things going? shot out in one quick blast, as if she were afraid a more gradual version would give her time to withdraw into herself and she would end up revealing nothing. She knew this wasn't news her father wanted to hear. No one in his family had ever been divorced, divorce was a sign of immaturity, of failure. In her dad's time, wives didn't work, men didn't help with the housework, and children required two parents to be whole. He and her mother's marriage had endured happily enough, she supposed, maybe because they had no options. Maybe her parents did not expect real intimacy, had thrown themselves into the family whirl and settled into a working relationship and made do.

For the last couple of years she had believed she could not make do. She wanted intimacy, the exchange of innermost feelings and desires. She wanted Shane to reveal himself and to respond when she poured out, as best she could, her urges and fears. She had expected him to be an equal core of the family, her partner and helpmate. Instead, they operated on the edge of civil, never falling off into the pool of emotions that surrounded them, as if afraid they might drown. She wanted to go out and do things, family things, for him to join in their games. The way he responded with monosyllables, his lack of initiative, frustrated her. He was the only other adult in the house and he wasn't even there. She and the children were on their own.

She told her father an abbreviated version of this.

"A divorce means that the children will be with you part-time and that in all probability down the road you will share them with Shane and a new wife," he said. "Are you up for that?"

Radley recoiled. The thought of being torn away from Megan and Larry was unbearable. "They're my life," she whispered. "It's the disciplining I hate, not them." It was important, she thought with alarm, that he understood the difference.

"Their untamed years will pass before you know it," Wilson said. "They need you."

But it seemed she needed them. She took a sip of ice water from the crystal stem glass, trying to clear her mind.

It's Shane's fault popped into her mind, then she gave a bitter chortle as the childishness of her words rang in her ears—the sessions with the therapist had taught her that it's never all one sided, that there is no such thing as a relationship with one partner sane and healthy and one broken and damaged. The counselor had held up a mirror—and she detested what she saw.

"When is Shane expected home from Fairview?" Her father's words broke into her thoughts. The night of the car accident she had phoned her parents, explaining that after a night of heavy drinking at Maury's Pub, Shane had lost control of the wheel and hit a tree head-on, totaling the Buick. Rushed to Fairview limp and bleeding, he was discovered to have broken three ribs and Radley was told it would take up to six weeks to heal.

"He got home yesterday, still bandaged up and tender." Radley thought of the hours spent at Shane's side at the hospital. It had sobered her. He had never appeared so helpless. "Later that evening I found him propped up in the living room, shoulders slumped, hands between his legs, looking devastated and lost. He turned towards me a desolate face, with his hair sticking out in tuffs, his shirt collar loose, the skin on his neck pale. I wanted to hug him."

"'What if someone else had been in the car?' he kept repeating. 'What if Megan had been with me?' Dad, now I'm not so sure. Shane's changed. He's trying. He's stopped drinking."

She saw a flicker of hope on her dad's face. Her parents were aware that Shane drank heavily, but such indulgence was not uncommon at popular social events where the liquor flowed freely.

"He's been attending AA meetings with a fellow from work, someone with fifteen years in the program. A volume of the AA Big Book sits on the bed table and he reads it every night while I lie next to him, reading my own book. Next week he wants us to get together so that he can make his amends. It makes me wonder about the amends I should be making myself!"

Nothing had been solved, she assured Wilson, but a burst of fresh air had entered the house. As she spoke, her tone mellowed, her anger all but disappeared. He cares, he tries, he suffers. What more could she ask?

Wilson listened to all this leaning forward over the table, arms on either side of his dinner plate. Now he sat back and laid his napkin on the table.

"Radley, don't overlook Shane's good qualities. Everyone here at the club likes Shane to a man. He's a congenial, modest, polite, and highly intelligent fellow. He gets along with everyone. During our annual Rose Bowl club dinners, my friends seek out his company. He listens to everyone and he tells a mighty good story."

Radley blinked. Silent Shane, who had to have words pried from him with a pruning hook, amusing people with stories? "He hardly talks at home."

"Why, last New Year's Day he had the group in stitches over a story about his pet cockatoo. When he was only eight he stood on a stool and opened the cage door to give the bird its freedom. He hasn't told you this one? His two maiden aunts chased the cockatoo around the apartment until one of them tripped and fell face first into a platter of spaghetti sauce, knocked the table over, and broke his mother's new set of dishes. He tells the story with a lot more detail and flourish than I ever could."

"I don't believe it! I've never heard that story." There must be an explanation, a key to this Jekyll and Hyde husband of hers, an element that differentiated the gregarious Shane in the exterior world from the withdrawn and somber Shane at home. She could think of only one—she hesitated to admit it, but it burst out at her from the debris of her confused thoughts, clear and inevitable—herself.

It must be her. How could Shane, how could anyone live under the barrage of put-downs and criticisms he had to endure? Married love required compliance and self-sacrifice and Shane with his undemanding acceptance gave her too much power. The image of herself as the persecutor struck her full in the face.

It wasn't just Shane. Maybe they were both broken and damaged, in different ways. Shane sought to have a happy, harmonious family around him. She craved freedom. Was there any way to reconcile these opposing drives and support together the family life they both valued?

Several nights later Radley heard a knocking at the front door. Putting down the dishtowel, she strode into the hallway. Who could it be? She wasn't expecting anyone. To her surprise, when she opened the door there stood Dean, shifting from foot to foot, clutching a white pouch in front of her. Just like her to ignore the doorbell—doing her own thing in her own way, as usual. Dean had already shown up with an apology for her part in the accident, at her parents' insistence. What could she want? She'd had enough of Dean's shenanigans.

At the sight of Dean's meek expression and the way she stood with drooped shoulders on the other side of the screen door, Radley mellowed. There was something different about her, standing so still and passive like that.

"Here, I brought Larry something." She held out the white pouch, which started to wiggle as Radley grasped the strings. "It's one of Tipsy's babies, I thought Larry might like it. Tipsy died," Dean blurted out, tears forming in her eyes. "It was my fault. I didn't feed her. Mama says I can keep two of the babies if I take care of them, and I will! One is so timid I have to pet it a lot. It nibbles my fingers, like kisses."

Radley eyed her with suspicion. This was hard to believe. How could such a turnaround have happened so quickly? Maybe this was a cover for some new trick. She did not, however, look or act like herself. Radley recalled that Adele and Adele's mother had recently taken her, without her sister Courtney, to the San Diego Zoo, where Dean fed the baby elephants. She had fallen in love with the elephants—*they're smart and they're powerful*—and had insisted on returning to see them three times.

"Tell Larry he can come over and see the other baby rabbits any time." With a sudden bright smile, Dean tripped down the curved front steps and was gone.

A short while later, as Radley was turning on the dishwasher, the doorbell rang. This time it was Adele, her smile fringed with seriousness. Radley led Adele into the living room where they could talk.

"I know Dean has just paid you a visit," Adele began after they were settled and Radley had switched on the bronze table lamp. "It was her idea to give Larry the rabbit." Adele adjusted the collar of her coral blouse. "I have something to tell you. Did you know Dean is adopted? It's a family secret; we don't want her to feel different from her classmates. Dean has known since she was little. Maybe that's why she's so different from Courtney.

"Dean has always been a handful, with her share of scrapes, but we had no idea the extent to which she had fallen into deception. Her involvement in Larry's accident was a wake-up call. Something had to be done; Dean is obviously in need of help. All our attention now is focused on her needs." She opened her purse, drew out a photo of herself, Dean and Dean's grandmother in California standing next to a dolphin tank. "This was taken on our recent vacation. Dean loved every minute of it. We did everything she liked. Her favorite was the San Diego Zoo. The meerkats also fascinated her, she begged us to buy one. She finally settled on the baby rabbits we have at home, which she guards like a hawk, now that Tipsy the mother has died."

Struck with amazement, Radley stared at Adele. *Such a character change—not possible unless the earth had suddenly become flat.*

"Oh, we know it takes time. Dean's seeing a counselor, seems to relish the chance to explain herself. She has a long way to go to earn our trust, but at least it's a start. I really believe, watching the babies snuggle up to her, that she is experiencing new feelings. She needs touch and affection to thrive, everyone does for that matter. And from now on she's going to get it."

Dean, Adele explained, had always been overshadowed by Courtney, two years her senior. A straight-A student, class leader, homecoming princess, admired by her fellow students, Courtney was a model of perfection. This year she won the Max Sitwell Award for her paper on American colonial history.

"Dean, on the other hand, is wiry and hyper, she never stops, she flies off without thinking. At school, she does the minimum to get by. Shunned by the pretty girls, she does her best to emphasize her ungainliness." Adele, engrossed in her work, had paid little attention to Dean, who shunned help, preferring to wander off and do her own thing. Hugh, absorbed at the bank, left the raising of the children in Adele's competent hands. Neither she nor Hugh were demonstrative, but Dean, the therapist had pointed out, needed hands-on nurturing. "Dean is now enrolled in Blanche Pearl's tap and jazz dance class, she practices faithfully every night and is selecting a costume for the spring recital," Adele said, a buoyant look on her face. "No more wandering around the neighborhood by herself; she has things she likes to do at home. The theory is if she acts properly long enough the feelings will be fed and engrained into her reality."

"I sure hope things work out," Radley responded, trying to conceal a residue of suspicion. But with Adele's skill, there was a good chance that Dean would make it. The girl had spunk, if it could just be pointed in the right direction.

The grandfather clock was striking ten as Radley turned down the thermostat, switched off the hall light, and approached the bedroom. She paused at the sight of Shane standing by the chest of drawers staring at a gilt-framed photo that showed the four of them posed in front of a ceiling-high Christmas tree sparkling with colored lights that weaved through icicle-drenched branches. Megan and Larry, wearing floppy slippers, gripped Santa-decorated cups of hot chocolate, their faces gleaming above their checkered bathrobes . Shane and Radley stood on either side of them gazing happily into the camera.

Shane looked relaxed in a pair of tweed slacks and the Irish green sweater she had given him, his full dark hair falling neatly at his neck. An image flashed in her mind of the handsome figure she'd seen for the first time at Louise Doyle's wedding on Long Island, standing by the punch bowl, two animated blondes at his side. She noticed that women's faces lit up when he approached, that they turned towards him and flooded him with their light. He responded with shy smiles, not saying much. Toward the end of the evening, she wandered onto the back terrace and to her surprise there he was, alone. They stood together, talking little. He seemed to like the quiet, kept looking at her, and they spoke of fox terriers and New York clam chowder and to her delight he drove her home. On the way, she twisted her gloves nervously in her lap and agreed with everything he said—not like her at all—and tried to quiet her quivering heart. After that, she never looked at another man.

He didn't seem to have heard her come in.

Suddenly she wanted to lay her head against the soft woolen fabric of his sweater and feel its warmth.

Unbuttoning her velveteen dress, she walked past him into the closet and slipped out of her clothes. A few minutes later she emerged wearing a rose cotton nightgown.

He turned and she saw his face was pale as he stood immobile, his gaze downcast. Here, in the stark quiet of the bedroom, the cleft between them stretched like a desert canyon.

He did not want a divorce.

"How are we going to survive, Shane?" she asked dejectedly. She was aware that all roads they had been down had led smack up against a wall. She couldn't fathom how this marriage could be made to supply the needs of two such different people. Once, she had simply wanted her freedom, but it was no longer only herself. And she had come to understand that the internal needs she had uncovered in herself didn't lead elsewhere.

He replaced the photo on the chest-of-drawers and took a deep drag on his cigarette. "I don't know. It's up to you."

She stopped, facing him. "Are you willing to make concessions?" she asked.

"Yes," he said quickly, looking at her steadily with his soft grey eyes.

"Will you discuss what's going on with us as we move along? Will you tell me how you feel about things? And will you tell me when I'm being too—whatever it is I'm being?"

"Yes to the first two. As to the last, I'll do my best. Critiquing is not in my nature, but I'll try to be helpful."

'Don't think of it as criticism, think of it as guidance," she said. She seemed to be admonishing herself, and she felt the balance of responsibility between the two of them shifting.

"I'm lucky to have you," she said suddenly.

Shane looked at her steadily, then lowered his gaze and placed one hand on the bureau. "I should have kept a better eye out for Larry, instead of holing up in the basement in front of the TV," he blurted out unexpectedly. "I can't forgive myself."

At the look on his face she felt the vestiges of her resentment dissolve. "You're human, like the rest of us," she said, going up to him.

His mouth relaxed slightly. "Will you be able to accept me and the children even if we don't meet all your needs?" he said.

Her needs? They were important. They were part of what she and her fellow feminists were fighting for. She would not capitulate totally. But they were only a part. "Yes. But Shane, I need to know who you are, and to be known by you."

"I'll reveal anything, but you might have to ask."

"And there's so much out in the world I want to be part of."

He stepped forward until their faces were inches apart. "Go ahead. I won't stop you," he said, looking gently into her eyes. He stood by her warm and open. The usual grumpy put-upon expression on his face was gone, replaced by a touch of sadness.

"I can do more. I can change," he said, and looking into the soft grey depth of his eyes, laced with colors that descended into the earth, she thought he already had.

He looked so despondent that she moved forward and curled her arm around his neck. He turned his head towards her.

With astonishing speed, she felt the tight mass within her loosen.

Something had happened.

Moving slowly, he undressed, put on his pajamas and climbed into bed.

It's a risk, she thought watching him. One shouldn't have to give up one's own actualization and be accommodating in all things—one couldn't endure under total submission. But once past self-centered childhood there were fuller, more communal paths to follow. A dance of tribal unity. She'd have to learn the steps.

"This weekend we'll go dancing," she said to Shane as she slipped between the covers and reached for his hand, "and learn how to move in step."

From the pillow next to her she heard a bright laugh. "Why wait?" and he pulled her towards him.

Chapter 34

⁓⌇⁓

They watched as Larry gobbled mashed potatoes, minute steak, and peas from a hospital tray. By now he had become skilled at feeding himself, finding dishes quickly with his hands and scooping food from the bowls with a right-handed scoop spoon. He could easily dress himself and navigated to the bathroom by feeling along the familiar shapes of the hospital furniture. Outlines he could see, vaguely, not well enough to walk in public on his own. Radley would be driving him to intensive physical therapy sessions, and they hoped that time alone would bring further healing. It still seemed unreal, seeing the immobile form they had gazed at for so many months back in motion, as if raised from the dead. Not only had he gained fourteen pounds in four weeks, he would be going home the next day. Home! Hard for Radley to believe, to absorb—a fantasy, a dream.

Megan, sitting by her parents, stabbed a piece of the glazed chicken on her plate with her chopstick and gnawed on it like a lollypop, tilting her head sideways. Shane and Radley exchanged glances over their dinner trays. They were going home! They would have their family back! Radley felt the overpowering presence of the four of them together amid the hum of breathing, the pulse of life that expanded and filled the room.

Dinner over, Shane carried the soiled trays to a side counter, murmured "Be back soon," and strode abruptly from the room. Radley peered after him. What was he up to? She puttered, straightening the room, dropping games into a toy chest, clearing a corner table of newspapers, adjusting the gold barrette in Megan's hair. Impossible to remain still, too much happening. The excitement of all of them returning home flooded through her.

No sooner had an orderly carted off the dinner trays than Radley felt an arm reach around her and a hand appeared, a gruff, shy hand holding a single yellow rose wrapped in yellow tissue. She turned. Shane stood next to her, barely able to contain his exuberance.

"Here, for you." He pushed the flower into her hands, and she felt the breath of his soft laugh against her ear. Curling her fingers carefully around the tissue, Radley looked down at the velvety petals, then looked up at Shane in amazement. He must have gone to the flower shop on the main floor. Something fluttered down her throat and into her stomach. To her surprise she giggled. What was happening inside her?

"This is the fourth one," she said, collecting herself. "Let's add it to the three roses Klara sent." She indicated a vase by the bed in which three butter yellow roses stood amid fans of feathery green. "Klara gave us three flowers, one for each of us. Now that Larry's back with us, we're four again. Four yellow roses. It's perfect." She lowered her head and, pressing her hands against her cheeks, began to shake with sobs, quivering the length of her body.

Shane slipped his arm around her. "You've been through a lot, Radley."

Radley—he rarely called her by name. It was a key, a magic password, and she felt her limbs relax and her breathing slow to a quiet, easy rhythm.

"I'm glad you gave up the studio," he said into her ear. His voice was close, mellow. "I missed you, it—wasn't the same with you gone. I hope you'll stay with us now." His voice was so soft she hardly heard the words. He coughed, almost like a sob. She attempted to say something, but the words stuck in her throat.

Hurriedly, she strained to think, to find an answer, but Shane's tall form standing next to her was more real than any concept she could devise.

She looked up at him.

"Let's move," he said suddenly. His voice grew. "Let's move closer to town. Larry can be near his visual therapist and you can find a job."

Job—the word rang out like a shot, a ripple of hope. Dabbling in photography in the studio had given her the satisfaction of a hobby. But a real job, with salary, responsibilities, co-workers! Such a daring idea to be voiced by Shane, a solid adversary of change. Could this be a new Shane? For so long she had pressed him to conform to her idea of what he should be, but was beginning to realize that it was useless to attempt to replace the existing husband with an idealized version. And now, just as she had given up her tenuous hopes and was looking inward for answers, Shane seemed to be moving in new directions after all.

Everything was happening so fast she couldn't keep up.

The four yellow roses drew a flash of bright color into the room, their sweet scent camouflaging the hint of camphor that lingered over Larry's bed. Her eyes followed Shane as he settled in the brown arm chair and leaned forward, elbows on knees and watched Megan show Larry how to sculpt an elephant out of modeling clay. Shane, along with his faults and irregularities—a complete package that, in the clear light of the bedside lamp, she accepted as her own.

EPILOGUE

"Welcome one and all. You will very soon learn your way around the decks. With so much to see in the scheduled time, if you are not at the gate on time you will be left behind. Take care of your valuables, better don't have any. If you do, make sure to use the ship's safe. Don't trust strangers, don't trust anyone, even the crew members. Our country is too poor to be honest. Don't let uniforms fool you, and don't worry about guns, the guards carry them to protect themselves, not you. Report anything that seems questionable.

"Warning: disease and deadly creatures are everywhere, but the adventures in each of these islands will compensate any danger, so forget worries and let whatever happens happen. You can follow the guide, which might be me, or the map you have each been given, otherwise you're on your own. Last thing: medical supplies are rationed this trip, so don't too many of you get in trouble.

"I talk too long. Any questions, direct them to the purser at the dining hall tonight. Again, my name is Ted-pau Gonzales. *Buen Viaje.*"

The fifteen passengers accumulated on deck at the appointed hour, hot and flushed in the tropical sun. Larry climbed down the ladder first, then Megan and Shane, and Radley followed. The tender bobbed through the waves until it came close to shore, then one-by-one people hopped out into knee-high water and waded onto the sandy beach. As she felt the water lap around her legs, Megan tossed her head back, raised her arms in the air and let out a peal of laughter. Along an upper ridge, blue-foot-ed boobies could be seen clomping between the rocks, and frigate birds perched with their black wings spread against the sky like soaring kites. Beyond them, sky-diving pelicans plunged one after another from the cliffs. The four of them stopped to gaze in fascination as an albatross ca-reened in free flight along the escarpment. Chattering with excitement, Megan and Larry raced along the sand toward the iguanas and fur seals basking lazily on the rocks, having been warned by their parents against disturbing or touching the animals.

"This way, folks!" While the other passengers lined up behind Ted-pau in his green canvas cap and disappeared into the brush, Shane found a comfortable rock by the ocean half-buried in the sand, spread down his beach towel and sprawled out, legs stretched in front of him. Let the oth-ers traipse off to see more of what was already right here on the beach. He had approved the cruise because they would have one central cabin to op-erate from, no continual messing with hotels and trains and luggage. On a tourist ship like this everything was taken care of and he could relax, which is what people are supposed to do on vacations. He'd enjoyed the trip to the wildlife center in Guayaquil, watching the kids running here and there excitedly, found the Old Town interesting, and stopped to gaze at the brilliant parrots behind the stalls in the handicraft market. Now he could take it easy and watch the vermillion fly catchers with their bright orange breasts flitting through the trees and land on the sand in front of him. He chuckled as two of them fought over a catch only ten yards down the beach. He could watch these creatures for hours. This trip was prov-ing to be more interesting than he had expected.

Here he was, never having ventured past the boundaries of New York, hardly beyond the modest Queens neighborhood where he grew up, until he married Radley and she had whisked him off to California to visit her college friend Melissa and husband. Then they had settled in Minnesota, and now here he was on another continent, thousands of miles from the spin of his citied youth, and he was loving it.

He adjusted the sponge pillow and leaned back against it comfortably. His ribs no longer gave him trouble, the pain was gone. He thought with satisfaction of the night he had ripped off the bulky elastic rib belt he'd worn for weeks and cheerfully hurled it into the garbage can. Larry and Megan had clapped and tugged on his arms—wait, you wildcats, no big hugs yet.

It had been six months since he carried a large crate of liquor to his office and offered the contents to his co-workers—the bottles had disappeared by lunch time. He hadn't touched a drop since. AA three nights a week, along with Radley's pledge to abstain along with him, eased the struggle, although images of golden drinks in tall glasses still waved in front of him from time to time. But he had made the pledge, would do whatever it took.

That fellow last night with his raucous laugh and thick Spanish accent you had to plow through with an axe had been great company. Emiliano, first officer of the watch, knew everything there was to know about the islands. As the moon lifted over the dark ocean, the two of them sat on the upper deck outside the officer's lounge drinking what Emiliano called holy punch, consisting of iced tea, honey, and Sanbokan lemon. He listened as Emiliano explained that the blue-footed boobies, named from the Spanish word *bobo*, meaning stupid due to their clumsiness on land, were actually exceptional and graceful flyers, diving for anchovies from as high as 80 feet. If you had told Shane that he would spend an evening thousands of miles from home discussing exotic birds with a foreigner he could barely understand, he would have demurred. *Not me.* And here he was, thrust miles into the tropics, enjoying every minute.

It had been fun planning for the cruise, with the help of a travel agent. The children couldn't stop talking about their upcoming venture out of the country. It was their first family trip together, to celebrate their move to the new house. They now resided in a small bungalow packed among a string of houses along a street that wound up a hill and disappeared in the direction of the nearby university. Built-in bookcases lined the living room walls and old oak woodwork framed the arched doorway leading to the dining room, where a wooden buffet filled one wall. Shane was satisfied. As much as he disliked giving up the house in Deephaven, the home that epitomized his every dream, Shane knew he would be happy in their Prospect Park home. He could live anywhere.

As for Radley, many of her women friends considered the return to her marriage traitorous—clinging to the institution of bondage was an abandonment of women's goals—she had capitulated, returned to the enemy camp, given up the great struggle for female independence. Freedom could never be found in the traditional institutions that were economically and legally dominated by men. Of course we'll stick by you, you must do what you think right, they told Radley, pointing out how much of herself she'd given up. Radley pointed out how much she had gained in its place.

It was true that she and Shane approached the world differently. They were two different souls, but they clung to the same desire to raise a family together and combine a life of shared values of devotion and support. Something that Radley became more and more certain she wanted.

Besides, the women's group had broken up as her friends became involved in major life changes. Klara was appointed teaching assistant for her TV writing class at the University, winning praise from the professor for her witty comic scripts. Maureen no longer attended group meetings, explaining that her new position as chair of the Global Poverty Campaign consumed her time. Mirat had taken the big step and left her husband, moved in with her sister in Anoka and enrolled in nursing classes at the local community college. Radley continued a close friendship with Klara, Trish, and Bette. The four often met for lunch in Dinkytown near Radley's new part-time job at the on the editorial staff of the University Extension Learning Center. Last week they attended Jane Fonda's Stop the War talk describing her recent visits to Hanoi and Haiphong. The previous month, Radley had driven Audrey and Klara to a remote adoption home, and on the way back they had all spent the day at a country spa immerced in volcanic mud baths and hot steam towels.

After spending the Christmas holidays in the new house, Radley and Shane had decided to build on the rekindled family unit and embark on an adventure.

"We're going to sail around the Ga-pa-los Islands!" Megan exclaimed when they informed Char and Wilson.

"Wonderful!" Char said.

"I'm taking my sling shot," Larry said.

"No way, you can't see," Megan cried.

"Yes, my vision is almost back to normal and with my glasses I can find things that move."

"No, no you can't hurt the animals!"

"I'm going to shoot flies," Larry said. "Maybe an animal too. Anything that bites."

"I'm afraid not, sweetheart," Radley said, laughing as she brushed a lock of blonde hair from his forehead. "You can't see well enough yet to hit the underbelly of a whale."

"My brother is always doing dumb things," Megan remarked as she climbed onto Wilson's lap.

Sitting on the beach, Shane chuckled at the recollection. Best of all, he thought, tipping his straw hat over his eyes, he was with his family. And he had already thought of things they could do back in Minneapolis—like attend ball games, go swimming at Lake Calhoun, play the board games he had stashed in the basement closet, ready for Sunday afternoons by the fire. Ah, the peaceful surge of water swishing against the shore, the playful antics of the animals, the musical calls issuing from the trees, so pleasant, so wonderfully simple. Except for that red ant crawling up his calf—with a swat it was gone.

Radley, who had returned for a swim, watched Shane relax on the sand, saw his smile spread beneath his straw hat, content in the warm sunshine. Down the beach, Megan lined up pebbles alongside the outline of a snoozing sea lion, taking care, Radley noted, not to disturb the animal. One of the sea lions gave a lazy bark and scraped his head in the sand to look at her. Megan gave a gleeful laugh.

"Larry, stop throwing those rocks all over the place," she heard Megan yell, becoming serious. "The sea lion is sleeping, don't step on him, here," and she took his hand and scrambling to her feet she wound him through the array of sea lions sunning themselves in the sand, down to the shore and into the shallows. "You can do what you want right here. We have the water by ourselves."

Larry looked out over the ocean rippled with light, making it hard to distinguish details, but he saw a distant rock formation surrounded by a circle of turquoise water, the dark form of a bird cruising overhead. Pressing his tinted prescription glasses tight against his nose, he pulled his other hand free and hopped into the lapping waves, whistling.

Radley tugged her bathing cap around her ears and waded into the water until it reached her waist, then breast-stroked out into the Pacific Ocean. She felt the waves lap against her cheeks and with each deep breath she drew in the odor of clam shells and seaweed. After several minutes, she flipped onto her back and opened her eyes to the sky. The water cradling her shoulders felt warm. She laughed for no reason. From the corner of her eye she could see Shane spread out on the beach in the distance. A flush of ecstasy flowed through her, a rush of plentitude and good will. The span of islands around which they had been cruising for the past week, Baltra, Isabella, San Cristobal, and the rest, each harbored unique varieties of life that flourished fearlessly, species she viewed with awe, witnessing the natural force of adaption playing out everywhere in front of their eyes.

Fluttering her feet in the water to keep afloat, she flashed on her encounter that morning on the upper ship deck. Not far from where she had stood leaning over the railing, a man dressed in black surveyed the wide expanse of ocean. He introduced himself as a monk from Venezuela who was touring the archipelago with two other monastics. "I come here to contemplate," he said. "Can you feel it? It is peaceful."

For a while, without speaking, they gazed out over the soft white caps of foam and the blue water and beyond that blue and more blue. He spent his time contemplating the Buddhist teachings on the value of being in the present, he told Radley. "Remember, the mind can go in a thousand directions . . . but with each single step a flower blooms," he said in a slow, even voice.

She very much liked this monk, was drawn to the calm of his soft grey eyes. It was unclear what he meant, but she felt a truth ring through his words that penetrated her in an organic way and made her think of peace and nature and creatures that knew where they belonged and the extent of their power.

The monk's words came back to her as she breast-stroked gently through the water. A lone figure waded ankle deep at the edge of the beach. It was Shane, watching a raft of sea of lions cavorting in the shallows. "I'm coming in," he waved. Turning on her back, she floated and let the blue mantle of ocean pull her to shore, to the real world, without thought of past or future.

www.ingramcontent.com/pod-product-compliance
Lightning Source LLC
Chambersburg PA
CBHW070304260626
47160CB00003B/709